Sarah Shoesmith writes uplifting stories inspired by kindness, community and beautiful countryside. She lives on a farm in Norfolk, UK with her family and their dog, Basil. When she isn't writing, Sarah spends her spare time reading, growing food and gardening for wildlife.

If you'd like to find out more about Sarah, you can sign up to her newsletter on www.sarahshoesmithauthor.com or visit her on social media channels. She would love to hear from you!

facebook.com/SarahShoesmithAuthor
x.com/gardeningshoe1
instagram.com/@sarah.shoesmith

A Garden of Hope in Sweetingfield

Sarah Shoesmith

Cosy Up Press

Cover design by Berni Stevens

Edited and proofread by Perfect Prose Services

ISBN 978-1-917257-05-3

For my brother, John Shoesmith,
a truly remarkable and inspiring man.
With love.

Chapter One

Dilly Pepper held her breath and crept up on a half-open purple crocus flower growing in Jessica's lawn. A smile lit her face as she knelt down on the damp, dew-spangled grass to get a closer look.

'You're my first of the year!' she exclaimed, peering into the crocus at a fluffy upended bumblebee. 'You look drunk on nectar. Did you spend the night in there and have breakfast in bed?'

The scuff of boots on the path alerted her to Jessica's arrival.

'Look at this beauty,' said Dilly as a shadow joined her on the lawn. She turned quickly, excited to show her client and friend. 'Oh! You're not Jessica.'

Amusement skittered across the stranger's face and danced in his moss green eyes, causing Dilly's heart to skip away at a thousand beats per minute. She gulped air into lungs that had forgotten to breathe and battled to bring order to her body, which until a few seconds ago had been functioning perfectly normally for a sunny Friday morning in Jessica's front garden.

She clambered to her feet, aware that her knees were muddy and she was most likely sporting a shrubbery in her tangled hair.

'I'm Dilly – Jessica's gardener,' she said, sliding off a thermal glove to reveal hands that at the best of times were lined with dirt, but at the worst of times, like now, seemed to have half a garden under her fingernails. She swiftly stuffed her embarrassment for a body part back into its thermal glove and made do with a nod.

'I guessed,' he said. She liked the warmth in his smile and the glossiness of his dark hair, which was too long to be sensible and too short to be playing it cool. 'I'm here to see my aunt Jessica.'

'You must be Alex. Jessica's told me all about you – and now we meet at last.'

'We do, but only briefly. Does my aunt pay you to talk to comatose bees?' Laughter sparked in his eyes, causing Dilly's stomach to flip.

'Amongst other things,' she said, then leant in closer to him and whispered, 'Don't worry, the few seconds I spent admiring my first bee of the season won't be stolen from your aunt. I'll make them up.'

'Glad to hear it.' He held her gaze for a few delicious moments, before turning away, his smile fading as he reached the path.

She watched him walk slowly towards the front door. He might be tall and strong, but there was a slight stoop of one shoulder, as if it were burdened with the weight of whatever worry he was carrying. He obviously wasn't looking forward to seeing Jessica, which was strange, because she was one of the kindest and most welcoming of Dilly's clients – and that was saying something, because they were all wonderful in different ways. Dilly not only adored her job, she loved her customers too, which made charging them a sticky subject, but she did have to eat, and contrary to the ribbing Alex had given her about being a slacker who whiled away his aunt's time and money talking to bees, Dilly did work very hard.

She returned to the border she had been weeding before Doctor Alex Hampton left her feeling all topsy-turvy like an upended bee. She suspected things weren't going well for the family, and she guessed it had something to do with Alex's brother, Nathan. If everything were fine, Alex Hampton would not have been there. He would have been in some fusty university study with his head in a book. She bent over the border as if working, but watched as he rang the bell and stood back to wait for his aunt to answer.

'Alex! You don't get any uglier.' Dilly heard Jessica laugh as she leant forward to kiss her nephew. He looked awkward, as if the last thing he wanted was human contact, which was exactly the opposite impression she had received from him when they met. His mood had changed in seconds, making Dilly wonder what life had done to him to make him so standoffish with Jessica. His aunt was affable and warm-hearted, while he was distinctly cold towards her. It was a sad and interesting contrast.

'The kettle's just boiled.' Jessica's voice was as friendly as ever, even though Alex's body language was screaming that he did not want to be there. 'Come in and tell your old aunt about everything you've been up to.'

Jessica bustled Alex from the glass-clad lean-to into the brick cottage. A trail of smoke wended its way from the chimney stack into the clear blue late February sky. Hoping that his iciness would thaw by the fire in Jessica's kitchen, Dilly turned her back on the house. Lovely though that fire would be, she was glad she was outside. She was always happiest with her head in the sun and her hands in the soil – even cold February soil.

Usually a garden would divert and absorb her, but today she couldn't stop thinking about Alex Hampton. She knew he was an academic. She knew from Jessica that he was on sabbatical and she knew from having seen his response to Jessica that this was probably the last place on earth that he wanted to be. All in all, she knew quite a lot about Alex Hampton. She hadn't realised that she'd be floored by his looks though. The power of attraction was beyond anything Dilly had felt in her thirty-five years. She wondered if that force got stronger with time, like a biological response to the reduction of fertility, and if she'd be attracted to anyone and everyone by Christmas.

She pushed the idea aside. Dilly wanted a family. She wanted a life partner. She didn't *need* either of them and she would not have them at any cost. If they came her way, all well and good, but if not? She had a job she loved, in a village where she was valued, and a best friend who happened to be the mother of the most amazing and wonderful child on the planet – and she was thankful for all of these things every second, of every hour, of every day. Even so, a few moments with Alex Hampton made her want more. A whole lot more.

'Dilly,' called Jessica, cutting through Dilly's thoughts. 'I've made tea and cake. Would you like to warm yourself by the fire?'

Dilly shook her head, aware of the glowering face behind his aunt in the kitchen. Whatever worry Alex Hampton was carrying hadn't burdened Jessica, as she seemed as happy and carefree as ever, but Dilly suspected that she was hiding some sadness, if only over Alex's reluctance to spend time in her company.

'No, thank you, Jessica. I'll have them out here and keep working while the sun's shining. If you pass me the container of birdseed, I'll fill the feeders for you.'

'That's so kind of you, Dilly, thank you, but we need to build up your strength for the pancake race this weekend, so let's feed you first.' She held out the tea and warm apple cake and Dilly went to the glass lean-to to collect it. As soon as she was in whispering distance, Jessica hissed, 'I can't help thinking that you and Alex would make an extremely handsome couple.'

Dilly laughed. 'You're an incorrigible matchmaker.'

'I simply want to see my nephew happy,' said Jessica, releasing the plate.

He seemed happy enough when I first met him, thought Dilly as she picked up the little fork Jessica always provided for her and dug it into the cake. 'I doubt we have anything in common.'

'Can't you find something?'

If only, thought Dilly, her mind straying to that strong, finely honed body, which even fully clothed and from a distance had stolen the breath from her lungs.

'Step out of your comfort zone and try something new,' said Jessica, decisively. 'Why not ask him out for a drink – see where it leads?'

Dilly spluttered on her cake. 'Don't you think I'm a bit too earthy for him?'

Jessica looked contemplative. 'I would argue that earthiness is precisely what he needs. That, and to relax a little.' She leant forward and whispered, 'He's dreadfully serious.'

'Perhaps he's just thoughtful,' said Dilly.

'Dear Dilly – those big blue eyes of yours are always looking on the bright side and searching for the best in people,' said Jessica, taking the container of birdseed from the cupboard. She sighed softly. 'He used to be such a fun-loving child. It's hard to believe he's the same person.'

Yes, thought Dilly, remembering his green eyes twinkling with merriment and the laughter waning from his delicious smile as he walked towards Jessica's cottage. What had happened to that beautiful man to sap the joy from him?

Chapter Two

A crowd had already gathered on the playing field in the bright late-winter sunshine by the time Dilly arrived for the annual Sweetingfield pancake race. The bunting Jessica had made ten years ago for the event fluttered on the breeze near the starting line, and a trestle table, covered in the same red gingham cloth that had been used for the previous seventeen pancake races, held stacks of cold pancakes waiting to be distributed to the runners.

Dilly sighed happily at the sight. 'Nothing ever changes,' she said as she embraced her best friend, Bella.

'Apart from your pinny,' said Bella, smoothing down her dark brown hair and tightening her ponytail, even though it didn't need it.

'And you can always count on me having a new one for the pancake race, so no change there either.' Dilly turned her back on Bella as she lifted this year's apron over her head and tied the ribbons around her waist. 'It's a bit big, but it was love at first sight.' She twirled round to reveal the bright yellow banana pinny she had bought at a local craft fair.

Bella laughed as she hugged her six-year-old son, Luke. 'That's quite something, Dilly,' she said, releasing him so she could slip her sensible, neatly pressed red-striped kitchen apron over her head.

'Steve,' shouted Luke, running towards Dilly's former schoolteacher. 'I'm watching the race with you.'

'You are,' said Steve, who had looked after Luke while his mum ran, every year since he was born. He turned to Dilly and nodded at her apron. 'Looking great!'

'Glad you like it. It's my favourite pancake race pinny of all time. I might not even donate it to the church hall this year. I reckon it's a keeper.'

Steve gasped. 'But you rarely cook.'

'I might not cook, Steve, but I spill food often enough.'

'You do,' said Bella, bending down to check that the laces on her trainers were properly tied. She stood up, and bounced up and down, which made Dilly smile. She had never seen her friend tie her trainers without double-checking they were secure and comfortable.

Bella grabbed her frying pan. 'Shall we go and line up?'

Dilly nudged Luke. 'Your mum's keen.'

'That's 'cos she wants to win again.'

Dilly faked shock. '*Again*? Don't you think it's my turn to finish first?'

Luke giggled. 'You don't take turns. You just win. And my mum's a winner.'

'There's no doubting that,' said Dilly.

Bella slipped her arm through Dilly's as they set off for the starting line. 'Shall we run together?'

'And steal the look of joy on Luke's face when he sees you do so well? And, even worse, have to deal with his disappointment when instead of winning, you get dragged down to my level?'

'It might be your year to win.'

Dilly held out her frying pan for a pancake. 'I hardly think so. I know my limitations and I'm comfortable with them, thank you very much.'

Jessica nestled in next to Bella. 'It's a good turnout,' she said, looking around at the other runners.

'It is,' said Bella. 'There must be at least thirty of us running today.'

Dilly eyed Jessica's cast-iron frying pan. 'Don't you have something lighter to run with?'

'I'm afraid not. It's a bit much for my ageing wrists, to be honest.'

'Here,' said Dilly, reaching across Bella to thrust her lightweight frying pan at Jessica, while making a grab for Jessica's cast-iron one with her free hand.

'You can't do that,' said Jessica.

'I just have.' Dilly flinched, burdened by the sudden weight. She was surprised Jessica had even managed to get as far as the starting line with the heavy pan.

A horn sounded, stifling the noise of the crowd.

'Are we ready for the eighteenth annual pancake race?' The vicar's voice boomed from the speakers and everyone shouted and cheered. 'Fantastic! So the rule is that you need to stop at each of the taped lines and toss your pancake before running to the next.'

The public address system squealed, causing people to block their ears and groan, but Dilly laughed delightedly. 'This happens every year – and every year the vicar ends up shouting.'

As soon as the noise stopped, the vicar yelled, 'Toes behind the starting line, runners.'

Dilly glanced down to see her foot halfway over the line, and swiftly stepped back. She felt that familiar, joyous adrenaline buzz, as she stood, ready to unleash her finest jog-trotting and pancake-tossing.

'On your marks... get set...' A horn sounded and the runners were away to the cheers of the crowd.

Jessica's pan required both hands to carry it, and its weight made it impossible to propel the pancake to a good height, so Dilly couldn't get the pancake to flip. After five attempts, she assumed a squat position in the hope of getting extra power beneath the pan. To her huge relief, she managed to launch the pancake high enough for it to flip, so she decided she would stick with the squat-toss position, even though she looked ridiculous.

Her arms had barely recovered from her exertions at the first taped line by the time she had to toss the pancake again. Bracing herself for the pain, she gritted her teeth, squatted and managed to propel the pancake into the air, only for it to land with a desultory plop on the floor.

A Labrador, spotting an opportunity for a light snack, broke free from the crowd and took a mammoth bite of it before Dilly had a chance to pick it up.

She recognised the dog immediately. 'No, Basil,' she ordered, giggles bursting through her attempt at sounding strict. Despite her laughter, Basil took her seriously and sat down while she grabbed what was left of her pancake and popped it in her pan. Ahead of her, Jessica had successfully caught her pancake and was walking towards the next pancake-tossing line. It made Dilly smile. At least Jessica was having a good race.

'Come on, Mary,' someone called.

Dilly glanced to her left and saw that she was keeping company with the oldest competitor in the race. 'Hello, Mary. I didn't see you at the start.'

'I was late.'

'That makes me feel so much better for being this far back in the pack!'

Try as she might, and even with the embarrassing squat position, the remainder of her pancake wouldn't flip. Meanwhile Mary's pancake was flipping, but kept missing the pan. 'At least your pancake is launching,' she called to her.

'I can catch it, too. I'm waiting for you,' said Mary.

'That's so sweet of you.'

'But please get a wriggle on with your pancake, Dilly, darling, I don't think I can keep throwing this thing forever.'

'It's this pan. It's so heavy.'

'Borrow mine,' said Mary, handing hers to Dilly.

Dilly took it gratefully. She flung her pancake from it and caught it straightaway.

'That's more like it, Dilly, although we'll probably both be disqualified for cheating,' said Mary, chuckling as she took her pan back and flipped and caught her pancake first time.

Dilly held out her arm to Mary. 'Shall we?'

'Why not?' said Mary, slipping her arm through Dilly's as they worked their way through the other pancake-tossing stations, using only Mary's pan.

As they approached the finishing line, a cheer went up and Dilly and Mary acknowledged the applause. Mary waved and Dilly danced in a circle and whooped back at the crowd.

'Go Dilly and Mary,' called Luke, and Dilly, beaming with happiness, did an extra turn for his benefit.

Her smile froze on her face as her foot caught in her over-sized banana apron, and she closed her eyes as she felt herself tumbling out of control to the ground. She lay there, bruised and embarrassed, but having checked that nothing hurt apart from her frying-pan-weary arms, she sat up. Mary held out her hand and helped her to her feet, before they crossed the finishing line arm in arm to the roar of the crowd.

'Thank you, Dilly,' said Mary as she received her competitors' medal. 'I had been dreading the race, as I've always run with dear Lois, but she isn't well enough this year. It's why I was late. I had decided not to take part, but Lois insisted I come. Now I'm glad I did. You made it so much fun. I hope you're not hurt.'

'Not one bit,' said Dilly, rubbing her bicep and hoping that she wouldn't be in need of any upper body strength at work this week.

Steve bustled to the front of the crowd and hugged her. 'Well done, Dilly,' he said relieving her of the frying pan. 'This is a bit weighty. What happened to yours?'

'I swapped with Jessica.'

'Is that Jessica who won the senior age group?' he asked.

'The very same,' said Dilly, glad that she had swapped and given Jessica the chance to come first.

'I've just realised,' gasped Steve, 'you and Bella book-ended the race!'

A warm smile flooded Dilly's face. 'She won?' Steve nodded. 'That's brilliant news,' cried Dilly, clapping her hands and immediately regretting it, as her forearms weren't up to so much action.

'Here she is, the winner,' he called as Bella approached them.

'Well done,' said Dilly, hugging her friend.

'And well done, you, for making Jessica and Mary's day,' said Bella. 'Have you seen Jessica?'

'Not since I watched her disappear over the horizon in the race,' said Dilly.

Bella glanced around, then pointed. 'There she is.'

Dilly followed the line of Bella's finger and spotted Jessica with Alex. Her heart sank and raced at the same time. It was heart multitasking gone mad. She smiled at Jessica as she fought to stem the colour threatening to flood her already flustered face.

'Here's my heroine. I couldn't have done it without you, Dilly,' she said, as they all set off towards the playing field gate. 'Are you okay? We were so worried when we saw you take that tumble.'

Nothing could stop Dilly blushing now. That Alex should have seen her trip over her massive banana pinny was bad enough, without considering that he had probably witnessed her assuming the ridiculous squat position to get power beneath the pan, while also being beaten by all but one of the seniors in the race. Add to that the fact that Mary had only come joint last because she had been kind enough to lend Dilly her pan to cheat with, and that Dilly had been helped up after her fall by a nonagenarian, and even Dilly's considerable and robust optimism had to bow to the truth that she had hardly proved herself to be the most desirable of women. She risked a glance at Alex. He was looking cool, calm and more than a little bemused. Who could blame him? she thought, as they shuffled with the crowd waiting to funnel through the playing field gate and on to the narrow path beyond.

He dropped his head slightly as if confiding in her. 'I've

only been here for forty-eight hours and I'm finding myself doing new things all the time.'

His voice was as rich and delicious as a vat of treacle. She turned to him, wanting to immerse herself in that sound. 'Like what?' she asked.

'Like shuffling in a crocodile to a barbecue in February with a woman dressed as a banana.'

'I can't believe you've never done that before,' said Dilly, delighting in the spark of amusement skipping across his face. 'If it's any consolation, I've never done the post-pancake barbecue hobble with a university professor, so we're both outside of our comfort zones.'

He rubbed a hand across his forehead. 'I'm way outside of mine, but surely you're still in yours?'

'Yes, thank goodness. Apart from you being here.'

'I can't imagine I make much difference,' he said. You have no idea, she thought. 'As far as I can see, I'm just another person for you to chat to, Dilly. Since we met, I've realised that you'll speak to anyone or any*thing*.' A smile played around his too sexy lips and she had the strongest desire to stand on tiptoe and kiss him. 'You even transformed coming last in a pancake race into a social event.'

Dilly glowed at how he had reframed what had been, without a doubt, one of her more embarrassing moments. He hadn't teased or mocked her about her pancake race experience as others might; instead he had found something positive to say about it, although heavens knew how. People who could do that were kind to their core, and she sensed that despite his brusque exterior, there was a depth to Alex Hampton that was steeped in kindness, and she liked that. She liked it a lot.

'I could hardly ignore Mary,' she said. 'She was like a mother to my late dad.'

A shadow crossed his face. He wore his emotions for all to see. 'I'm very sorry about your dad.'

Dilly felt familiar sorrow nudge her. 'It was a long time ago.' She shored herself up. Her dad would not want her to be sad on pancake race day and she certainly didn't want to burden Alex with her loss. She grinned at him. 'It was a treat to finish the race with Mary. I've known her all my life.'

'It seems to me that you know everyone.'

'That's what living in a village is all about.'

He nodded. 'So I'm learning. I feel like everyone already knows who I am.'

Why wouldn't they? she thought. You're new. You're gorgeous. You're turning heads –you've certainly turned mine. 'I think it's lovely that people are interested in who you are.'

He didn't have a chance to respond as they arrived at the pub car park where her friends immediately welcomed them, proving his point.

She breathed in the heady fragrance of barbecue smoke. It smelt so good that she swore she could taste the food in it. 'The first barbecue of the season.' She sighed. 'Is anything better?'

'Yes,' said Steve. 'The second one. This one is so early in the year, it can be freezing and wet. The next one will be sunny and warm.'

'Perhaps in your house,' said Bella. 'But Dilly loves eating outdoors. If there were only cold, rain-drenched barbecues on offer all season, she'd be there.'

'You know me too well,' said Dilly.

'There's a big queue,' said Jessica, eyeing the throng of

racegoers who were already stacking their plates high with grilled food and side salads. 'Why don't Luke and I save a table in the garden while you get the drinks? Hopefully the queue will have died down by then.'

Luke immediately reached up to take her hand and she smiled down fondly at him.

Dilly glanced at Alex. The fun she had seen earlier had drained from him again.

'I need to make a call,' he said. 'Please eat without me.'

What was that about? wondered Dilly, as she watched him walk away. He had been polite, but the warmth had gone. It was like spring sunshine being eclipsed by clouds and the day turning cooler, and it definitely had something to do with Jessica. What had his aunt done to make him hide his sunniness?

Chapter Three

Even in winter, the whitewashed walls of The Yew Tree pub were hidden behind an array of bright bedding plants. Dilly loved the colours; they were so welcome in the darkest months. As she passed by, she kept an eye out for any dying or diseased leaves which might spread an outbreak of botrytis, and as always, there were none. Jeff, the landlord, was as meticulous with his plants as he was with the rest of his pub. She had barely stepped over the threshold when she heard his voice.

'Don't think I didn't see you casting your professional eye over my plant display, Dilly Pepper,' he called, making her laugh. 'They look alright?' he added, with less certainty.

'As always, Jeff.'

The bar was busy. Jeff happily provided a warm welcome to everyone involved in any village event. It was great for business and even better for the community that had taken this burly man with a bushy beard to its heart.

'Where would we be without this place?' said Dilly as the heat from the fire hit their faces.

'And where would I be without you lot boosting my takings?' said Jeff, his eyes having never once left the pint he was pulling when they walked in, confirming, yet again, what Dilly had suspected for years: that Jeff had to have a second set of eyes hidden somewhere in that glorious bird's nest of a beard. 'Are you all having the usual?'

He was met with a chorus of agreement. 'And lemonades for Jessica and Luke, please,' said Dilly.

Jeff nodded. 'I'll get your drinks sent out to you. Great pinny, by the way, Dilly,' he added, his eyes still focussed on the beer glass.

'That confirms it,' said Dilly.

'We know your pinny's great,' said Steve.

'Not that! That Jeff has more than one set of eyes. He hasn't stopped looking at the pints, yet he saw my apron.'

'Your pinny is visible from outer space,' said Steve. 'It's certainly not going to be missed by Jeff's peripheral vision.'

Dilly was already leading the way to the door. 'Shall we go outside?'

'Spoken like a true gardener,' said Jeff. 'She's been indoors for all of a minute.'

'And the food's in the garden,' said Dilly, holding the door open for her friends and doing her best to ignore the dull ache in her arms. 'I'm ravenous.'

'You could have snacked on your pancake,' said Steve.

Dilly grimaced. 'Not after Basil had eaten half of it.'

They went to load up their plates, plus two for Jessica and Luke, then joined them at the table where their drinks were already waiting for them. Steve squeezed onto the picnic bench next to Jessica and Luke, and Dilly and Bella sat opposite them.

'This is delicious,' said Steve, tucking into his food.

Dilly swigged thirstily from her shandy. 'Leave room for the pancake puddings, Steve.'

'Haven't you had enough of pancakes for one day?' he asked.

'As long as I don't have to toss them, I'll be fine,' she said.

'So you won't be giving them up for Lent,' said Jessica.

'No way.'

'I used to love choosing what to give up for Lent when I was at school,' said Steve. 'Will you be giving up anything, Luke?'

'You know ice cream with sprinkles?'

'Hmm?' said Jessica, faking a shiver. '*Very* seasonal. So, ice cream?'

'No. Ice cream with sprinkles.'

'So ice cream without sprinkles is allowed?' asked Steve.

Luke nodded so hard that Dilly felt sure his head would fall off.

Bella laughed. 'That's going to be a challenge... especially in chilly March!'

'What about you, Dilly?' asked Jessica. 'What are you giving up?'

'I was thinking of joining Luke on the ice cream and sprinkles front.'

'Not allowed,' declared Steve. 'It's got to be your own idea.'

Dilly crammed a huge bite of veggie burger into her mouth. The bun was stacked with salad and she had given it a generous douse of sriracha. The whole lot squeezed out at the sides, and a large dollop landed on the front of her banana apron, then ricocheted downhill until it came to a halt in her lap.

Dilly set about cleaning up the mess with a paper

napkin, starting with her chin, which had taken the first hit. She tried to rub the blobs of sriracha off her cotton apron, but instead of coming away cleanly, the sauce smeared across the banana, leaving bits of disintegrated paper napkin in its wake.

Steve chuckled. 'You're worse than a child, Dilly.'

'I don't do that,' said Luke indignantly, causing Dilly to break into a fit of giggles, which grew into a full-blown laughter attack when she felt Bella's body convulse with laughter next to her. Gasping for breath, she put her hand over her mouth, which was still full of veggie burger.

'The lengths you go to, to avoid committing to giving something up for Lent, Dilly Pepper,' said Steve, making her laugh even harder.

'Alex, there you are,' said Jessica. 'Come and join us.'

'Are you all right, Dilly?' He sounded concerned.

'There's nothing wrong with her,' said Steve. 'She took a gluttonous mouthful of burger to avoid telling us what she's giving up for Lent. Chew the thing, Dilly. We're waiting.'

Had her mouth not been full of food, she would have reminded Steve that he had retired from school life years ago, and teased him about practising teacher-speak on pub picnic benches. Instead, she grabbed her almost empty glass of shandy and hoped that the dregs would be enough to help her to swallow her food.

She watched Alex walk around the picnic table and slide onto the bench next to her. His muscular leg against hers caused an involuntary sharp intake of breath and she began to choke. Tears that had been welling in her eyes cascaded down her face like waterfalls, and Dilly flapped her arms, fearing she might never breathe properly again.

'You're the nearest, Alex. Do the honours, will you, and hit Dilly on the back?' said Steve, making Dilly gasp again. Before she could stop him, Alex was on his feet and pummelling her on the back in an attempt to save her life, when quite frankly no amount of back-slapping and Heimlich manoeuvres could save a woman dying from embarrassment.

'I'm okay,' she panted, lifting a hand to stop him and hoping that if Alex could reframe the end of the pancake race, he might also manage to rework the past few seconds into something less mortifying. It was unlikely.

'How long will you be here?' Steve asked him, taking the spotlight from her, for which she was thankful.

'Three months max,' said Alex, sitting back down next to her and causing a wave of longing to ripple through her.

'Three lovely months with my nephew in Sweetingfield,' said Jessica. Her happiness was visible for everyone to see. Dilly managed a half-smile which barely hid her disappointment. He would be here for thirteen weeks and then he would be gone forever.

'Alex is an expert on the Romans.' Jessica sounded as if she might burst with pride.

'Ah well, you're in the right place,' said Steve. 'Bits of Roman life are always popping up in the fields here.'

'That's what I thought. It might inspire me to live amongst it,' said Alex. Dilly spotted a pulse in his jaw and sensed he wasn't telling the whole story. She was sure he didn't want to be in Sweetingfield, so why was he? After all, there were Roman remains all over the place, so why choose this village? She was certain that he didn't make an error of judgement and end up in Sweetingfield by accident. He didn't seem like an accidental soul. Unlike me, she thought, glancing down at her banana apron spattered with sriracha and dotted with a not particularly decorative mosaic of white napkin glued hither and thither, like loo roll stuck over nicks after a catastrophic wet shave.

He turned to her. 'Are you okay now?'

'I am, thanks,' she said, touched that he had cared enough to ask. She shuffled slightly so she could see his face. There was warmth in his eyes now and not a trace of the shadow of sadness that had haunted him earlier remained.

'Thank you for swapping frying pans with my aunt,' he whispered. 'It made her day.'

He looked genuinely delighted about this, so Dilly guessed that whatever made him guarded and caused him to be standoffish with Jessica didn't stop him from caring about her happiness, and she was relieved. She would never comprehend anyone wishing another person anything but joy.

'No problem.' Dilly wished that her arms didn't think it was a problem. She bet Alex wouldn't have struggled with the heavy pan. She had always assumed that Nathan's younger, academic brother would be weak from study, but here was a man whose body was honed and strong. 'Do you work out?' she asked.

'That came from nowhere.' He laughed and the edges of his eyes crinkled delightfully. Dilly loved those crinkles. They were like a troupe of happy smiles.

'Not really. I was just thinking that you're very muscular for a nerd.' Dilly wanted to swallow down the words, but it was too late now. She'd probably choke on them like she had the veggie burger.

'Some nerds exercise. I'm one of them. It offsets all the sitting down I do when I work. While you...'

She nodded. Neither of them needed to finish that sentence. They were polar opposites. There was absolutely no common ground, and even if there were, he would only be in Sweetingfield for three months, so there was no point in even thinking about what-ifs.

Chapter Four

Dilly always looked forward to working in the garden surrounding the cottage that Mary shared with her longtime friend, Lois. She had known the garden all her life, and she loved it. She had climbed every apple tree as a child, plucked sweet raspberries dangling tantalisingly from canes from summer through to autumn, and scrambled in the dirt to find the treasure of potatoes that had magically grown and swollen beneath the ground. It had been the backdrop to her life, either as a playground in which to discover the natural world around her, or as a place of work, where she now put the knowledge and experience she had gained to good use.

Mary and Lois lived in one of the prettiest cottages in Sweetingfield. A weathered double wooden gate opened from the track around the village green, and a gravel drive led to a welcoming front door which was surrounded by winter-flowering jasmine or fragrant summer roses. Nobody used the front door, preferring instead the stable door at the side of the detached brick house, which opened onto a small utility area with open shelves stacked with well-used trugs and baskets. The top of the door was always open if Mary was awake; and Mary was generally awake. Lois was a different matter. She had always been a lively, fit sparrow of a woman who flitted around the village at top speed, throwing herself physically into life, but recently she had slowed down and often snoozed away whole afternoons, aided by the whisky that had always been her tipple of choice.

The more Lois slept, the more the responsibility for taking care of them both fell onto Mary's shoulders. This worried Dilly, especially as Mary and Lois were in their nineties. They guarded their independence jealously, so Dilly treated the top of the stable-style door at the side of their cottage as a barometer. Every day she checked from a distance that it was open, and only then could she reassure herself that Mary and Lois were fine.

As Dilly closed the gate behind her, she heard a familiar bark. Keaton was the latest in a long line of Norfolk terriers Mary and Lois had welcomed into their home. He had arrived courtesy of a local charity which loaned dogs to elderly owners, and Dilly adored him. She was certain that he must love her, too, as he always leapt up and greeted her enthusiastically.

'You do know you'll be in trouble if Mary catches you jumping up, don't you?' She leant down to pat him and he immediately rolled onto his back for a tummy rub.

'Is that you, Dilly?' called Mary from the back garden.

'It is!'

'Keaton, are you waylaying Dilly?' Her voice wobbled slightly as she called. Dilly had noticed that Mary's voice had lost a little of its strength and she hoped that the rest of her body wasn't following it and weakening, too.

'Come on, Keaton. You don't want to be in trouble,' said

Dilly, standing up. She went over to the oak tree at the side of the house, where glorious golden winter aconites had self-seeded to create a vast swathe of colour. The path had disappeared under the throng of yellow petals which crowded every centimetre of space. Other clients would have wanted them weeded out for tidiness, but not Mary. Mary loved their free-spiritedness and the joyfulness of their bright colour, as did Dilly.

'You can hear the bees buzzing on the aconites,' she said as Mary joined her. They stood and admired the yellow flowers jostling for space and swamping the path.

'Aren't they spectacular?' said Mary. 'They positively glow as well as buzz. And if they keep you, me and the bees happy, I don't give two hoots about what anyone else thinks. Although perhaps their waywardness isn't the best advert for your gardening services.'

'They're a great advert for respecting wildlife though,' said Dilly.

'Too true. We can be too tidy.'

Dilly dragged her eyes from the display to Mary. 'How are you today? Have you recovered from the pancake race?'

'I have! Wasn't it fun?'

Dilly hugged herself and rubbed her arms. Fun wasn't quite how she'd describe her humiliation; then again, they had raised plenty of money for the church hall, so two sore arms and a dented ego were a small price to pay.

'What are we doing today?' she asked. Apart from being one of her favourite people on the planet, Mary was also one of Dilly's favourite clients, because she worked alongside her. Dilly always enjoyed the company of other gardeners, especially those who were already knowledgeable, yet keen to learn more, like Mary. Once upon a time, Lois would have accompanied them, too, as long as the weather was warm, but Mary had always joined Dilly outside come rain, come shine.

'I want to make some changes,' said Mary, leading the way to the large back garden. 'I'm thinking of making a clashing border of bright colours along here to lift the spirits. Everything is so tired and weary. It needs a jolly good fillip.'

'That's a big job.'

'It is. And I want a couple more fruit trees to step up to the plate when the older ones begin to fail. I'd like the next owners to have plenty of fresh fruit after I've shuffled off this mortal coil.'

'We're just in time to get them in,' said Dilly, pushing aside any thought of Mary and Lois not being here forever. 'Do you know which ones you want?'

'You choose. You know what's there and the pollination groups. I'll trust your judgement – and please make sure they have good flavour. I don't want my successors to be disappointed.'

'I'm sure they won't be,' said Dilly, wishing they weren't having a conversation about the thing she had dreaded most since she lost her dad seven years before.

The back garden was almost an acre and sat behind a protective high wall that separated it from Jessica's cottage. Nurturing the garden had been a labour of love for Mary and Lois. Lois had always grown the vegetables, while Mary concentrated on flowers, and since becoming their gardener, Dilly had done whatever they asked on any given week. Now all of the work fell to Mary and Dilly.

'So what do you think of Jessica's handsome nephew?' asked Mary.

Dilly examined a seed head rather than look at her friend. 'I don't really know him.'

'Truly?' asked Mary. 'I saw you with him after the race. You seemed to be chatting about plenty then. I thought you made a striking couple.'

'What? Me in my big banana pinny?' And a general air of being a loser with sriracha slops down my front? she thought, but didn't add.

'You with your halo of glorious red curls that bounce back just like you do, and him with a body to die for.'

Dilly couldn't help laughing. Mary had never married and had never, in all the years that Dilly had known her, commented on the attractiveness of any man. Ninety-five was a peculiar age to suddenly start doing so.

'You might giggle, young lady, but I do have eyes in my head... just.'

'I don't doubt it, but a body to die for or not, I think the eyes in *his* head are firmly fixed on getting back to where he came from.'

'That's a shame. I was hoping to pair you off.'

Dilly spluttered. 'He's not staying, you know.'

Mary leant on her old garden fork. 'That's what they all say. Lois only came for a holiday, and here we are thirty years later, still muddling along. Now, you and I had better get on with our work. It'll be summer before we know it, and I want this done so that I can enjoy looking at it – and you never know, a jolly border might entice Lois outside again. She did so love gardening. It's strange being out here without her.'

Dilly rested her hand on Mary's arm. 'I know. At least *we* can still garden together.'

'Yes, and we can plant a new border together and keep the faith that Lois will be able to come outside and enjoy it. What was it that Audrey Hepburn said?'

'"To plant a garden is to believe in tomorrow",' they chorused.

'Well then,' said Mary, 'to plant a border is to believe that Lois will be able to enjoy it in summer.'

'I can't argue with that,' said Dilly.

'And you can't argue with the look I saw in your eyes when you were sitting next to Jessica's nephew,' said Mary, plucking her old wooden-handled fork from the border.

'Dilly, is that you?' came a voice from the other side of the high wall.

'It is,' Dilly called, hoping that Jessica hadn't heard what Mary had said.

'Are you muscling in on my Dilly time, Jessica?' asked Mary, rolling her eyes in mock umbrage.

'I am, Mary. And I'm sorry. I wouldn't usually, but it's an emergency.'

Dilly immediately set off down the garden. 'I'm on my way,' she shouted.

'Not that much of an emergency,' called a male voice, stopping Dilly in her tracks. She sensed the heat of a fully fledged blush flooding her face. Had Alex been listening to everything she and Mary had said?

'We heard you in the garden, Dilly,' called Jessica, confirming the worst. 'And it occurred to me that Alex knows nothing about gardening, so please could you teach him something so he can knock the nursery cottage garden into shape?'

'I'm sure that Dilly's too busy,' said Alex.

Gardening with her was clearly the last thing he wanted, and Dilly felt gut-deep humiliation at being forced upon him in this way.

'Do you have time for him?' Jessica wasn't giving up.

'Of course she does,' said Mary before Dilly had time to formulate a polite but negative response.

Dilly frowned. 'Do I?' she hissed.

'Yes, you do,' said Mary firmly. 'Spring hasn't properly started yet. Give it another couple of weeks and we know you'll be rushed off your feet with enquiries. What is it you always say? Make hay while the sun shines? Well then, Dilly, my girl, go and make hay with an exceedingly handsome man.' Then she added more quietly, although Dilly was already so mortified that she needn't have bothered. 'And if you don't have time, then make some. It will do you both good.' Dilly was relieved that she was hidden behind the eight-foot wall separating Jessica's and Mary's gardens.

'What was that you said, Mary? I missed the last bit,' called Jessica.

Dilly sighed and with a pleading glance urged Mary not to repeat herself. Mary simply returned her gaze with a questioning look. 'Well?' she challenged. 'Will you, or won't you?'

Lovely though Mary and Jessica were, their interference wasn't at all welcome and Dilly was exasperated with them for putting her in this position. They both knew her well enough to be certain that whatever she might be thinking of them at this moment, there was no way that she would say no, as she was so fond of them both.

'Okay,' she said, barely concealing her reluctance. 'Will Friday morning suit?'

'Perfect!' said Jessica, and Dilly could only imagine poor Alex's appalled face on the other side of the wall.

'Why were you so reluctant to help?' asked Mary, far more loudly than Dilly was comfortable with.

'I wasn't.' Dilly smiled through her embarrassment.

'I thought you'd be glad of the work.'

'Thank you. I am,' she said.

Mary knew that Dilly's savings were always severely depleted by the end of winter and she needed all the work she could get. Even so, Dilly couldn't help but think that this was all a ruse and the ladies were trying to get Alex and her together. So long as Alex believed it was only work and not his interfering aunt and her nonagenarian neighbour match-making, she would be able to carry it off, she decided, feeling bamboozled and embarrassed, but immediately forgiving Mary and Jessica for meddling, as she knew they only had her best interests at heart. Despite the embarrassment and excitement gurgling together uncomfortably in the pit of her stomach, she had to admit that the idea of being able to spend time working side by side with Alex, no matter who had organised it, was thrilling.

Chapter Five

A chill wind caught Dilly's hair as she loaded up her bike trailer. The forecast was for strong wind and showers, but she was ready for it, as she firmly believed there was no such thing as the wrong weather if she was dressed appropriately.

She went back to the house to fill two flasks. One with sweet coffee, the other with warming tomato soup. On days like these, she wished she had learnt to drive, so she could shelter in her car while she drank her soup at lunch. Memories of the great tomato soup spillage two winters ago made her double-check that the lid was screwed on tightly. There was nothing sadder than realising that there was hardly anything left for lunch and what there was, was cold. Add that to the ignominy of leaving a trail of red soup through the village and the shuddering stories the schoolchildren had made up to explain the trail emanating from her bike, and Dilly never wanted to spill another drop of soup again.

At least my legs aren't aching like my frying-pan-weary arms, she thought, as she set off on her bike towards her first call of the day in a garden that was in a kind of no man's land between Sweetingfield and the next village. She cycled up the high street and turned right past the school, where some of the parents and carers were chatting after dropping off their charges. She gave them a friendly smile as she cycled by and they all waved back at her, gladdening her heart. *This* is what I love about Sweetingfield! It's like a big hug I've been wrapped in all my life, she thought as she acknowledged a call of 'Morning, Dilly,' from an allotmenteer she had known since she had been at the village school.

Today's client, Barry, lived in a bungalow hidden behind tall hedges and high metal gates. As Dilly pedalled along his road, she felt a familiar excitement about seeing the bulbs she had planted last autumn peeping through the soil in his garden. It would be a wonderful show by the time warmer spring days were with them. She wondered if they would make Barry's heart sing, as they would hers. She hoped so, although that was optimism above experience, for Barry was a golfer who had no interest in his garden, apart from for holding drinks parties there in the summer. The only opinions he had ever expressed regarding his plot were that it should be tidy, his terrace regularly pressure-washed and that his lawn should resemble a green on a golf course. To underline the fact, there were three golf holes cut into the grass with flags protruding out of them. Dilly compensated for the garden's rigorous tidiness with little log piles hidden behind shrubs and flowers for bees and butterflies. So long as it appeared to be neat from the terrace, Barry was happy.

A white van was parked in the middle of his drive, blocking her way to the back garden. There was no way she could get her trailer around it, so she abandoned her bike and squeezed past the van. She could hear machinery that sounded like a strimmer, but she guessed it must be some kind of saw. She went around the side of the house and into the back garden, a smile on her face, ready to ask the van owner to allow her through, and couldn't believe her eyes. A man was strimming the bulbs she had planted. How dare he wreck *any* plant just as it was about to bloom?

'What are you doing?' She tried to shout above the noise of the strimmer, but the man carried on, his back to her and his head hidden beneath a large black woollen hat as he destroyed all of her hard work. She didn't want to get any closer as unopened early tulip flower buds were flying through the air and she didn't want to surprise him in case it caused an injury. This can't be allowed to continue, she thought, rushing to the door to try to rouse Barry.

It was then she saw the shrubs. She had always taken good care of them, allowing them to flourish and flower. All had been cut into shapeless blobs, even those that should not be cut back in spring. There would be no flowers this year. This man had no idea what he was doing.

She hit Barry's doorbell, then kept ringing it repeatedly to get his attention. Surely he would have heard the noise and stopped the intruder massacring his precious plants?

There was no reply, so she phoned him.

'Barry!' she yelled above the din. 'I'm sorry to shout, but there's a man strimming your garden.'

'Ah, yes. I thought it must be getting on top of you, what with the long grass at the sides.'

'That's not long grass. They're bulbs. Do you remember we said we'd put them where they wouldn't trouble anyone?'

'Did we? I forgot. Anyway, he's cheap.'

'Barry, he's cut back your shrubs.' And they all look like hideous blobs, she thought, mourning the mullered plants.

'Already? Aha! He's a fast worker. Efficient and good

value. It would have taken you hours. I guess you're not up to the job.' Dilly felt sick. *Not up to the job?* This man hadn't a clue what he was doing. 'I'm not sure what I was paying you for,' Barry added. It was an arrow through her heart. She was more hurt and angrier than she had ever been in the whole of her life.

'You were paying for my expertise,' she shouted above the sound of the strimmer, battling to keep the anger from her voice. She needed to remain professional, despite Barry's heartless words. It was his garden and his decision – even if it was the wrong one.

'He's a fraction of the price you are,' said Barry. 'And I'm seeing a lot more bang for my buck.'

Dilly sighed. 'Well, if that's how you feel, I wish you all the best. Thank you for the past work.'

'No prob, Dilly,' he said. 'Got to go. Time and golf wait for no man.'

Dilly climbed forlornly back onto her bike. She had hoped that she might convince Barry to like his garden more, but he only wanted tidiness and a lawn like a putting green. There would be no flowers for butterflies and bees. Probably the slash-and-run man would leave no stalks for wildlife, hidden away, and there would be no birds feeding on seed heads and minibeasts. The loss of their precious habitat saddened her as much as the loss of her income.

As she pedalled slowly back to the village, Dilly thought her head would explode from the force of her increasing fury at the contemptuous way Barry had thrown precious plants for wildlife to the wolves, or at least to an ignorant man with too much kit and not enough knowledge. Her own expertise had been undervalued – and that hurt. She could already sense that Barry's treatment of her would dent her confidence, but wouldn't it be the same for anyone turning up to work to find they hadn't got a job any more? He could have told me that he'd fired me, instead of letting me find out like that though, she thought indignantly. What if I had needed that money to buy my supper tonight?

'Done already, Dilly? That was quick.' The words came crashing through her misery and she immediately put a smile on her face.

'Something like that,' she called back to the allotmenteer.

It wasn't their fault she had lost her job. She wasn't going to inflict her sadness on them. She kept the smile in place as she went past the school, then held out her arm, ready to turn left back down the high street to the safety of her home. Her stomach knotted with the unfairness of having been treated so shabbily, and shame that she had been so unceremoniously kicked out from her job because Barry didn't think she was good enough. It saddened her that she would never see the garden again. It had been a part of her life for six years and she would miss it. While Barry's garden might not have been to her taste, she had loved and tended it as her own, and spent more hours in it than Barry and the slash-and-run man put together. All her careful nurturing had been ripped away, along with much-needed annual income. However would she replace the work for next winter? Year-round clients were rarer than they should be. Too few people appreciated that gardens didn't stop moving forward simply because the house owner had gone inside for winter. They benefitted from being tended all year round, and Dilly needed that income.

She wheeled her bike back into the garage and closed the door, her flasks nestled in the crook of her arm.

'Are you okay, Dilly?'

She looked up to see Bella walking towards her, and rushed to open the kitchen door to let them both in. Once closed, the tears flowed as she gasped out the story of her morning.

'It's officially the worst day of my entire career.' Tears racked her body. 'What if Barry tells people I'm not worth the money and I can't keep on top of the work?'

'You can and you are,' Bella insisted, rubbing her friend's arm reassuringly. 'You have always had so many happy clients.'

'But my reputation is now at stake. All those years of hard work and goodwill could be wiped out by a golfer and a slash-and-run man who know nothing about gardening.'

Dilly furiously unscrewed the lid on her flask and poured out some coffee, spilling it on the table, and Bella immediately grabbed a cloth to wipe it up, then carefully placed the cup in Dilly's hands.

'Thank you.' Dilly cautiously sipped the steaming brew. 'At least it's still warm.' The anger was abating and now she was flailing around for a bright side to cling on to so that she could right her world again. 'And at least you're here, dear sister-friend,' she added, taking one hand from the cup and reaching out for Bella.

'I can't stay for long, though. I'm sorry. I was about to leave for work when I saw you cycle past.'

Dilly's heart swelled with gratitude. 'Are you going in early for a reason?' she asked, flicking the tears from her face.

Bella sighed. 'Nathan isn't around, so Dave and I are having to pull more than our weight.'

'Where's Nathan?' Dilly hadn't seen Bella's boss for ages, but she had assumed their paths hadn't crossed because he had been busy, or away.

'I don't know. I think he must be really struggling,' said Bella, a frown gathering on her forehead and concern clouding her deep brown eyes. 'He hasn't made it into work much lately, and now he's stopped coming in altogether and we can't get hold of him. Dave and I are pitching in as much as we can, but there are so many things we can't do. I mean, I haven't a clue about the plants we're selling. It's Nathan's business and customers want his expertise.'

Dilly's heart went out to Nathan. It was very out of character for him to be absent from work for any length of time. He was five years older than her, and had set up The Treasure Trove Nursery when he was only eighteen. It was, without question, the most beautiful nursery that Dilly had ever visited, but it was the atmosphere there that made the place so special. Nathan hadn't only created a treasure trove of plants; he had employed some much-loved villagers and created a treasure trove of people, too.

'I haven't seen him since we went for a drink together,' said Bella suddenly. 'What if it's my fault?'

Dilly reached out to reassure her friend. 'Of course it isn't. That wouldn't cause Nathan to go to ground. It's Nathan. He's reliable. He's—'

'Gone AWOL,' said Bella sadly. 'I'm worried about him. I thought he was over his marriage split. Everything seemed happy and settled again, but now he's stopped coming to work and it feels as if he's given up.' Her voice dropped to barely a whisper. 'I can't see how the nursery can survive without him.'

Dilly couldn't believe what she was hearing. Bella was the most no-nonsense person she knew. It wasn't like her to be dramatic.

'Of course it will survive,' she insisted, despite a sickening stab of concern. 'It's a wonderful nursery. Everybody loves it. It's part of all of our lives, and that won't change. Nathan will be back in no time. He won't be able to stay away, and everything will return to normal before we know it.'

'I hope you're right, Dilly. Apart from loving working there and missing Nathan—' Bella chewed her lip and Dilly shot her a suspicious glance. There was definitely something Bella was keeping to herself about that date '—on a selfish level, I'm concerned that if I can't work at the nursery, I'd struggle to find a boss as understanding as Nathan, who'll give me so much freedom to be there for Luke when he needs me.'

Dilly's heart sank. Without a job in Sweetingfield, Bella might have to move away, and she couldn't bear the thought of losing her neighbour and friend. She glanced at the clock on the kitchen wall. Much as she wanted Bella to stay, she knew that she needed to go to work. 'You'd better be on your way,' she said.

'Will you be okay?'

'Of course I will. I needed to rant, that's all,' said Dilly, hugging her friend. 'And now I'm all ranted out.' Plus, I have a new worry to think about, she thought, but didn't add. At least her instincts about Doctor Alex Hampton were right. He *was* in Sweetingfield for a reason. It had nothing to do with the Holy Roman Empire and everything to do with the fact that Nathan was his older brother. It was clearly no accident that he was living at the nursery cottage, either. Dilly had assumed he didn't want to stay with Jessica and that Nathan's flat was too small, but now she suspected it had more to do with the running of The Treasure Trove. All she could hope now was that Nathan was okay and that

Alex could do something to help to keep the nursery running.

As Bella closed the kitchen door behind her, Dilly sipped her coffee thoughtfully and watched the bronze leaves that still clung to the beech hedge quiver in the breeze. The wind was picking up. The weather was changing, and since losing the work at Barry's, her life was changing, too. She shuddered. Change was never good.

She couldn't do anything to help Bella and Nathan right now, but she would, she vowed, as soon as she could work out what was going on and what was needed. Her time today was better spent doing something about increasing her income this spring so she could save money to cover the loss of a year-round client next winter. At least it had happened now, rather than at the end of autumn when she had less chance of replacing the income, *and* she had said yes to working alongside Alex, even though it had been the last thing she had wanted to do at the time. She could be grateful for that, she reassured herself, but no amount of sensible reasoning and gratitude could erase the hurt she felt at Barry's treatment of her.

The coffee was cooling and Dilly wished the pain would follow suit, but Barry's words and actions had stung her, and like a bee sting, the pain was intensifying after the initial shock.

Chapter Six

'Another new morning, another fresh start. Give this new day a chance. It might be a golden one. You wouldn't want to miss its delights just because you're upset and cross with Barry,' Dilly told herself as she stepped outside and scurried into her back garden.

It was bitterly cold, but she knew it would warm up to a more tolerable temperature later, just as she was certain the pain she felt from Barry's wounding, thoughtless words would become more bearable with time.

She took down the bird feeder and began to top it up. 'I'm starting today by keeping everybody fed,' she told the robin sitting on the bare stems of a Japanese quince by the kitchen window. 'First you and your friends, then Bella and Luke. Oh! How lovely. Those quince buds will soon open and match your red breast perfectly. What a sight that will be!' She carefully pushed down the lid on the feeder, then looked back to the robin. 'Now I've got to pop next door to get Luke to school and after that I'll be teaching Alex to garden.' A flurry of butterflies unleashed itself in her stomach. That's what new jobs do, she told herself. They make you nervous. It's perfectly normal. 'Have a lovely day, dear robin. Enjoy your breakfast.'

She returned to the warmth of her kitchen and took a few moments to stand and stare at her garden through the window. A couple of blue tits joined the robin, and she smiled as she watched them flit between the Japanese quince and the feeder. It was such a simple pleasure.

'I could stand and watch you all day, but it's time I wasn't here,' she said decisively, turning towards the door.

She strode down her short gravel drive and took a second to glance across the high street towards Mary and Lois' cottage on the edge of the village green. Satisfied that the top of the stable door was open and all was well, Dilly walked up the path to Bella's home. She felt hugely blessed to share more than a thin party wall with her friend. There wasn't much that went on in one house that couldn't be heard in the other. This might have caused some people to fall out with their neighbours, but for her and Bella, it just made them feel even more like one happy family. They had been that way since the day Bella moved in. Pregnant and battling to come to terms with the realisation that Luke's father had no interest in their unborn child, her love, strength and determination shone through as she created a cosy home into which she would welcome her baby.

Now that baby was six, and Dilly liked to help to get him ready for school a couple of times a week when things were quiet at work in the colder months, so that Bella could have some time to herself and a break from routine, but once spring and summer, with their earlier starts and lighter evenings, kicked in, Dilly focussed on work and making as much money as she could to carry her through the harsh winter days when she would have fewer clients requiring her services. She shuddered. What if this year was different? What if she didn't pick up enough work to carry her through now that the slash-and-run man was operating in the local area? Her fears were never far from the surface.

Thankfully, Mary and Jessica stuck with her through any weather. What she would do without them, she did not know, and at least she had the work with Alex at the nursery cottage. Despite being railroaded into the job, she was now grateful for Mary and Jessica's meddling. The hours would help to replace those she had lost at Barry's for a few weeks. Then when Alex left, she would doubtless need to find a new and reliable winter client. She sighed. Now was not the time to worry; now was the time to help Bella.

She let herself into Bella's cottage and popped her head around the sitting room door. The joyous little Tête-à-tête daffodils she had planted in a glazed turquoise bowl last autumn with Luke took centre stage on the fireplace next to stacks of drawings and messages of love scrawled in his gradually neatening handwriting. Dilly loved being in Bella and Luke's home. It made her feel safe, and cocooned from the reality of life alone.

'Breakfast chef is here,' she sang. 'What would sir wish to break his fast with today?'

Luke leapt up from his morning fix of children's programmes and laughed. 'Why are you talking like that?'

Dilly bowed. 'I am merely wishing to ascertain what sir would like for breakfast. Would it be soldiers constructed entirely from the finest bread in Sweetingfield, accompanied by an egg boiled to perfection for said soldiers? Or Sweetingfield's finest bread, dipped into broken egg and fried in the household's prizewinner's frying pan?'

'Eggy bread!' squealed Luke.

'You've got it,' since it's the only meal I can cook with any level of confidence, thought Dilly.

'And the word's *please,* Luke,' called Bella, appearing in the doorway, clad in her running gear.

'I don't know how you can run so soon after the race,' said Dilly, as she broke an egg into a bowl.

Bella stretched and bent down to touch her toes. 'It was ages ago.'

Dilly nodded to her friend's upside-down head. 'And I certainly have no idea how you do *that.* I'm struggling with the prospect of lifting the frying pan, although your pancake race frying pan prize is very smart.'

Bella seemed unconvinced by Dilly's bravado. 'Are you okay?'

Dilly knew that she was referring to their conversation the day before, but neither of them would mention it, as nothing was ever private with a six-year-old repeating every word spoken at home.

'I'm fine,' said Dilly, splashing some milk at the bowl and missing. How she wished that nerves and excitement for her new job didn't make her so clumsy.

'Are you working today?'

'I am,' said Dilly, wiping up the mess. 'I'll be at the nursery cottage.'

'So I might see you at The Treasure Trove,' said Bella, jogging on the spot.

'I hope so.' Dilly seasoned the egg mix and tried not to spill any more. 'I also need to buy some plants for Mary.'

'She is unstoppable.' Bella deposited a kiss on Luke's head before opening the back door. 'See you later, Lukey. Love you.'

'Love you, too, Mum.'

Dilly began to dip slices of bread into the egg mix. Even with the spillages, there would be enough for all three of them, which was a relief, because Bella was always hungry after a run.

Dilly loved walking Luke to school. It made her so happy to see him clambering over the village stocks and being excited to see his friends. It reminded her of her own happy childhood, before it all went wrong. She adored chatting with parents and grandparents at the school gate, just as her mum had done when she was in the infants. Dilly always made the most of her time with them, as she knew that once spring started in earnest, she would miss their catch-ups.

This morning was no different from any other, except for the butterflies, which were multiplying and fluttering about more wildly in her stomach with every minute that passed. She tried to reassure herself that a frisson of nervous excitement was perfectly normal when she started with a new client, but this was a frisson with bells on and Dilly was growing increasingly concerned that the butterflies might break loose of her stomach by lunch time.

Once she had kissed Luke goodbye at the school gates and spent a few minutes catching up with everyone's news, Dilly hurried home to load her bike trailer with tools. She took care and more than a little pleasure in packing extra tools for Alex to help her. She thought of his hands, which did nothing for her nervous excitement, and found her largest gloves to protect them, then added extra secateurs and the loppers she had replaced last season with new. He could have the new ones. They were easier to use. She would make gardening as fun and easy for him as she could, and he would become a convert. She allowed herself a few moments of imagining them together in the nursery cottage garden as she sowed the seeds of a lifetime love of gardening in him. Not only was the garden a project, she realised, but so was Alex. She was excited to share the joy of gardening with him. He might be a hugely intelligent academic, but there wasn't much about local nature, gardens and wildlife that Dilly hadn't encountered before. It would be a meeting of minds and, she hoped, bodies.

Please calm down, Dilly, she begged herself as she wheeled her bike with its trailer out of the little garage at the rear of her cottage. If Alex was as interested in you, as you are in him, he would have asked you himself, and his aunt would not have had to force you on him. Even so, she couldn't help feeling optimistic that magical things would be happening between them before the day was over.

The myriad butterflies that had taken flight in her stomach earlier were now metamorphosing into a murder of agitated crows, and the nearer she got to the nursery, the wilder they became. As she put out a wobbly arm to indicate her left turn into the nursery track, the butterfly-crows were flapping so vigorously that Dilly was convinced her stomach would take flight from her bicycle and her whole body would be dragged buffeting hither and thither with it.

She clung on tightly to the handlebars and cycled cautiously along the pot-holed dirt track towards the large shed which housed the tender plants, the office and two tills. Instead of going inside to see Bella, Dilly continued behind the shed and along a smaller track through the container sales and past the stock beds towards the cottage at the far end of the nursery. The stock beds were a sorry sight in early spring, but in a couple of months, the picture would be entirely different, and if Alex stayed long enough, he would be able to enjoy a tapestry of colour.

Alex's brother, Nathan, had always had a passion for plants, and after a visit to his aunt Jessica, he had decided not to take up his place at university, preferring to rent a field and set up The Treasure Trove. The nursery had gone from strength to strength, and as the business expanded, Nathan had bought the field, along with a tiny cottage at the far end of it, which was where Alex was staying. Nathan had never lived there. He wanted space away from the nursery, so had bought a home nearby. That had gone, along with his marriage, and now he rented a poky flat above the hairdresser's.

Originally, a gamekeeper for the big house on the edge of the village had inhabited the cottage, and he had become Nathan's tenant when Nathan bought the plot, but after the gamekeeper died, the garden became neglected, and Dilly guessed that Nathan's responsibilities at the nursery had taken all of his energies.

She reached the cottage gate and peered over at the tangled mess passing as a garden. On the one hand, it was a paradise for wildlife; on the other, it was as far from looking like most people's idea of a garden as it was possible to be. If this was the level of neglect outside, Dilly could only guess at the state of the internal décor.

After a moment's hesitation, she mentally grabbed herself by the scruff of the neck. If not now, Dilly, when? she challenged herself. Before she had time to reply, she leant her bike against the hedge marking the boundary between the cottage and the nursery, and taking her courage in both hands, she walked through the gate and bent down to test the soil. It was cold, yet as she rolled it around her palm she could almost feel the goodness springing from it. No wonder the weeds are so happy, she thought, replacing the soil in what had once been a border. Weeds were making a play for supremacy and delicate flowers didn't stand a chance. Old man's beard tangled with brambles and deseeded thistles, and judging by the dry brown seedless stems, the garden was home to the national collection of docks.

She wandered around the side of the cottage, past an old barrel doubling up as a water butt at the bottom of a drain-pipe. The broken brick path led down one side of what had once been lawn, but was now like a tiny uncut, un-grazed meadow. Further away, two gnarled plum trees, their branches held aloft by old props, half-hid a dilapidated chicken coop. This little garden had once been so bounteous, it made Dilly grieve. She needed to rescue it – and fast. She wanted to create somewhere that Alex might like to be. Somewhere he might want to make his home.

'You can run away if you like.'

Dilly spun around to see Alex standing at the back door. The sparkle was back. There was no trace of the wariness that seemed to beset him when he was in Jessica's company. He was more handsome than ever. Black jeans gripped deliciously strong thighs, and his toned body was swathed in a deep burgundy sweater. The sight of him made Dilly gulp.

'I could,' she said, hoping he would think that the gulp was about the state of the garden, 'but one of these thuggish plants would probably trip me up, so I'll stay where I am and wrestle with them.'

'Sounds fun,' he said, a smile gently lighting those moss green eyes.

'Can I ask you – is it as bad indoors as it is out here?'

She was surprised when he stood to one side to allow her in. 'Be my guest.'

'Oh! I wasn't being nosy. Just... concerned,' she said, grabbing the opportunity to get a deeper insight into his life.

She squeezed through the narrow doorway and her body revelled in his closeness. The faintest fragrance of citrus as she passed him left her wishing she could hold it in her lungs for evermore. She would have gladly never taken another breath ever again to keep it there, but since she was already light-headed enough, she carried on breathing and tried to focus her attention on the interior of the cottage rather than its temporary inhabitant.

'This is surprisingly lovely.' She glanced around the kitchen, then looked down at her muddy boots.

'Don't worry about them,' he said. 'These floors were made for mud.'

The grey flagstones would have been harsh, but they were softened by the gentle tones of duck-egg-blue painted cupboards and a warming Rayburn. In the centre stood a small pine table with four chairs around it. Files were neatly stacked on three of the chairs, and in front of the fourth stood an empty mug, a laptop and an open document.

He must have seen her look at them. 'I do have a lot of work to do,' he said. 'So, I'm sorry I won't be able to throw myself into gardening as my aunt suggested.' Dilly's heart sank. 'To be honest, I wouldn't care what's outside the door, but Aunt Jessica has got a bee in her bonnet about me getting fresh air and clearing the mess out there.'

If the cottage had a basement, Dilly's heart would have been down there by now. It was beyond her how anyone could not like being outside.

'Fine,' she said sharply as she turned on her heel. 'Leave it with me.'

So much for spending time together and sharing this magical world with him, she thought as she grabbed her gauntlets from the trailer.

She had endured one too many brambles in the face over the years, so she set about hacking them out. First, get rid of anything that will hurt you, she reminded herself. It was a pity she couldn't do the same with Alex Hampton. She was already reeling from Barry's dismissal, so Alex's rejection cut even more deeply. She gritted her teeth as if it would stifle her disappointment, and took her frustrations out on the weeds rampaging through the cottage garden.

After she had cleared the brambles and thistles, she could see the stubs of dormant geraniums lining the path. Already she couldn't wait to see what colour they would be. Were they all white, pink or a sea of blues and purples? There was so much to look forward to here.

She grabbed her spade to dig out a deep-rooted dock from the border and unearthed a cyclamen corm. 'I'm so sorry,' she said, hastily putting it back and patting the soil down.

'Do you always talk to bulbs and bees?'

Dilly turned, red-faced to see Alex. 'Not always, and anyway, it was a corm.'

Fascination shone from his eyes, which seemed to change with sunlight and now shone like emeralds. 'And the difference is?'

'Corms are swollen stem bases. Bulbs are basically modified leaves.'

Dilly could see he was enjoying absorbing this information. Some people loved learning about things and he was clearly one of them.

'And do they both get an apology from you?' he asked.

'Yes, if I dig them up. Why wouldn't they?'

'Will digging it up have killed it?'

'Not once I've apologised,' she said, her face straight.

'And that makes all the difference?' His eyes twinkled with fun.

'It was an accident. I apologised. There'll be cyclamen flowering here in autumn. You'll see.'

He shook his head. 'I'll wonder what's gone wrong if I'm still here in the autumn.'

Dilly returned to her work. She didn't want to think of him leaving, any more than she wanted to think about things going wrong for him.

'What brought you outside?' she asked, finally pulling out the recalcitrant dock root.

'I came to offer you a coffee.'

'That's so kind. Thank you. White, two sugars, please.'

'I don't have any sugar.'

'Okay, I'll have white coffee with no sugar then,' she said. She wasn't going to miss out on drinking a cup of coffee in his company.

'That's unusual. Most sweetened-coffee drinkers wouldn't entertain a coffee without sugar in it.'

Dilly busied herself with weeding the border. Alex was right. She would usually have refused the coffee, especially as she had a perfectly sweetened flask of it on her trailer, but not today. When Alex returned, she was glad to see he had brought one for himself. He held out a pale lemon and white spotted mug to her, and she tore off her gardening gloves to take it.

As she did, her fingers brushed his and she was thrilled to feel that buzz of electricity she had read so much about in the romantic novels she devoured snuggled by the warmth of her cottage fire on those long winter nights alone. Had he felt it too? Her eyes caught his.

'Thank you,' she said, confidently, while hoping that she wasn't blushing too much, or even worse, that she didn't have a smear of dirt on her blushing face.

She took a sip. It was as bitter as a pollinated cucumber and her instant reaction was to spit the vile, unsweetened drink into the border, but instead she kept what she hoped was a self-assured smile on her face and swallowed the devil's drink. Whoever thought that coffee without sugar was a good thing? she wondered as she held on to the mug, torn between wanting him to stay and chat, and hoping he wasn't going to wait with her until she had drunk it all.

'Lovely,' she said, and in an attempt to sidetrack him from the disgustingness of the drink, she talked to him about the plants she had already found in the garden. 'It's going to be gorgeous,' she exclaimed.

'That's good,' he said. 'It sounds as if there'll be enough here not to have to raid the nursery.'

'It might be worth doing though, to showcase some of the plants in a garden situation. Sometimes it's hard for people to imagine them. We could do another garden over there with that land. That belongs to Nathan too, doesn't it?'

'It does, but I think he has enough on with this place at the moment,' said Alex.

Dilly thought about Bella's concerns. All wasn't well with Nathan. Usually he'd have been down here, chatting about plants with her.

'Perhaps I'll mention it to him. Is he in the nursery office?' she asked, probing for more information.

A glimpse of something clouded Alex's face for a second, and Dilly worried that it was hopelessness, then he straightened his shoulders.

'I don't think he's in the office today,' he said, then strode towards the open door.

That doesn't sound encouraging, thought Dilly.

'Just one thing before you head back in time with your Roman friends.'

He turned back to her and she caught sight of a quirk of his mouth, which quickened her heart.

'Where shall I put the brambles and dead stems?'

'Around the back. Behind the garage.' He wafted a hand towards the river, where a solitary garage stood.

She watched him close the door and waited a few seconds before throwing the coffee into the hedge, then she grabbed the bag from her trailer and replenished the mug with sweet, but cooler coffee. Next week, she thought, I'll bring my own sugar. She took the mug to the back garden and spent some time exploring. There was definitely hope in this garden, but was there hope for Nathan? And what about her dreams of gardening with Alex? She looked back at the house and saw him standing at the window, watching her. Was it wishful thinking, or was he simply counting how many minutes she wasn't working?

She turned her back on him so she could gather her thoughts. She was determined to show him that she was a hard worker, although quite what she had to prove, she couldn't fathom. No heart was ever won by hard work. Even so, it niggled that he might think she was a skiver and not giving his aunt good value for her money. She pulled herself up short. She had spotted Alex's kindness and his ability to find the good in situations after the pancake race. He wasn't keeping tabs on her work; she was being oversensitive. It was hardly a surprise after what had happened with Barry. Barry's words had cut her to the quick, and her fears that her reputation could end up in tatters weighed heavily on her.

When her time working in the cottage garden drew to a close, she left the lemon spotted mug on the front doorstep and went to collect the tarpaulin of brambles. Part of her wanted to knock on the door, but he was clearly a busy man and it didn't seem appropriate to disturb his work to hand him a mug. He would find the mug easily enough without her pointing it out.

She cautiously wrapped the tarpaulin around the spiny brambles and dragged them through the garden gate and along the lane towards the brick garage. Stark in its basic design, with red wooden doors which were glazed at the top, it would have looked more at home in a suburb than down a dirt track in the countryside. Still, it was a good place to hide the garden refuse until she had a chance to deal with it.

A few long-dead thorny stems lay scattered down the side of the garage and rather than risk tearing the tarpaulin as she dragged its weight over them, Dilly abandoned her haul of brambles in favour of clearing the path. She took the spiky deadwood around the back of the building and gasped. Instead of a diminishing heap of long-dead wood, she was confronted by a fresh pile of abandoned shrubbery. Her heart raced as her eyes roamed the heap. At the top of it were plants she knew grew in Barry's garden. Had the slash-and-run man been dumping his refuse on Nathan's land? Tears sprang to her eyes as she examined a branch, hacked roughly from what had once been a beautifully shaped plant. Scattered amongst the shrubs' severed limbs were flower heads for early tulips that would never provide nectar to the early bees they had been planted for.

A sob rose in Dilly's throat. 'How could he?' she cried.

Finding the remains was worse than seeing what had remained. Everything the garden had lost and everything she had lost – her income and her reputation – lay abandoned in that unloved heap.

Before she knew what she was doing, she was running towards Alex's house. This was a crime. Dumping garden refuse was against the law, and she was going to stop the thug who had trampled over her reputation and stolen her client, once and for all. She hammered on Alex's door without a second thought to the pain pulsing through her hand and up her arm.

'What is it?' He seemed scared and concerned all at once. 'What's happened, Dilly?'

'Come and look,' she cried.

He followed her, not stopping to close the door. Down the lane they ran, him asking her what she had found and her unable to speak because she was out of breath.

'We need to call the police,' she finally gasped as they rounded the back of the garage.

He stood looking at the pile of plants, worry written across his face. 'Did you find something in there?'

'What? No! That *is* it,' she yelled. 'Someone has been dumping rubbish on your land.'

He looked confused. 'No they haven't.'

'Well, where did it come from?' she demanded, tears streaking her face.

'I did it.'

'You?'

That melting smile, those shining eyes crinkling at the corners. She stood speechlessly staring back at him, fury crackling in the air between them.

'Yes. I helped someone out and dumped the stuff here.'

She had never, in her entire life, been so angry.

'*You?*' she hissed. 'You did it?'

She watched his smile fade. 'What did I do wrong? A guy came into the nursery and said he needed a hand clearing his garden, then another guy said he'd lend me his van, and at that price I could do his, too.'

'*At that price*?' She spoke slowly, her words laden with venom she hadn't known she was capable of feeling.

'What's wrong with that? Someone wanted a service and I provided it. It's all for the nursery.'

'You haven't a clue what you're doing.'

She could see colour rising up his neck. 'The nursery is in trouble,' he said, his voice barely audible. 'I need every penny I can get to keep it afloat.'

'At any cost,' she spat.

He flinched. 'What cost?'

'The cost to wildlife. The cost to my livelihood.'

'You don't have a monopoly on gardens, Dilly.'

Dilly felt as if she would explode with rage. 'Since you don't understand plants and gardens, I can hardly expect you to even begin to comprehend a gardener's finances. I depended on a regular income from Barry to help me to eat and pay my basic bills through the winter. You've steamed in, lost me my client, wrecked his garden and left me losing sleep over how I will manage next winter. I hope you're extremely proud of yourself, *Professor*.'

She couldn't bear to spend another second with him. She stormed away and rushed around the nursery cottage garden, collecting her tools. The yellow spotted mug sat insouciantly on the step where she had left it only a few blissful moments ago, before she had discovered the truth about Alex Hampton. She threw her tools into her trailer and hopped onto her bike. He had ruined everything. Her wonderful working life; her security; the garden she had cared for, for the past six years; her reputation; her faith in the goodness of others; her faith in *his* goodness. He was a wrecking ball, and he didn't care about anything that mattered. 'How could he?' she cried as she cycled down the bumpy track, away from the source of all her pain and worry.

Chapter Seven

'Where were you today, Dilly? I thought you were collecting Mary's plants.'

Bella held out one of the mugs of tea she was carrying. Dilly was sitting on the bench that had once belonged to her dad. She only ever sat on it if she was upset and needed to feel close to him. She looked up at her best friend, her face still wet with tears.

'Oh, Dilly, what on earth has happened?' Bella dumped the mugs in a border and rushed forward to hug her.

'Not here,' Dilly whispered as she stood up. She smiled gratefully at her friend. 'Thanks for the tea.'

'It's half-slopped on the soil,' said Bella, picking up the mugs. 'I'll make you another.'

Dilly led the way to the kitchen door at the side of her cottage, her head down in case anyone saw her. She closed the door quickly and pulled out a chair at her kitchen table. Bella set her tea down and Dilly took a grateful sip.

'And to think, I drank disgusting sugarless coffee just to

spend time getting to know him,' she said. 'And now I'm every bit as bitter as the coffee I chucked in the hedge.'

Bella seemed confused, so Dilly took a deep breath and told her the story of her discovery behind the garage. It was garbled and disjointed, veering from polka-dot mugs to beheaded tulips, and she could tell from Bella's bewildered face that she was making a poor job of getting her tale across.

'So let me get this right. Alex Hampton is the slash-and-run man,' Bella said eventually. Dilly nodded. Somewhere in the melee of words, Bella had found the nub of what had happened. She shook her head. 'I can't believe it, Dilly.'

Fresh tears flowed with another wave of sadness. 'He'll be gone in under three months and will leave me almost jobless and with my reputation in tatters. How could he?'

'Did he know?'

'He didn't know anything. Not how to prune. Not that the tulips weren't grass. He was completely ignorant.'

'I meant, did he know Barry was your client?' Bella asked gently.

'I haven't a clue. And what difference does it make? I'm still a customer down for next winter.'

'I know it makes no difference to where you are now, but what if it was a genuine error? That he didn't know Barry was your client?'

Dilly went quiet for a few moments. 'He shouldn't have been doing the work anyway. He's not a gardener.'

'I guess he must have really needed the money then.'

Dilly reached out for her friend. 'I'm so sorry,' she said, shame supplanting her own sadness as she grasped what this meant for Bella's future at the nursery and in the village. 'I had promised myself that I would do everything I could to help, but instead I didn't buy Mary's plants and I've been prattling on about my own problems instead of realising what this means for you. Please forgive me.'

'There's nothing to forgive.'

'I'll find a way to help,' said Dilly decisively.

Bella squeezed her hand. 'I know you will.' She sighed. 'I'll make you a fresh cup of tea, then I have to go and collect Luke from a birthday party. Will you be okay?'

'Don't worry about the tea. I'll be fine,' said Dilly, sounding more confident than she felt.

'That's good to hear. And you'll be in for Mary's plants tomorrow?'

Dilly's stomach lurched. She wasn't ready to risk seeing Alex Hampton again yet. He had upset her quiet life and brought her nothing but heartache. She swallowed down her anger. She had no choice. She had to support the nursery in every way she could, to protect Bella's future there.

'Of course I'll be at the nursery tomorrow,' she said as she hugged her friend goodbye.

'I'll just have to hope that my path and Alex's don't cross,' she told the plants on her kitchen windowsill. 'At least you all stay the same, unlike almost everything else at the moment.' She ran a little water from the tap into the sink and sat a tray of seedlings in it. 'Have a lovely drink, little ones. I'll see you in a while.'

She went upstairs to the spare bedroom and sat on the floor in front of the bookcase which housed her work files and diaries. Every diary since childhood was there, standing in age order, forming a rainbow of colours across the shelf. Their contents had changed over the years, from childhood scraps, to teenage crushes and then the names of clients. She never lifted the older ones from the shelf. It hurt too much to look back. The past was a place of security and safety that had been crushed in moments and then rebuilt thanks to her dad, only to be crushed again when he died. She could never look back. Those changes had been too painful. This moment and all the tomorrows were all she could think about. She didn't want anything to change, and she was absolutely not going to let Alex Hampton and Barry get under her skin and wreck her happy, secure life. She would book her spring tidy clients in now and get ahead of the game. She would not be beaten.

She took out her previous year's paper diary. It was a mass of colourful squiggles and arrows as always. She should probably use pencil and rub it out, but who wanted a load of shavings of rubbings-out scattered across the kitchen table? It might look messier in her diary, but the coloured squiggles were joyful, and she had always done it that way.

She carried the diary downstairs and sat down at the kitchen table to make a list of the clients who usually had one-off spring tidies. She would book them in, then place advertisements in the shop, on the village website and in the nursery. She hadn't had to advertise for years. Word of mouth usually brought clients to her, but now, what would the word of mouth sound like? She shuddered at the prospect of fighting for her reputation as well as her livelihood.

'Well, fight, I will,' she said, as she went to lift the seedlings onto the draining board.

She filled the kettle with water, and as she waited for it to boil, she readied herself to phone her first client. The butterflies were back, she realised as the kettle began to sing. Nothing had been comfortable since Alex Hampton had arrived in the village, and she craved the stability of normality.

A gentle knock came at the front door. That was odd. No

one ever knocked there. They always came to the side of her cottage. Instead of answering it, she went out of the kitchen door and made her way to the front of the house, her feet crunching on the gravel. When she saw who it was, she spun around to creep back indoors, hoping with every sinew that he hadn't seen her.

'Dilly,' Alex called.

A tidal wave of emotion swamped her. Pure undiluted lust followed by incredulity, sadness and anger so acute she was sure she could have killed him with just one look. She couldn't ignore Alex, but she wasn't ready to see him again. As she walked away, she could hear him following her. She had to face him now.

'I'm just returning this,' he called.

Dilly eyed her tarpaulin, neatly folded and looking like new. 'Are you sure you won't need it for any more of your slash-and-dump behind Nathan's garage, money-making, client-thieving, reputation-shattering ventures?' she spat.

His eyes looked deep into hers. He didn't fear her venom. 'I'm sorry. I messed up. I never meant to harm you, or your business.'

'Too late for that, now,' she hissed.

'Please can we talk?'

'What have we got to say? You came swaggering into Sweetingfield, meddled, upset people, and you'll disappear back over the horizon as soon as you can. In fact—' she added, because now that she had started to speak up for herself and vent her spleen, she couldn't seem to stop '—I'm surprised you haven't already gone.'

He sighed. 'Believe me, I would if I could.'

'That's so easy for you to do, isn't it? Meanwhile I end up picking up the pieces, probably without even a friend to rely on, because her job will go and she won't be able to stay, thanks to your harebrained ideas to save the nursery.'

'I don't understand.'

'Something else you don't understand, *Doctor* Hampton,' she hissed spitefully, then wanted to swallow the words back as he looked so crestfallen. 'Barry called my reputation into question. Nathan employs my best friend. She needs that job, with an employer who understands the demands of parenthood.'

He flinched as if the truth was too painful. 'I really am very sorry, Dilly.' His body seemed burdened with regret, which made her feel worse.

'So you've said.' She snatched the tarpaulin from him. 'Thanks for bringing this back.'

He shrugged as if it were nothing, but Dilly recognised the courage it must have taken to walk straight into her wrath. He had absorbed every vengeful word she had flung at him. He hadn't deflected, bitten back or defended his actions. Instead, he had taken her vitriol on the chin, not out of fear – if he had been fearful, he would never have sought her out – but out of respect for her right to be outraged by what he had done. He was kind, she knew, and she had been crueller than she had ever been in her life.

He breathed in deeply as if steeling himself for another onslaught of her fury, but still he spoke, his eyes engaging hers. 'Do you fancy a drink and a bite to eat at the pub?'

'No. I don't. If you were me, would you? Listen, Alex—' She managed to stop herself from telling him that he was the last person in the world she would want to spend even a second with. How could she say anything so mean when she already felt sick with herself over her outburst and needed to back off? She sighed. 'Alex, I've been crying. I look terrible.'

'You honestly don't, Dilly. If you're not keen on my company, I understand, but I feel awful about what I've done and I would do anything to make things right between us.'

She looked into eyes that brimmed with the need for her forgiveness, and thought of Bella's words. He hadn't done it on purpose and she had been harsh on him. She needed to find a way to protect Bella's job, or else she would never live with herself. Most of all, for her own peace of mind, she needed to apologise to him. She had been rude and cross. He was a fish out of water in a village where he knew too few people. He was flailing around trying to save his brother's nursery and was probably lonely, worried and hated himself as much as she would have, had she inadvertently stolen his client.

'Okay,' she said. 'But I need to put this tarp away and splash some water on my face first, so I'll see you there in fifteen.'

Relief nudged at his lips. 'I'll get the drinks in.'

'Mine's a shandy,' she said, thankful that despite her cruel and hurtful outburst, and all of his and her regrets, they were trying to find a way to build bridges rather than harbour grudges. A surge of hope pinged through her from the tip of her toes to the top of her head.

She immediately stashed the tarpaulin and went indoors to try to repair her tear-stained cheeks.

'You'll have to do,' she told the puffy face staring back at her from the mirror. At least her eyes shone as brightly as ever. The cry must have done them good.

She hurried along the high street and pushed open the door to The Yew Tree pub. She had never felt tense stepping over the threshold. Usually she was embraced by its walls and buffered from the world outside by the warmth of their welcome, but now nothing was normal, and this familiar place where she had always felt safe was unable to calm her. *That's the Alex Hampton effect,* she told herself. *He's done nothing but upset your life since he arrived.*

She glanced around. She couldn't see him at first, then she spotted him sitting at a table discreetly tucked away in an alcove. His face lit up as she walked towards him, and despite her earlier outburst, she couldn't stop her smile reflecting his.

'I'm glad you could make it,' he said, passing her a menu as she sat down.

She placed it on the table, then picked up her glass of shandy and took a gulp of it to try to quell the sudden attack of nervous excitement that had hit her full force in the gut when their eyes met.

'I said I would,' she said, embarrassed for sounding like a petulant child. 'I mean,' she said more gently this time, 'that I would never say I'd do something, then not do it.'

He nodded. 'I know you're reliable, Dilly. My aunt has given me an extremely strong talking-to on that point.'

Dilly wondered what had caused Jessica to go to so much trouble on her behalf, then pushed the thought away in case it was in response to him complaining about her whiling away her time talking to upended bees.

'I'm glad to hear it,' she said, then sighed heavily. 'Alex, I am so sorry about the way I spoke to you earlier.'

'You have no need to apologise. I upset you. It's entirely my fault.'

His eyes were kind, and she relaxed. She knew she was forgiven. He had never meant to hurt her. No one was perfect, but how they responded to their mistakes mattered, and Alex had owned his and apologised quickly, and so had she. They might be different in so many ways, but when it came to something that mattered, like this, she knew they were a perfect match.

'Let's put it behind us.' She reached forward to hold his hand, then realising what was happening, she suddenly grabbed her menu and began to peruse it as if she had never seen it before, and now that she had, it was the most absorbing read of her life.

'What do you recommend?' he asked.

If he had seen her move to grasp his hand, he wasn't drawing attention to it, for which she felt grateful.

'It's all good,' she said, looking up to find his eyes watching her. 'I think I'll have the vegetable moussaka.'

He stood to place the order. 'Another drink to have with your meal?'

She nodded. 'Thank you.' Now, Dilly, she told herself as she dragged her eyes away from him, if you can find a way to relax without trying to grab his hand while thinking inappropriate thoughts about him, this could be the best night in The Yew in a very long time. It's ages since you've been out alone with a man and none of them were ever as attractive as Alex.

If her brain was listening, her eyes had their own agenda and sought him out again. He was leaning against the bar, looking confident and at ease as he chatted with Jeff. Her breathing changed as a thunderbolt of desire tore through her body. What are you doing, Dilly? her brain cried. It was as if her whole body was dispatching all its emergency services to subdue the rioting, lusting cells.

She was still struggling to regain control of her body when he carefully set her drink in front of her. In the second it took him to sit down, Dilly decided to focus on helping Bella. That was what mattered.

'Tell me, Alex—' her voice sounded higher than usual, so

she made a concerted effort to drop it a couple of tones '– why are you helping out at the nursery, instead of working in your usual job?'

He looked like a rabbit caught in headlights. He took a long drink, just as she would have done to give her time to formulate an answer.

'Cut to the chase, why don't you?'

A teasing spark flashed in those captivating green eyes, causing lust to fell her again.

'Are you going to tell me?' she asked, knowing how big her own eyes probably appeared. She could never help it when she wanted to know something. Bella called them 'spotlights of interrogation'.

He sighed, then stared down at the table. 'Jessica says I should trust you with this, but I'm not comfortable with telling anybody.'

The weight of the worries he was burdened with was visible and almost palpable. It did more to quash her desire than her brain ever could. Her heart went out to him. She couldn't push him for answers, much as she wanted, or needed, to know, to honour her promise to Bella. She remained silent, hoping the food wouldn't arrive and interrupt them. She could wait quietly for as long as it took for him to speak.

Dragging a hand across his brow, he said, 'Please don't tell anyone. Not even Bella. I hate talking about other people and private business.'

'You have my word,' she said, holding firmly on to her own hand in an attempt to prevent it reaching out for his.

'When Nathan and his wife divorced, rather than lose the nursery, I bought out his wife's share. It took all of my savings and I had to borrow some money, so I used the value in my flat as a guarantee. Now that Nathan's not... around, I need to keep the nursery going, or else...'

'Or else you both stand to lose everything,' she said softly.

Alex nodded. The situation was worse than Dilly could have ever imagined. 'And there I was whining about losing one client. I'm so sorry,' she said, her hand breaking free of the other as she grasped his. He didn't draw back, and as his fingers curled around hers, she felt a deeper connection to him than she had to any other man she had ever met.

'Please don't apologise, Dilly. There's no need.'

'There's plenty of need. You were trying to do a good thing. I can see that now.'

'I won't ever do it again,' he said, looking at her as if relieved to have unburdened himself.

'What? No more good things from you?'

He laughed and she was delighted to have helped to raise his mood. His eyes caught hers and he became more serious again. 'Thank you.'

'My pleasure,' she said, her hand still holding his. 'So what about you?'

He seemed embarrassed, as if talking about himself was the last thing he wanted to do, and Dilly liked him all the more for it. It made her immediately want to know more, so she asked, 'What *don't* you like – apart from talking about yourself?'

He laughed. 'I would have thought that upbeat Dilly Pepper would only want to talk about things I like.'

Dilly was delighted that he had spotted that she was an optimist. 'I think you learn more about a person from their dislikes – and hopefully there are fewer of them than their likes.'

He shrugged. 'Fair comment. You start.'

'I can see what you're doing, you know. Deflecting from talking about yourself, but I'll start the ball rolling... I hate change.'

'I'm with you on that,' he said, and Dilly, had she not been holding his hand, would have leapt up and punched the air with glee. They had found common ground in this, at least. 'What do you hate about it, Dilly?'

'It's never for the better. Or it never has been for me. I'll be chugging happily along and something will come in, slide-tackle me off my comfy course and ruin it all.'

'Like...?'

She sighed. She didn't want to put a damper on their evening by talking about losing her parents. 'Like everything. Chocolate bars getting smaller...'

'Agreed,' he said, his eyes sparkling. 'What else?'

'Plant names – botanists are forever discovering new things about plants and renaming them, which I guess isn't something that happens with the Romans. I mean, they're reliably Romans.'

He looked suddenly pensive and Dilly realised that she could read his moods so easily. He was like an open book and she liked that.

'I hadn't thought about it before, but you're right,' he said reflectively and Dilly could almost see his brain working. Romans were safe, just as life in Sweetingfield was safe for her. She knew why she needed the comfort of this security, but what on earth had happened to him to make him need it, too?

She might have asked him, but she didn't want to break the silence as they gazed at one another. Being with him like this comforted her yet exhilarated her at the same time, and she would have happily stayed there, staring into those exquisite green eyes forever, had the three little words she had been dreading not interrupted them.

'Two veggie moussakas,' called the barmaid, setting their meals before them.

They snatched back their hands and the moment was ruined.

Dilly usually loved food, but suddenly she couldn't care less about eating. They had held hands; his eyes had held hers; they were in agreement about change; he had confided in her, even if it was at Jessica's insistence and probably only because Jessica knew that Dilly understood more about the business than he did. Even so, these were huge, great strides and she wanted to know what else this evening might hold for them, but the food was getting in the way of her finding out.

Like with any job that she didn't like, Dilly decided to wolf down the moussaka, to get it out of the way. She didn't do it justice by savouring every mouthful as she usually would, but at least her empty plate would give the chef the impression that his food had been enjoyed, rather than shovelled into a mouth that would rather be kissing.

Between forkfuls, she filled Alex in on her life, such as it was, she now realised. Although it was wonderful to have lived in, been to school in and worked in the same village, it was hardly on the scale of seeing the world, as Alex had.

He listened with interest and made her feel as if she was the most intriguing person on the planet, even though she was a normal woman who hadn't been to many places, and whose only ambition had always been to stay in Sweetingfield and maintain the status quo. Somehow though, it didn't seem enough any more. Now she had a new and very intense ambition to throw herself bodily across the table and into Alex's arms.

The meal was over quickly. She hoped that was because he couldn't wait to be alone with her and not because he had tried to keep up with her speed of moussaka-eating and now felt like she did: bloated and unable to manage another drink, let alone pudding.

'So what's your situation with Jessica?' she asked as they walked to the door. A small wrinkle formed between his eyes as emotion clouded his face. 'I mean,' she carried on, as she stepped outside, 'why do you always seem as if she's the last person you want to see?'

'That's not the case at all,' he said briskly. 'She isn't.'

The more relaxed Alex, the one who let her be closer to him, seemed to have disappeared behind invisible barriers. She could see him clamming up before her eyes.

The short walk home passed in silence. When they reached the end of her drive, he whispered, 'I would really appreciate it if you would keep quiet about what we've discussed.'

It was as if a chasm had opened up between them, and Dilly sensed that it was filled with mistrust.

'You know I will,' she said firmly.

'I don't though,' he said. 'It now seems ridiculous to have shared my private concerns with someone I barely know.'

'And now you have a whole new worry weighing on you.' He regarded her sharply. 'You know the one,' she continued. 'You don't know whether or not I'll be discreet, even though I have promised not to tell a soul.' That made him smile slightly. 'I won't let you down,' she reassured him.

'Thank you,' he said.

'And thank you for a delicious meal and for trusting me with your worries.'

She turned away from him. She didn't want him to see her regret at having accidentally shattered the closeness they had shared earlier in the evening. Surely he had felt that connection too? She was certain they had a bond, but for some reason, asking him about dear, lovely Jessica had got in the way, and she had no idea why.

Chapter Eight

It's impossible to be down on a day like this, thought Dilly as she strode across the village green to Jessica's cottage. The sun was shining, the birds were singing and there was an unmistakeable surge in the plants as they burst into life. The sap rising was almost palpable; it was as if the whole world was being dragged upwards from the soil, taking Dilly's mood with it. Her worries over replacing her lost income from Barry and her disappointment with how her meal with Alex had ended were eased by the hope that a bright and beautiful spring day brings. She couldn't stop herself from wondering why Alex was so uncomfortable with his aunt. Jessica was hardly the type to upset people, but Dilly asking about her had certainly troubled him.

She wished she had never mentioned his aunt, but there was nothing she could do about it now. It hadn't been ill-intentioned, and in the same way, he hadn't meant to lose her the job at Barry's. She spotted a flirty pair of blue tits flitting amongst the branches of the oak outside Mary and Lois', and her thoughts immediately wandered to what might have happened with Alex had she not asked about Jessica. The shift from friendliness to guardedness had been immediate and surprising, but at least he had relaxed and trusted her for a while, and that was better than not trusting her at all.

She lifted her face to the sun, which would surely have enough power later to replenish her freckles, and enjoyed the promise of warm summer days ahead. She had taken care to apply suncream for the first time this year before leaving for work. The smell of it was so redolent of long days spent amongst plants and wildlife that she could have done a merry dance. There was a real sense that winter was over, that they had made it through to the other side and now there would be hard work and happiness for months to come. She planned to make the most of this glimpse of long, warm days while it lasted, because spring was a capricious creature and perfectly capable of switching from high summer one day, to deepest, darkest winter the next.

She closed the gate to Jessica's cottage and strolled with a spring in her step to match the season along the long, straight path to her front door. The garden had changed so much in only one week that she could almost hear the plants yawning and stretching as they woke up.

Jessica wasted no time in bringing tea and homemade chocolate cake out to her.

'Breakfast cake. Thank you,' exclaimed Dilly, tucking into Jessica's delicious home baking.

'I'm fuelling you up,' said Jessica, as the church clock struck eight.

'Are you expecting high-energy gardening?' said Dilly between mouthfuls.

'Naturally. You *are* Sweetingfield's gardening heroine.'

'Am I?'

'Yes, indeed. I popped up to the nursery after you'd left and found Alex folding up the tarpaulin like it was a precious hand-crocheted blanket.' Dilly's heart swelled at the thought of him taking such care of it. 'The cottage garden already looks like it's been hit by a human dynamo. You must have both worked jolly hard.'

I did, thought Dilly. What with the work at Nursery Cottage and the pancake race last weekend, her arms were already screaming for their winter holiday and it was only the first week in March. 'The front garden should be under control soon,' she said reassuringly.

'You are amazing. And how did Alex do? Did he pull his weight, or leave it all to you?'

'He was the perfect client,' said Dilly. If perfect clients watch over you like a hawk and give you sugarless coffee, she added mentally.

'That's good to hear. I do worry that he's always got his eyes on words, his feet in the house, his head in the past and not one bit of him enjoying the great outdoors in the here and now. It'll do him a world of good to do something practical outside, instead of getting his exercise from those weights and that cross-trainer thing he keeps in the cottage, taking up all the dining room. What's wrong with being outdoors?'

Dilly thought that she'd be happier if Alex never went outdoors again, if only to protect her income and to stop any more gardens being razed to the ground. Then she pulled herself up sharply. He had apologised and it was only right that she should let it go, even though the thought of the loss of regular income sent a shiver of fear down her spine.

'Perhaps he's so used to city life that he hasn't developed a love of his hands in the soil,' she said kindly.

'You'll soon sort that out for him, won't you?'

'I'll do what I can,' she said. 'Thank you for the cake, Jessica. It was delicious.'

'My pleasure. I'll pop indoors and clear up the kitchen, then I'll come and join you for half an hour, if that's all right with you.'

'That's perfectly fine with me. I'll be as glad of your company as I always am,' said Dilly, as she went on her way to collect some tools for Jessica.

Jessica's garden shed was the outbuilding of Dilly's dreams. Constructed from brick and set into the garden wall, it was pure heaven and Dilly loved spending time in it. There were hooks for every tool, and terracotta pots stacked on shelves. Slate labels, already inscribed with the names of the crops Jessica would tend this summer, were alphabetically filed in a wooden seed tray on the potting bench that stood under a window looking out onto a border which was a butterfly oasis in summer.

Dilly heard footsteps on the path that led to it and was surprised to hear Alex's voice.

'Please don't tell me that my aunt's trying to get me working on her garden, too.'

Dilly swung round to find the doorframe filled with the very man who had been crowding her mind, and despite yesterday's disappointment, she couldn't have been happier to see him.

'Hi, Alex,' she said, unable to stop the flood of colour to her face. 'I was—' She began to speak, but now that she had started, she had no clue where the sentence was going, and her discomfit wasn't helped by the look of expectation on his face as he waited for her to grasp the words swirling around her brain and put them in some sort of order.

'So glad you could make it, Alex,' called Jessica.

Dilly heaved a sigh of relief. Saved by Jessica. Where have all my words gone? she wondered. He must think I'm ridiculous.

Dilly faced the tools hanging from the wall and pretended she was examining them thoughtfully while she tried to hide her embarrassment at having lost the ability to form a coherent sentence.

'I usually help Dilly, and if you're not too busy, I thought it would be lovely if we all gardened together.'

'Jessica.' His voice was further away from Dilly now, so she felt safe to turn and watch what was happening outside.

He reluctantly received a hug from his aunt. His unwillingness to be close to Jessica didn't surprise Dilly now, although why he didn't want to hug lovely Jessica was beyond her. There had to be a reason for it, because he wasn't a shallow man who was given to holding grudges, as he had shown when Dilly had been angry with him, so what had happened to make him be so guarded around his aunt? Dilly looked at Jessica. If his coldness towards her bothered her, she didn't show it. Even so, it must have hurt, and Dilly could see that Alex was hurting, too. What on earth had gone on between them to make their relationship so uncomfortable?

'I am in Sweetingfield to work,' he explained.

'Good,' said Jessica. 'Dilly will show you what's what.'

'Work, as in research.' He sounded patient, but Dilly didn't doubt there was exasperation hidden beneath the surface.

Jessica crossed her arms and tilted her head to one side. 'And you haven't time to help your old aunt?'

There was nothing old about Jessica. She was seventy, fit and healthy and as sharp as a pin. She was clearly playing a part, intent on getting her nephew out into the fresh air every day. She was a woman on a mission and no one would get in her way, it seemed.

'I will always make time to help you. You know that.' He sounded respectful, but firm. 'But I only have thirty minutes right now.'

'Perfect. Half an hour in the great outdoors is all I ask, then you can go and hole yourself up in that little cottage with a laptop for the rest of the day. Far better to get your vitamin D out here than in a capsule from the chemist.' She popped her head around the shed door. 'I'll join you later, Dilly, when Alex has done his thirty minutes.'

The look on Alex's face as Jessica left them together spoke volumes and made Dilly laugh. 'I can read you like a book, you know.'

His eyes twinkled naughtily. 'In which case, I must apologise for the page of swearing.'

Dilly gasped. 'You're hurling silent swear words at your aunt?'

'I would never do that. I'm swearing at myself for not saying no, but I can never say no to Aunt Jessica.'

'Me neither,' said Dilly, remembering Jessica and Mary's mortifying efforts to get her to work with Alex. She and Alex were in the same boat and Dilly couldn't have been happier as they shared a conspiratorial smile. 'We'd better get this half hour over with,' she said, and her heart did a flip when she saw her smile reflected in his. 'Do you know how to use one of these?' she asked, handing him a garden hoe.

His brow knitted. 'Is there a method?'

'There is,' she said, walking towards a border. 'Stand, legs apart at a slight angle, like this.' She showed him. 'Then sweep the blade through the soil and it should cut the weeds away. After that, you can leave them to wither in the sun.'

He did as she had shown him, taking out a few seedlings that really should have been left. 'Keep an eye out for self-seeded honeywort, and forget-me-nots,' she said. 'Your aunt loves forget-me-nots.'

He stared blankly at her. 'You've lost me. Which are they?'

Dilly prodded her hoe in the direction of a glaucous leaf. 'Alex, meet *Cerinthe major* – known as honeywort to her friends. And these little babies here are forget-me-nots.'

'They look the same as that.' He pointed at a cluster of daisy leaves.

'Look more closely,' said Dilly. 'Its leaves are more serrated and a slightly different shape.'

'So it's in the detail. They all look green to me.' Alex bent down to inspect the daisy. 'Ah... I've got you.'

You have, thought Dilly, only you don't know it. 'And since a weed is a plant that's growing in the wrong place, I'm afraid this daisy has to go. Now, are you ready for a gardener's workout?'

'As I'll ever be,' he said, copying her stance and moving the hoe through the soil.

Dilly smiled. Jessica obviously wanted him to spend time outside, clearing his head and not thinking about work, the problems at the nursery and whatever was happening to Nathan, so she would let him do that while enjoying his company. She watched him for a moment. She had thought he was handsome before, but now, with a healthy hint of pink to his cheeks from exerting himself on a sunny early spring day enhancing a body honed by the gym equipment she now knew he had moved into the cottage, he was even more attractive. He was so close – only a couple of steps away from her – but miles away from where she really wanted him to be. The sense of longing mingling with the pain of the unbridgeable gap between them was unbearable. Oh, Dilly Pepper, she thought, you have it bad. She saw him slice through a forget-me-not.

'No,' he said, picking up the upper part of the broken seedling. 'Is there anything I can do for it?'

'You could always apologise and pop it back in the soil.'

'I'm not falling for that one, Dilly.'

'In which case, you'd better take greater care going forward or else Jessica will be in for a disappointing May.'

'I wouldn't want that. At least I'll be out of here around then.'

Dilly's happiness evaporated. He didn't want to be here. He was spending time with her to please his aunt because he was a good nephew and a kind man, but he would be gone as soon as he could.

'Do you hate it here so much?' she dared to ask.

'I don't hate it. It's just not what I'm used to, that's all. But it's good to spend time with family.'

You could have fooled me, she thought, remembering his reaction to her questioning his coolness towards Jessica.

'It is,' she agreed, even though she hadn't spent any time with her own family for a very long time. She had briefly seen distant relatives at her dad's funeral seven years ago, but they all lived so far away that catching up never happened. It made her sad to think of it, so she tried not to, and anyway, Mary, Lois, Bella and Luke were her family now, and she loved each one as if they had been her family forever.

He stopped work and lifted his face to the sun, which

made Dilly smile. Jessica will be pleased to see this, she thought.

'This is harder work than it looks,' he said. 'My arms are going to ache tomorrow.'

'They will,' she said, her own arms having barely recovered from the pancake race. 'But it's a good pain.'

'Is there such a thing?'

'Only when it comes from working in a garden in the early spring sunshine.'

'I feel guilty doing nothing,' he said, making no move to assuage his guilt, which made Dilly smile. He clearly needed to relax more.

'You shouldn't feel guilty. When you're not used to gardening you should take regular breaks.' She looked up and found him watching her.

'Are you suggesting that I'm unfit?'

'I'm suggesting that you're not used to gardening.'

'I can't argue with that,' he said, shaking out his arm. 'All respect to you, Dilly, this isn't a light workout.'

All respect to me? A smile flooded Dilly's face. She needed to hear those words so badly after Barry's treatment of her. She had Alex's respect. All was not lost.

Chapter Nine

Dilly threw back the curtains and gasped. While the weather warnings had been loud and clamouring, the arrival of snow had been silent and stealthy. Nothing ever prepared her for the wonderful romanticism of waking and discovering that her world had been transformed overnight. The village green was like a Christmas card and every house was topped with a thick duvet of purest white. Not a single tyre track marked the pristine snow blanketing the road. The urge to be out in it and playing snowballs with Luke was overwhelming. She pulled on her thermals, topped them off with her warmest trousers and grabbed a coffee.

While everyone else seemed to dream of a white Christmas, Dilly generally wished for snow in January, when it wouldn't affect her income. Snow this late in the year couldn't be more catastrophic for her finances and for getting on top of gardening jobs. Still, it did make her heart flutter, just like Alex did, she thought. And like Alex, it will be gone in no time, she reminded herself firmly. There was no point in dreaming of what might be, when the reality was a snow day waiting to be filled with fun memories.

She glanced over to Mary and Lois' cottage and despite the snow, the upper part of the stable door was open. Reassured that all was well, Dilly went to Bella's.

Bella laughed when she saw her. 'I wondered how long you could bear to wait. I can guess what you want.'

'Is Luke coming out to play?' asked Dilly.

'Yessss!' Luke punched the air. 'Please, Mum?'

'You can, but not in your pyjamas. Go and change first. I'll find you some warm clothes. Are you coming in, Dilly, or staying on the doorstep?'

Dilly could feel the warmth of Bella's cottage on her face. If she went indoors, she would have to strip off all the layers again and she really couldn't be bothered.

'I'll wait outside for him,' she said.

'He won't be long,' said Bella.

'I know,' sang Dilly, remembering how desperate she had been to play in the snow at his age. *At any age*, she corrected herself.

Dilly glanced around Bella's garden. Plants that she had put there for just this moment sat sweetly under white hats. All through the snowless winter she had waited patiently to see those little hats and now they were bigger than she could ever have hoped for. It had to be the heaviest snowfall Sweetingfield had seen in over a decade. She pushed aside the sadness tingeing her happiest memories of playing in the last thick snow with her dad, even though they had both been adults at the time.

'Look at the snow hats,' she called to Luke as he stamped his feet into his wellies. 'Do you know why we left the seed heads on?'

'For birds and minibeasts,' he said, skidding to her side.

'Well remembered. Now we get the joy of seeing the flowers with their snow hats on. Aren't they cute?'

Luke smiled that gappy smile of his. He clearly wanted to play, not talk.

'Shall we head up to the playing fields so we can have loads of space?'

'Yes,' he said, slipping his gloved hand into hers.

They walked as speedily as Dilly dared, the snow making the delightfully satisfying squeaky crunching sound beneath their feet that she had loved since childhood.

When they arrived at the playing fields, there were already several families enjoying the snow, and a group of teens honing some spectacular slides.

'So, Lukey, what's first? Snow man, woman, dog, caterpillar, angel, or since we're not too far from Easter, a snow bunny? Or would you prefer a snowball fight?'

'Fight,' he shouted, his puny arms raised in a boxing stance while the rest of his body looked ready to run away.

'Okay, Luke, you've asked for it!' she said, bending down to pick up some snow. Taking care to make sure it wasn't pushed together too hard, she tossed it in his direction and missed completely. She bent down to make another snowball, and Luke, with none of Dilly's regard for not causing discomfort, ran up to her and rubbed snow in her face.

'Luke.' She spat the snow away, hoping it was clean. 'You're in trouble now!' She mock-growled and chased him around the field with a handful of snow.

'Let's do snow angels!' he shouted, and Dilly, recognising the fear he was trying to hide, flung herself down and made an angel.

Luke immediately took advantage of her position and

rubbed a second handful of snow in her face, leaving her flat in the snow, her arms and legs flailing, and spitting like a snow fountain.

Luke was laughing so hard that Dilly feared he might be sick.

'What have you done to Dilly?' said a male voice she knew so well.

She blushed as she always did when she saw Alex, but she took solace from the possibility that it might return her to her usual skin colour, as she was so cold, she suspected her lips had turned an unbecoming shade of cobalt.

'Thank goodness you're here,' she managed to gasp. 'Help me, Alex.'

'I will not. You're twice the height of Luke. I'll help him.'

'No,' she cried, getting to her feet to run away.

'Come on, Alex. Get her!' shouted Luke, and Dilly ran for all she was worth, laughing loudly, until she slipped on a snow slide some older children had made and went hurtling along it, through a break in the net fencing and plummeted into a deep ditch on the other side. She yelped as she crashed through the thick snow and landed in icy, filthy water at the bottom. Mud splashed up into her screaming mouth as Luke piled down the slope next to her, his gloved hands full of snow ready to rub in her face.

Dilly's mind worked fast. She didn't want to spoil Luke's fun, but she had no intention of sitting too long in ice-cold muddy water. Fortunately, Luke was laughing so hard he was unable to deposit more than a couple of handfuls of snow in her face.

'I think you win,' Alex said to Luke. 'And the honourable thing for a winner to do is to shake the other competitor's hand, and in this instance, help her out of a ditch.'

He held on to the back of Luke's coat while Luke tried to haul Dilly out.

'I can't do it,' said Luke. 'She's stuck.'

Well, this is embarrassing, thought Dilly, shuffling into a position where she could get some purchase with her foot. She reluctantly put her boot into the mud at the bottom, and icy water seeped through her socks and onto her already cold toes. If she could have, she would have cried, but there was no way she was sullying Luke's snow day memories just because she'd taken a tumble. She had forgotten that the excitement of snow always turned into a muddy mess and cold extremities, although she'd never had such catastrophic extremity issues in all of her thirty-five years.

Alex reached down and his strength was reassuring as he hauled her out of the deep, muddy ditch. The sludge released her with a mortifying squelch, but her relief at being back on firmer ground was tempered by the sensation of her trousers and thermals dripping cold water down between her legs.

Luke doubled up with laughter. 'Dilly's wet her pants,' he cried.

Oh joy, she thought. My humiliation is complete.

'I think you'd better go home and get under a warm shower,' said Alex.

'I think so, too.' Dilly felt her pink cheeks blushing a shade deeper as a fleeting image of her and Alex showering together flashed unbidden into her mind.

'This is what Dilly looks like,' shrieked Luke, dragging her back to reality by walking wide-legged, like a toddler with a full nappy.

'You've made his day,' Alex whispered to her.

'I aim to please,' she said. 'What brought you to the playing fields? Were you building a snowman?'

Alex laughed and shook his head. 'I was with Jonty.'

'Jonty's great. It's good you've met.'

She might have guessed that Jonty would welcome Alex into the village community. Like Dilly, Jonty was Sweetingfield born and bred, but unlike her, he had gone away to work in Silicon Valley for a few years, and then like a homing pigeon, he had returned, because village life and daily catch-ups with his demanding and loving grandmother suited him better. He was a little younger than Dilly, and tall and lean, with different-coloured eyes that Dilly thought made him look very cool.

'He was showing me an area where there are signs of Roman habitation,' explained Alex. 'You can see it more clearly when the land is under snow.'

'Was it worth seeing?' she asked, glancing up at him.

'It was.'

His eyes radiated contentment. She hadn't seen that in them before. He might not have realised he was doing it, but he was revealing little glimpses of his character to her, and it delighted her, even if his happiness was simply because he'd spent some time with his precious Romans.

The cool air had brought gentle colour to his face and he was even more handsome for it. Then again, Dilly rationalised, you've always had a thing for ruddy-faced outdoor types. That was why it was so odd she had fallen for him straightaway. He wasn't at all her usual type, but with the fresh air bringing out the colour in his cheeks, he absolutely *was* her type. He definitely needed to be outside every day, instead of cooped up behind a desk, she decided. What was she thinking about? Why on earth should she change him? It was one thing for his aunt to get him outside for half an hour a day for some healthy fresh air and quite another for Dilly to want him to be rugged and outdoorsy. Imagine how I'd feel if anyone tried to change me, she thought. Considering her strange gait, she had to concede that it was a moot point in this instance.

When they reached Bella's cottage, Luke ran ahead and repeatedly rang the doorbell until Bella answered. Her delight at seeing him changed to a look of concern immediately she saw the state of Dilly.

'What happened to you?' she asked.

'It was so funny, Mum,' began Luke.

He chatted away while Bella mouthed to Dilly, "Are you okay?"

Dilly nodded and smiled broadly. "I'll just go and warm up," she mouthed.

'Wait a second, Luke,' Bella said, interrupting his long tale of Dilly's demise. 'You can tell me all of this over a mug of hot chocolate while we let Dilly go home and warm up. What do you say to Dilly?'

'Thank you.' He beamed at her. 'It was the best snow day ever!'

Dilly's heart warmed, even though the rest of her was frozen. 'So happy you enjoyed it, Lukey.'

'And sorry you wet your pants,' he added.

'Lu-u-uke,' growled Bella as Dilly walked away.

'Would you like a coffee?' Dilly asked Alex.

He smiled. 'Yes, please.'

They walked towards her back door and kicked off their boots on the step, then carried them in to warm them by the log burner in the kitchen.

'You go and get changed. I'll make the coffee,' said Alex,

and Dilly, relieved at being handed the opportunity to get out of her wet clothes, hurried upstairs to the bathroom.

One look in the mirror told her everything she needed to know. Her lips were blue, her freckle count had increased significantly courtesy of mud spatters and her hair dripped down her front, causing wet patches around her boobs. It was by far the least attractive she had ever looked. She was grateful the bathroom didn't have a full-length mirror to kill the minuscule shred of hope she still harboured that the appearance of her lower regions had, in some miraculous way, escaped being as completely mortifying as Luke's impersonation implied.

She leant into the shower to turn on the flow. The hot water limped into action. With any luck, it would be approaching an endurable temperature by the time she had finished peeling her sodden, muddy clothes from her body.

Despite her optimism, the shower failed to live up to her hopes for it and was only lukewarm by the time she stepped in and closed the door. Even in this cold state, she couldn't wait any longer for the water to heat up. The very idea of any more of it dropping into the water collection system without cleansing the dirt from her body first was even more unbearable than the temperature of the shower. Her legs were blotched and red, her fingers tinged with a shade of blue that nearly matched her chattering lips and the shower was doing little to warm her, but she reasoned that at least she wasn't going to shock her body by going from cold to hot in an instant.

As the water finally edged towards being warm and Dilly began to thaw, her sense of mortification intensified. She thought back to the humiliation of landing bottom first in the ditch. At least it had been a soft landing in the icy mud, or else she might have sustained an injury. There is still much to be thankful for, she reminded herself as the water finally became hot and her toes tingled painfully back to life. Now she was warming up, she didn't want to stay under the water for too long. Alex was downstairs, and she had already wasted a shower's worth of water waiting for it to heat up.

Having wrapped her wayward hair in a towel, she began to dry her body. The mirror had steamed up, so she could only assume the water had cleansed the mud from her face. She wasn't so desperate for an update on the mud spatters that she was willing to risk leaving wipe marks on the mirror that would stare back at her, reminding her of her humiliation in the muddy ditch long after her brain had done the kind thing and filed it under experiences best forgotten.

With no clean clothes in the bathroom, Dilly wrapped herself in her fluffy yellow towel and stepped out onto the landing, just as Alex came upstairs. They stood opposite one another on the tiny landing, neither speaking, as if all their words had been stolen by the air being sucked from her lungs. He stopped dead, his eyes shining as if she were the most magical creature he had ever seen. Her body tingled with the need for him. His lips parted and he leant towards her. She felt powerful like never before, yet powerless to resist her desires. The urge to let go of the towel was overwhelming. Her fingers slackened against the fabric.

What are you doing? her brain screamed. You are Dilly Pepper from Sweetingfield, not a heroine from one of the novels you lose yourself in every winter. You have hideous purple, pink and blue blotchiness on your ankles, which, thankfully, are the only bit of your body sticking out of the towel you want to drop like some sexy film siren.

She clamped the towel under one arm, mortified by her

body's response to being near him, and took the mug of coffee he was holding. 'Thank you,' she said brightly, as if jollity could possibly mask the deep, heavy longing overwhelming her.

'Shall I take your wet clothes?' he asked.

'No need – I'll bring everything down in a minute,' she said, horrified at the idea of him seeing the thermals torn from her cold, damp body, and left inside out with her knickers still clinging to their legs. 'I need to...' She nodded towards her bedroom door, and taking the hint, he went downstairs as she scuttled away, her feet almost tripping over one another in their haste.

She glimpsed herself in her bedroom mirror. The bright pink towel on her head matched her cheeks, and her biggest, most bulky, yellow fluffy towel wrapped around her body showed her blotchy ankles and swollen pink toes. She looked less like a romantic heroine and more like an uncooked sausage roll.

As she pulled the warm, dry clothes over her damp body, she was still shaken that Alex had caused such a seismic shift in her sense of reality, in her sense of herself and in her common sense. For a few seconds, she had felt amazing, and while a little part of her wished that prudence hadn't prevailed, most of her was grateful that she hadn't made a fool of herself.

That *would* have been embarrassing, she thought as she examined her face in the mirror for any remaining spatters of mud. Her lips were fading to a paler blue now, with shades of lilac and even a little soft pink. She was getting warmer, just as Alex had since they first met. Perhaps he was like the shower and warming slowly.

Enveloped in a snuggly rainbow-coloured Fair Isle

jumper and indigo trousers, with two pairs of thick fluffy socks warming her tingling toes, Dilly raked her fingers through her damp hair to check that no remnants of whatever else was lying in the ditch still clung onto its curls. Convinced that she was back to normal, she went to the bathroom to disentangle her knickers from her thermals and bundled everything together to carry downstairs to the washing machine.

As she entered the kitchen the toaster popped. Alex was standing at the kitchen side. His coat hung from the drying rack suspended above the log burner, and his thick jumper had been jettisoned over the back of one of the kitchen chairs. Dressed in a tight black roll-neck, trousers and socks, he looked like an academic James Bond who was very much at home in her kitchen, and Dilly felt decidedly at home with him being there. It was thrilling and reassuring all at once.

'Hot toast and butter?' he asked.

She smiled. 'Perfect.' How could she have dropped into a stinking ditch and landed in heaven with the man of her dreams creating a food of the gods desert island snack?

'I arranged to meet Jonty at the pub. Will you join us?'

'I would love to,' she said, happily tucking into two slices of lavishly buttered hot toast. 'What happened to Jonty? Did you chase him into a ditch, too?'

He laughed. 'In my defence, that was definitely Luke chasing you.'

'You could have stopped him.'

'And ruin his fun?'

Despite her demise in a ditch, Dilly was happy to know that Alex had seen the importance of Luke making happy memories, too.

'So what *did* happen to Jonty?'

'He went to check in with some of the older members of the village.'

Dilly laughed. 'He'll be having a cup of tea with every last one of them. We'll be lucky to see him this side of Easter.'

'I've not been here long, but even I've noticed that he drinks a lot of tea.'

'Jonty's ninety-eight percent tea, while the rest of us are around sixty percent water.'

'I could have sworn you and your clothes were tipping towards one hundred percent earlier.'

'Give or take a percent for mud and whatever else was in that ditch,' she said, watching his delicious smile light his eyes.

'You're extremely kind to Luke,' he said.

Dilly was happy that he noticed kindness. Kindness mattered, and too many people failed to spot it, or took it for granted.

'He's like family to me,' she said.

'And you're so patient. I'm not sure many people would have been happy to let a boy rub snow in their face.'

'I didn't have much choice. He's getting quicker and stronger every year.'

'Even so...' He tipped his head, as if he knew she was brushing it off.

'And it's so good to make fun memories,' she said, realising if Alex wanted Luke to make memories, then perhaps he had loved snow as a child, and she wanted to know everything about this beautiful man. 'Do you have fond memories of snow days when you were younger?'

'Yes... I loved them.'

'Me too. Happy memories. Snowballs, angels, snowmen...'

'Not for me,' he said. 'I didn't go out in it. I just loved the opportunity to stay home and read.'

'You're teasing.'

'I'm not. Ask Nathan.'

'I would, if I ever saw him these days...'

Had she pushed it too far? She hoped not, but surely he would see that she wanted to help.

'Next time you see him, you can ask him,' he said, dodging her clumsy attempt to get to the bottom of whatever was going on.

'I will,' she said, wondering when she would see Nathan again. She licked the butter from her fingers and became aware of him watching her intently. 'Shall we go?' she asked.

He seemed shaken, as if drawn out of whatever had been holding his attention, then he nodded speechlessly. And they call me Dilly Daydream, she tutted to herself as she stood up to grab her boots and coat, ready for the short walk along the high street.

The path to the door of The Yew Tree pub had been cleared, but the eponymous yew outside was being dragged down by snow-laden branches. Dilly's first thought was to take a brush to them to remove the snow, but when she entered the bar, she was met with such joy from the drinkers about the yew looking like a Christmas tree, that she decided to wait until after dark to relieve the tree of its burden. At least the clocks haven't sprung forward yet, she reassured herself, so those poor branches won't have long to wait.

Jeff stood behind the bar with his arms wide, embracing his beer pumps and the weather, in his Christmas sweater and a flashing knitted Christmas bobble hat.

'You're looking unseasonably festive,' said Dilly.

'Weather called for it,' said Jeff, his bushy beard waggling with every word. 'What can I get you?'

'A pint of shandy for me, please,' said Dilly.

'The special for me,' said Alex.

Dilly squinted at Jeff's sweater. 'Do you have the lights twinkling on your Christmas jumper to match your Christmas hat, Jeff?'

'I do. I swear they warm me up a bit.'

'You should get some for your beard,' called Jonty, stamping the snow from his boots in the doorway.

'Are you suggesting that Jeff's luxuriant mop of facial hair isn't thick enough to warm the cockles of his chin?' asked Dilly, and Alex laughed, making Dilly want to punch the air with happiness. She loved making anyone smile – especially Alex.

'Not out playing in the snow, Dilly?' asked Jeff as he placed her pint before her.

'I've already done that,' she said.

'Why doesn't that surprise me?'

'Have you been out in it yet?' she asked.

'No way. I'm a grown-up and snow days are usually good business for me,' he said, looking around the pub.

'My loss, your gain,' said Dilly.

'Sorry about that,' said Jeff. 'Will you be able to make up for the impromptu day off?'

Dilly shrugged. 'Probably not. I'll just have to bite the bullet and hope it doesn't last too long.'

'I hadn't thought about how weather-dependent your income is,' said Alex. He wasn't only interested in learning about her life; he was also unafraid to say when he didn't know something, too, and Dilly admired him for it. 'I should have realised.'

'There's no reason you should. Sometimes when we get a bad spell, I go up to the nursery and help Nathan pot up containers to sell, which helps a bit.' She lowered her voice. 'But he hasn't been in touch and I kind of half-expected to hear from him when snow was forecast.'

Alex coloured slightly and Dilly was certain it wasn't the warmth in the pub causing it. Something was definitely not right.

'I'll have a chat with him later if you like.'

Dilly gazed into compassionate eyes. She hadn't seen that before and it made her feel inexplicably safe. How could that happen? She barely knew him. Even so, she pocketed a feeling she hadn't had since she was a child, safe in the gaze of her loving parents. It was like stepping back in time, only with an added frisson of excitement. Did he sense this, too? Or was he simply a caring human being and she was projecting her feelings onto him, like she did with plants and animals?

Jeff sat the final pint on the bar. 'My round,' said Alex firmly. 'I've enjoyed this morning more than I usually enjoy the snow.'

'Have you been checking on the elderly as usual, Jonty?' asked Jeff.

'I have. Dilly will be keeping an eye out for Mary and Lois, and I rang around a few and popped in on the rest. Everything's good so far. They all seem to have stocked up ready for a week of snow.'

Jeff harrumphed. 'If it lasts that long, I'll run out of beer.'

'It won't,' said Jonty reassuringly.

'Thank goodness for that,' said Dilly, lifting her pint. 'Cheers! And thanks for the drink, Alex.'

As she lifted her glass, four people by the fire began to

put on their coats. Jeff nodded towards them. 'Looks like it's your lucky day.'

It feels like it too, thought Dilly, glancing at Alex and meeting his smiling eyes.

No one was waiting for a drink at the bar, so Jeff followed them to the fire.

'I'll just have a warm-up before the next lot of snow day drinkers arrive,' he said, leaning against the huge beam above the fireplace that straddled two brick pillars and rubbing his hands together. 'It gets a bit nippy behind the bar.'

Dilly shuffled along a settle by the huge inglenook fireplace and Alex followed her. She thought she would shoot like a rocket through the ceiling at any moment with excitement. Forget the heat from the inglenook, she thought as she enjoyed the sensation of being close to him, the flames of passion are alive and sparking into life all over my body.

'If I were to have a sabbatical, I'd take it in summer,' said Jonty, who seemed unaware that the hot, glowing logs in the grate were no match for the sizzling fire raging in Dilly's body.

She couldn't focus on anything but the pressure of the top of Alex's thigh on hers. It was an intoxicating agony. There was no way she could stop it by moving away from him. She was held captive by a force she neither understood, nor wanted to fight.

'What do you think, Dilly?'

Jeff saying her name dragged her back to reality. She gasped. Had Jeff seen her reaction to being so close to Alex? What had Jeff been talking about?

'What else can I think?' she said in the hope that the vagueness of her response might match the question.

'So, that's agreed then,' said Jeff. 'Thailand next weekend.'

Dilly's jaw dropped and Jeff roared with laughter. 'I don't know where your mind was then, Dilly Pepper, but it certainly wasn't on the history of Sweetingfield.'

Dilly could feel her face turning puce. It was the same as when she had been at school and she was caught not listening, only in those days it was because her brain wasn't on the work or even in the classroom; it was roaming the great outdoors and filled with plants and wildlife. How could anything – any*one* – ever be a match for her beloved outdoors?

She glanced across at Alex. He looked shell-shocked. He had felt the spark, too. He had to have done.

'So long as you weren't worrying about money,' said Jonty.

Dilly was grateful for his concern. 'I'll be okay.'

'I'll get you another pint. I feel bad for doing that now,' said Jeff.

'There's no need,' said Dilly.

'Oh, there's every need. I don't offer a drink on the house often.'

'According to the village records,' said Jonty, 'this has never happened in the entire history of Sweetingfield.'

'Careful,' said Jeff, heading back to the bar. 'I won't be doing it again in a hurry.'

'In which case, I'll get a round in and you keep that free pint for when you want to claim it.' Alex's smile seemed to have Dilly's name written all over it and she nearly passed out with longing.

Chapter Ten

The cold air caught in Dilly's lungs as she stepped from her cottage into a silent darkness that might have felt oppressive if it wasn't for the gentle twinkling of freezing snow. It had been the most memorable of snow days, for all the most unusual reasons. Never before had she experienced such heat. Never had she known such longing, or been so wanton in her mind, even if it hadn't stretched to her brain and the towel had stayed in place. Her body's response to Alex had surprised her. Every man before him paled into insignificance. She had believed herself to be in love before, but she had never felt desire like this. She now knew what was missing from her previous relationships. They had been the pipe and slippers of love, but this was raw, red-hot, fiery lust, mingled with a sense of coming home – of safety and security. Her foot slipped as she stepped from her drive onto the pavement where trampled snow had turned to ice. It would be perilous by morning. Take it easy, Dilly, she told herself. Focus on keeping safe, not on Alex. The last thing you need is to get hurt.

The village green was dotted with snowmen and igloos, which sparkled in the diffused light cast from street lamps. The pub path was clear, just as it had been earlier. Jeff took his responsibility to keep his punters safe extremely seriously, ensuring that they made it to his bar in one piece, even if they left four sheets to the wind.

Jeff spotted her as soon as she popped her head around the pub door.

'Are you claiming your free pint already?' he called.

'Not yet.' Dilly approached the bar and leant over it towards Jeff so she could speak without being overheard. 'I'm here to clear the yew. It was looking too laden earlier.'

'You do know you'll upset the punters?'

'Which is why I waited until after dark,' she whispered. 'I thought a little stealth snow clearance wouldn't upset a soul. They could believe the tree had catapulted its load from its branches, so is it okay if I clear it now?'

'Do what you will, but my offer of a pint still stands at one.'

'I would expect nothing less.'

'You can expect less, Dilly, just don't expect more,' he said, as he opened the cupboard to grab a broom.

Dilly stood beneath the tree, her breath illuminated by the pub lights.

'Let's make this lighter for you,' she said, poking at its snow-laden branches with the broom.

Clods of snow plummeted to the ground, causing the branches to ping heavenwards. As more branches sloughed off the weight bowing them down, it set off further mini-avalanches of snow. She moved swiftly around the tree, keen to get the job done and return to the warmth of her little cottage before anyone complained about her ruining the delightful effect of snow on a Christmas tree outside the pub. Hopefully those who wanted to would have taken pictures by now. She prodded another branch.

'I bet that feels better,' she said to it as it unburdened itself of its load.

'So it's not only bees and corms you talk to?' came that sonorous voice that made her go weak at the knees.

Dilly smiled into the darkness. 'Were you in the pub?'

'No, I popped in to see Jessica and saw you striding out like a woman on a mission with a brush, and was intrigued.'

Pleased that she was intriguing, if only for striding into the darkness brandishing a broom, which made her sound more like a witch than a siren, she poked the brush at the next set of branches. Snow cascaded down and landed a direct hit on them both.

He laughed. 'That's no way to treat a man who's here to offer you work.'

'Work?' She stopped what she was doing.

'If you'd like to come to the nursery and plant up containers as you usually would during bad weather.'

'I would. Very much. Thank you,' she said, smiling broadly at him.

'Good.' He reached up and caught the branches above her, causing a light flutter of snow to land on her.

'Oi! And that's no way to treat a woman with a broom. Although it's kind of you to help.' She prodded more branches and a wedge of snow plummeted onto them both. Cold iciness slid down the back of her neck and she hopped around. 'It's freezing,' she yelped.

'You did it.' He was laughing. She loved his laugh.

'I was trying to get you,' she said indignantly.

'And that makes it better?' He brushed his arm along a branch and snow fell onto her.

She bent down, grabbed a handful of fallen snow and threw it at him, scoring a direct hit in his face. There was a second's silence and Dilly panicked in case she had gone too far.

'Right,' growled Alex. 'This is war.'

Snow flew, mingling with the sparks she was convinced she could actually see lighting the icy air around them. The joy of spending time together and the warmth of her feelings for him kept out the cold. They chased one another like a pair of teenagers around the yew tree, throwing snowballs and hurling threats, as the sound of breathless laughter filled the air.

'So much for keeping quiet about unburdening the yew,' called Jeff from the pub door.

Dilly panted breathlessly. Wonderful though her life was, and thankful though she was for everyone and everything in it, she had not had this much fun in far too long. Even better, she had uncovered Alex's playful side. Now that she had discovered this about him, she wanted to shout from the rooftops that she was utterly, absolutely convinced that he was The One. She could not stifle the smile splitting her face in two. What was it about playing together and staying together? They just had to *get* together first, she thought as she bent over in the hope of curbing any would-be stitches.

Alex was nowhere near as out of breath as she was. 'I haven't had this much fun in a long time,' he said.

'You really should get out more.'

'So Jessica keeps telling me.'

'She's a wise woman.' Dilly stood straighter as her breathing eased. 'You don't behave like an academic.'

'Aren't academics allowed out to play?' he asked.

'They're allowed, but I never thought they did.'

'You have a lot to learn, Dilly.'

'We both do,' she said, looking into his eyes.

Their warm breath mingled in the cold night air between them. Was it weird to be jealous of breath?

'I'll see you tomorrow,' he said, stepping away from her.

Dilly nodded, their breath dispersing as if nothing had happened. Only it had.

Chapter Eleven

Dilly was bored with lying in bed, waiting to hear any signs of life from next door to indicate that Bella and Luke were awake, so she got up. It took another two hours of pottering about her cottage before she heard Luke's surprisingly heavy footsteps running downstairs. Certain that Bella was awake at last, she phoned her.

'I'm doing pots at the nursery today.'

'Fantastic,' exclaimed Bella. 'Did you hear from Nathan?'

The excitement in Bella's voice betrayed how much she wanted Nathan back at work.

'No, I'm sorry. It wasn't Nathan,' said Dilly. 'Alex told me,' she added, hoping she sounded neutral and not as elated as she felt about their fun together in the snow the night before.

'So he's properly stepping up to the plate at the nursery?'

'I don't know,' said Dilly.

'I guess it's hopeful if you're doing the planters though.'

Dilly could hear the relief in her friend's voice. 'Will I see you at work?'

Bella laughed. 'No chance. School's called another snow day. Needless to say, Luke is ecstatic.'

'I'm sorry.'

'What for? Please don't tell me you're feeling bad about going to work. If you are, don't, Dilly. Honestly, I'm delighted to spend a bit of downtime with Luke. It'll be a treat.'

Dilly bit her lip. She hated being unavailable to support Bella. 'If you're sure.'

'I'm completely sure. It'll be fun... until he starts missing school. Fingers crossed they reopen tomorrow as I think that'll be his breaking point,' said Bella.

'You'd better make the most of today then. Have a lovely time together. Hit him with a snowball from me.'

'I most certainly won't. I saw the state of you after your snowball fight and I'm definitely not risking that.'

The snow that had been compacted by people the day before was now frozen solid and more perilous than ever. Even though the high street had been gritted, all the side roads and country lanes were treacherous, so cycling to the nursery was not an option.

Clad in her warmest boots with two pairs of socks and her thermal gardening gloves instead of mittens, Dilly set off on foot for The Treasure Trove Nursery. She only needed a pair of snips to tidy any plants requiring attention, her hot water bottle, and some milk and sugar, in case there was none left. She knew how cold polytunnels could get and she would be standing in one place for hours, so she would need hot drinks, and plenty of them, to keep warm. It was a bright start to the day and her sunny mood matched the morning, with the exception of the chilly air. Despite the sub-zero temperatures, Dilly felt warm through to the marrow, thanks to the excitement of yesterday's turn of events coupled with hope that she would see Alex again.

As she passed Mary's house, she noted that the top section of the barn door was closed, but smoke was coming from the chimney. It's too cold and dangerous even for Mary to be outdoors, she thought, making a mental note to pop in on her after work, ostensibly to talk about the new border and to tell them about her day at the nursery, but really to see if they needed any wood brought in, or something fetched from the village shop. Mary and Lois wouldn't want a fuss made of them just because of the snow. Even so, Dilly didn't like the idea of them taking any risks in this weather.

The nursery was like a winter wonderland. No cars had driven up the long track leading to the shop, which wasn't surprising. Snow was bad news for many businesses. It was the last thing The Treasure Trove needed at this time of year, and it felt as if it was underlining in triplicate the precariousness of Bella's job there and her future in Dilly's life.

Christmas trees, not yet big enough to sell, grew in the fields bordering the track and looked at home under the scattering of white snow clinging to their branches and sparkling in the cool, low sunlight. It was as romantic as any scene in Sweetingfield could be, made even more special because every step of her journey brought her closer to Alex. She had lost count of how many times she had relived the thrill of seeing him last night, but reliving it again now would do no harm. She happily immersed herself in her memories. The world no longer existed. Only her and Alex, their warm breath mingling and a tantalising silence.

'Dilly!'

She screamed just in time to stop Bella's colleague, Dave, shouting her name right next to her ear again.

'You made me jump out of my skin, Dave – or at least out of my winter weather gear.'

'I've been calling you for ages. Thought you must have some of those pea pods in.'

'Pea pods?'

'You know—' Dave wafted around his deerstalker-clad ears '—listening devices.'

'Ear buds?'

'Yes, them. I thought you were listening to one of those passionate, fruity dramas.'

Dilly laughed. Her thoughts may have been fruitier than usual for a weekday morning, but, disappointingly, there was no passionate drama.

'No. Just me, alone with my thoughts.'

'Ah, yes... Dilly Daydream. You don't change. So you're here to do the pots at last?'

'I am. And what do you mean "at last"? I was only asked to come along last night.'

'What I mean,' said Dave, leaning in and lowering his voice, 'is that all the plants were ready to pot up weeks ago, and usually we'd have an eye-catching display of them arranged in containers to entice the public, but instead nothing. *Niente*. Zilch.'

'No need to go multi-lingual on me, Dave. So no one has done any pots at all?'

'Not a single one.'

Clearly the task was bigger than Dilly could have guessed. The pots made good money in spring, when people wanted a pop of colour on their doorsteps. The lack of snow until recently had meant that Nathan wouldn't have asked Dilly to step in, but the fact that no one had been brought in to fill any of the pots in his absence was very worrying indeed.

Dave unlocked the door to the shop and office. 'I don't expect we'll be seeing anyone up here today, but I'll keep an eye out for any intrepid visitors, just in case. Coffee?'

'Yes, please. Don't worry – I'll make it. You get on with what you need to do,' said Dilly.

'I'm going to try to find you a little heater for the polytunnel. The thing in there keeps the frost off, but it's not enough if you're going to be standing still all day.'

'Thanks. I have my hot water bottle.'

'That won't keep your feet warm,' he said, unplugging the heater beneath the till. 'Take this. We shouldn't need it today.'

'But you'll still open?'

'I'm here to check for any frozen pipes and deal with any urgent stuff, so I may as well open up, too.'

She took the heater from him. 'Let me know if there's a rush.'

'Chance'd be a fine thing.'

Dilly poured the coffees and refilled the empty sugar canister. There was some milk left from the previous week, but it smelt off. Nathan had always made sure that his little band of employees were well-looked-after. It was sad to see that his care for them had gone the same way as his love for his nursery. The Treasure Trove had been such a happy place, but the magic had somehow been drained from it.

She filled her hot water bottle and stuffed it down her jacket, then took her coffee and the little fan heater outside and carried them along the rows of potted plants she always imagined were waiting for their forever homes in gardens. She set the coffee down on the snow while she pulled open the door to the polytunnel. The mustiness of baby pelargoniums mingling with compost and a hint of petrichor hit her nostrils. Bella couldn't stand that smell, but to Dilly it was pure heaven. She grabbed her coffee before it got too cold and took it inside. Table after table of spring flowers shone and performed with no one to enjoy them. Stuck here with nothing but spent organic traps and an automated watering system for company, it was as if their lives didn't matter any longer. They appeared to be fine, but Dilly wondered if anyone had bothered with their feeding regime recently. It felt as if nobody cared about them, yet she knew that Nathan had lovingly tended them all before things went wrong for him. It was so sad. She mentally rolled up her sleeves, since she wasn't going to actually roll anything up in these temperatures, and set herself up at an empty bench near a plug socket for the heater.

She began by unwrapping the pots. They were made of pale terracotta clay with a trail of grey streaks meandering through them.

'You're gorgeous,' she told them as she lifted them onto the bench. They were heavy, but her muscles were craving a workout after her snow day off. She examined the rows of plants. 'How can I choose?' she asked. 'You're all so pretty.'

'I can hear you talking to the flowers,' came a voice from the other side of the door.

'Someone has to,' she replied, a smile readily spreading across her face. 'The poor things look as if they're in need of conversation.'

The door opened and she was transfixed. Every time she saw him, he grew more irresistible. His black puffa jacket stopped at his waist, highlighting the length of his muscly legs and a dark khaki hat brought out the mossiness of his green eyes, which shone with the playfulness she now knew was there.

'I wondered if you might appreciate some help,' he said.

'I would,' she said, gathering her senses. 'Come in and be creative.'

'I can't do that. I was thinking more of brawn than creativity.'

'I've already done the heavy work, so you'll have to embrace your creative side.'

Dilly did a double-check. No, tempting though it was to say 'embrace *me*' instead of his creative side, she had stuck to creativity. Now she came to think of it, she might have said 'me'. The colour rose in her face as she wrestled with the prospect of having embarrassed herself again.

'Why are you looking so perplexed?' he asked.

Phew, she thought. I mustn't have said it out loud. Concentrate, Dilly.

'There's a lot to do here. Shall we get on?' She vowed not to think about him embracing her. It would be a challenge. 'Try to do different designs, but also two matching, or similar, so people can have a pair of pots by the front door if they want.'

'Do they want that?'

'Sometimes. Nathan said he'd seen people come in for one and walk out with two, just because they matched, so it's worth offering the option.'

'Will you show me what to do?'

'Gladly,' she said, as he moved to stand behind the potting bench. 'Now for the compost.' She handed him a scoop, and having seen her begin to fill her terracotta pot, he followed suit.

'So far, so good,' he said, and she basked in the glow of him watching her as she prepared the pot for planting.

'You've enough compost in there, so you're ready to plant it up now. Grab some bulbs.' She gestured to the swordlike leaves of miniature daffodils. 'Then one from the top table.' She pointed to a bench filled with miniature shrubs. 'And five others.' She wafted her arms in the direction of the smiling pansy faces, delicate primroses and pastel pompom daisies.

'Like on *Countdown*?'

'I didn't realise that academics watched daytime telly.'

'In my defence, I can't live in the past all the time.'

'Would you, if you could?'

'I'm happier with my brain in the past.'

'That's funny, because like a lot of gardeners, my brain's default setting is six months ahead.'

'So mentally you're in midsummer?'

'Yes, and it's toasty warm where I am.'

'Lucky you.' They went together to the tables of bulbs to consider their selections. He paused. 'Do I choose any colour of flowers?'

'Any that sit comfortably with a terracotta pot and its neighbouring plants. Remember, we all have different tastes. One person will want sumptuous purples, while another will want cool blues and whites. Start with something you'd like.'

Dilly was astonished to see him going for the hotter colours. Burnt orange, umber and red. I didn't expect that, she thought, as she selected a cooler palette.

'That's surprising,' he said, eyeing her selection. 'You're such a colourful person. I thought you were all about vibrant colours.'

Dilly flushed at the thought he had noticed her love of

bright colours and then reminded herself that it was difficult to miss a girl with red hair and a rainbow collection of clashing clothes. Still, he *had* noticed.

'I'm all about something that works and will sell,' she said sensibly.

'And this won't?' He seemed genuinely concerned and her heart went out to him. 'I thought you'd like them.'

'I do. And if I like them, someone else will, too. You stick to making up pots of hot colours and I'll stay cool.'

'Hard to stay anything else in this weather.'

His nose was reddening at the end. He was clearly colder than he was letting on.

'Here.' She reached under her coat and pulled out her hot water bottle.

His eyes were like saucers. 'I was wondering what you were doing then. So this is your secret weapon against the cold. That explains why you were looking so pink.'

She blushed deeper. At least he was putting her heightened colour down to the hot water bottle and not her reaction to being so close to him.

'You can borrow it for a while. You can't beat a hotty on your chest.' What am I saying? she inwardly yelped, wishing she could swallow the words as soon as they were out.

His eyes sparkled with naughtiness as he took the hot water bottle from her, then he dipped his head while he unzipped his jacket. It meant she couldn't see his face and she wondered momentarily if he was hiding some thoughts from her.

They worked together in silence. It suited Dilly. She liked him being there and while she wasn't speaking, she couldn't say anything else she regretted. Soon, they had eight pots ready for sale and she couldn't have been happier. These containers of spring flowers signified hope.

His phone vibrated on the surface of the bench and a name flashed up on the screen: Nathan. Even looking at his phone felt like an intrusion into whatever was playing out in the life of his family. Alex shook off a glove, took out the hot water bottle and handed it to her, before walking away, the phone still vibrating in his hand as he slid open the door.

Warmth left the room with him. The chill cut into her toes and the silence was oppressive, in stark contrast to a few moments ago.

She picked up Nathan's trusty transistor radio and hit the on button in the hope that it might bring relief to the lonely emptiness, only to hear 'Cold Heart' blaring tinnily from its tiny speaker. She left it playing. It was better than nothing. She stamped her feet in an attempt to keep warm as she began to fill another pot, ready to plant. Instead of focussing on the freezing here and now, or her garden plans for the future, she allowed her mind to linger in the past, when he was there. Warm memories, pocketed for lonelier times. She had a great life, but with Alex there, it was even better. She took a pale lilac pansy from its pot and absent-mindedly checked its root system before nestling it into its new home.

'Grow and bloom, little flower,' she whispered. 'Here's to believing in tomorrow.' Left alone with her thoughts, which were the very best kind, she waited for Alex to return. Only he didn't.

Chapter Twelve

It was dusk by the time Dilly left the nursery and made her way back down the snowy track towards the centre of the village. Alex hadn't been in the shop when she said goodbye to Dave and she feared that whatever Nathan had called him about was bad news. Still, she reminded herself, she was doing what she could to help The Treasure Trove. It now had a great selection of pretty containers filled with plants to sell. She wanted to buy one for herself as a souvenir of their time together. Preferably, one that Alex had created, but she couldn't lug it home with her, so she would have to wait until it was safe to cycle with her trailer.

The village green glistened in the glow of the street lamps, and little patches of iced grass peeped between the white, where snow had been dragged from its blades to make snowmen. The biggest, plumpest snowman remained undiminished and proudly took centre stage with its twig arms held wide, as if graciously accepting applause from the shrunken snow audience surrounding it.

The upper part of the stable door at Mary and Lois' cottage was still closed, so Dilly grabbed the fraying rope and rattled the cast-iron bell which hung outside. Snow tumbled from its frame as it jangled and Dilly smiled when Keaton barked and hurled himself at the door, as if he believed that a Norfolk terrier could bodily break it down. The snow covering much of the garden was only marked by the imprints of birds' feet, while nearer the house, boots and dog prints had trampled the snow flat. Dilly didn't think there was much she would be able to do in the garden the next day, but at least she could make sure they had enough logs for their fire.

'Come in. You look frozen.' Mary flung open the door and Dilly climbed up the steps and rushed inside, closing the door quickly behind her to keep in the heat. Keaton immediately leapt up, resting his front legs on Dilly's knees.

'Paws on the floor there, buddy.' She bent down to make a fuss over him once he had stopped jumping up on her, then she grinned at Mary. 'He's learning.'

Mary laughed. 'Only for you,' she said, and Dilly worried that one day Keaton might knock one of the ladies over.

'I'll have to start getting stricter with you, mate,' she said, kissing Keaton on the head, before turning her attention to Mary. 'I'm here because I had an idea for the border.'

'No you're not, Dilly,' said Mary. 'You're here to check up on us.'

Dilly smiled. 'And to see if you need anything. Wood, kindling, food, drink...'

'Only your company, dear Dilly. Everything else is taken care of. Go and sit by the fire and I'll make you a warm drink. A nip of whisky in it wouldn't go amiss. Your lips are blue.'

'Perhaps just a finger of whisky and no hot drink might be better,' said Dilly, trying to minimise the work for Mary.

'How about both? I'll make Irish coffee,' said Mary decisively.

So much for simplifying things, thought Dilly. 'I'll put on the kettle while you sit down.'

Mary held up her hand. 'Dilly, I've been sitting for the better part of the past half hour. I need to move, or else my joints will seize up in the cold.'

Dilly shook her head. Mary always got her way. While Mary filled the kettle, Dilly began to dry the cups on the sink drainer.

'What are you doing, Dilly? Put that tea towel down.'

'I'm cold, Mary. I'm keeping moving,' she teased.

'You're incorrigible. Go and sit by the fire with Lois,' said Mary, taking the tea towel from her, giving Dilly little choice but to do as she had been ordered.

The sitting room ran from the front to the back of the cottage, and in the half closest to the front garden two chairs were positioned either side of the fire for Mary and Lois. The room smelt as it always did in early spring: wood smoke, whisky and wet dog mingling peculiarly, yet happily, with hyacinths, which were always blue, always planted in the same chipped blue and white floral patterned bowl, and always later than they should be because Mary couldn't bear the idea of forcing them for Christmas as it sounded so barbaric.

Lois slumbered in one chair, and the other, surrounded by books heaped on the floor since the tiny nest table was already piled high with them, was Mary's. A richly tapestried ottoman sat between a small two-seater guest sofa and the fire. The furnishings were a mix of faded antiques, passed down through generations of their families, and pops of colour from chartreuse and lemon cushions and a brightly patterned kantha throw slung nonchalantly over the guest sofa. Dilly sat down quietly on the sofa, hoping her presence wouldn't wake Lois, who was so tired these days, and a shadow of the feisty woman she had once been. The warmth of the sitting room began to permeate Dilly's clothes and she was soon stripping off her layers and piling them next to her on the cushions.

'Here we are,' called Mary from the doorway, startling Lois from her slumbers. 'Hot drinks with whisky, Lois,' she said, setting the tray between two open books on the ottoman.

'Ah, whisky. Just what the doctor ordered,' said Lois, and Dilly wondered when, in the history of medicine, a doctor had recommended whisky as a waking beverage.

Dilly handed the ladies their drinks, then sat back with her own, cradling it in her hands for extra warmth.

Mary immediately placed her drink back on the tray and took the poker to stab at the fire. She reached into a log basket and before Dilly could stop her, took a branch and brought it down on her skinny leg with a harsh snap. Dilly's heart was in her mouth. She could have sworn that Mary's leg was more brittle than the branch. Checking the log store to ensure all the wood was cut to a small enough size to fit in their tiny fire went straight to the top of Dilly's to-do list. She would never forgive herself if Mary fractured her leg, having forgotten that with age comes fragility.

'Doesn't that hurt?' she asked.

'Not as much as it hurts the wood,' said Mary, positioning the broken branches on the fire. 'So what have you found to do with yourself today, Dilly?'

'Potting up planters at the nursery.'

'Oh good. Is Nathan back?'

News of Nathan's long absence was clearly doing the rounds.

'No. Just me, Dave and Alex.'

Mary sighed heavily. 'Things aren't right there, are they?'

Dilly, not wishing to lie to Mary nor to betray Alex's trust, shrugged. 'It's a snow day,' she said by way of explanation.

Mary shot her a look that told her loud and clear she knew she wasn't telling her the whole story, but Lois finishing her coffee noisily saved Dilly from any further interrogation.

Mary laughed. 'Did you enjoy that?'

'It was delicious. Thank you.'

'I'll fetch you another,' said Mary, hauling herself up out of her chair.

'Please allow me,' said Dilly.

'Absolutely not. Your job is to stay here and not let the fire go out, nor allow Lois to fall asleep now that I've gone to the trouble of getting her a drink,' said Mary as she headed for the door.

'I worry about her,' hissed Lois, once Mary had left the room.

Dilly felt as if she had taken a punch to the gut. There couldn't be something wrong with Mary.

'Why?' she asked, not wanting to hear the reply in case anything serious was the matter.

'The less I'm able to do, the more she does,' said Lois. 'We need help to do the things I once did, but Mary won't have it.'

Dilly leant across to Lois and lowered her voice. 'Is there anything I can do?'

Lois sighed. 'You might do a few more hours outside if Mary would let you. I can't keep trailing down to the greenhouse to water the tomatoes every day this summer.'

'Why don't I set up a watering system to save you both from trekking down there, without increasing my hours here?' suggested Dilly.

Lois smiled warmly at her. Her dear dark eyes, set into a narrow face wizened by time and her love of being outdoors, shone gently. The light had not gone out yet and it warmed Dilly's heart.

'What are you two plotting?' asked Mary, arriving with Lois' drink and a plate of cheese and biscuits.

'Nothing, dear,' said Lois, reaching up to take her drink from Mary.

Mary immediately lifted it out of her way. 'Spill first!'

'You will if you keep waltzing around with my Irish coffee like that,' said Lois.

'Well?' Mary wasn't going to concede. It made Dilly smile. Mary's inquisitive nature was still glowing brightly.

Lois sighed. 'Dilly kindly offered to put in a watering system for the tomatoes.'

'I see,' said Mary, lowering the drink into Lois' shaking, waiting hands, spilling a drop on the antimacassar, which Lois swiftly mopped up with the sleeve of her navy hand-knitted cardigan. 'Well, that's rather spoilt my fun.'

'What fun is there in watering?' asked Lois.

'Even I have to admit it can be a bit boring at times,' said Dilly.

'I'm not talking about watering,' exclaimed Mary. 'I'm talking about my new project.'

Another one? wondered Dilly, thinking of the huge job of lifting, dividing, redesigning and replanting the long border.

Lois took a sip of her drink. She was more shaky than ever, thought Dilly sadly. A splash of coffee hit the front of the jumper below the cardigan, and she mopped it up with the same sleeve she had used earlier.

'Are you going to tell us about this project, or is it top secret?' Dilly asked.

'Not secret,' said Mary, delving behind her armchair for a book. She set it on her lap with its front cover facing towards Dilly and Lois. 'I'm going to embrace the prickly world of cacti,' she proclaimed.

'Sounds painful,' quipped Lois.

Dilly smiled. Good for Mary, making the most of a less than ideal situation.

'You know nothing about cacti,' said Lois. 'Nor do I.'

'In which case, we shall learn together,' exclaimed Mary. 'I've always fancied a cactus house.'

'Since when?' asked Lois.

'Since I was wondering what to do with the greenhouse now we're getting a little long in the tooth to keep traipsing down there to tend tomatoes.'

Lois' mouth drooped. 'I shall miss my tomatoes.'

'No you won't,' insisted Mary.'We'll grow a couple outside, right by the back door, so we can easily water, feed and pick them, and we shall find out all we can about cacti.'

'Mary, I'm ninety-six.'

'And you're never too old to learn. Come on, Lois, it'll be fun. Get the old grey matter working. You know what they say – use it or lose it.'

Another drop of Irish coffee fell onto Lois' chest. 'Like my drinking skills,' she cackled.

Dilly laughed. She loved to see Lois finding humour in her situation and Mary seeking out new things to learn and opportunities to enrich their lives when they could both so easily have focussed solely on the heartache of Lois' deteriorating health.

'I guess that replacing the tomatoes with cacti is like that saying about life giving you lemons and making lemonade,' she said.

'Please don't give her ideas of growing citrus,' said Lois.

'Now that is a good idea. I'll learn about that once I've conquered the world of cacti,' said Mary, using her chair arms to haul herself to her feet. 'We can put a seat in the greenhouse for you to enjoy the plants, Lois.'

'Or we could put two there so we can enjoy them together,' countered Lois.

Mary patted her arm. 'Your sleeve's soaking. I'll go and get you another cardi.'

'I'll get it,' said Dilly, putting her drink onto the tray.

'You will not,' said Mary firmly.

"See?" Lois mouthed to Dilly, concern written all over her tired, aged face.

Dilly nodded. 'I'll do what I can,' she said reassuringly.

'Thank you,' said Lois, her eyelids looking heavy, as if the effort of waiting for Mary to return with a dry cardigan was too great.

Dilly sat in the silence, pondering the problems around her. At least she would be paid for today, so that was an immediate issue she didn't need to worry about. The loss of her longer-term income from Barry would have to be replaced, although once the weather settled, she should be able to make up some of that with extra spring tidies. Then there was Mary and Lois who needed her help, as did the nursery. Something must have happened to keep Alex away from The Treasure Trove today, and Dilly could only hope that it was nothing too serious. She took a nervous breath in and shivered. Juggling so many people's needs with her own felt overwhelming, but there had to be a way to do it. She would find a way.

Chapter Thirteen

Dilly woke in the early hours, her mind swimming with ideas and no way of fulfilling them in the wrong weather.

'Par for the course in early spring,' she reminded herself, reaching over to her bedside table to flick on the lamp.

On the floor by her bed lay a book filled with scrawls and notes from previous awakenings. Why does my brain work best at five in the morning? she wondered, finding a clean page on which to note her latest ideas. For the first time ever, they involved the nursery. She had to do what she could to secure Bella and Luke's future in the village. She doubted that The Treasure Trove could afford to employ someone to replace Nathan, but something definitely needed to be done until he returned to work. At least while the business stayed afloat, there was hope.

It couldn't have come at a worse time. Spring was here, even if it wasn't showing its full beauty right now, but it was only a matter of time before the weather would turn on a pinhead, as it so often had, and people would flock to the nursery for plants and planters. Then there was Mothering

Sunday. Usually there were pretty pots of joyous spring flowers to put smiles on the faces of loved ones. As for the summer planters and hanging baskets they created every May and June for clients, she had no idea if Alex knew about them, let alone if they had the stock to fill them, given the state of the business. None of this would happen without Nathan. He was a one-man planting powerhouse. Only he wasn't any more, she thought, chewing the end of the pen.

She drew a chart and mapped out her week. If the nursery could afford to pay her for the hours she worked there, it would help her to make up for the loss of her regular income from Barry. If they couldn't? Then what? They needed the planters. She was certain they were key to boosting sales this spring.

She stood up to draw back the curtains so she could look out of the window, as if the silent morning world beyond her cottage might clarify her thoughts. Instead she saw the milkman and gave him a friendly wave. He must think I never sleep, she thought as he nodded his acknowledgement. The trampled-down snow on the pavement glistened in the moonlight. It had been another clear night, plunging temperatures below zero. At least the road has been gritted, thought Dilly, as the milk float crawled silently to the next house.

She went downstairs to make herself a warm drink. Today she would track down Alex and make a proposition. A business one, she reminded herself, regretting that it wasn't a proposition of a more romantic kind. The thrill of their breath mingling, of his thigh against hers, of that moment when her body's needs overtook sense and had she dared, she might have let go of the towel – none of that could be suppressed by the practicality of earning enough money. It was as if her private needs were overwhelming her outward needs. It was a new feeling – fresh, exciting and scary.

'But not as scary as not being able to pay the bills next winter, losing Bella as a neighbour and the beautiful Treasure Trove closing down for good,' she told herself firmly. 'Alex might be an intellectual whizz and you might not head a multinational company, but you are a businesswoman and you do have the skills required for this, unlike him,' she said aloud, as if hearing it might shore up her confidence in her ability to convince Alex that she could help in a meaningful way.

Having reviewed her notes and drunk her coffee, she made herself a bowl of steaming porridge and stirred in a generous drizzle of sticky maple syrup. She was not going to let the cold get to her.

Dilly waited a while longer before she left her cottage. It was not quite light, and a little early for social calls, but if her offer of help was going to be accepted, she wanted to fit in a long day's work at the nursery. She had to focus on what needed to be done, she decided. She would stay away from any discussion about Nathan. Clearly Alex's loyalty to his brother would not allow him to speak about whatever was the matter, but why did she need to know anyway? That he was suffering in some way, and that the future of his beloved nursery and Bella's livelihood and Alex's money were in jeopardy, was all the information she needed. Private details were irrelevant.

Footprints in the snow on the path leading to his cottage showed the imprints of only his boots. She trod alongside his footprints. Two sets of prints from two solitary people. Did he feel alone like she did sometimes? The thought saddened her. She pressed her smaller footprint into one of his and smiled to herself as she lengthened her stride and walked in his footsteps towards his garden.

Pale smoke meandered into the air above the chimney at the cottage. At least that meant that he was likely to be awake, she thought as she closed the garden gate.

She knocked on the door and waited, then realised she had stopped breathing. Passing out on his doorstep would not be clever, she told herself, forcing air into her lungs.

He opened the door and her inability to get air into her lungs was miraculously cured by a sharp intake of breath. Alex in his day clothes was a captivating sight, but Alex in navy checked pyjama bottoms and a navy long-sleeved tee, topped off with mussed-up bed hair was too exciting to do business with. She looked down and immediately regretted it. Bare toes on the stone and the most perfect feet she had ever set eyes on. She bit her lip and tried to rally her thoughts, which had been catapulted all over the place by the sight of him.

'Are you okay?' he said.

How can you even ask, when your body does this to my mine? she wanted to scream. She stood motionless, like a rabbit caught in headlights for a few seconds, before being hit by the full force of her befuddled body going into fight or flight mode. She swallowed hard and clung to the edge of the porch as if it would stop her from fleeing down the snowy garden path.

'Yes,' she finally managed. 'I'm fine. I'm worried about the nursery though, and I have a proposition to make.'

She blushed at the word and wondered why she hadn't sought out a synonym. Even if she had, she would have said it, but she'd still have been thinking of propositioning him.

'You'd better come in.' He stepped to one side to let her pass.

Being so close to this astonishing man, who smelt of sleep and sexiness and wood smoke was more than she could bear, and she was alarmed to physically weaken in his presence. Willing her legs not to give way under her, she stepped into the cottage.

'It's warmest in the kitchen,' he said, his voice soft, as he closed the door behind her.

Come on, Dilly, she told herself firmly, do not be put off by his body. You have work to do. She stepped unsteadily towards the Rayburn as if to warm herself, but it was really to get further away from him so that she could pay attention to what she was here to achieve, rather than get sidetracked by her body's needs. You can do this, she reassured herself. You have the expertise, the experience, the knowledge and the desire. No! Don't think about desire.

As she began to recover from the initial excitement of seeing him so recently out of bed, she examined his handsome face and was shocked to see tiredness around his eyes. He mustn't have slept properly, she realised. This man needed her help, even if he didn't want it.

'To what do I owe this pleasure?' he asked.

She smiled confidently. 'The pleasure's all mine,' she said, and immediately regretted it, a grimace replacing her self-assured smile. 'Well, actually it isn't a pleasure.'

'That sounds worrying.'

He looked so together, while she felt like she was falling apart. She needed to regroup.

As if sensing this, he said. 'I was about to make a coffee. Would you like one?'

'No, thanks.' Much as she would have loved one, she had

no sugar with her and no means of easily throwing the bitter brew into a hedge.

'I have sugar.' He tilted his head and smiled teasingly at her.

'Ah... well, in that case, yes, please.'

She could have danced around the kitchen with happiness. He had thought of her and bought her some sugar.

'I thought I should. After all, I don't want the hedge dying of caffeine poisoning.'

He raised an eyebrow, causing Dilly to blush from a combination of pure desire and complete mortification at having been spotted tipping his sugarless coffee into the garden hedge. Even so, as he turned away to make their drinks, her embarrassment was drowned by lust as she admired his broad shoulders and strong back.

She glanced away as soon as she heard the base of the mug scratch against the work surface. He set the mug on the table, then cleared the papers from the chair and Dilly gratefully sat down. If she was going to slip into any more unforeseen and extremely unprofessional swoons, she would be far safer doing it from a seated position.

'So what is this proposition about?' he asked.

There was that bewitching twinkle in his eyes again and it took every ounce of strength she had to ignore it and smile with the confidence she knew she ought to have, even if she didn't quite feel it one hundred percent.

'First,' she said, stiffly, 'I was wondering if you wanted me back in today to make up some containers for the nursery. Nathan usually sells a lot of them in spring.'

He looked regretful. 'I'm sorry, Dilly. I don't think the nursery can afford you.'

Dilly shook her head in disbelief. Were things really that

bad? She took a slow sip of hot coffee while she corralled her thoughts. 'So who will do the pots?'

'I guess that will fall to me.'

Speaks volumes, thought Dilly. 'The ground still hasn't thawed so I have nothing pressing today. Let me help as a volunteer.'

'I can't allow you to work for nothing.'

'Why not? I'm offering. As a friend.'

'It's not right.'

'And it's not right that this wonderful nursery isn't thriving. I want it to thrive. I need it to thrive, both for my clients and my best friend.' And you, you gorgeous, stubborn, proud man, she thought.

'But Dilly, it can't afford you, and it's not right that you should offer your considerable expertise for free.'

Considerable expertise? She was glad she wasn't holding her coffee at that moment. She might have dropped it with relief and gratitude. After everything Barry had said, she needed to hear those words more than ever. She felt a warm glow of happiness. Times might be dire, but Alex respected her abilities, so there was a chance that she could convince him he needed her.

'Okay,' she said, calmly. 'How about I make up containers and if they sell, I take a cut? That way, I'll be paid and you don't have to spend any money on me upfront.'

'I'm not sure it would work.'

'It *would* work. Trust me,' she said. She hoped her confidence, which was growing by the second, and the serenity she felt about the solution transferred to him. His brow furrowed, and she quashed all desire to kiss away those worry lines. She would have to ease them with practical action instead, she thought with a pang of regret.

He looked out of the window and she followed his gaze. The hedgerows had been stripped of all berries and there was little food out there for the birds. She was about to say something about them, but reminded herself to stay on track. *One step at a time, Dilly. You can put food out for the birds once you get his agreement.* She regarded him expectantly. He wasn't looking thrilled at the prospect of her offer, which didn't make any sense at all, since it was the perfect solution. She would have to try harder.

'Look, Alex. It's no skin off my nose if you want to sink your money into a business and let it fail.' Too hard? she wondered. Somehow, the plight of hungry birds and the thought of a delayed opportunity to feed them was chivvying her on and intensifying the sense of urgency about Alex's and Bella's situations.

She watched his Adam's apple jump nervously in his throat. She wanted to kiss its bobbing loveliness, which was hardly an appropriate response, given that she was here to talk business.

He heaved a heavy sigh. 'I'm not comfortable with it,' he said, and she believed him. He hadn't been consistently comfortable since the day they had met. He seemed to be open one minute, then closed like a crocus flower on a cold day when he was with Jessica. Dilly reached out to touch his arm and reassure him, which was hardly proper business protocol, but she didn't like to see him suffering like this and she wanted to make everything better for him. He leapt away as if she had injected a thousand volts into him while he was standing in a bucket of water.

'Sorry,' she said, and he looked back at her, shocked. 'I was only trying to help.'

'I know,' he said, colour rising in his face.

She was ashamed of herself for touching him and making things worse, but she immediately put her humiliation and the pain of his rejection to one side, because she was here to accomplish one thing, and she would not leave until she had achieved it.

'If it helps,' she said, the calmness of her voice at odds with her shame, 'I can buy into the business.'

She had no idea how she would fund this, but she would find a way. She would do anything to save The Treasure Trove and secure Bella's future in Sweetingfield.

'That won't do.'

'So please let me help by making up the baskets and containers. It will cost you nothing. We can sit down and bash out an agreement, not that it's needed, because I trust you.'

He glanced sharply into her eyes, as if stung by her words, then shook his head. 'I feel at a disadvantage talking business in my pyjamas.'

I feel at a disadvantage looking at you in them, she thought, then, against every bodily plea, she said, 'Why not get dressed while I make more coffee? Have a shower and a think. Phone Nathan. Chat it through with him. I'm sure he'll see it's a good solution. Mothering Sunday will be on us before we know it, and after that, Nathan makes good money refilling people's hanging baskets for them, and I usually help out whenever I can. I know what his customers like. I get involved every year and see their baskets outside their homes all summer long.'

He rubbed his eyes as if bored with hearing her, then he scraped back his chair with such determination that she was worried he would ask her to leave. Resolutely, she stayed where she was. If he wanted her to go, he would have to physically eject her. Even thinking about it sent a thrill through her.

As he reached the door, he turned to her. 'Deal,' he said.

'Deal, I plant up containers, or deal, I make coffee while you think about my offer?'

He smiled. 'Deal, you make coffee while I shower. I think best in the shower.'

She nodded reassuringly and stood to put the kettle under the tap as he left the kitchen. The creak of floorboards above her head stopped her in her tracks. Reasoning that if he had a shower, she would only have to boil the water again when he finished, she held off making the coffee and used the time to stand by the sink and study the garden through the window. As she watched the sun rise, she pondered what she could do to create the best possible view from the kitchen. She wanted to create a haven for Alex that might be a salve to his troubles. Somewhere that would soothe him. Somewhere he might want to stay. To plant a garden is to believe in tomorrow, she reminded herself as she placed her hope in the scrubby patch of land beyond the pane.

There would have to be changes. The lavender was well past its best and not cut back. Perhaps it hadn't been for years, she thought, looking at the splayed plants flopping over a scrappy lawn that needed resowing. So many shrubs had outgrown their spaces and were blocking the view down the garden. Thugs played for garden dominance. It was like a battle zone. She would create a gentler space, one in which anyone in the kitchen could find diversion, solace and a refuge without going outdoors, so that even if he was working at the kitchen table, Alex would have scenery into which to escape. She sat at the chair in front of his closed laptop and looked out. Yes, she would make this a diverting view – and she would start by bringing him some bird feeders and keeping them topped up. Or perhaps she might even convince Alex to fill them. She would spark his interest in the garden somehow. Jessica would be delighted.

She was so absorbed in her plans that Alex's arrival back in the kitchen, hair damp from the shower, took her by surprise. She wasn't sure which she preferred, Alex's hair all messy from a bad night's sleep, or Alex's hair clumping divinely and dripping slightly after a shower. Both were spectacular, and to see them one after the other made her want to spend every morning alternating between them for the rest of her life. This won't do, she reminded herself sternly. You are here to persuade Alex to let you help, not to visibly drool every time he enters the room.

'I thought you were making coffee.' He sounded accusatory, as if he couldn't even trust her to do that, so how could he trust her to keep her half of a business deal?

'I am,' she said confidently. 'But I didn't know how long you'd be and I didn't want to waste electricity by brewing up twice, so I waited.'

'Very thrifty.'

'I like to think of it as an efficient use of my time.'

'While you sit and stare?'

'While I plan the renovation of your back garden, actually.'

'I'll fill the kettle then, shall I?' He cocked his eyebrow in that teasing way of his.

She scraped back her chair. 'Ah, no. You sit down. I'll make the coffee. I'm not having you accusing me of reneging on my half of the deal. Have you kept to yours?'

'I'm dressed. What more do you want?'

A whole lot more, she thought, and congratulated herself

for managing to keep that thought to herself. 'An answer,' she said, tilting her head on one side. 'Did you speak to Nathan?'

'It's a bit early in the day.'

'Can you take decisions about the nursery without him?'

He rubbed his eyes as if he was weary of the problems at The Treasure Trove, or perhaps he was fed up with her. She went to fill the kettle, feeling a little deflated.

'I'm not used to any of this.' His voice was barely audible.

Her shoulders relaxed a little. He was vulnerable and opening up to her. She remained facing away from him, scared to spoil the moment. 'So let me do what I can.'

He sighed heavily. 'I'm not used to falling back on others for help.'

'I can imagine you're not,' she said. 'But we all need support sometimes.'

'Perhaps.' He was silent for a few seconds and Dilly waited. 'Do I have to give you an answer now?'

'You don't have to give me an answer at all, but time is of the essence,' she said, her eyes firmly fixed on the kettle. 'Those containers won't plant themselves.'

She finally turned around and caught him nodding thoughtfully. He would let her help him. She knew it.

'I suppose.' He sounded exhausted. 'We need to do something, but I value discretion.'

'Discretion is my middle name,' she said confidently.

He laughed, as if relieved to break the tension. 'Dilly Discretion Pepper? It suits you.'

'I like to think so,' she said brightly, then dropped her voice to almost a whisper. 'I won't leave you in the lurch, I promise.'

'I don't know why not,' he said, his eyes seeking out hers and holding them there, as if they were the most precious of stones. She hadn't felt this treasured since her parents were alive, and it was wonderful to be in the warmth of his gaze.

'My problems aren't yours.' His voice was gentle, but laden with regret.

They are, she silently insisted, because I want to share them. I want to share everything with you.

They felt so close, yet an invisible, unnamed chasm separated them. It was as if there was more than a kitchen table standing between them and stopping them from becoming what she was certain he wanted, too.

Chapter Fourteen

Dilly sat at her kitchen table, rummaging through the packets of seeds stored in her tin. She had collected plenty from her and Bella's gardens, dried them and put them into used envelopes. All were carefully labelled and dated. She always thought of them as little envelopes of hope.

Two pigeons caught her eye as they flapped about on the garage roof. She watched them hop, bow and preen in their mating dance. They have no qualms about throwing themselves into their love lives, she thought. Why can't I be more pigeon and less Dilly?

She caught sight of the Valentine's card in pride of place on the front of her fridge, and smiled. Luke had made it for her. It featured a wild-looking woman with wonky eyes and a big red smile surrounded by a mass of orange scribbling for her hair. Round the border were wobbly love hearts, some looking more like livers and lungs, as Bella had pointed out, but Dilly loved them, livers, lungs and all.

It had been eight years since Dilly had last received a

romantic, rather than a love-filled, Valentine card. That had been an envelope of hope and it had lived up to her expectations, fulfilling all her dreams of a romantic gesture, until the gesture wasn't matched by his behaviour. I might be Dilly Daydream, but I'm not a fool, she thought. She set aside some verbena seeds for the swap. If previous years were anything to go by, her garden would present her with enough self-seeded plants for her requirements and she would probably be able to dig up a few to share once they were a little bigger.

Dilly loved the annual seed swap. There was so much temptation and none of it cost a penny. There was only one thing that could improve the morning in Dilly's mind and that was if Alex went, but there was no chance of that happening. It's the last place he'd be, she thought as she grabbed her coat from the hook on the back of the kitchen door.

She hurried along the high street to the village hall and flung open the door to be met by the familiar smell of bleach, coffee and cake. This seed swap is the same as all the previous ones. It's wonderful that it never changes, thought Dilly, smiling broadly at Joanna, the vicar, who was at the helm of the tea team. In front of the serving hatch stood a cluster of tables, where seed swappers were already refuelling on tea and cake. The remainder of the hall's Formica-topped tables were arranged in an L-shape in front of two of the walls, behind which Steve and Jonty stood, ready to help gardeners to make their swaps. On the tabletops were scattered an assortment of seeds housed in an array of packaging. Some commercial ones were brand new and unopened, while others were half-used, and all of them were jumbled together with paper bags and envelopes which housed seeds collected by gardeners from their own plots, labelled in a variety of handwriting styles,

Dilly made a beeline for the nearest table and began to rummage excitedly through the packets on offer.

Steve chuckled. 'You're like a kid in a candy store.'

'*You're* the kid in a candy store,' said Steve's husband, Mark. He leant nearer to Dilly. 'I'm only here to make sure he doesn't come home with more than he brought to swap.'

Dilly laughed. There was no chance of Steve doing that since he was one of the main donors to the event. Knowing Steve, he would donate thirty packets of seeds and go home with only two. He was, without question, one of the most generous-spirited people she had ever met.

Mary was examining a small brown envelope. 'Is this the colourful blue, red and yellow corn, Dilly?'

Dilly read the label. 'It is. Are you going to have that?'

'I think I will. It's always good to try something new in life. It might even entice Lois outside. Speaking of which, are there any bright flowers for the new border?'

Dilly searched through the ornamental seeds on offer. 'Red snapdragons, our usual yellow sunflowers and bright orange Mexican sunflowers.'

'They sound perfect. I'll put the corn back.'

'Why?' asked Steve.

'I only brought three packets to swap.'

'Who cares?' exclaimed Steve. 'Have the corn on me.'

'I couldn't do that. It feels dishonest.'

Dilly smiled. 'I need sunflower seeds, so why don't I take these, then you have the other two and the corn?'

'I couldn't do that,' said Mary.

'You must,' insisted Dilly. 'I only need three plants. It wouldn't do for the rest of the pack to go to waste.'

Mary hugged her. 'Thank you, Dilly.'

Dilly felt someone's gaze burning into her. She glanced up to see Alex. Their eyes met and the world disappeared momentarily until Steve's voice slammed it back into place and Dilly crashed back down to reality with such force that she found herself blinking blindly at the village hall as if she had never seen it before.

'Have you been bitten by the gardening bug too, Alex?' Steve was looking earnestly at him.

'Hardly.' Alex laughed. 'Jessica's on a mission to get me to garden. She's constantly trying to inflict me on poor Dilly.' He threw a cheeky smile in her direction, and she both swooned and grew in stature all at once.

She struggled to regain her composure. It was one thing to control her body when she knew she was going to see him, but quite another when he arrived without warning where she least expected him and her reactions ambushed her. It was like a knock-out sucker punch and she felt winded and elated all at once.

'I'm sure Dilly doesn't mind, do you, Dilly?' said Steve.

What did Steve know? Colour rose in her face. Were her feelings for Alex so obvious?

'No... not at all,' she managed, turning her back on them to focus on the packets of seeds, while willing her face to lose its red glow.

'You're in extremely capable hands,' continued Steve, causing Dilly to battle with the urge to crawl under the table and hide.

'Is Jessica here?' she asked, hiding her embarrassment by keeping her back to them.

'Sadly not,' Alex replied.

His lack of an explanation for Jessica's absence from an

event she had always supported didn't surprise Dilly. Alex was discretion personified and guarded other people's secrets and respected their right to privacy. Perhaps Jessica was with Nathan. If that was the case, it was no wonder Alex was being evasive about her whereabouts.

'So which seeds are you going to choose and sow, Alex?' asked Steve.

'They're not for me. I'll be long gone by the time anything grows.'

Dilly's heart sank. She wished her heart would stop being so excitable then deflated. It was like a balloon being buffeted joyously about on a windy November day only to pop on a barbed-wire fence.

'There's plenty of time to grow pea shoots and harvest them,' she said, seizing the moment to involve him in growing things and to spend some extra time in his company.

Steve rummaged through the seeds. 'Eureka!' He held out a packet of peas. 'Dilly will help you, won't you?'

Dilly beamed with happiness. She would convert Alex to gardening yet, and maybe that would encourage him to come back and visit more often once he left. She tried to tone down her bright smile to something akin to one of professional competence,

'Of course I will. You'll be self-sufficient for pea shoots in no time.'

'If you say so,' he said, but he didn't look convinced.

'What did you bring to swap?' asked Steve, nodding at the envelopes in Alex's hand.

'Forget-me-nots and honeywort.'

'Jessica's favourites,' said Steve.

'I don't think she'll begrudge me a packet of peas, but what should I take for her?'

'Dilly knows her best,' said Steve. 'I'd trust her judgement.'

Dilly couldn't have stopped her joy at Steve's words from showing on her face even if she'd been paid a million pounds to hide it. Honestly, she thought happily, my buffeting balloon of a heart is getting put through its paces today.

She went over to Jonty's tables and browsed the seeds there. 'She hasn't got any nigella in her garden,' she said, picking out a packet.

Alex's brow crinkled. 'I'm no expert, but I have severe doubts that Jessica will want to grow TV chefs on her plot.'

Dilly laughed. 'I could certainly do with a clump of chefs.'

'Do you still hate cooking for yourself?' asked Jonty.

'Always have, always will. How about you, Alex?'

'I love cooking,' he said. A perfect match for me, then, thought Dilly. 'So tell me about nigella. I know the seeds we cook with, but what about the plant?' he asked, promptly batting the subject of their conversation away from him, Dilly noticed.

'Love-in-a-mist,' said Dilly, blushing ever so slightly at even discussing love, which was ridiculous, but he'd shown an interest by asking, so she ploughed on with her explanation and hoped her skin tone would calm down soon. 'So called because of the ruff of feathery bracts around the flower, making it seem as if it's in a misty haze. It has the most gorgeous plump seed pods, too. Jessica will love it, I promise you.'

'You know so much about plants,' he said, and Dilly wanted to hug him and dance around the village hall right there and then. He leant in closer to her and it took her by surprise. 'When will you teach me how to sow these seeds?' His breath was hot against her cheek.

Desire shot through her body. Sense and reason were crushed by longing. 'Now,' she gasped, feeling helpless, yet fearless. Waiting was no longer an option. She needed to get away from the hall with him this second.

Even though she had been brought up to leave any event well, by saying goodbye and thank you to the hosts, be it a party, a playdate, or in this case, a seed swap, manners flew out of the window, along with any care for what anyone else thought of her. She was a woman on a mission to beat her brain, which might kick in at any moment and override her bodily desires, as it had when she had backed out of dropping the towel. She and Alex left the village hall without uttering a word to anyone. She was absolutely certain they were both intent on only one thing.

They came to a halt on the high street. 'Your place or mine?' she asked, then laughed in embarrassment at her own words. 'Actually, I know the answer. Yours. Otherwise, you'll have a job carrying the seed tray home with you.'

He smiled that easy smile of his. 'Ever the pragmatist,' he teased.

Not today, she promised herself, despite the fact they were hardly running hand in hand towards the nursery like in a romantic novel or film. Instead, they tramped slowly in single file, thanks to the icy patches and sharp peaks of grey-streaked frozen snow mounded to one side of the pavement.

When they spoke, she had to turn back and shout to him, and she regretted her pragmatism more than ever. If she had simply plumped for her place, even though it didn't make sense for transporting the sown seeds, they would already have been snug in her cottage, without any of this frustrating rigmarole of getting there.

Still, there isn't long to wait now, she promised herself, as her hands grew colder. She hadn't been expecting to trek to the nursery, so she hadn't worn her gloves, and her fingers were already hurting from the cold. She would have shoved her hands in her pockets, but she was frightened of not having a hand free to protect her if she fell. Always scared, Dilly, she thought, daring herself to act, and compromising by popping only the fingertips of one hand in her pocket. It was better than nothing.

Once they reached the nursery turning, their pace slowed further as the track hadn't been cleared, but at least they could now walk side by side and speak properly.

Alex glanced down at Dilly's hand. 'You haven't got gloves – you must be freezing.'

'See? I'm not so pragmatic, after all,' she said.

He held out a gloved hand. 'Here,' he said, and a shiver of excitement pulsed through her body as she placed her hand in his and he put them both in his pocket.

The simple act of kindness was shot through with a charge so powerful that Dilly's body heated immediately. If this was its reaction to being so close to him, swathed in winter clothing, what might it be without those clothes? The anticipation was killing her. Her mouth began to chatter as if it had suddenly developed a personality of its own, and she couldn't shut it up. Stop showing your nerves, she wanted to shout at it, but it was too full of words of its own, filling the void left wordless by his silence.

'I think this hand's warm enough now,' she heard her mouth say as she swapped sides. 'It's this hand's turn. It's feeling left out.'

His laughter rang out across the countryside. Deep and resonant, warm and filled with joy. It made her body sing with happiness. They plunged their hands into his other coat pocket and she beamed up at him. His smile matched hers, and her whole body tingled in anticipation. His darkening eyes stole her endless words away. In that silent moment, she knew they were going to kiss. She felt beautiful and sexy and powerful. You're going to get hurt, screamed her brain at such a level of decibels, she could have sworn the whole of Sweetingfield heard it.

Every cell of her body shouted down her thoughts. She wanted this. She could live in a moment filled with opportunity and delight. She would not think of all of the painful tomorrows when he had gone, but her brain knew what her impulsive body didn't – couldn't – comprehend: that pain lasts longer than pleasure ever could.

She stepped back abruptly. 'Come on,' she said. 'Let's get those seeds into some compost.'

Confusion and hurt tore across his face, and she saw then that she had let them both down. Her heart went out to him, but she could no more turn back time than she could turn herself into a person she wasn't. If only she could.

She was kicking herself so hard for having been scared of being in the moment that it was a miracle she could walk. They reached the polytunnel and Alex pushed open the door.

'It feels colder than ever,' he said, and Dilly wondered if he was talking about more than the temperature of the polytunnel.

Yet again, she had sabotaged something that could have been wonderfully romantic, and for what? She scrutinised the thermometer when a glance in its direction could have told her all she needed to know, but she wanted to take a few seconds to bury her embarrassment at having run from the thing she wanted more than anything in the world.

It's all very well being Dilly Daydream, she thought, but why can't I, for once, let my daydreams be reality? Her brow crinkled. The temperature between her and Alex was cooling, but it wasn't half as cold as the temperature in the polytunnel.

'It's borderline concerning.' Her voice sounded serious and nothing like the nervously excited chatty one that had run away with itself on the nursery track. She needed to focus on practicalities. She had messed up their moment, and now she was doing her best to pretend that their moment had never existed. 'The last thing we need is for temperatures to drop further in here.' In more ways than one, she thought.

'Will it kill the plants?' Alex was examining the thermometer too, as if it were the most exciting piece of kit in the universe.

Could focussing on the mundane assuage her grief for the lost kiss? *Lost?* she demanded of herself furiously. Murdered, more like.

Shame flooded her face with a guilty blush. She was a fearful, embarrassing ingenue, and she needed a familiar footing to right herself. 'They won't like it.' She turned away from the thermometer to examine a tray of violas. 'But you'll cope, won't you?' she said to their happy, smiling faces, which were oblivious to the cold and the awkwardness Dilly felt now she had broken the spell between her and Alex.

'Is there anything you won't speak to?' he asked. It was disappointing to be back on steady, safe, recognisable territory, but she was grateful to Alex for returning there with her. She racked her brains to find a single thing she wouldn't give the time of day to.

'Actually, no. Everything deserves a few kind words,' she said.

'If you say so.' The warmth radiating from his eyes made her feel better.

She watched a flicker of thought sail across his face and laughed. 'What was that expression for?'

His eyes didn't leave hers and when he spoke, his voice was gentle, reverent even. 'I've never met anyone like you.'

Dilly's heart skipped a beat. That had to be good, didn't it? All wasn't lost. Unless he meant he had never met anyone like her because he steered clear of people like that as he couldn't stand them. Don't overthink it, Dilly, she told herself firmly.

'Likewise,' she said, then looked away, frightened by how exposed she felt about sharing her feelings. She hastily reached for a seed tray and began to show him how to sow the seeds.

They stood side by side at the potting bench and together they nestled dried peas into a tray of compost. His head was down and he was focussing on the task. She could tell he had closed off. She prodded a seed into the compost. *Why*, Dilly? *Why* are you so scared? she cried inwardly.

She missed those twinkling eyes flirting with her. She missed those intense eyes lusting after her. Now he only had eyes for the task at hand. There were more changes from sunshine to wintry days between them than there were in spring. I had better watch the barometer, she thought, looking over at it to see if, or when, the atmosphere between them would thaw after this freeze.

The barometer didn't budge, but Alex did. As soon as the

seeds were sown, he left, claiming he had somewhere to be. She couldn't blame him.

'I'll stay and make some planters while I'm here,' she said, hoping he would stay too, but instead she watched him stride away, while she felt overwhelmed with sadness at how their time together had fallen so far short of her expectations.

And whose fault is that? demanded the voice in her head. *You have no one to blame but yourself.*

Dave pushed open the door to the polytunnel. 'I'll give you more than a penny for those thoughts, Dilly. They look worth at least a quid.'

'Thank you, Dave, for suggesting that I have deep and meaningful thoughts,' she said, shaken from her regrets.

'I don't know about deep and meaningful. That look on your face would have felled a grown man.'

'That fabulous, huh?'

'That scary.' He nodded in the direction of the office. 'What's going on?'

Dilly shrugged innocently.

'Don't act as if you haven't a clue, Dilly Pepper. Last week he was shut away in the office mumbling away on the phone. That office door's never shut. I tell you, it wouldn't surprise me if it was to the bank. Or an estate agent. Or—'

'That's how rumours start, Dave, and any rumour that the nursery might be having problems could lead customers to go elsewhere, so it would be best to keep those kinds of thoughts to yourself to protect jobs.'

'Woah... I was only saying it to you,' he said. 'You don't count.'

'Charming.' Her laughter sounded hollow.

'You know what I mean.'

'I do,' she said, more gently. 'And you know what I mean about keeping quiet about any worries about the nursery.'

'Understood,' he said. 'I don't want this place to go under.'

'No one does. Let's do what we can to help it to ride out this storm.'

Dave nodded, and Dilly was relieved that he was on board, even if he had sown the seed of doubt that Alex might sell the business, or the land from under them. After all, Alex owned at least half of The Treasure Trove and he had no real interest in keeping it.

A quiver of panic rose in Dilly's throat. What if she was making all this effort to try to rescue a nursery Alex had no intention of saving? She didn't know how his mind worked. All she knew was he would be gone within a matter of weeks. Was this why he had come to Sweetingfield – to put the nursery on the market? How could she trust him when it was in his best interests to sell?

Dilly didn't hear Dave leave. She was lost in thought, unable to contain her fears, which were growing quicker than weeds on a warm, wet day. His suggestion had rattled her and she wondered if she was wasting her time making up planters for a nursery which might not be in business for much longer. She shook her head. Surely Alex wouldn't do that.

She nestled a delicate cream viola into the compost and admired its dear little face. Believe in Alex, she told herself firmly. Of course he won't sell up.

Too cold and disconsolate to carry on planting, she left quietly, glancing towards Alex's temporary home. Suddenly, believing in tomorrow wasn't enough. She had no control over what Alex would do. She couldn't even control her own body and brain at the moment. They felt like they were constantly at war when she was near him.

As she made her way down the nursery track towards the village, she remembered the moment they had been there together with their hands in his coat pocket. The look she had seen in his eyes was an image she would never erase. She could have lived her dream, but instead she had behaved in a way which, if their situations had been reversed, she would have known without question meant only one thing. She had rejected him.

Chapter Fifteen

After a night given over to a battle of conflicting emotions, pragmatism finally won through and Dilly accepted that it was as well that her brain had kicked in when it had, otherwise fear of rejection might have plagued her night. It could have been a night of pleasure, she reminded herself. The final stab of regret might have punctured her defences for a moment, but it wouldn't win. There was only ever going to be one winner, and that was self-preservation. If Alex was planning to sell the nursery, she would be devastated; complicate that with a physical relationship, and she would be drowning in regret, anger and a whole host of other negative emotions. Her rejection of him and her own body's needs was for the best. She had learnt enough in thirty-five years on this planet to know that she was safer in her comfort zone. She was Dilly Pepper, practical hands-on gardener, not Dilly Pepper, hands on Doctor Alex Hampton, who would be gone within weeks.

She flung open her bedroom curtains to reveal a glorious spring morning. The snow had melted, leaving behind a couple of carrots, a battered hat and two sorry scarves languishing soggily on the village green. Doubtless they will be gathered up before long, she thought as she assessed her own garden. The gravel drive needed to be weeded. There was a fine line between a thoughtfully planted flowering strip for under a vehicle, if she were to actually own one, and weedy mayhem. It was nonsense to have a drive at all, given she didn't have a car, but she needed the little garage it led to, and the drive gave her the perfect opportunity to inspire other villagers to plant up their driveways for bees and butterflies.

Dilly liked to use the little front gardens at her and Bella's cottages to showcase what could be done. Situated on the high street and close to the shop, they were like display gardens, and while some might think she was advertising her expertise, her true purpose was to inspire. This year, she planned to mingle a few homegrown vegetables in with the flowers to encourage people to grow their own food, however small their patch. Now, though, the more urgent job was to weed the gravel drive that was the perfect medium for a weed seedbed.

Leading what she thought of as a revolution from the front garden was all very well, but every year there were times when she was so busy, her garden became the equivalent of the cobbler's unshod kids. What if that didn't happen this year? She shuddered at the thought. Her concerns for her income and the hurt she still felt about losing Barry were never far from the surface. She could only hope that once spring really sprang, she would be as busy as always and her worries would be a distant memory. Dilly shook her head, then jutted out her chin. There was no point in worrying about things that might never happen. It was far better to go outside and make the most of this beautiful day,

She wrapped up warmly, as although the sun was shining, there would doubtless be a cool nip in the air that would be magnified because she wouldn't be moving around much as she weeded. She plonked her bright pink bobble hat on her head and grinned at her reflection in the mirror. She loved this hat. It had been a Christmas gift from Mary, who said it clashed joyously with her hair, and she was right. It made Dilly smile every time she wore it, although it only got an outing at weekends as she didn't want to ruin it at work.

She grabbed a small weeding tool, a watering can, a Tupperware box and a trug, then she headed down to the far end of the drive to commence work. Villagers on the way to the shop greeted her, and she soon caught up with all the news. Plenty of people stopped to tell her how much they had loved her apron at the pancake race, and asked if she had seen her photo in the local paper.

She hadn't and she didn't want to look. It was probably the least flattering photograph in the history of local papers, which was saying something. Memories of her mortification after the publication of a photo of her and her school friends raising money for charity came flooding back. She had never wanted to leave her bedroom again as the graininess of the photo and the weird printing pixels highlighted her freckles, which she'd loathed at the time, not to mention her teenage spots. Surely photos have improved since then? she thought, digging out a clump of groundsel and putting it in an old ice-cream box for Luke's pet rabbit.

'Are you rescuing and repurposing weeds?'

She glanced up to see Alex standing at the end of the drive. Relief drowned any shame she had felt at her unintentional rejection of him the day before. While they were still talking, there was still hope.

'Naturally,' she said, tapping the lid of the box. 'Stay safe, little groundsel. You'll soon be nestled comfortably in Jessica's garden, seeding yourself about and making work for me every week of the year.'

'A sound business plan.' His eyes shone in the morning sunlight, reminding Dilly of gently unfurling spring leaves.

'And don't worry, little weed,' she whispered to the ice-cream container loudly enough for Alex to hear. 'I have an under-gardener who doesn't know his weeds from his forget-me-nots, so you'll be perfectly safe.' She wiggled her eyebrows to indicate she was teasing before realising they were hidden under her woollen hat.

'I thought that was our secret.'

'It is,' she said.

'You told that weed.'

'She'll keep it quiet. She won't want to terrify the forget-me-nots.'

'She?'

'Obviously.' Dilly dug a Jacob's ladder seedling from the gravel and planted it straightaway in the border, before grabbing the watering can next to her and dousing the seedling with water.

'And you're transplanting that one because?'

'Right plant, wrong place. And if I move swiftly enough, he won't know what's hit him.'

'No apologies to that one, I see.'

She shook her head. 'I wouldn't want to alert him to the fact he's moved half a metre to the right.'

'You're so thoughtful, although I'm intrigued to learn why he's a he.'

'You honestly want me to give you a talk about the birds and the bees?' she said, her face flaming. You could do with giving yourself that talk after what happened yesterday, she told herself sternly.

His eyes twinkled naughtily. 'Now that *would* be interesting,' he said, turning to leave.

Dilly watched him walk away. From the ground, his legs seemed to go on forever and his thighs appeared even more powerful. She shook her head. This wouldn't do. Still, a smile crept across her face. They were making inroads towards friendship again. It was a sunny morning, she had seen Alex and everything had seemed fine between them. More than fine.

She and Alex getting along despite her embarrassing behaviour after the seed swap was the best gift Dilly could imagine. It buoyed her up for the rest of the day, until the sun set too early, as it always did in early spring, and she packed up her things and went indoors to face reality. The fears she had been hiding from in the garden hadn't gone away. It was as good a time as any to make some calls and shore up her income.

She poured herself a cup of calming camomile tea, took a sip, even though it was too hot, then spluttered when her first client answered immediately. When will you ever learn, Dilly Pepper? she admonished herself.

'Mr Thompson,' she managed, her tongue burning, 'it's Dilly Pepper, the gardener. It's a courtesy call really. My slots for spring tidies are filling fast, and since I've done your garden for the past few years, I didn't want you to miss out.'

'That's incredibly thoughtful of you, Dilly. Thank you,' he said, and she opened her diary, ready to insert his name. 'But I've already had the garden cut back.'

'That's early,' she said, narrowing her eyes. Alex had mentioned a second client. Perhaps Mr Thompson and Barry were golf friends. What's done is done, she told herself firmly. Alex has apologised and there's nothing more you can say, or do. Even so, her heart was breaking at the implications for minibeasts and the birds that feed on them. There was nothing she could do for them either.

'Truth to tell, the chap was a fraction of the cost, and was in and out in a matter of hours, rather than two days.'

'So long as you haven't been overlooked,' she said. It was as if all her years of work on his garden had been well and truly forgotten.

'Thanks for calling anyway, Dilly. It sounds as if business is booming if you're running out of slots.'

Dilly swallowed. 'No problem.' She was relieved that he couldn't see the tears threatening to spill.

She shook as she put a cross next to his name, but she shored herself up to move on to the next call. Two clients lost would take more replacing, but it wasn't impossible, she reassured herself. She took a deep breath and dialled her next client. She summoned up her most friendly voice.

'Mrs Weaver, it's Dilly Pepper,' she began. 'I noticed you haven't booked in for a spring tidy, and since I'm—'

'Ah, Dilly. Let me stop you there. A man came over to check out the garden and I've booked him in to do it.'

'Wh-when?' she whispered.

'He only popped in today.'

'Today?' said Dilly, grabbing the edge of the table with her free hand. How could he? After everything he had said.

Six more calls, five of which were answered, confirmed her worst suspicions. Alex hadn't stuck to his word. He had stolen all her spring tidy clients despite his apologies and promises. No wonder he was willing to do half an hour in Jessica's garden. He was learning while keeping Jessica happy, and lulling Dilly into a false sense of security.

She left a message for the non-answering client, then pulled on her coat. Alex had lied to her. He didn't care about her, or her income at all. So much for his friendly smiles and chatty conversation earlier. He had duped her.

Well, that's it, she seethed. It doesn't matter how good-looking he is, his behaviour makes him the ugliest man alive, and I've had enough.

Chapter Sixteen

Dilly pushed furiously at her bicycle pedals and leant forward over the handlebars as if it would bring her closer to Alex more quickly, so she could tell him exactly what she thought of him. Fuelled by anger with him, and shame at herself for having ever imagined that he was the most desirable man she had ever seen, she sped up.

The cold night air cut like a knife at the back of her throat, only to be melted with every furious breath.

'Lies are hideous and ugly,' she hissed as she swung her bicycle from the road and rounded the corner onto the nursery track. She gritted her teeth and pedalled harder. 'I should be at home in the warm, safe in the knowledge that I have enough money to pay the bills, not confronting a liar.' She spat the words like weapons as her front wheel hit a pothole, flinging her over the handlebars and onto the cold dirt with an excruciating thud.

The impact of her body clashing with the hard ground forced the air from her lungs. For a moment she was numb, then a wave of shock and panic hit, threatening to overwhelm her.

'Why me?' she cried, as the pain intensified. It felt as if every centimetre of her body was a mass of seething agonies. She lay on the ice-cold ground, winded, unable to even flex a muscle for fear that she would hurt more and pass out from the pain.

She tried to rally her thoughts. Hypothermia wouldn't be far away on a night like this, but standing up brought its own risks. What if she caused more damage? If she had broken anything, she wouldn't be able to work. As if it wasn't enough that Alex was stealing her business. Slowly, cautiously, she tried to move her fingers. All good, she reassured herself as she battled to control the sense of panic engulfing her.

Certain that no bones in her hands or arms were broken, she reached into her pocket for her phone. Bella couldn't leave Luke, but Jonty would be there in minutes. All would be well.

'No,' she wailed, as she realised that in her haste to tell Alex Hampton exactly what she thought of him, she had left her phone on her kitchen table with her half-drunk mug of camomile tea.

She had to get herself to safety as soon as she could. She grimaced as she tried to roll onto her side. Her back hurt, but not as badly as she had imagined it would. She continued onto her front, then carefully raised her aching body until she was on her knees. The world seemed to spin, making her feel nauseous, so she remained in a foetal position on the cold dirt track, waiting and hoping that the dizziness and sickness would pass. Breathe, she reminded herself, counting her breath in and slowing down her breath out, while trying to focus on anything but the cold, the pain and the fear that she might pass out.

The dizzy spell abated. Slowly, warily, she pushed herself onto her feet. It seemed to take an age to stand at her full height, and when she did, she was frightened that she might plummet back to earth. Steadying her breath, she reassured herself that she would be fine, so long as she got into the warm. Her bicycle was too damaged to move, so she abandoned it and limped along the dirt track towards the nearest point of safety. The nursery cottage was the last place in the world she wanted to be. She would ask Alex to call Jonty for her, then get out of the way. She didn't want to see Alex now. She never wanted to see him again. He had stolen her work from her, lied to her, and now she was battered and bruised in more ways than one, with a mangled bicycle she couldn't afford to have repaired. If Alex hadn't come to Sweetingfield she would never have been in this position. *This*, she thought as tears plummeted down her face, *this* is why I hate change. It's never good. It's never for the better.

She plodded on, scared to go too fast, yet frightened that if she didn't get to his door soon, she might never find safety. Fuelled by fear and fury, she willed her body to stay awake and get to the nursery cottage. Once through the gate, she threw herself towards the safety of the porch and pummelled maniacally on the door. It would be the cruellest blow to have made it this far and then not be heard, or for Alex to be out, she realised, as fear gripped her again.

When the door opened, relief overwhelmed her and she crumpled against the frame.

'Dilly. What the—?'

He stepped forward, caught her in his strong arms and

lifted her over the threshold and into the warmth of the sitting room. Gently, he lay her on the sofa by the fire, his eyes roaming her face as if seeking an explanation.

'I fell off my bike. Please can you remove it from the track? I'm worried it might cause an accident.' Her voice shook, just like her body.

He nodded his agreement, but he didn't leave her side. Heavenly green eyes, full of compassion, looked deep into hers.

'You're shaking.' His visible concern deepened to worry. 'I'll get you to hospital,' he said decisively.

'No.'

'But you're in shock.'

'I'll be okay.'

'Did you hit your head?'

'Am I not making sense?'

'You're making perfect sense as always.' He placed his hands over hers, causing a jolt of electricity to course through her. She withdrew her hand. She would not be sidetracked from the reason for her visit. Much as she would have once loved to have lain there holding hands all night with this man, the scales had now fallen from her eyes and she knew without any doubt she couldn't trust him. 'But your hands are freezing.'

'I'm a gardener. Cold hands come with the job.' It was hell to talk, but she couldn't stay quiet.

'Your lips are blue.'

'And that comes with the job too, but you'd know that, wouldn't you?' Why was he pretending to be so kind after he'd stolen her work? Her anger towards him surged. 'Now that you're the expert in gardening,' she said, pulling herself up into a seated position and immediately regretting it as her head spun. Everything seemed to hurt, but she ploughed on regardless. She had risked life and limb to have this out with him and she was going to tell him what she thought once and for all. 'Well, I've got news for you, sunshine... one short lesson in hoeing and knowing the difference between a daisy and a honeywort does not make you an expert. You're as dangerous out there as you ever were. Stop leading people on and wrecking their gardens and precious wildlife habitats.' Her eyes narrowed. 'I have worked for years to build up my client base, and you have swept in and taken my customers without a care for the fact you're wiping out my livelihood. Now I'm paying the price for what you've done. Big time... because none of this—' she swept an arm over her aching body '—would have happened if you hadn't come here stealing my work and lying to my face.'

He shook his head, then leant closer to her. 'Lying?'

'Don't look so shocked. Doubtless it's all part of your pretence of innocence.'

'Dilly, I genuinely haven't a clue what you're talking about.'

'And you expect me to believe you? I need to go home. I've said what I came here to say. Now please call Jonty – I haven't got my phone.'

'I'll give you a lift, but I'm concerned that you did hit your head. You sound so confused.'

'*Confused*? So now the professor is gaslighting?'

'What?' Anger matching hers flashed across his face. 'I would never gaslight anyone. How could you even suggest it?'

'I can see right through you, Doctor Alex Hampton, so you can stop playing the innocent right now. If it wasn't for your lies, I wouldn't have been cycling along the track. I wouldn't have had the accident. I wouldn't have lost work and I wouldn't have to pay to repair my bike. You caused all of this and the sooner you get out of all our lives the better.'

'Believe me'—his voice was loaded with frustration—'the sooner I get out of here, the sooner my life will be better.'

The silence seemed to last an eternity. Anger crackled in the air between them. Neither was backing down, neither spoke and neither one looked at the other. How could I have ever found this irritating man attractive? Dilly wondered, staring furiously into the fire.

It was Alex who finally broke the silence. 'I'll give you a lift home, Dilly,' he said. 'But not before you've had a warm drink and cleaned up your knuckles.' She inspected the gritty puncture wounds caused when the backs of her hands scraped along the ground as she landed. 'And since it's apparently my fault that you came off your bike, I'll pay for the repairs, but I promise you, I have never knowingly lied to you, so if I have, I'm sorry. It wasn't intentional.'

'Yeah, right,' she muttered.

The tea was sweetened and drunk in a silent rage as he tenderly cleaned her wounds. Brimming with fury mingled with the injustice of life having handed her a handsome man who was helping her, but who was, as it turned out, a client-thieving liar, she stared hard at the wall ahead and tried not to focus on his gentle touch and the frisson of excitement coursing through her traitorous body. She had never, in her whole life, been so angry with anyone. She couldn't see his face, so she had no clue as to what was going through his mind, but she didn't care. He wasn't to be trusted. He wanted to leave Sweetingfield, and she wanted her old life back with a diary filled with clients, and no complications.

Once he had finished cleaning her wounds, manners forced a hostile thank you from her lips.

'Wait there for a minute while I bring my car to the gate,' he said. Civilised words uttered with barely concealed exasperation. He arrived back in the room within a minute and reached down to help her to her feet.

'I can manage,' she said, even though she wasn't convinced she could.

They drove slowly along the track and she was begrudgingly grateful to him for that. A drop down a pothole would have been agony. The sight of her mangled bicycle made her want to cry, but she bit her lip. She was okay. She hadn't broken anything. She would get through this. Alex stopped the car and went to move her bicycle from the farm track, then they continued their journey in silence. She couldn't wait to get out of the car and away from him.

They arrived at her cottage and he looked at her, his eyes pleading. 'Take it easy, please, Dilly.'

'As if you care,' she snapped. He went to her side of the car to help her, but she waved him away. 'No need. I can manage.'

He lowered his head as he stood back to allow her to push her way painfully out of the seat. It hurt more than she cared to admit, or wanted to show, but she needed to stand on her own two feet, both physically and mentally. She couldn't trust him and she would never trust him again.

His car remained outside her cottage while she trudged up her drive and let herself into her kitchen. Her whole body ached. Doubtless there would be bruising from her landing, which was softer than it might have been, thanks to her warm clothes, but not soft enough, she thought, rubbing her back. Seconds later, the phone she had abandoned on the kitchen table sounded with the arrival of two messages. The first was from Bella. It was as pragmatic and generous-hearted as her dear friend, but she didn't need to take Bella's bed, and she didn't want fussing over. Then she opened Jonty's. *Can I do anything to help?* The thought that Alex had told them cranked up her hostility towards him. She was perfectly capable of contacting her own friends.

'*I'm completely fine xx*,' she replied to them both, then slowly crept upstairs for a proper cry.

Chapter Seventeen

There was a blissful moment as Dilly's brain emerged from sleep, when she had forgotten what had happened. Then reality dawned in all its agonising misery. Waking up like this brought back distressing memories she would rather have forgotten, of when she had lost her mum, and later, her dad. Back then, trouble-free waking followed by the pain of reality had dragged on for months. She hoped that this time it was a one-off and that tomorrow she would wake up as normal, with a reality she loved rather than the one she now found herself in.

She eased her aching body out of bed and went downstairs to make herself a cup of coffee. There would be no work today. Apart from her not having her bike, her body needed to heal, and the grazes and puncture marks across her knuckles ought to scab over properly before she plunged them back into the soil. She might have been vaccinated against tetanus, but she wasn't going to take a chance with any other infections, nor was she going to risk seeing Alex. She needed time to heal from him as well. She had been too trusting, and she would have gladly walked away from the nursery cottage garden job had she not been so desperate for the income.

'And why am I so desperate for the income?' she demanded of the plump, unopened buds of an Easter cactus on the windowsill. 'Because Alex Hampton stole my clients.'

She bristled with rage and slammed her empty coffee mug into the sink. The frustration of an enforced day off was already overwhelming her. She hated being stuck indoors. It was such a waste of a perfectly good day. She glanced out of the window. It was drizzling, so not perfectly good if she was completely honest, but workable in the right clothing. She had slept later than usual and she could hear from next door that Luke was already having his breakfast, so she was too late to do that for Bella, but she could walk him to school. She messaged Bella, offering to help and got a swift reply back.

'Rest, Dilly. Let me know if there's anything you need from the shop x'

Bless Bella, she thought. At least I can rely on her, but she has her own life and can't be round here entertaining me all day. She began to pace the kitchen, even though every painful step brought with it a reminder of what had happened. Her fear as she flew over the handlebars. How scared she had been as she lay on the cold, hard ground. The spark when Alex had held her hand. She shook her head to try to erase the memory, and continued to pace. The day stretched ahead of her and she hadn't a clue what to do with it. She felt trapped like a pot-bound plant desperately seeking space to grow.

'Oh, this is too much.' She grabbed her first aid box from the cupboard and covered the wounds on her hands, then took the washing-up gloves she never used from under the sink. She would double-glove and go to Jessica's, and Mary and Lois' to work. She couldn't do nothing all day.

A knock at the kitchen door stopped her in her tracks. Doubtless it would be Jonty calling by to drink tea and offer sympathy, she thought, happy to see her friend. She flung open the door to find Alex standing there with a bunch of daffodils.

He held them out to her. 'Peace offering,' he said, a hopeful smile playing around those too delectable lips.

'A bunch of daffodils won't bring back my lost income.'

'No. I'm sorry. I didn't mean to sound flippant. Please can I come in?'

'I'm about to go to work,' she said.

'Work? After the accident?'

'If I don't work, I don't earn, and I need to look after my clients, or else you'll steam in and steal them.'

'That's what I need to talk to you about,' he said.

'Oh – you want a full client list so you know where to go poaching them next? Well, I'm sorry I haven't got around to printing you one off yet. You'll have to call back later.'

'Dilly, I honestly haven't been taking your clients. Please believe me.'

'Well, if you haven't, who has?'

'I don't know, but I promise it isn't me.'

'How can I believe you?'

He stared at the ground and shook his head. 'I don't know. I'm the last person who'd be able to answer that.'

What does that mean? she wondered. He did look genuinely shaken by what had happened.

'I suppose you might ask one of them who their new gardener is.'

She eyed him suspiciously. 'And how do I know you haven't been giving them a false name?'

'You didn't strike me as a mistrustful sceptic.'

'It's a new skill I've been learning since I met you.'

He flinched and was silent for a beat. 'It isn't healthy, you know,' he said. 'Dilly, I'm genuinely sorry you're going through a tough time, but apart from the mistake I made at Barry's, I haven't attempted any garden clearance.'

Dilly remained unconvinced by his claims. She couldn't trust him.

'I need to get to the nursery,' he continued, 'but I wanted to drop these off first and let you know that I'll get your bike back to you as soon as I can.'

'Thank you,' she said, taking the flowers. 'They're lovely. You shouldn't have bought them for me.'

'I didn't. I picked them at Jessica's.'

'You stole Jessica's early daffs?' she gasped.

He held out his hands as if to plead his defence. 'Not all of them.'

'I'm glad to hear it.'

'But only because Jessica caught me.'

'Well, at least you're honest about *that,*' she said.

'She told me that pleased though she was that I was developing an interest in cut flowers, her gardener would have my guts for garters if I cleared the lot of them.'

'Very true. Now, if you don't mind, I have things to do,' she said, closing the door behind him.

That man is too charming for my own good, she thought, shaking her head. She sniffed the flowers. It was a shame she couldn't trust him. She would have to find a way to get along with him, though. There was never a falling out in the village without collateral damage and she was absolutely *not* going to be associated with that kind of behaviour. Far better to enjoy the flowers, accept his apology and secretly not trust him, than to risk any more drama.

She reached into the cupboard for a jug for the flowers and took it to the tap to fill with water. He wasn't staying in Sweetingfield for long, so she only had to be civil to him for a few weeks. She could do that, she reassured herself. How difficult could it be?

Chapter Eighteen

Dilly opened Jessica's garden gate and gasped. Tiny blue flowers, shining like sapphires, fringed the length of the path. As she got nearer to the house, she bent down to take a closer look at their white centres.

'No wonder they call you glory-of-the-snow,' she exclaimed. 'You are *glorious*.'

'Aren't they adorable?' called Jessica. 'You were right, as always. The river of blue along the path does make my heart sing every time I step out of the door. Thank you for suggesting them and for planting them... And these winter pots you made up. They put a smile on my face every time I see them. You are so clever at putting smiles on faces, Dilly.'

'What a lovely thing to say! Thank you.'

'And I hear you've been working your magic on that serious-minded nephew of mine. He was even in here scrumping my daffs this morning. I ask you! So, well done, Dilly.'

Dilly plucked a bird's feather from a pot filled with hyacinths and primroses. He clearly hadn't told Jessica who the daffodils were for. Remember, you will have to live in this village long after he has flown, she warned herself, and you definitely don't want to upset dear Jessica. It's not her fault Alex is her nephew.

'I'm doing my best,' she said, neutrally.

'Well, your best is marvellous,' enthused Jessica. 'Would you like a cup of coffee? You look cold.'

Dilly had already lost the feeling in the end of her nose. 'Yes, please. I'm going to be training the roses on the wall today. I know you love leaving them as long as possible for the hips, but they really do need to be done now.' Not least because my poor body aches after the accident, thought Dilly. Alex clearly hadn't mentioned that to Jessica either.

'I understand. And there'll be no Alex today sadly. Apparently he has an important meeting this morning and he absolutely can't miss it. Personally, I think it's simply too cold for him.' She laughed and Dilly joined in, despite drowning in an unpalatable cocktail of anger at him, mingling with fear that the meeting was about selling the nursery, served on a bed of crushing disappointment that he wasn't the man she had hoped he was.

Dilly usually loved training roses. She took care to cut the stems and tie them in to create a strong framework that would show the structure of the plant and its flowers off to their best in summer, but today her mind was elsewhere. She was like Keaton chewing on a bone. Once she'd had the thought that Alex might have a meeting with bankers or estate agents or someone who might develop The Treasure Trove into a soulless garden centre, she simply couldn't shake it off. Surely he wouldn't, she reassured herself. She wanted him to return right there and then and tell her all about it. Not that he would tell her anything. It was hardly her business.

After a quick sandwich lunch in her kitchen, when she did little more than worry about who Alex was meeting, Dilly went over to Mary and Lois'. Perhaps it had something to do with his university work, she reasoned as she opened the gate, but she could tell herself anything she liked; she wasn't listening.

Keaton bounded over to her and leapt up in greeting. 'I'm going round in circles. I mustn't fret about the nursery any more today,' she told the little dog. 'Shall we go and find Mary?'

Since Keaton was in the garden, Dilly knew that Mary was somewhere outside. They ambled together to the back of the cottage, Keaton occasionally stopping to sniff a plant or follow the trail of some creature that had traversed his territory. She couldn't see Mary in the back garden, so she took the narrow gravel path that skirted the boundary furthest from Jessica's cottage, under the wisteria walk, and towards the greenhouse, where she found Mary holding a clipboard.

'What do you think of my plans?'

Dilly examined the rough, spindly-lined drawings that Mary had made. 'You've been busy.'

Mary's blue eyes sparkled. 'It doesn't do to dwell; far better to do.'

Dilly understood. Keeping busy helped her, too. It stopped her mind from thinking and dulled the pain. It always had.

'Here is what I hope to achieve,' continued Mary. 'I'm going to need benches down each side that are strong enough to hold the sand I plan to sink the pots into.'

'Have you ordered benches?' asked Dilly.

'Better than that, Dilly, I've bought some at auction online. Reuse, recycle, re- whatever the other thing is.'

'Repurpose,' said Dilly.

'And that's precisely what I'm doing. But I was wondering what to do with all this luscious soil. I don't want it to go to waste under the benches.'

'Shall I repurpose it for you?' asked Dilly, even though her body was crying out for rest.

'If you wouldn't mind. Also, I've made a list.' She took a piece of paper from behind her drawings. 'Please source these cacti for me. Preferably locally – if possible from The Treasure Trove. I know it's not Nathan's thing, but if he can get hold of them on my behalf, I'll pay him whatever markup he wants to put on, and you a sourcing fee, naturally.'

'Thank you.' Dilly checked the list. Mary was taking her new hobby very seriously. 'I'll do my best,' she said.

'You always do, dear Dilly. Now, I'd better go and see if Lois needs anything.'

Dilly watched Mary walk away with Keaton at her heels. She was getting slower; there was no denying it. Perhaps the worry over Lois and all the extra responsibilities were taking their toll. At least she had let Dilly get on with sourcing the plants for her. Dilly knew that Mary could have bought them herself. First the apple trees, then the perennials and now cacti. It was strange that this was the third time Mary had asked her to source plants for her recently.

Dilly went to the potting shed to collect a spade and smiled as she saw a blackbird pecking on an apple that Mary had thrown onto the lawn for him. Mary was doing her best for nature, for Dilly and for The Treasure Trove, and while villagers wanted the nursery to be there, the support could be found. She would simply have to convince Alex that it was worth it. She placed the spade in the wheelbarrow and returned to the greenhouse, confident that once Alex realised the village was supporting him, he couldn't possibly do anything desperate like sell up and walk away. Could he?

When Dilly returned from Mary and Lois' garden, the first thing she saw, leant against the shelves of her porch, was her bicycle with a new straight wheel. She walked it into her garage, grateful that although her body still hurt from the accident, her bicycle, at least, was back to its old self.

The warmth of the kitchen had opened the daffodils and their fragrance lifted Dilly's spirits further. She might have made no inroads into finding replacement clients, and she was still a little sore, but she had enjoyed working in Mary and Lois' garden and she had come home to her favourite sunshine flowers.

Bella had been in touch with her earlier to check she was okay, and Dilly had reassured her that she was, but now the evening stretched before her and she wanted company. She messaged her friend, hoping that she would be free. '*Do you fancy a catch-up later?*'

Bella replied straightaway. '*Come over when Luke's in bed. I have wine x*'

Dilly didn't need inviting twice. As soon as she heard Bella and Luke's cottage go quiet, she grabbed her coat, wrapped a scarf around her neck and went next door.

'I'm so glad you messaged,' said Bella. 'I was properly in the mood for a glass of wine, but I couldn't justify having one.'

'You could have messaged me to come over,' said Dilly, wrestling herself from her coat.

'I didn't like to – you get so busy in spring.'

Chance would be a fine thing this year, thought Dilly, then she was chastened. Had Bella always felt sidelined when Dilly focussed on her work in spring and summer?

'I'm never too busy for you,' she said, hugging her friend.

Bella drew away from her to inspect her plaster-covered knuckles. 'I know you've been telling me all day that you're fine, but how are you really after the accident?'

'Bruised, but not beaten,' said Dilly, rubbing her backside and making Bella laugh.

'I'm glad to hear it.' Bella unscrewed the lid on a bottle of Pinot Grigio while Dilly opened a kitchen cupboard and took out two wine glasses.

'So, dear Bella, why are you in such a mood for wine?'

'Oh... I don't know... the nursery... Nathan not being around, and Alex is there one day, but gone the next. I don't think he's interested in the nursery at all.'

Dilly's heart sank. Was he going missing because he had lied about stealing her clients? It made her sad and angry at the same time.

'Take today, for instance,' continued Bella. 'He wasn't there when I arrived. Then he came in and stayed a little while, before disappearing again.'

Dilly was humbled. He had probably gone missing to sort out her bicycle.

Bella took a long sip, then smiled at Dilly. 'Anyway, less about me. More about you. What's happening in your life?'

What isn't? thought Dilly. She sighed. 'Someone's taken most of my spring tidies.'

Bella gasped. 'Who would do such a thing?'

I have an idea who, thought Dilly. She didn't believe Alex's denials, but while she didn't have proof, she couldn't very well go around spreading rumours. 'I haven't a clue,' she said.

'What are you going to do?'

'I don't know. Some of my spring tidies have already

been slashed down, and others are booked in. I've only seen what happened to Barry's garden. Honestly, Bella, it was heartbreaking.'

'Can you replace Barry?'

'I hope so, in time, but it's now that's concerning me. I usually save the extra money I make on spring tidies to help to carry me through winter, but the way things are going at the moment, plus having lost a regular like Barry, I'm not sure I'll get through next winter at all.'

Bella squeezed Dilly's arm. 'That's terrible. What are you going to do?'

'Apart from worrying? I'm not sure. It's as if this slash-and-run person has taken a chainsaw to everything I've built up and felled it.'

'It's not only whoever is doing this, Dilly. Your clients are supremely disloyal. I'd gladly go round there and—'

Dilly held her friend's hand. 'I love that you want to fight my corner for me, Bella, but please don't get angry on my behalf.'

Bella slammed her hand holding Dilly's onto her thigh. 'Dilly, I'm furious with them. Aren't you?'

'I feel let down and hurt.'

'The problem is that they don't know the value of your knowledge.'

'Perhaps there is no value to my knowledge,' said Dilly forlornly.

'Oh, there most definitely is, but people won't see it until something goes catastrophically wrong,' said Bella, displaying a worrying amount of schadenfreude.

'I hope it doesn't,' said Dilly.

'You're too nice.'

'No such thing as too nice. Just one thing, Bella, please

don't tell anyone what's going on. I feel so ashamed about losing clients.'

'You have nothing to be ashamed about.' The force of Bella's voice surprised Dilly.

'Maybe I don't, but that's how I feel. I'm scared that if other people hear, they might not want to employ me.'

Bella hugged her tightly. 'You'll be okay, Dilly. I know you will.'

'Perhaps, but everything was rubbing along so well. I loved my work, I love my friends, and now everything's gone wrong.'

'Not everything,' said Bella, compassion shining from her dark eyes. 'You still have us.'

Not if the nursery goes under, thought Dilly, awash with sadness. However angry she might be with Alex, and however little she might trust him not to sell The Treasure Trove, she would have to face up to working alongside him to secure the nursery's future. If The Treasure Trove couldn't be saved, she stood to lose so much more than Barry and a few spring tidies. She could lose her best friend in the world and the child who had made her life so much brighter since she had lost her own family.

Chapter Nineteen

Dilly's body was healing, but her fears for her income and the future of the nursery weighed heavily upon her. They penetrated each breath and every waking moment. At least Mary's ambitious plans for her garden and greenhouse meant more hours for Dilly now, and for that she was thankful, but it wouldn't chase away her niggling concerns about next winter.

She closed the gate to Mary and Lois' cottage and set off along the village green track towards home. The sun was low in the sky and without the blanket of cloud to protect the ground, it was already cold. There would be another frost tonight. Dilly shivered. Now that she had finished for the day, there seemed little left to do apart from to allow her brain free rein, and she was soon lost on the same endless spiral of worry surrounding Alex and the nursery. She was abruptly torn from her pondering by someone calling her name.

'You look cold, Dilly. Fancy a pint by a warm fire?'

She was delighted to see Steve's friendly face. That's

exactly the kind of distraction I need, she thought. All of this worrying is exhausting. I need to live in the moment a little. A pang of regret about her failure to live in the moment with Alex after the seed swap cut into her, but she couldn't rewrite history. She was who she was and she couldn't change that.

'You've read my mind,' she said, walking briskly towards him. 'How are you doing?'

'Not bad at all, thanks, but let's go inside before your lips turn any bluer.'

'Are they blue?'

'Dilly, they're violet. How long have you been outside?'

Dilly shrugged. 'Most of the day, but I was busy so I didn't notice the cold. *Now* it's hit me.'

As they pushed open the door, a wall of warm air met them and Dilly's nose began to tingle.

'Sit down by the fire, Dilly. I'll get them in.'

Dilly gratefully plonked herself on the settle by the fire and took off her bobble hat.

'You look like the wild woman of the garden,' he called over to her, and she patted her hair down in a vain attempt to impose some kind of order.

The fire soon warmed her and she began to strip off her layers of clothes. First her coat, then she dragged a tight-necked fleece over her head, swiftly followed by her bright purple holey jumper.

'That's done nothing for your hair,' said Steve as he placed a pint in front of her.

She shook her head to try to restore some kind of bounce, then ran her fingers through her curls to clear some of the knots. 'That'll have to do. This pint needs my fullest attention.'

The door to the pub opened and Jonty strode in, rubbing his glove-clad hands together as if it would warm them up, and holding the door open with his foot for Alex. She drew in a sharp breath and gulped back the longing she felt every time she saw him.

Hating herself for caring that her lips might be deep purple, her nose pink and her eyes bloodshot with cold after a day of wrestling with plants, she focussed on her pint. It wasn't easy. Alex was too distracting. Typical, she thought, taking a moment to appreciate his teal jumper, which highlighted the solidity of his chest muscles while bringing out the sea green shades in his eyes.

'Just the man I was hoping to see.' Jeff's booming voice reverberated across the bar as he grabbed a glass and set it beneath a beer tap.

'Me, or Alex?' asked Jonty.

'Alex,' said Jeff. 'What's happening with my babies?'

'Babies?' Alex's body language screamed that he had been caught on the back foot. This wasn't good. Concern drowned any mistrust or animosity Dilly harboured towards him. She stood up, fearing Alex might not know about Jeff's exacting requirements for the pub's hanging baskets. His baskets were well known in the region and people came to the pub just to look at them, and to have a drink and a meal. Jeff's love of aerial gardening was legendary and his biannual plant orders to The Treasure Trove were as valued and profitable as they came, but would Alex know this?

'Babies.' Jeff's eyes had actually left the pint for once, and he was staring directly at Alex. 'Baby plants.'

'The plug plants are coming on a treat, Jeff,' said Dilly with more confidence than she felt. 'Everything is growing beautifully.'

'Well, that's a relief, I can tell you. I had been starting to get a bit worried, what with Nathan not confirming my order. Then I thought, he's never let me down yet, so I decided I'd wait to catch him when he came in, but I haven't seen him in ages. What is he up to?'

Dilly watched Alex rub his neck. He mustn't know about the plants and he certainly didn't want to speak about Nathan, but most worryingly, he would have no idea how important Jeff's order was. To top all of this off, Dilly still couldn't shake the idea that Alex might have attended a meeting yesterday to decide the fate of the nursery. Even if the nursery was going to close, it should honour Jeff's order. He had always been the most loyal of customers and regularly dispatched any visitors who commented on his hanging baskets and window boxes to The Treasure Trove once they had contributed to his profits with a meal and some drinks. To sell Jeff short on an order that was fresh and inspiring for his punters could impact his business, too.

'His dry January extended past the month end,' said Alex.

If anything underlines the dishonesty of the man, that answer does, she thought, her hackles rising. Although, she reluctantly conceded, Nathan might not be drinking at the moment, in which case Alex was telling the truth. It was too confusing. She sighed and ran her fingers through her hair, only for a knot to trap them. She wrenched them free and hoped that he was telling the truth. Not that it matters, she reminded herself sharply. He's not to be trusted.

'I can't stand dry January myself,' said Jeff, placing the pint before Alex. 'It plays havoc with my takings. I've never heard of one lasting til March though. This is a hugely worrying development.'

'Don't worry, Jeff. Summer will soon be here and everyone will have a thirst on,' said Dilly.

'A thirst and an appetite are two things of wonder,' he said as the card payment went through.

Reassured that Jeff wasn't going to ask any more questions about his order, Dilly returned to her seat next to her mountain of discarded clothes by the fire. She didn't care if Alex hadn't wanted her input, or if she had crossed an invisible line into interfering in his private business; she was ferociously protective of The Treasure Trove and Bella's future there, and Bella was her priority.

As Alex turned away from the bar, he threw her a glance laden with gratitude. It made her feel sick with worry. What if Alex couldn't find Jeff's order, nor fulfil it? Jeff was a lovely man, but he ran a tight ship and his hanging baskets were a source of pride and income. She knew he spent ages researching and planning new colour palettes every season. If all that time and effort had gone to waste, he might take his business elsewhere. What type of time-poor businessman wouldn't want to take the path of least resistance? The path of least resistance for Alex was to sell. That made sound business sense. It was scant consolation that Alex appeared to be as worried as she was.

'Are you Nathan Hampton's brother?' She heard a voice she recognised all too well, and it never meant good news.

'Yes.' The word was barely out of Alex's mouth when the onslaught began.

'You'd better have a word with him then. I was up at the nursery today. Fat lot of good that did. No one was any use up there whatsoever.'

Dilly had never felt so indignant. How dare he speak about Bella and Dave like that?

'I'm sorry. I—' Alex tried to speak to the man who Dilly's dad used to call Negative Nigel.

'If he doesn't sort it out, he'll be slapped with a fine and a criminal record.' Nigel cut through Alex's words. If Alex was angered or embarrassed by the sudden public onslaught, or fearful about whatever Nathan had done, he kept calm and didn't let it show. 'This is his final warning,' barked Nigel. 'I'll get the authorities involved.'

Alex's brow knitted. 'I'm very sorry about this.' His words were measured, making Nigel's high-handed superiority sound even more ridiculous. 'Perhaps you could tell me exactly what's troubling you.'

'He has blocked a public right of way,' shouted Nigel and the rest of the pub fell silent. The louder Nigel shouted, the more reasonable Alex sounded. Dilly admired his strength under attack. By behaving appropriately, he made Nigel look like a ridiculous, snappy Chihuahua.

'Where is the right of way?'

'Your brother will know. Tell him to clear that path by the end of the day tomorrow. I'll be over to check.'

Nigel stormed out of the pub before Alex could respond. Dilly watched Alex take a deep breath. If anything would make him want to rid himself of the responsibility of the nursery, it was having Negative Nigel on his case so soon after she'd had a go at him. She saw him blink as if he couldn't quite believe what had just happened, then his eyes sought hers as he shook his head.

'I bet you wish you had never come out for a pint,' she said. 'Don't worry. We can sort this out.' He looked beaten and weary, but grateful.

Jonty squeezed in next to Dilly and her discarded

clothes. Having swigged his pint, as if refuelling himself for action, he leant forward. 'To business!'

His words made Dilly smile. Jonty was a help-seeking missile. If something needed doing in the village, you could guarantee that he would set up some kind of committee or party. It would be wonderful if it was a party, she thought. She hadn't had a good excuse to get dressed up in ages. Still, whatever it was, she would be happy to help if she could.

'I think Nigel was talking about the right of way leading to the river,' said Dilly.

She had fond memories of the path from her childhood. She had strolled along it with her dad as a girl. How she had loved to amble in the countryside around the village with him, spotting birds and other wildlife, until she began to work outdoors, then she needed a rest more than exercise in her downtime. With a jolt, she realised that she hadn't taken a walk in the countryside for pleasure since her dad had died, and that was seven years ago.

'It runs behind Alex's cottage,' said Jonty.

Alex's cottage makes him sound like a permanent fixture, thought Dilly. If only that were true.

'Does Nathan have power tools there?' asked Steve.

Alex nodded and sneaked a meaningful and apologetic glance at Dilly. Now was not the time to brood on Alex's use of them, she decided. She needed to make sure that Alex saved the nursery and didn't sell it, so she parked her feelings about the power tools and remained silent.

'I can work on it tomorrow morning,' said Jonty. 'Dilly?'

'I can't, I'm afraid. I'm scheduled to work.' She didn't need to tell the others that the job she was doing would be on a commission basis at the nursery: commission she might never receive if Alex were to sell the nursery, or if the nursery went under.

'I can help,' said Steve.

'That's settled then,' said Jonty.

'I hadn't realised there was a path down there, so thanks.' Alex smiled tenderly at Dilly, and the barriers she had erected to protect herself from him crumbled quicker than the Norfolk coast in a storm. 'To be honest, I thought it was just a patch of brambles behind the cottage.'

Sadness washed over Dilly. It wasn't like Nathan to let this happen. How long had something been the matter? she wondered. And how had he kept it so secret that no one noticed? She hoped the growth across the path was recent. Perhaps the odd branch had fallen during winter storms and blocked it. If it was more congested than that, if it was caused by plants that had grown last year, she would know that poor Nathan had been suffering in silence for far longer than she had suspected. The thought made her heart break a little more for Nathan, The Treasure Trove and Bella's future there.

Chapter Twenty

Dilly hadn't had the chance to speak to Alex at the pub about what had happened to Jeff's order, nor had she made any inroads into ascertaining whether his meeting yesterday had been about selling the business. Now, she was determined to find out what was going on. She cycled along the nursery track, a shiver running down her spine when she saw the spot where she had come off her bike. The pothole had been filled. That was considerate of Alex, she thought with a smile. Pushing any feelings about him caring enough to mend the road to one side, she pedalled on purposefully. She had a lot to achieve today. There was no room for emotion.

Steve's car was already in the car park, along with a couple of other vehicles. She hopped off her bicycle, leant it against a pallet at the back of the polytunnel and went into the shop to see if any containers had been sold and urgently needed replacing. The nursery wasn't yet busy, but it would be later in the day. It only took one morning of sunshine, and the gardeners of Sweetingfield and the surrounding villages and towns would emerge from their winter hibernation and their thoughts would turn once again to their gardens.

She saw Alex talking to one of the school mums. Dilly could see she was basking in his attention and an unwelcome dart of envy shot through her. So much for containing your emotions, Dilly. Nothing good ever came of jealousy, she told herself fiercely. Even so, she couldn't help being envious of the easy smile he was bestowing on the mum. His body language was open, confident, and not at all as if he was a man fighting for the life of the nursery. Perhaps he isn't, thought Dilly crossly. Perhaps he's making the most of this woman's attention before he sells the nursery from under us.

'Ah... Dilly.' She had never seen him so relieved to see her, which took the force from her fury. 'Do you happen to know where Nathan keeps his japonicas?'

Dilly saw the woman battling to suppress a giggle and caught the horrified look on Alex's face when he realised the effect his question was having on the mum.

'I have a thousand answers to that one,' said Dilly with a wry smile.

The woman snorted. 'I bet you do.'

'Because gardeners use the word japonica to describe so many plants.' Dilly spoke as if she hadn't any idea of where this woman's mind was taking her. 'Why don't I show you some of the things it might be and we can see if any of them is the one you're looking for?'

'I need to get to the office,' said Alex. 'Excuse me. Good luck with your plant hunting.'

He couldn't get away quickly enough. Dilly's resolve strengthened. He was accessing her knowledge for nothing. Knowledge that her clients paid for. She pulled herself up sharply. It was knowledge she would have given freely under usual circumstances, since she had gleaned so much information from Nathan over the years and was definitely in his debt.

She led the mother to the shrub section, and having found a skimmia, its dark red flower buds already opening to reveal fragrant white blooms, she carried the plant to Liv, the student who covered for Bella on the till at weekends and when she needed time off during the school holidays. Having checked that the mum understood the care the plant required, Dilly left her with Liv and headed straight to the office to find Alex. He was sitting at Nathan's desk, which looked uncharacteristically as if a bomb had hit it. She quietly closed the door behind her.

'Can I help?' she asked.

He shook his head. 'It's okay, thanks. I'm sorry. I shouldn't have dumped that customer on you without warning. I had no idea what she was talking about. It was so awkward. I was having to fake confidence and I hate doing that.'

'Don't worry about it,' said Dilly, embarrassed by how angry she had been with him at the time.

She moved a pile of files from a chair to the floor, while wondering if there was ever a chair without files on it when Alex was around, then she sat down on the vacated seat. The arms were dusty. Nathan had always run a clean and tidy nursery and the state of the office shocked her. Her concern that Alex was selling The Treasure Trove niggled more worryingly than ever. She needed to work out what was going on.

'Please let me help out more,' she said.

'Thanks for the offer, but I just needed a bit of help with that customer. That's all. Everything is in hand.'

She flicked at her elbow to brush away the dust that had caught on it as she sat down. 'And Jeff's order?'

'Dilly, you don't work here.'

'I know, but I have a vested interest.'

'I hadn't realised that you had invested in the nursery, too.'

Dilly could have screamed at him in frustration, but instead she balled her fists and contained her emotions. She would not leave this office without his acceptance of her help. She took a deep breath in to try to calm her desperation. 'My reputation is on the line, Alex. I told Jeff it was all in hand.'

'Why did you lie for me?'

'I didn't. I'm the world's worst liar and I hate lies,' she said indignantly. 'I just wanted to buy you a little time to sort yourself out and find the order. It'll be here somewhere.'

'But what if I can't fulfil it?'

Dilly was shocked. 'Can't you?'

He looked up at her, and despite all her resolve, she wanted to dive into those deeply troubled eyes. 'I don't know.'

'Would you mind me taking a look at it?'

'I wouldn't mind... if I could find it.' He ran his fingers through his hair, mussing it up, and Dilly's mind immediately flitted back to seeing him in his pyjamas, fresh out of his bed. This is not the time, Dilly, she told herself sternly.

'Would you like me to look for it?'

'I'll wait until Bella comes in on Monday. Perhaps she knows about it.'

'Okay. Let's just hope Jeff doesn't chase for news again before that, and that no one else comes in for their orders.'

He rubbed his eyes. She could see the worry for his

brother and the business weighing on him. So much for his sabbatical.

'Are you getting any of your own work done?' she asked.

He shook his head. 'The nursery is taking over, and I'm not a businessperson.'

'But I am. Alex, you can trust me,' she said, forcing her own mistrust into a back seat. Bella needed this job, and Dilly would fight tooth and nail to save it as she had promised. 'Let me loose in the office this weekend, and I'll try to make the next few weeks as manageable as I can for you. It's not Bella's job to sort out this mess, nor is it Dave's.'

'Nor yours,' he said.

'Nor yours,' she replied.

'But I've invested in the business, so I need to pull my weight.'

'So have I. It might not be money, but the time I spent planting up those containers was my investment and I won't get a return if the business goes under.'

'I didn't realise you were so hard-nosed.'

'I am when it matters. Alex, the sun is shining and the nursery is likely to get busy today. I can answer any questions about plants that customers have, pot up a few containers, then sort things out in the office later.'

'I can't ask you to do that.'

'You didn't, and you may as well accept that I'm going to do it whether you want me to or not,' she said, getting to her feet and picking the files up off the floor, then placing them back on the chair. She nodded to them. 'Just in case chairs are a vital part of your filing system.'

A smile flickered around his mouth. It was a welcome sight and warmed Dilly's heart. Whether she trusted this man or not, keeping the nursery she and Bella loved in business was all that mattered.

It was a busy day at The Treasure Trove, and Dilly enjoyed helping people to make well-considered selections for their gardens. As daylight faded and the business of selling plants slowed, Dilly asked Liv to help her to arrange a few containers and small pots of bulbs and primroses into a display ready for Mothering Sunday. There was something there for all pockets, she reasoned, as they positioned the pretty containers and plants.

She went to the stockroom and found some old bunting to draw attention to the display.

'That looks a bit grim,' said Liv as Dilly tried to untangle it.

'It has seen better days.' Dilly sighed and wrapped it up again. 'I'll ask Jessica if she has any. She's got a thing about making bunting from fabric scraps. It wouldn't surprise me if she had something suitable already made up.'

They stood back to assess their arrangement of plants. It hurt Dilly to think about Mothering Sunday. As a child, she had cried when she saw other children making cards, and her dear dad, realising she was struggling, suggested she make a grandmother card for Mary. Mary had been delighted and told her it had made her year. She still remembered Mary every Mothering Sunday – and every single time Mary told her it had made her year. Her dad had helped her to look beyond her own heartache to try to make Mary happier. He was a good man and she still missed him badly.

'It seems a shame to spoil the display by selling something,' said Liv.

'Good point,' said Dilly, focussing on Liv instead of her own sadness. 'I'll do some extra containers tomorrow to place along that wall for anyone who feels the same way as you do, so they don't need to wreck the display by buying something.'

'You'll be back?' asked Liv.

'Oh yes. More sunshine is forecast tomorrow and that'll bring the punters in.' She checked the clock on the wall. 'You'd better be heading off, Liv. Thanks for all your help.'

As the bell on the door jangled behind Liv, Dilly shuddered with fear. Even though she had enjoyed chatting to people at the nursery all day, she had never been able to shake off the dread of what she might find ignored and unactioned amongst Nathan's paperwork and emails.

She went into the office. Its vast window, which had once shed light onto Nathan's immaculate desk, was now grey and spattered with dust-laden dried raindrops. Files that had once stood regimented across the tops of four filing cabinets lolled drunkenly. Some had collapsed completely and lay on their sides, stacked as they landed, with pages blundering out from within their usually ordered confines. It was immediately clear that the office was a victim of time constraint. Dilly knew from her own busy summers that tidiness was a luxury for those with a few minutes of spare time. By the end of summer, Dilly's own home became dusty and a dumping ground for whatever she didn't have time to put away, as her energies were diverted into earning money.

She stood, her hands on her hips, and took in a deep breath to steady her nerves. She guessed, from the state of the office, why Jeff's order hadn't been confirmed, and she also guessed it probably hadn't been attended to, which was deeply concerning, but until she knew otherwise, there was a sliver of hope. There was always hope, she reminded herself, casting her eye over the chaos and trying to work out where to start. It would have made sense to begin with the files on the chair, but her most urgent task was to find the order sheet or email for Jeff's plants.

'I've already been through the stack of papers on the desk.' Alex was leaning against the doorframe, looking half-apologetic, half-grateful and one hundred percent gorgeous. Did that make him two hundred percent man? *At least you know he's one hundred percent untrustworthy*, she told herself as she pulled the mud-encrusted chair, laden with bits of paper, out from under the desk.

'I need to go through these chair documents though, to make sure there are no other surprises lying in wait. At the very least, they should be filed somewhere,' she said, glancing to the pile of files on the cabinets.

'Is there a system?'

'There would have been one once. Nathan always kept this place ordered, if a little muddy.'

He sighed. 'I wish I'd been able to come over sooner.'

'It's not your fault.'

'It doesn't matter whose fault it is. It changes nothing.' He picked up a stack. 'Shall I go through these papers?'

'I'm afraid they all need checking against the online system,' she said.

'In which case, I'll log you in,' he said, typing his password quickly. 'We'll check any paperwork and I'll file it if necessary.'

'Putting your research skills to good use?'

'Are you suggesting they're not usually put to good use?' He cocked an eyebrow at her, and Dilly's resolve to mistrust this man was engulfed by an ocean of longing.

'Not at all. You're simply expanding their application,' she managed, before dragging her traitorous lusting eyes back to her screen. 'Shall I start going through the emails too?' she asked, determined not to look at him again.

'Good idea.'

'How far should I go back?'

'When was the last reply he sent?'

Dilly clicked on the sent emails and panicked. 'Four months? No. That can't be right.'

'It could be,' he said, his voice sombre.

This was worse than Dilly could have ever imagined. She had believed that all had been well over the Christmas period. Perhaps prior planning had helped the nursery initially, and although Dave was no plantsman, he would have easily carried the nursery through the Christmas tree season with a little help from Bella and Liv. What had happened to poor Nathan in November? She thought back to New Year at The Yew. Nathan hadn't been there. She had believed he was away on a much-needed, well-deserved holiday. It made sense at the time and Dilly hadn't thought twice about it, apart from to hope that he had a great time.

Slowly and methodically they worked through their tasks. Correspondence requesting calls and emails remained unanswered. How had this been allowed to happen? It was fascinating to observe at first hand the workings of the nursery, but horrifying to see how many clients had been neglected and how many orders risked being unfulfilled now that spring was upon them.

Dilly soon learnt that every sigh meant that Alex's list of unconfirmed orders had grown by another previously well-nurtured client. Her own list made for uncomfortable reading. It took a lot of hard work to gain client loyalty, she knew, even though her own customers had been disloyal the second that cheap labour was waved under their noses. She suspected that if Nathan's neglected clients had not already taken their precious business elsewhere, they soon would. It didn't take much to lose a client, as she had discovered recently.

'I've found Jeff's order,' she said, staring at the screen. 'No communication after Jeff firmed up the order, so we've no idea if anything's been done about it.'

Alex pinched the bridge of his nose. 'That's not going to sit well.'

Dilly read the long list and wished she hadn't promised Jeff he would have his babies. 'Were any of these plants sown?'

'I don't know.'

'It's too dark to check now,' she said. 'Let's just make sure we have a complete list of orders, then we can see what we can do about fulfilling them.'

'Isn't it too late to fulfil them?' He looked at her, his eyes sad. 'This one was dated the fifteenth of November and hasn't been confirmed.'

'I guess some clients will already have gone elsewhere.'

'Perhaps more than some.'

'Let's remain optimistic, shall we?' she said, looking at the concern etched across his face.

It spoke volumes. There was no way on the planet that Alex was thinking of selling. Even though she couldn't quite quash the thought that he might be using her to get the paperwork organised for a sale, the stress taking its toll on his strong body and the sadness and concern emanating from those beautiful, caring eyes told a different story. Here was a man who was already worried about his brother, and now his savings were likely to be eaten up, too. At best, the chances of the nursery making a profit this year were almost zero – at worst, all his money would be gone and Bella would lose the job she loved.

It broke Dilly's heart. She hated the thought of Bella and Luke having to move away and she couldn't bear to see Alex suffering like this. She desperately wanted to wrap her arms around him and make everything better, but that would serve no purpose apart from to confuse things between them. She needed to be practical, so she crushed her natural instincts and did what little she could to support him by working on in silence, her shoulders hunched over the keyboard and her body begging to be allowed out of the chair. It was one agonising discovery after another.

Dilly didn't stop until her tummy let out the most unseemly and embarrassingly loud growl of hunger, shattering the silence.

'I'm sorry. I didn't realise the time,' said Alex, pushing his chair away from the desk. 'How about I cook us something?'

I didn't expect that, thought Dilly, her excitement at him cooking for her at odds with the desperation that hung heavily in the office air. 'That sounds amazing.'

'Don't get too excited. It'll only be risotto.'

Dilly's stomach leapt with joy. She didn't care if it was only two curled slices of last week's bread. She loved being cooked for. He mightn't be able to pay her for her work this evening, but sharing his dinner on a night when she might have been at home with nothing more than a tin of soup for company was happiness on a plate.

'That would be lovely,' she said, doing her best to contain her elation.

It was a cold, clear night and the moon was full, so there was no need to use phone torches to light their path through the stock beds towards the cottage. The welcome there was warm and cosy, its thick walls retaining the heat and protecting them from the biting cold outside. She smiled to herself as she remembered how uncomfortable and uncared for she had imagined it would be when she first visited him there.

'Would you like a glass of wine, Dilly?'

The way he said her name made her want to hear it over and over again. She stamped on the thought. She could not afford any distractions and she would do everything she could to prevent any more pain spoiling her safe life.

'I would love one, thanks. White if you have it,' she said.

He opened the fridge and took out a bottle of French wine. 'Are you warm enough?' he asked, as he uncorked the bottle.

'I'm fine, thanks. Compared with the nursery, this kitchen is practically tropical,' she said, shedding her jacket and hanging it over the back of a chair, which in true Alex style was stacked with files.

He set a crystal glass and a small turquoise bowl of olives on the table in front of her, then disappeared into the pantry before returning with rice and vegetables. I could get used to this, thought Dilly, watching him work for a few blissful moments before asking, 'Can I help?'

'I think you've done more than your fair share of helping. Sit back and relax,' he said, taking a knife from the block.

Dilly's eyes shot out like organ stops. She had never seen anyone wield a kitchen knife with such precision and confidence. 'You chop like a chef.'

'I'm a bit rusty to be honest.'

'If that's rusty, I'd love to see you at full tilt. I probably wouldn't be able to see the knife.' She saw a small smile play around his lips. She was thankful for it. It was always good to raise someone's spirits.

The wine slipped down far more easily than felt decent, while Dilly absorbed the details of this new, relaxed version of Alex at home with an audience watching him cook, pocketing it for future lonely evenings once he had returned to his other, more sophisticated life.

'Are you studying my risotto-making technique?'

Was I staring so obviously? she wondered. 'I am indeed,' she said, emboldened by the wine. 'I want to make sure you get it right.'

'Now you're making me nervous.'

'There's no reason to be. I make the worst risotto in the world.'

'I don't believe that for one second,' he said, adding stock to the rice.

'It's true. I only tried it once. It ended up being a massive lumpy rice rock that harboured interesting shocks of undiluted stock cube.' She shuddered at the memory and he laughed.

'I bet your guests enjoyed those little surprises.'

'Mercifully no guests were involved.'

'Did you stir it all the time?' he asked.

'No.'

'That's probably what happened. Try it again with homemade stock. You'll get it right next time.'

'You really think so?'

'I do. I also think your glass needs topping up, so why don't you take over stirring the risotto while I grab the bottle?'

Dilly panicked. 'Can't it be the other way around? I'll wreck the risotto.'

'I trust you.'

The words were music to Dilly's ears. She might not fully trust him, but at least he trusted her, if only with his risotto, and that was in spite of the fact she hadn't a clue what she was doing and had confessed to being a culinary nightmare. Her homemade risotto wasn't even the worst meal she had ever cooked for herself. Still, she couldn't let him see she didn't trust herself to make a pan of food, so she pushed back her chair and took over at the hob.

Much to her astonishment, he was right. The risotto didn't end up being a solid rock in the pan. They sat down to eat and the meal disappeared in a blur. Conversation and wine flowed, and too soon it was time to leave. Having stacked the dishwasher, she turned to him, slightly tipsy and full of risotto and gratitude.

'I ought to be going.' Ought to, but I don't want to, she thought, reaching for her coat.

'Let me walk you.'

'You don't need to,' she said. She might have wanted to prolong her time with him, but not to the point of him doing it out of a sense of duty. She didn't want him to think that he *had* to make sure she was home safely.

'Weren't you the one trying to get me to go outside?'

Dilly laughed. 'I was. In daylight, with your hands in the soil, filling your body with good endorphins, and anyway, I have my bike and trailer.'

'Should you be cycling after wine?'

'Probably not.'

'I'll walk you,' he said decisively, causing a meltdown of what remained of Dilly's defences.

No one had cooked her dinner and walked her home after it for so long that she thought she had crash-landed in someone else's normality. Her own life had definitely become a little restricted over the years.

They stepped into the cold night and Dilly was glad that even though the moon was full, it didn't give off enough light to capture the glow of her face, which was afire with anticipation and excitement. She was fast realising that not only could she not trust Alex, she couldn't even trust her own body these days.

They arrived far too soon at the end of her drive. Should I invite him in for coffee? she wondered, or would that be too movie-clichéd? She shook her head. Dilly Pepper, it absolutely would be. Don't you dare, she told herself firmly. 'Thank you for a delicious dinner, for the amazing wine and for walking me home,' she said instead.

'And thank you for all of your hard work today.'

'I'll see you tomorrow.'

'You won't have your bike.'

'A walk will do me good.'

'I can collect you.'

She smiled. 'No need. I have great legs. I mean...' she said breezily, stepping backwards along her drive and stumbling on a creeping thyme. 'Sorry!'

He leapt forward to catch her arm and set her back on her feet.

'Was that apology to me or the plant you trod on?'

'The plant, obviously,' she said. She couldn't hide her smile. He had reached out and stopped her falling, and despite all of her efforts to build barriers and put a safe distance between them, she couldn't deny that the strength of his arm felt good. She also couldn't deny he had always been there to help her when she needed him.

Chapter Twenty-One

There was an icing of frost on the pavement the next morning as Dilly trod with trepidation along the high street towards the nursery, her breath clouding the air before her. She wanted to walk more speedily, to get there sooner and put herself out of her misery, or realise the extent of her misery, whichever it was. Not knowing was the worst thing. She needed to find out how far Nathan had got with his orders before it had all gone wrong. A new worry now bothered her. Had she and Alex unwittingly been filling containers with precious plants that should have gone to clients? Clients, she now knew, who had come to Nathan as a result of him providing great plants to Jeff? Recommendation was a wonderful thing. The last thing she wanted was to be contributing to anyone's diminishing reputation.

She could see a human form in the polytunnel and she knew immediately it was Alex. She opened the door and stepped in briskly, to keep any heat in there with them.

'You're early, Dilly.'

'So are you. Have you found anything?'

Alex rubbed the back of his neck. 'I have, but nowhere near enough. The plants labelled in here don't tie in with the ones we need, and there's nothing of Jeff's order. Could they be outside?'

'If they were, they'd be dead by now. They're not built for frost.'

'Not even an apology will resuscitate them?'

'Not even a million apologies.' She stepped towards him and peered at the screen he was holding. 'You uploaded it all?'

'I thought it would be easier,' he said.

He mustn't have slept, she thought sadly.

'Only now I realise I'm trying to pair eggs with oranges,' he continued. Much like I used to dream about doing with us, she thought as she watched him rub his eyes in the way he always did. 'What are we going to do?'

'I think we need an inventory of every plant on the nursery. The last one was done in November. Once we know what we have, we can offer substitutions, or....' She held her hands wide, as if willing the solution to land in her open, waiting arms. The sentence remained unfinished. They were both painfully aware that unless they could source the plants, the only option remaining was to admit they couldn't supply Jeff's order.

'Will we be able to do this once the nursery opens?' he asked.

'I don't see why not. Let's start in here first, then I can update the inventory outside while helping customers.'

'Which leaves me with?'

'Your own work. Remember the Romans? Unless Jonty and Steve didn't finish clearing the path.'

'They did – they were such a help.'

'And doubtless Nigel has already assessed their work.'

'He has, and it passed muster.'

'In which case, there's nothing we can do about the orders until tomorrow, when I'll ring round some of my contacts and see if I can buy plants in to sell on to Nathan's clients.'

'That isn't how Nathan runs the nursery. He grows everything from seed or cuttings.'

'*Most* things,' corrected Dilly.

'What doesn't he grow? He even has a field of Christmas trees.'

'And he supplements them sometimes,' said Dilly.

'How do you know?'

She smiled kindly. 'I know my plants. I also know he supplements summer bedding at times and he certainly buys in the bulbs. Speaking of which, at least they were all planted, and there are more here than we know what to do with. We have a choice. Sell them at a reduced price now, or keep them for next year and hope Nathan can work his magic on them.'

'Sell now.' He sounded resigned, rather than decisive.

Things must be even worse than I suspected, she thought. Still, while there are plants, there is hope. 'Why not give me a chance to make a profit on them first?' she said. 'There are plenty of pots, bowls and baskets. I can make more expensive arrangements for Mothering Sunday. Fingers crossed they will sell to last-minute shoppers.'

He nodded. He looked beaten, and it broke her heart.

She held on to the bench as she watched him leave, in case her body rushed towards him, to wrap him in a hug. It was unnatural not to put an encouraging arm around someone in need, but she needed to focus on the inventory and she knew from experience that getting too close to him muddled her brain. She picked up the list and began the task of finding which, if any, of the plants on the list were already on the nursery. She hadn't made much headway when Dave arrived for work.

'So what's happening, Dilly?' He slammed the door to the polytunnel closed behind him.

'In what way, Dave?'

'You're here. Something's happening. It's one thing for you to be here when it's snowing, but now isn't normal.'

'It's perfectly normal, Dave. I'm here because I have a clear day and I offered to help while Nathan's off.' It wasn't a lie, but it wasn't the whole truth. Not telling the complete truth didn't sit comfortably with her and she was certain her face was giving her away. She only hoped the crisis could be averted and Dave need never know how dire things were. If not, she would never forgive herself.

Dave stood, hands on hips. He certainly didn't look as if the matter was closed. 'Something's not right.'

Dilly blushed. She was a terrible liar, so she wasn't even going to try. Dave was too switched on to believe any denials.

'Morning, Dave.' The door to the polytunnel rattled open and Dilly was relieved to see Alex was back. 'All okay?' Alex sounded as chirpy as a blackbird in spring despite all the problems he was dealing with.

'As okay as a man with a clogged nozzle can be,' he said.

Dilly laughed. Typical Dave, she thought. As serious as anything and then he dumps a line like that on me. 'Sounds painful,' she said.

'Only on the bank balance,' he said. 'This irrigation system is on its last legs. It could do with being replaced.'

That wiped the grin off Dilly's face. The weather would soon be warming up. You couldn't run a nursery – even a relatively small one like The Treasure Trove – without a fully functioning irrigation system.

'Will it last the summer?' she asked.

'I'm spending so much time patching it up that it's not worth keeping. Last autumn, Nathan seemed pretty keen to install a new one over the winter. But... '

'I'll have a word with him,' said Alex. News of the ailing irrigation system did nothing for the worry lines forming on his forehead, but he rallied himself. 'See you in the office when you're ready, Dilly,' he said as he left.

Dave went to stand next to her. 'That doesn't sound hopeful. Look, Dilly, are you sure you're okay? You're looking a bit flushed.'

'I'm wearing too many layers,' she said, heading out of the polytunnel to make some strong coffee to take with her to the office. They had a long and difficult day ahead and Alex had clearly already had a sleepless night.

She paused at the office door with the mugs of steaming coffee, waiting for a natural break in Alex's concentration. His body screamed silently with tension. She spotted a pulse in his jaw, suggesting he was gritting his teeth so hard they might shatter. The urge to massage away the stress was overwhelming. He looked up and smiled wearily. Dilly walked towards him and set their coffees down on the desk.

'Thank you,' he said. The words sounded as if he was thanking her for everything, rather than just a mug of mediocre coffee, and she revelled in the warmth of his appreciation.

She sat down opposite him and clicked on the unfulfilled

order list file on the computer. The screen filled with the work she needed to do, causing her to let out a deep sigh.

'That sounds like an uncharacteristically defeatist sigh for an optimist like Dilly Pepper.'

'That wasn't an admission of defeat, I'll have you know. That was the unmistakeable sound of me girding my loins.' *What am I saying? I can't say loins in front of this man.* Her face flamed.

He laughed. 'I'm glad to hear it.'

I'm not glad I said it, thought Dilly. 'My plan is to contact local growers first, rather than a large supplier, as keeping plant miles down is Nathan's ethos.' Or it used to be, she thought sadly.

'That sounds like a plan.'

'In any case, Jeff has gone a bit exotic this year. I can't imagine that the big suppliers would grow anything as niche as he's looking for.'

'Does he have a budget?'

'Unfortunately he does. Nathan quoted for the plants back in October and Jeff gave him the go-ahead for them on that basis.'

'So we can't put the price up.'

'No. We need to honour Nathan's quote. To do anything else could cause us even more problems.'

'And there's no way we could alter the plants?'

'What? Swap in?'

He nodded.

'Jeff spends all year designing and tweaking those hanging baskets. He'll already have spent hours on them. To make any major changes at this stage would be to let him down big time. I'm not comfortable with that... not that it's my business.'

'It's not, but like you said, you reassured him and I wouldn't want your good name to be called into question simply because...'

There was no need for her to finish his sentence. Any joy that she might have felt about him preserving her good name was wiped out by his despair. She needed to be strong and shore him up.

She took a deep breath and bundled all the confidence she could muster into her words. 'The good news is that we should be able to source the plants from a niche nursery somewhere. The bad news is that they will cost more – potentially double the amount that Nathan quoted, as the plants we buy in will be a decent size by now. So what do you want to do?'

'Take the hit on the chin.'

Ouch. On the chin and in your bank balance, she thought. 'Are you sure? It's a lot of money.'

'My brother is worth it,' said Alex. 'And so is your good name.'

His words cheered her. Even though this was a dark time, he cared about her good name. Under other circumstances she might have been on cloud nine and punched the air with glee, but now, in this moment, a subdued thank you had to suffice.

'I could grow some of the plants myself.' She hadn't meant to say her thoughts aloud, but now she had, she could see a possible solution. 'They'll be small, but at least we would stand a chance of fulfilling Jeff's order and possibly reducing the financial strain.'

'It's a lot of work,' said Alex.

'I love sowing seeds, so it won't feel like work. I can take a shot at growing the gerberas, for example. They'll be cheaper than buying in, which will go some way to offsetting the expense of the plants we need to buy in as they take longer to grow,' she said.

'Would you really do that?'

'I can try. They can be a bit tricksy, but I'll give them my best shot.'

'Thanks, Dilly,' he said. 'Let me know how much I owe you for the seeds.'

'I may have to buy extra, as I'm not sure about germination rates,' she confessed.

'Whatever is needed. I trust your judgement,' he said, and Dilly felt a welcome rush of gratitude and pride. She was securing the confidence of a private and mistrustful man. If every cloud had a silver lining, this was certainly a sterling silver one.

'Will they be ready in time?' he asked.

'All being well,' she said, mustering all of her optimism. 'We have time on our side – not as much as I would like, but enough for us to get the plants to a decent size for transplanting. Also, Jeff is a bit of a trendsetter in these parts. People will want the plants he has, so it will be good business to grow a few extra for them and certainly to add the plants to next year's bedding selection, too.'

'You think he'll want them again?'

'Jeff won't, but people will have loved his hanging baskets this year and will want to copy them next.'

'I hadn't realised he had such power.'

'He does. That's why we need to fulfil his order,' she said, standing up to go and check on a plant she was certain she had seen, but which hadn't been added to the stock list yet.

The Mothering Sunday display caught her attention as

she passed by and she stopped momentarily to admire it. It looked tempting with Jessica's new pastel bunting. Jessica had been so delighted to find a new outlet for her sewing that she had offered to make Easter bunting, too. Nathan had never created a Mothering Sunday display. He'd always left containers there for customers to buy for whatever reason they might fancy one. Some of the planters she had created had already gone, which filled her with hope. If they were popular, then hopefully the nursery might sell enough of them to keep going for a while. It was a baby step, but it was in the right direction, she thought, making a mental note to replace the ones that had been sold, before she left for the day.

'How lovely!' A lady with a baby strapped to her front approached the display with her friend.

'Perfect for anyone wanting a pop of colour on a dull March day,' said Dilly. 'As well as for Mother's Day gifts.'

'They are,' said the lady with the baby.

Her friend pointed at one of the brighter arrangements. 'I think my mum would love that one.'

'I don't know about your mum, but I'd love one by my door,' said the lady with the baby. 'Actually, I'd like two. I'm going to treat myself.'

'Let me put them on a trolley for you,' said Dilly. 'I'll leave them by the till, and when you're ready to pay, ask Liv to fetch me – I'm Dilly, by the way – and I'll take them to your car.'

'Thank you, Dilly,' said the lady with the baby.

'And to think, we only popped in for a little thyme,' said her friend.

Dilly lifted the planters onto the trolley. The lady with

the baby had given her an idea. She left the women to peruse the plants and went over to the herb area. The stock was already available. All she had to do was to combine the herbs to create decorative and useful culinary herb planters, fragrant herb planters and herbal tea planters. As she loaded the herbs into a trolley, she felt a fizz of hope.

Chapter Twenty-Two

Luke and Dilly were robed in Dilly's oldest shirts. Luke's was like a ginormous dress and she'd had to turn his sleeves over several times to roll them out of the way so they could see his hands. They sat at her kitchen table, which was covered with a water- and paint-repellent wipe-clean cloth, ready for action. In front of them was a pair of chipped dinner plates, three times as much cardboard as they could possibly need, paintbrushes, colourful pens and bottles of yellow and green paint.

'Yuck,' squealed Luke, as they plunged their hands into a plate of yellow paint.

Dilly yelped. 'It feels like a handful of slugs.'

They pressed their hands onto their pieces of card, then peeled them away to reveal yellow palm prints.

'Now the next one.' She grimaced as they repeated the process, placing their hands along from the print already on the card. 'What do you think?' she asked.

He giggled, looking pleased with himself. 'Daffodil handprints!'

'So all we need to do now is paint some green leaves and add a message,' she said.

His face dropped. His handwriting might be improving, but writing was still Luke's least favourite thing in all the world. Dilly was surprised he hadn't announced that he had given it up for Lent.

By the time they finished, there were paint splotches on the floor, kitchen cupboards and all over the sink and taps, and two plates with newly grouted yellow and green cracks, but it was worth it. Bella would receive another special handmade Mother's Day card from Luke, and Mary would have one to match.

'When the paint dries, I'll hide them in my biggest gardening book as usual,' said Dilly.

'Don't tell Mum about the card, will you?' he hissed.

'I promise I won't,' she said, as she grabbed his coat from the newel post. 'Let's go and sow some sunflowers.'

It was cold in the garage, but they wouldn't be there long enough for him to notice the chill. She smiled as his chubby little hands plunged the seeds into the compost, and she hoped this moment together was helping to create a lifelong love of nurturing things.

Once she had delivered him home, she set off for Mary and Lois'. She had a favour to ask and it was a big one, given Mary's plans for the greenhouse.

Mary was delighted to see her. Dilly suspected that Mary missed Lois now she was asleep for so much of the day, and she worried that she might be lonely.

'I could grow them at the nursery,' she explained to Mary in hushed tones while Lois slept. 'But Dave's already suspicious about the amount of time I'm spending up there and I don't want to rock the boat.'

'So it's stealth seed sowing,' said Mary. 'Like seed bombers?'

'Only I'm not bombing. I'm asking your permission.'

'I'm glad you have, and I insist you use the greenhouse. I can delay my foray into cacti for a few weeks. It will be lovely to have you pottering down the garden.'

'I'll come and potter in your garden any time,' said Dilly fondly.

'But then you'd be gardening for me for nothing, and that wouldn't do.'

Dilly nodded. Mary treasured her independence and respected Dilly's job. 'I'd like to get started on them today, if that's okay with you.'

'That's absolutely fine. Lois has heated mats and grow lights in the cupboard under the trug shelves, so please help yourself to those. The greenhouse electrics are working and safe – I had them checked a couple of months ago, so it's all yours.'

'Thank you,' said Dilly. 'I'll go and get the compost and seeds.'

When Dilly got home, she took the stairs two at a time to her bedroom and grabbed a pair of tweezers. Some of those seeds would be tiny and she didn't want to sacrifice a single one of them by over-sowing. Then she loaded up her trailer with compost and trays from the nursery, and put the seeds in the panniers. As she arrived at Mary and Lois', the heavens opened, so she cycled down the garden to the greenhouse and got to work.

Rain pummelled the roof and the wind blew, but under the glass, she was cosseted and safe from the storm. It gave her an opportunity to set herself back on course and to reflect on how her life had changed since winter. Change was never good. She had lost work; the nursery was under threat; she had stupidly fallen for a man she couldn't trust, but she was dealing with that. She was being professional, friendly and working with him towards what she hoped was a common goal, but she couldn't stop the niggling suspicion that he might sell the nursery. She felt sick thinking about it all, so she focussed on clinging to what was the same. She was still in Sweetingfield and still single, she thought with a stab of regret at not having been brave enough to act on her body's needs, but, she reminded herself, she had to be thankful she hadn't acted, as Alex was not to be trusted. Most importantly, she was still surrounded by the people she loved most in all the world; the thought of them made her feel warm and safe in the same way as the greenhouse protected her from the storm. When you think about it like that, not much has changed at all, she thought, happily popping a seed into the compost.

The storm passed quickly and the sun was shining again by the time she was ready to go home. She had spent the most wonderful morning doing a job she loved. She had truly rediscovered her equilibrium, thanks to spending time doing a familiar task. There had been hope for the future with every little seed she had nestled into its new home, and as she closed the gate to Mary and Lois' cottage behind her, she realised she hadn't felt this relaxed in weeks.

The sound of a hedge trimmer further along the high street shook her from her reverie. Who trims hedges in spring? she thought crossly. She stormed down the street to see what was happening and was shocked to see a van like the one that had been at Barry's parked with two wheels up on the kerb. Was Alex cutting back gardens again?

How could he have lied to her? She had been right not to trust him. This might not be her client, but that was irrelevant when there were nesting birds to protect. Dilly despaired at the danger he was inflicting on innocent creatures. She stormed down the short drive and around the back of the house, tears tumbling down cold cheeks.

'You promised me,' she yelled. 'How could you?' But she couldn't make herself heard above the racket. 'Alex!' she screamed, blinded by fury and pain. His name died on her lips and the scales of rage fell from her eyes as she realised it wasn't him. Relief flooded her body before anger welled again. This man needed to be stopped. She rushed into his line of vision and flapped her arms wildly.

Now she had the man's attention, the hedge trimmer cut out, to be replaced by a second of furious silence while she took in the sight before her. He was younger than her by a good decade, and tall and strapping, like Alex, but potentially someone she shouldn't be confronting so aggressively. His eyes flashed with anger and disdain, but she would not back down. She had to stop him risking birds' lives, not to mention his own, she thought, noting the lack of ear defenders, safety goggles and gloves.

'Can I help you?' He managed to make the words sound like a threat.

'I need a quiet word.' She tried to sound reasonable, even though seconds earlier she had been screaming like a banshee.

'If it's about the noise, I'll be done soon enough. You can't make an omelette without cracking eggs.'

'If you crack a single egg, you'll be in trouble,' she warned.

A sneer crept across his face, making her feel like an irritating nobody. 'Unless you're here to hire me, I suggest you leave me to get on with my job. Time is money, and all that.'

'You'll be spending a whole lot more money if you don't stop cutting that hedge.' The words shot like hot arrows from her mouth. 'Did you know that it is an offence to intentionally damage or destroy birds' nests, or to intentionally kill or injure chicks, or adult birds?'

'Huh?'

'There are nests in there. If you continue to cut it as you are doing, now that I have told you there are nests in there, someone, not necessarily me, but a neighbour perhaps, will report you.'

'They wouldn't.'

'Sweetingfield has six tree wardens.'

'It's not a tree.'

'It's a yew hedge. Yew can be grown as a tree. The tree wardens will be keeping a watch on what's going on with it. Add all of the village's nature lovers and birdwatchers to the tree wardens and the chances of you continuing to cut that hedge without landing yourself in some seriously hot water are next to nothing.'

'You're just trying to do me out of work.'

Dilly's neck was aching with looking up at him. 'I'm not. I wouldn't do that. Unlike some,' she said meaningfully.

'How can I trust you?'

'You can trust her,' came a familiar voice behind her.

How long had Alex been there? she wondered. It felt great that he had her back and even better to hear him saying aloud that she could be trusted.

'Dilly knows what she's talking about,' he continued, and Dilly glowed inwardly with pride.

'You clearly aren't aware of the law protecting nesting birds, which worries me,' she told the man. 'I'm also worried about the fact you're not protecting *yourself* while doing this job. There can be some nasty accidents.'

He looked at her as if there was about to be another nasty accident. 'Health and safety.' He spat out the words as if they were filth.

'Boring, but there to protect us,' she said.

'Another thing to stop honest people making a living.'

'I'd hardly call protecting your body stopping you making a living. If you had an accident, it would definitely stop you. Look, it's none of my business. I could have left you to cut that hedge and potentially disturb or destroy a nest, then be reported and face a fine, but I took time out to mention it to you. What you do with that information is your business.'

He sighed. 'Okay. I won't cut the hedge today.'

'I'm afraid you'll have to explain to your clients that you found an active nest in the hedge – as I'm sure you will if you look – and that you will not be able to cut their hedge until the chicks have fledged.'

'Meanwhile you'll steam in and steal my business.'

'I won't. You have my word.'

'Well, someone else will.'

'If you explain the situation to your client, I'm sure they won't allow anyone else in. Why not tell them that you'll diary them for later in the year, when the chicks have fledged?'

'My diary only runs to a couple of weeks.'

'In which case you have a lovely job to look forward to,' she said brightly.

'And what about the work I've already done here?'

'Bill them for it,' she said, looking at a load of early spring bulb foliage he had cut to the ground. She swiftly reminded herself to take baby steps. She had doubtless saved some birds' lives today. That was enough.

She sauntered away from him towards Alex, a big smile on her face. She *had* saved baby birds' lives, and Alex had told the man that he could trust her. The adrenaline high was intoxicating and she loved it. Alex's face was clouded and unreadable. What was going on with him?

'Fancy a drink?' she asked brightly.

'No, thank you,' he said coldly.

'What's the matter, Alex?'

His eyes searched her face. 'You really don't know?'

'I haven't a clue. Tell me.'

'You thought he was me. I heard you – probably everyone except that guy with the chainsaw did.'

Dilly's mouth dropped open.

'You didn't trust me. You didn't believe me when I told you I wouldn't cut back any more gardens. It's gutting to think that you actually thought I would knowingly undermine your business. Even worse, you believed I would undermine it when you had done so much to protect my business interests. I thought we were on the same team.'

'We are,' she whispered.

'How can we be when you don't trust me?'

'You let me down once.'

'Without even knowing what I was doing. It was a genuine mistake. I thought I had explained that. I thought you had forgiven me.' His arms were wide, his palms open to the heavens as if seeking help with something. 'I was ignorant. I was wrong. I apologised.'

'I know,' she said. 'I was only...'

'You don't trust me, Dilly.' He looked hurt as he shook his

head. 'Trust is a two-way thing, and for once in my life I trusted someone and that trust wasn't reciprocated. That's a bitter pill to swallow.'

He walked away from her, leaving her feeling sick to her core. She had hurt him again and she didn't know how she could even begin to put things right.

Chapter Twenty-Three

Dilly wrapped her hands around her mug of coffee, seeking consolation from its warmth. She was now deeply ashamed of ever having believed that Alex had lied to her. She had spent so long trying to gain the trust of an untrusting man that she had failed to realise the value he placed on her trust. He was right. It was mutual, and because she had mistrusted him, he would now not trust her. It was a hopeless cycle.

She watched the birds flitting from the feeder to the hedges in her back garden. At least thanks to yesterday's intervention, some more birds would be safe in their nests. She spotted one perched on the garage guttering, its beak loaded with moss. It flitted into the hedgerow to line its nest. Dilly smiled to herself. Sure as spring followed winter, the birds would be busy nesting. It was never a surprise, but always a joy. There is hope for the future right there, she thought as she sipped her coffee.

'Are we ready?' Jonty popped his head around the kitchen door. There was no more time to brood on what had happened the day before with Alex.

'I don't know about you, but I've been ready for hours,' said Dilly, dumping her mug in the sink.

'In which case, let's go. Steve's chomping at the bit to get on the road. You know what he's like.'

Dilly smiled. 'Yes, a big excitable kid. Why didn't you park in the drive?'

'And put those little saxifrage flowers growing up the middle in the shade?'

'They wouldn't have minded for a moment.'

'But I wouldn't want my old car spoiling the view. It's looking great, Dilly.'

'Thanks. I can only hope it inspires someone else to plant up theirs.' She flung open the back door of the car and was greeted by a whirl of excitement.

'I've planned my day, Dilly,' said Steve, before she had even closed the car door. 'How about you?'

'I'm going to take things as I find them,' said Dilly. 'Which appears to involve being dragged along in your slipstream.'

'Steve has arranged it all exactly like a school trip,' said Jonty, climbing into the driver's seat.

'I hope we don't have to do a write-up about our visit, or a poster afterwards,' said Dilly. 'Those things always used to spoil a good day out.'

'A day out, but *not* a day off,' Steve said firmly.

'This *is* my day off,' countered Dilly.

'And a proper busman's holiday at that,' said Steve. 'You do know that it's a specialist daffodil day?'

'If you love plants, you love plants,' sang Dilly as they drove away.

'Please don't sing, Dilly,' said Jonty.

'We always used to sing on school trips,' she said.

'Trust me, if anyone starts singing while I'm driving, you'll be asked to leave my vehicle.'

'OooOOOOoooo,' chorused Steve and Dilly.

'Because trying to remember the words to songs is way too distracting.' Jonty chuckled and Steve and Dilly joined him.

It was a happy journey, filled with chatter, news and an appreciation of the countryside bursting into life. There wasn't a verge on the roads that didn't bring gasps of appreciation and excitement, and once they had left Norfolk, no tree escaped comparison with the trees in their own area of the countryside, where spring was a few days behind.

Signs for the festival heralded their arrival at the village of Silstone. They drove away from the main road and down a single-track lane edged with daffodils.

'Isn't this gorgeous?' cried Dilly as they approached the fields nearest the centre of the village, which had been given over to parking.

'It's busy,' gasped Steve, acknowledging a volunteer in a yellow hi-viz jacket and daffodil hat, who was directing them past lines of cars to the next available parking spot.

No sooner had Jonty stopped the car than Steve was out of the door and forging his way to the first of the three daffodil talks he had been so excited to attend.

'He's like a dog being released from a vehicle after a long journey,' said Jonty.

'Only dogs would get sidetracked and sniff around en route,' said Dilly, as Jonty locked the car.

'I'm planning to have a cup of tea first,' said Jonty. 'How about you?'

'I'm going to look around and see what takes my fancy,' she said. 'Shall I meet you later at the car as planned?'

'Good idea, unless we bump into one another beforehand. Have a great day.'

'I will,' said Dilly, smiling broadly. 'I've been looking forward to this!'

Dilly ambled around the glorious bright yellow and white displays, which were usually offset by blue flowers. She took photos of any exciting or satisfying plant combinations to copy when planting bulbs in autumn, or more immediately on a smaller scale in the containers at The Treasure Trove. A variety of daffodil she had never seen before caught her eye. She couldn't wait for the person who was leaning in to get a closer look at the flower to finish their inspection, so that she could get down and have a proper look at it.

It was his reaction to her when he stood up that drew her attention to him. She was so enamoured with this pretty little daffodil that had he not reacted, she would probably never have spotted him.

'Nathan,' she gasped.

There was a greyish pallor to his skin and he was stooped, as if the burden of standing tall was too great to bear. Even his dark wavy hair seemed to have given up and hung lankly around a face that was once round and exuded joy, but now drooped as if clinging to his bones was too much effort. His hazel eyes, which had shone so brightly, were dull and heavy bags weighed down the skin beneath them. It was as if a light had been extinguished in his soul. There was less of him. He looked, without question, ill.

'Dilly. How are you?'

She smiled through her shock at his appearance.

'I'm great, thanks. All the better for seeing you.' As she spoke the words, she regretted their triteness, but she was genuinely relieved to see him.

He seemed to panic. 'Are you here alone?'

'I'm with Steve and Jonty. Steve's all over the talks, as you might guess. Do you fancy a cup of tea?' she asked, wanting to prolong their time together now she had finally found him.

He hesitated. 'I was about to go.'

'Please stay and have a cup of tea with me.'

'I don't feel up to catching up with lots of people, to be honest.'

Steve and Jonty were hardly lots of people, she thought sadly. 'How about we go somewhere away from here for a cuppa?'

He looked as if it were the last thing he wanted, but he acquiesced. 'I'm staying at my brother's flat. We could have a cup of tea there, if you don't mind leaving the festival.'

She would have trailed to the other side of the earth on her hands and knees for a cuppa and a chat with Nathan, but she had never imagined for a second that following him would lead her to Alex's flat.

'That would be lovely,' she said.

They slunk off to Nathan's car in silence and drove away from the event towards the city. Dilly had expected Nathan to say something about The Treasure Trove, but instead he talked about the displays at Silstone and the pretty new daffodil. It was reassuring to see that whatever else was happening in his life, he hadn't lost his enthusiasm for plants.

Eventually, they drew into a car park behind a tall Victorian building and Nathan parked up. As Dilly climbed the stairs, she could barely believe she was going to see something so connected with Alex. He was still mysterious to her in so many ways. She watched Nathan unlock a shiny black front door that was much sturdier and grander than she had ever imagined the front door of a flat could be. Big, strong and dependable, she thought as she stepped over the threshold, into a narrow hallway with doors spaced equidistantly along it. Balanced, she thought as she watched Nathan deposit his keys on an antique table that shone and was well-looked-after, and was without question the most exquisite one she had ever seen. Just like Alex, she thought, shaking her head at likening Alex to a collection of doors and a hall table.

She glimpsed the high-ceilinged drawing room and it stopped her in her tracks. Nothing was too ostentatious, she was pleased to see, apart from the bookshelves lining the walls all the way up to the cornicing.

'Wow,' she gasped.

'Yeah, it is a bit much for plantaholics like us,' said Nathan.

'Do you think he's read them all?' she asked, following Nathan to the end of the corridor.

'I know he has,' said Nathan.

'So not all show.'

'My brother, all show? Definitely not,' he said, pushing open the kitchen door.

It wasn't a large kitchen. There was a small two-seater table by the huge sash window, and quality wooden cupboards that were obviously handmade, as the upper ones were taller than any she had seen in a kitchen before. An array of dried herbs and spices took up the space between the wall and base cupboards nearest the cooker, and a small bowl of sea salt sat next to the hob. She could imagine his long, sensual fingers dipping into that bowl and scattering the crystals into a cooking pot on the stove. This is ridiculous, she told herself firmly. Stop gawping

'Can I help?' she asked.

'No, I'll do it. Sit down.'

She did as she was told and took a seat at the table. *Alex's* table.

Oblivious to the thoughts racing through Dilly's brain, Nathan filled the kettle, then sat down opposite her, as if he was too tired to stand while it boiled. She wanted to ask him so many questions about what was happening in his life, but she bit her lip and waited. When no words came from him, she stared out of the window to the pavement below. The trees lining the road were yet to show signs of leaf burst.

She pointed to them. 'I bet they'll be amazing in a few weeks.'

'They will be,' he said, scraping back his chair to take mugs from the overhead cupboard nearest the sink. It was odd. Nathan was as uptight with her as Alex was with Jessica.

Two cream and navy mugs were set on the side. They weren't hefty, nor were they too small and dainty.

'I guess there won't be any sugar,' she said.

'There is. Don't worry. Still two?'

Dilly nodded. Nathan hadn't stopped caring about the little details that mattered so much to other people.

He dropped two teabags into the mugs. 'I won't use the teapot. Save on washing up.'

Dilly readily agreed. Who was she to argue? She was too concerned about Nathan's well-being to give two hoots about his tea-making technique.

They sipped their mugs of tea in silence for so long that they had almost finished their drinks by the time Nathan finally spoke.

'I guess you're wondering why my brother and I have swapped lives,' he said. Dilly nodded. She wanted to tell him he didn't need to explain, but she knew Nathan well enough to know he wouldn't even think of telling her anything if he didn't want to. 'I know you won't say anything to anyone, Dilly. I...'

Dilly sat motionless lest the slightest movement distract him and stop him speaking when he finally felt able to continue.

'I've had a rough time. I haven't coped with it.' Dilly wanted to give him a huge hug and to beg him to come home to Sweetingfield where he was loved, but she waited for him to speak. 'You know about the divorce,' he said, matter-of-factly.

Dilly nodded. She had thought he had ridden that pretty well, all things considered. He and Kim had seemed perfectly happy, then it was as if a grain of sand had got in between them, and niggled and annoyed them, then grown into a huge beach and rocks that were insurmountable.

'We had been trying for a baby,' he said simply. 'It didn't happen. It was too much pressure, and that was what broke us up.'

'I'm sorry,' she whispered, her heart breaking for them both.

'I was okay with it, I guess. I was fine when she met someone else too, or at least I thought I was.'

There was another long silence. Dilly waited. There was more. Perhaps it was too painful to say.

'She's a mother, now.'

Dilly was out of her seat with her arms wrapped around Nathan before she had a chance to think. It was the cruellest blow to a man who was a natural nurturer. Of course he wanted children. They cried together. She felt his pain to her core. No wonder he had run away from the nursery. It wasn't only the reminder of the life he and Kim had shared together. It was also that the nursery was all about raising and nurturing. Poor Nathan. Had he been here alone all along? Surely he would be better surrounded by people who cared about him?

They stayed, him sitting, her bending over him, enveloping him in the love of friendship, until long after the tears had dried.

'Why not come home?' she finally said. 'If you don't want to run the nursery any longer, then don't. But please come back to Sweetingfield where you'll be amongst friends. We miss you.' For a split second she wondered if she should say more, and then found she couldn't hold back the words. 'Bella does, especially.'

He sighed. Had she said too much? He remained silent for the longest beat, then spoke. 'I miss Sweetingfield... I miss...'

She guessed he missed Bella, but he wasn't ready, or able, to say so. She released him slightly so that she could see his face. 'Then come home,' she urged.

'I can't.' The words were heavy with hopelessness. He stood up slowly. 'I'll drop you back near Silstone.'

Speechlessly, she bade farewell to Alex's elegant flat and they went downstairs to Nathan's car. He didn't start the engine, but sat quietly, staring at the wall in front of them. Dilly resolved to stay silent. He had something else to say and she could wait for him to be ready.

'I've always believed I should look after Alex,' he said eventually, his voice cracking with emotion. 'That's what's tearing me apart about all of this. I'm not the heroic, strong big brother he can rely on. He's having to look after me and it's not right.'

Dilly couldn't bear for Nathan to blame himself, so she broke her silence. 'He's a grown man. He can cope.'

'I've let him down, Dilly. Ever since he was fourteen, when I promised I'd always be there for him, I always have been. Only, I'm not any more. He's having to be there for me.'

Dilly's brow knitted. 'What happened when he was fourteen?'

He rubbed his face. 'Our parents had itchy feet. They had always wanted to live abroad, so when Alex was fourteen they moved to a tiny Caribbean island and he was sent to boarding school. It doesn't sound like a big deal, but it was for Alex. He had lost everything he loved.' He went quiet again, then took a deep, weary breath before continuing. 'He was homesick, only he couldn't go home any more because they'd sold it to buy a place out there. No one talked it through with him, or considered his feelings. He had been such a happy little kid, but this wrecked things for him. Our parents shattered his trust.' He sighed heavily. Dilly felt wretched. It made Alex's trust in her more precious than ever. And she had failed him by not trusting him back. 'Alex believed he didn't matter to the people who were meant to love him the most,' continued Nathan. 'He couldn't be sure of anyone. Jessica tried. She wanted him to stay with her in the holidays – to give him a home and a mother figure, but he wouldn't go. It hurt her terribly, but he was still a boy. She didn't stand a chance.'

'Why? Because he was so damaged by what had happened?' she asked.

'I guess it's because she's our mother's identical twin. Every time he sees her, he sees our mother, only Jessica is loving and affectionate, and everything he wanted our mother to be.'

Now Dilly understood his standoffishness with Jessica. Poor Jessica, whose only crime was to remind Alex of everything he had lost. 'He only trusted me,' Nathan continued, 'and now I've let him down, too.'

Dilly shook her head. 'Nathan...' she said. She wanted to tell him he hadn't let Alex down, but he shot her a look that made the words wither in her throat. His mind was made up and her denials of his truth would change nothing. She spoke very softly. 'What would you say if you were speaking to me in this situation, and I was in your shoes?'

He rested his head on the steering wheel for what seemed like forever. Dilly sat still, barely allowing herself to breathe fully in case she broke the silence. Eventually he turned so that he was looking directly at her. He smiled weakly, then lifted his head and nodded, before turning the ignition key.

She had sown the seed of a thought; she knew that from the nod of his head. Now she needed to wait and see if that seed would germinate.

* * *

It was a subdued journey back to Sweetingfield with Jonty and Steve, and unrecognisable from the one to Silstone earlier in the day.

'You're quiet in the back,' said Jonty.

'I must be tired,' she said.

'Like our over-excitable child here?' He nodded to the passenger seat where Steve dozed, his mouth lolling open.

'He's had an exciting day,' she said fondly, then sat wordlessly with her thoughts. Alex had taken a risk and trusted her despite everything, yet she had been so ready to put up barriers against trusting him, just because he had made one mistake. She hadn't truly forgiven him, she realised, and by not fully forgiving, she had made herself unhappy. She wished she could go back to the moment they had met and allow herself to free-fall into love.

Her mind turned to Nathan. He was alone, yet so very loved. She had always known him to be a carer and nurturer, and now she knew that even as a teenager, when he should have been grasping life and freedom with both hands, he had taken responsibility for his homesick little brother. Nathan had been forced to grow up quickly and he had shown himself to be strong and resilient, but even the strongest people had a breaking point. She could only hope he would find a way to forgive himself for needing the support of his brother, and that perhaps their conversation today might encourage him to come home to his friends. It had to be better than being alone.

Chapter Twenty-Four

Dilly woke the next morning in low spirits. Sadness weighed on her as she got ready for the day. Poor Alex. It must have taken so much for him to trust her, and she had thrown his trust back in his face. And poor Nathan. Why was he trying to deal with this awful situation alone when he could have love and friendship? Dilly couldn't imagine wanting to be anywhere that she wasn't surrounded by love.

She unhooked the trailer from her bike and left it in her garage, before walking to the end of her drive and clambering aboard her bike to head down the road to The Treasure Trove. She needed to see Alex. How could she rebuild his trust in her and show him that she trusted him now, if she didn't spend time with him? She felt awful for hurting him, and guilty about honouring her agreement to go to the daffodil day rather than helping out at the nursery. It had been the right thing to do though, as it turned out, since she had been able to reassure Nathan that he was loved and wanted back in Sweetingfield, if, or when, he was ready to come home. She took solace from the fact he was showing an interest in plants. They had both been drawn to the new variety of daffodil, as plants-people are wont to be. That he had been examining it and finding out about it meant that all was not lost. Perhaps plants would help to lead him back to a better place. She could only hope so. Then there was Alex. He must have felt abandoned by his parents. She couldn't imagine how much that must have hurt. She had lost her mum at a young age and it had been the worst imaginable time, but there was never any question about her parents' love for her. No wonder Alex was so mistrustful and wary.

When she arrived at the nursery, she was surprised to find Alex helping Liv at the tills. The nursery was busier than Dilly had ever seen it. The change in the weather must have rattled shoppers into action. Relief washed over her. If the nursery was to survive, it needed to sell more than a handful of plants.

'Would you like some help?' she asked.

'Yes, please,' he said breezily, as if she hadn't hurt him the last time they had seen one another. He didn't catch her eye as he usually did, though. He was faking being okay and she could see through the facade, just as she had when he had been polite yet cold with Jessica.

He stood to one side to let Dilly in at the till. 'I'll help people to their cars with the plants,' he said, taking hold of the handle of a trolley-load of plants, and rushing away from her.

There was nothing she could do about the situation with Alex now, so Dilly threw herself into work. She wondered fleetingly if Nathan were to see this, would he be reassured that the nursery was in good hands and want to stay away, or would he stay and join in? She hoped it was the latter. The nursery simply wasn't the same without him.

It was a busy morning, but by lunch time the shop was quieter. 'They're probably all at the pub,' mumbled Dave. 'Which is where I should be.'

'I'll buy you a pint after work to thank you for coming in today,' said Alex.

'No can do, I'm afraid. I've got to go home for my Sunday roast.'

'And if you weren't here, you probably wouldn't be in The Yew anyway, as there'd be spuds to peel at your house,' said Dilly. 'So it's an ill wind, Dave.'

'And you get to enjoy our company,' said Alex. Dave muttered something to himself and shuffled off. 'Now I feel guilty for asking him to come in.'

'Don't be,' said Dilly. 'Dave is never happier than when he's grumbling, so he's probably ecstatic right now. He should be thanking you for bringing him in on a Sunday. You've most likely made his day.'

Alex laughed. She loved to hear him laugh. Perhaps there was a chance she might be able to break down the barriers he had put up after he realised their trust wasn't mutual. He spotted someone approaching the till with a trolley laden with plants. 'I'll go and help them,' he said, already striding away from her.

Dilly swallowed hard. He still hadn't looked her in the eye, and that hurt. I can play at pretending everything's okay and that you're not putting on a brave front as long as you want, Alex Hampton, but at some point we will have to speak properly, she told him silently. A shiver of uncertainty rippled through her and she quelled it immediately. There's still time, she reassured herself.

As the nursery was quieter, Dilly took the opportunity to stroll around the stock with a Danish trolley. She selected individual plants that would make good gifts and trundled them back into the shop to create a new display, using some pale blue and lemon ribbon she had brought from Jessica's craft room and the Easter bunting Jessica had made.

'I'm not sure Nathan would like this,' said Dave as he watched her work. Dilly kept her counsel. Dave didn't know how close they were to closing for good. Whether Nathan liked it or not, it was necessary to increase his profits and keep the nursery going until he returned. Then, he could go back to how things were.

Dilly tied a yellow ribbon around a rose in a container to make it look like a gift. 'It's only a ribbon or two, Dave.'

'And the flags.'

'It's bunting,' she said. 'And I think it's lovely.'

'Me too,' said a lady passing with her trolley. 'I'd like to buy some. Do you have any for sale?'

Dilly heard Dave snort. She didn't want to turn The Treasure Trove into a garden centre any more than he did, but money needed to be made. 'You can buy this one the week after Easter if you'd like,' she said.

'I would love it for my summerhouse. I'll come back then,' she said.

As she ambled away, Dave hissed at Dilly, 'What's got into you? You'll turn money on a pebble given half a chance. You're nothing more than a mercenary profiteer.'

'Recycling the bunting isn't profiteering, Dave,' said Dilly, trying not to sound defensive. 'It's saving on landfill.'

'For a price.'

She smiled. 'A small price, Dave, but a bargain to that lady.' Not wishing to be drawn into an argument, Dilly walked away. She needed to speak to Alex. If she was going to rebuild his trust, she had to start by being herself and keeping secrets was really not her thing.

She saw him walking towards the office. 'Alex,' she called. 'Please can I have a word?'

His eyes finally met hers and the desolation in them winded her. 'You sound serious all of a sudden.'

Now that she understood something of his issues with trust, she worried about how he would take the news of her speaking to Nathan; of her being in his flat; and of her knowing so much.

She followed him into the office and closed the door behind her. 'I saw Nathan yesterday.'

His body tensed. She wanted to reach out and hold him and to promise him that he could trust her. Instead, she said, 'I won't tell a soul. I thought you would want to know so there are no secrets between us.'

If he asked her to recount every word that had been said, she would, but he just stared down at his feet as if trying to compute the implications of what had happened.

'How did you think he was?' he asked eventually, his eyes filled with concern.

'Not good,' she said. 'But I hope I reassured him.'

'Thank you,' he whispered.

She smiled weakly. 'I'd better get back.'

He nodded. If that was a first step towards building trust, it was a minuscule fairy one, but it didn't matter how small it was, it was still a step.

Chapter Twenty-Five

Dilly pushed open Jessica's garden gate and allowed the beauty of her surroundings to claim her. As always, Jessica was ready with a cup of coffee and a slice of cake.

'You do know I am fuelled by breakfast cake when I work in your garden,' said Dilly, enjoying the sweetness and lightness of the sponge playing on her tongue. 'Coffee and walnut... Delicious!' She stepped slightly to one side to enjoy the weak rays of sunshine sneaking through between the clouds.

'I had been hoping that Alex would be here for a half hour of Gardening with Dilly, as I call it, but he's busy again today.'

Dilly's heart sank. He was most likely avoiding her, and who could blame him? 'I'm going to have to work harder to make up for his absence,' she said, slapping a broad smile on her face.

'Nonsense. Work at the normal speed and I'll join you. Let me get my gloves.'

Dilly's heart went out to Jessica. She was such a generous, kind soul. Her love for Alex and her pride in his achievements were obvious, yet he had built an impenetrable barrier around himself and would not let her in. It must hurt her, she thought. If only there was a way to build a bridge between them.

She was delighted to have Jessica's company. She was in too much of a thoughtful mood today to be alone, and none of the thoughts were as happy as they should be. Perhaps she was missing the hustle and bustle of life at the nursery. She enjoyed her days at The Treasure Trove, and when she wasn't there, she missed it more than she dared to admit. It was becoming like a second home to her, and she cared so deeply about its future that it hurt.

'I had forgotten all about the seeds that Alex brought back from the seed swap,' said Jessica, rattling the brown envelope of love-in-a-mist seeds.

Dilly flinched inwardly with regret and embarrassment at having ruined what could have been a very special moment with Alex after the seed swap. How might things have been between them now had she acted on her feelings then? she wondered, then she swiftly pushed the thought aside. She hadn't acted, so there was no point in even thinking about it.

'I had been worried that he might come back with something dull, like turnips,' continued Jessica. 'But he surprised me with this choice. He told me that you'd had a hand in his decision, so thank you, Dilly.'

'All part of the service.'

'Credit where credit's due,' said Jessica, opening the envelope.

Dilly was pleased that Alex had discussed her part in Jessica's seed selection. He made her feel good about her work. He always saw people's strengths, rather than their weaknesses, and the more she thought about him, the more she admired his qualities and his respect for others.

As she and Jessica sowed the seeds, she wondered if he would see them bloom and if not, how she would ever be able to look at these pretty love-in-a-mist flowers without thinking of all the wonderful tomorrows they might have shared had she trusted. Perhaps trust would have made no difference, she rationalised, even though she couldn't help thinking that had she trusted herself to let go of her fears, and believed him when he promised he wouldn't make the same mistake twice, they might have had a wonderful future together.

Was a future together still a possibility if she made things right with him, or was it too late? She sighed. Her belief in tomorrow had never felt so fragile.

Chapter Twenty-Six

At the end of a morning in Jessica's garden, Dilly returned home to find a container of vegetable soup in the shelter of her tiny porch. A note in Steve's handwriting sellotaped to it said, *I made too much.* Gratitude surged through her. She loved thoughtful tokens of friendship like this. Steve knew how busy spring and summer could be for her. He was also aware that she was no chef and the last thing she ever wanted to do was cook. All she had to do was microwave a bowl of Steve's soup and a few minutes later she would be tasting the delights of homegrown, home-cooked food.

Full of soup and hope, Dilly strode out to her own front garden and without thinking, she glanced across to Mary and Lois' cottage as she always did, to check that the stable door was open.

'What the—?' She ran out of her drive and across the green, her heart thumping in her chest. What was that van doing blocking their drive?

To her horror, she saw that the man she had confronted about hedge-cutting was spraying weedkiller along the path where aconites and windflowers flourished so freely. He wore no mask, and no other protection of any kind, which was hardly surprising since he had made his views on health and safety perfectly clear last time she saw him. What was Mary thinking, letting him into her garden? She was hurt that Mary had employed this man without consulting her first, even though it wasn't Dilly's garden and she didn't have the right to insist that she was consulted on everything. But hadn't Mary loved the way flowers spread across the path? Dilly was sure she had. Mary wouldn't do this, she decided, and she certainly wouldn't arrange for this to happen without discussing it first.

As Dilly approached the little wall separating the cottage garden from the village green track, she saw Keaton sniffing around the area that the man was spraying.

'Keaton,' she sang, trying to get him away from the weed-killer without alarming him. Where is Mary? she wondered.

She squeezed past the van, which was parked across the driveway and blocking the entrance. She guessed it would have taken too long to park considerately, so he had abandoned it there, as time was money according to him.

As she stepped through the gate, Keaton came rushing towards her. She immediately scooped him up into her arms, and safety. The stuff stank and so did Keaton. He would need a bath and a vet. She had no desire to hold on to all the chemicals on his coat, but she had to protect the poor dog.

'What *are* you doing?' she shouted.

'Spraying dandelions. What does it look like?'

Furious with him for putting Keaton's health at risk, not to mention spraying Mary's precious flowery path, she said. 'Killing much-loved garden plants.'

'It's what I was told to do. There are no birds' nests here.'

'But there is a dog and you might harm him.'

'It's not my fault that the guy let his dog out.'

Dilly glanced around her, looking for the mystery man who had taken the liberty of letting Keaton into the garden while it was being sprayed. 'What guy?' she demanded.

'Jim Jones.'

Dilly's eyes narrowed. 'Jim Jones lives on the corner.'

'Huh?'

'This is not Jim Jones' house, nor are they dandelions. If you knew anything about plants, you'd know an aconite leaf from a dandelion one. Come to think of it, you'd also know not to prune summer-flowering shrubs in spring, nor to cut back daffodils for at least six weeks after flowering, nor to spray whatever it is in that knapsack anywhere near a dog.'

'How was I to know?'

'Training.' The word seemed to explode from Dilly's mouth. 'If you're not qualified for a job, you need to get qualified.'

'You don't need qualifications to spray a few weeds.'

'You do need certification, as it happens.'

'Do you have a weed-killing certificate?'

'No.'

The man smirked. 'Well then, why are you bothered about me not having one?'

'I don't want to spray gardens. If I did, I would have certification. What are you using on here?'

'I dunno. Just some stuff my granddad had in the shed.'

Dilly panicked. 'How long has it been in your granddad's shed?'

'I dunno.'

'I need to see the label.'

'What for?'

'Because the vet will need to know what this little dog has been exposed to.'

'It won't harm him, will it?' The man suddenly seemed concerned.

'We won't know until we read the label.'

He rushed to the van. He might have been ignorant about gardening, but there was no mistaking that he was upset that he might have hurt a dog. It was only a shame he didn't feel the same about the plants he was wiping out, she thought crossly as a new fear gripped her. If he didn't know what he was using, heaven knew if he had calculated the dosage correctly.

She read the container and gasped. 'This was banned in this country years ago.'

'What for? It does a good job.'

'It does a good job of increasing your risk of cancer, and not wearing protection will doubtless increase that again.' It was cruel, but she had to get the message across to him.

Now he looked really worried. Dilly picked up her phone.

'Who are you calling? Don't call the police,' he pleaded. 'I'll make it right.'

'How exactly?' She shot him a challenging look. He clamped his mouth shut. 'And for your information, I'm ringing the vet. If anything happens to Keaton...' Her voice changed as the call was answered. 'Ah, hello... I'm concerned that a dog has been exposed to toxic garden chemicals. I'm not sure about the effects of the poison...'

'Poison?' the man exclaimed. 'But I didn't know.'

Dilly flashed him an angry look. 'Ignorance is no defence,' she spat. 'It's still poison.' Her voice changed again as she spoke on the phone. 'Yes, yes, we'll bring him in.'

'I'll do it, Dilly,' said Alex. How long had he been there? wondered Dilly. 'My car's in Jessica's drive. Tell me where I'm going.'

'I want to come too,' said the man. 'I'm worried.'

'Don't you think you should be rectifying the damage?'

'Hello, Dilly.' Mary ambled around the side of the cottage. 'What a lovely surprise!' Her smile quickly became a gurn. 'There's an awful smell of weedkiller around here. Have they been doing the verges?'

'Are you going to tell Mary, or am I?' Dilly challenged the man.

She saw his face crumple. He might have seemed hard, but he was a piece of putty when it came to elderly ladies and dogs, it seemed.

'As if I'd let you do it,' she hissed at him as she stepped forward to break the news to her dear friend. 'I'm afraid there's been a muddle, Mary. This man mixed up your house with Jim Jones'.'

'Ah well,' said Mary. 'It's easily done, what with us being Village Green Cottage and him being Village Green Corner.'

'Unfortunately, he sprayed weedkiller while Keaton was in the garden,' said Dilly.

'Oh no. My poor Keaton,' cried Mary.

'I've called the vet,' said Dilly. 'They're expecting him.'

'I'm coming.' Mary sped towards the van, causing Dilly to panic. No one in their nineties should be rushing anywhere like that. Even worse, she was about to climb into the passenger seat. If his driving was anything like his gardening skills, there was no way that dear Mary was getting into his van with Keaton. 'Alex is taking him,' she said, trying not to let Mary see her own panic.

'What can I do?' asked the man.

'Apart from to get some qualifications?' snapped Dilly. 'You can start by moving your van out of the way so Alex can bring his car round to collect Mary.'

She half-expected the man to drive off, but he returned to the garden once he'd moved his van, which was something in his favour, she supposed.

'I am sorry, you know,' he said.

'Not half so sorry as we are,' she muttered, climbing into Alex's car with Keaton in her arms.

Chapter Twenty-Seven

The stench of the weedkiller was overpowering, yet the windows in the car remained only slightly down to let a little air in, rather than open all the way to blast the smell out of the car. Dilly hadn't asked Alex to put them down further, because she didn't want Mary to get cold after the shock she'd had. She guessed Alex hadn't lowered the windows for the same reason. He was always considerate. He had offered to help Mary without a second thought. She bet the same had happened when Nathan needed help to buy out Kim during their divorce. He had never complained about the situation that loan had put him in, nor would she ever hear any grumbles about the additional stress that giving up precious time today placed on his already demanding life. There was a lot to love about this man, she thought as she sat in the back with Keaton on her lap, her gaze switching between the poor dog and Alex's profile in the mirror, as he concentrated on getting them safely to the vet.

Alex drove carefully, but with enough haste; even so, it

was not a fast or smooth enough journey for poor Keaton, who began to retch.

'How much further?' Alex asked Mary, who was sitting in the passenger seat and giving him directions.

'Not far. Hold on, Keaton,' Mary tried to command, but her voice sounded more wobbly than ever.

This was the last thing this beautiful soul needed. Dilly swallowed down the fury that rose within her for the act that the thoughtless, ignorant man had committed. She needed to focus on the poor, stinking, retching animal on her lap.

'You'll be okay, Keaton,' she said, every ounce of her wanting to cuddle him closer and give him a kiss, but she couldn't when he needed it most, because of the weedkiller.

Mary was beginning to look a little green around the gills. 'Is it possible to open a window all the way?' she asked, much to Dilly's relief.

'I'll do it for you,' said Alex, his eyes never leaving the road as they drew closer to the vet's.

He had barely stopped the car, when Dilly sprang from her seat with Keaton, grabbing the weedkiller container from the boot. She rushed through the doors without a backward glance, leaving Alex to follow in her wake with Mary.

The vet had been waiting for Keaton and took him in immediately, along with the container, and Mary. Dilly went to wash her hands. She scrubbed hard, desperate to erase every molecule of heinous toxicity from her skin. No matter how many times she washed them with the stringent lime-scented soap, the smell would not disappear. She needed to stop. Her hands were getting sore. A tear-stained face stared back at her from the mirror. This won't do, she told it silently. You need to be strong for Mary. She dried her hands and face, then went to the waiting area.

Alex was sitting opposite the door to the consulting room and Dilly sat quietly next to him. He glanced at her, nodded, then returned his gaze to the closed door.

'You don't need to stay,' she said.

'I want to,' he said simply, then fell silent.

They sat side by side, concentrating on the closed door as if willing good news from behind it. The wait was interminable, and Dilly couldn't bear it. She needed to pace, or be outside, or do *something*. She heaved a sigh.

'Thank you,' she said, turning towards Alex.

A pulse ticked in his jaw. Concern was etched across his face. 'I'm glad I could help.' Those bewitching mossy green eyes met hers. His gaze was tender and caring, and Dilly felt inexplicably safe and wrapped in love. Suddenly there was no need to pace and be outside.

'I'm sorry,' she whispered, tears welling up.

'What for?' His eyes searched hers.

'For not trusting you.'

'It's okay. I'm an expert in not trusting.'

'Professor of Not Trusting?'

An apologetic smile quirked at his lips. 'It's a bit of a kick in the teeth that the one new person who has come into my life and I've managed to trust, doesn't trust me.'

'I'm sorry.'

'You don't need to apologise. Not trusting can't be helped, believe me, I know, but now I understand how hurtful it is not to be trusted, so thank you. You've taught me something, and I do love discovering new things.'

She thought back to the pancake race and to all the other instances when she had felt inadequate or embarrassed. He had reframed all of those snapshots of shame into something positive and wonderful. Now he had done it again and she realised that he was a magnificent pearl of a man... not that he resembled a crusty barnacled oyster, she thought with a little smile.

'I do trust you, you know,' she said. A challenging twinkle in his eye sent delightful tingles up her spine. 'Well... I'm learning to.'

'That's good to hear,' he said, taking her hand and lacing her fingers through his. She leant her head on his shoulder and despite the pain of what had happened, she was relieved they had been able to speak and glad that he was here with her, sharing the bad times and being her friend. She looked down at his fingers and a jolt of longing darted through her. If only they could be more than friends. If only she hadn't slammed that door shut out of fear.

Chapter Twenty Eight

Dilly could have stayed there holding Alex's hand, feeling the warmth of his body and the strength of his shoulder forever, but the door to the consulting room eventually opened and they sprang from their chairs, desperate for news of Keaton.

'They think he'll be fine,' said Mary.

'But he was so sick,' said Dilly, unable to believe he was okay.

'That was no bad thing in this instance,' said Mary. 'They think it was travel sickness.'

'That'll be my driving,' said Alex, his eyes still twinkling, and causing Dilly's stomach to turn somersaults.

'Your driving was excellent, Alex,' said Mary. 'Thank you, and thank you for waiting.'

'Where is Keaton?' asked Dilly.

'He's staying in for observation, but he's on good form and loving all the attention.'

'I bet he is,' said Dilly. 'Shall we go home?'

Mary led the way and they followed her to the car. It still stank, and Dilly wondered if the smell would ever leave it.

'It's a good job you were at Jessica's with your car,' said Mary. 'Imagine what would have happened if you hadn't been there.'

'It was lucky timing. Five minutes later and I would have been at the nursery,' he said as they drove away.

'So where had you been?' asked Mary, ever-inquisitive.

'Back to my flat. I needed to check on something.'

Or someone, thought Dilly sadly. Alex must be shattered. He has so much to cope with and yet he still found the time to wait with me at the vet's. She had wanted his reassuring presence and he hadn't let her down. Those shoulders are not just broad in the physical sense, she realised with a surge of gratitude and the profoundest of respect. Alex was strong in every way.

As they drove back down Sweetingfield High Street, they spotted the man's van parked near the village green, and Dilly's heart sank.

'What's he doing now?' she said crossly. 'There won't be a decent garden left in Norfolk if he carries on like this.'

They parked outside Mary and Lois' cottage, and as they stepped out of the car, the smell of weedkiller hit them.

'I didn't think anything could smell worse than your car, Alex, but I was wrong,' said Dilly as she pushed open the gate.

Alex held the car door open for Mary while she got to her feet, and trundled with her up the drive. 'Let me pay to have your car valeted,' said Mary.

'Thank you, but there's no need,' he said.

They heard a rush of footsteps behind them. 'How's the

little dog?' asked the man. Dilly could see fear written all over his face.

'They're keeping him in for observation,' said Alex.

'But will he be okay?' The man was visibly shaken.

'I hope so,' said Mary. 'Now if you don't mind, it's been an unusually tiring day.' She turned away before the man had time to speak, and Alex escorted her up the steps into the cottage.

'I didn't know,' the man said helplessly to Dilly.

She stepped towards him as he towered over her. 'I guess that's what they call learning on the job,' she said. 'Although it's a very costly way to go about it – not only for Mary with the vet's bill.'

'I'll pay.'

'So it's costly for you since you're going to cover the bill, but your mistakes could be costly for wildlife as well as for you. Why don't you work with me?' she said before she had even thought it through.

'Are you trying to get your hands on my business?'

'What business? One that uses an unlicensed weedkiller to kill someone's much-loved garden plants without their permission... not to mention risking the life of their beloved pet dog.' His face dropped. 'If you carry on like this, you're going to be fined more than you earn, and get a terrible reputation, too. What's your name?'

'Carl.'

'Well, Carl, for the sake of wildlife, pets, gardens and yourself, think about working alongside me, please. Now, I have to go.'

She hurried inside to check on Mary. Lois had managed to sleep through the whole ordeal, which was a huge relief. Mary was sitting by her, explaining what had happened, and Alex was in the kitchen making them a restorative pot of tea.

'You've done well.' Dilly nodded to the kettle. 'Mary doesn't usually allow anyone to wait on them.'

He laughed. 'She hasn't. She insisted on putting the kettle on and the tea in the pot, then went to tell Lois about what happened.'

'That sounds about right.'

'I didn't mean to eavesdrop, but I couldn't help hearing what you said to that guy. You are incredible.'

A blush crept up Dilly's face. 'No, I'm not.'

'You are,' he insisted. 'You were upset – and quite rightly too – but most people would have hauled him over the coals and gone public about what he's done, whereas you're trying to guide and teach him so that he can become better at his job.'

'I don't know if he'll join me.'

'But you made the offer,' he said. 'You couldn't have done more.'

And nor could you, she thought, as she remembered how reassured she had been by his presence at the vet's, and the security of her hand in his when she needed his support. She wanted that feeling again, and drew closer to him to reach out for his hand. Their fingers brushed, but instead of the sense of security she expected, a shock of desire coursed through her. This man had it all.

'Oh, and Dilly,' called Mary as she neared the kitchen, 'don't even think about making the tea.'

Their hands were already apart. Dilly was left with more sparks crackling through her body than she knew what to do with. The kettle boiled and she envied it being able to release its pent-up energy.

'We could have brought it through to you,' said Dilly, her eyes not leaving his.

'Nonsense,' said Mary. 'You've done enough today to help, and in any case, you stink like a poke of devils.'

Laughter danced in Alex's eyes, and Dilly felt hers match his. 'I'll take a shower, then I'll be back with home-made soup.' Mary gurned. She had tried and failed to eat Dilly's cooking before. 'Not mine, Mary. There's no need to worry about any more poisonings. Steve left it earlier.'

'In which case, we look forward to sharing some,' said Mary. 'Alex?'

'I'm afraid I have to get back to the nursery.'

Yes, thought Dilly. I bet this time away has caused you all kinds of problems.

'Thank you, Alex, for all your help,' said Mary. 'You're our hero, isn't he, Dilly?'

Dilly blushed. 'You are.' She held her arms out to Mary. 'I would hug you, but...' She wafted her hands over her smelly clothes.

'Quite right, too. No one wants to touch you smelling like that,' said Mary.

Apart from Alex, thought Dilly. Alex did. They walked out of the cottage together to his car.

'Thank you, Alex, for everything.'

He gazed tenderly into her eyes. 'My pleasure, Dilly.' The way he said her name had changed. It seemed as though the world was shrinking until they were the only two people on the planet.

'Okay. How are we going to work this?' Carl shouted from the other side of the gate.

'Incredible,' said Alex, and as Dilly went to speak to

Carl, she had no idea whether he was talking about her, the moment or the untimely shattering of it.

Chapter Twenty Nine

Dilly couldn't wait to get to work the next day. She would divide her time between Alex's garden and the nursery. She parked her bicycle, her heart fluttering with excitement at the prospect of seeing Alex, then strode happily around the cottage to the back garden and gasped. Alex was sitting on a chair by the kitchen door, drinking his morning coffee.

'Now there's something I never thought I'd see,' she said delightedly.

'Me neither. You've had a hugely positive influence on this crusty old professor.'

'I consider my work to be done.'

'How can you say that? There are weeds over there.'

'And now you're the gardening expert too?' she teased. 'Will you be helping me?'

'Sadly not. I was just having a coffee before work. It's strange. I didn't want to be cooped up. I guess my body's adapting to a new level of fresh air. I'll have to start going for walks along the river when I go back to my flat.'

The reminder of his limited time in Sweetingfield had a

sobering effect on her mood, but she wasn't going to let it spoil this giant step forward in the quest to get Alex to spend time outdoors.

'I'm glad to hear it,' she said. 'I bet Jessica's pleased.'

'I haven't told her yet. I thought I'd save it for you to tell her.'

'Because you didn't want to see her gloating?'

'Exactly! She's a terrible gloater. She's still crowing over winning the seniors' pancake race.'

'And so she should,' said Dilly.

'I'm scared she might explode with smugness when she hears about this.' He stood to take his empty mug to the kitchen. 'Will I see you later?'

'You will,' she said, their eyes locking for a moment.

She could not stop smiling. Jessica would be delighted to hear that her handsome, serious, indoorsy nephew had finally found his own way into the garden and discovered the pleasure of relaxing there. All that was needed now was for Alex to accept his aunt for who she was, rather than as his mother's lookalike.

Dilly's morning disappeared in a flurry of clearing borders of choking weeds and rediscovering the gems of plants hidden beneath. She took her lunch from her bicycle pannier and sat where Alex had drunk his coffee, enjoying the warmth of the spring sunshine. It had been a great morning's work, enhanced by seeing Alex, and now she would see him again. She decided to leave her bicycle at his cottage. When had she stopped thinking of it as the gamekeeper's or Nursery Cottage, and started thinking of it as Alex's? She would probably call it Alex's Cottage for years after he had gone back to his flat, leaving Sweetingfield and her life emptier.

A weed caught her eye as she passed through the nursery stock beds. She knew that Nathan didn't spray the paths, so any weed needed to be removed before the seeds set. Focus on the here and now, not on Alex's inevitable departure, she told herself firmly as she bent down to pull the weed from the edge of the path. She popped it in her pocket rather than lie it down to die, as it might set seed, and then they'd be inundated with them.

'Put that back,' shouted Alex. 'I saw you. Are you saving it for later, you weed thief.' His eyes sparked with laughter as he feigned fury.

A broad grin tore across her face. She stood firm, placed her hands on her hips, and jutting out her chin, she faced him full on. 'And what are you going to do about it?'

A smile played about his delicious mouth and naughtiness tripped across his face.

'That's for me to know.'

She cocked an eyebrow. 'And for me to find out?' The air between them sizzled. She was caught in a forcefield stronger than her. Pure lust coursed through every cell of her body.

'Excuse me. Will this grow in dry shade?'

Someone was wafting a plant under Dilly's nose, and she stared at it as if she had never seen a plant before in her life. At that moment, she couldn't have christened it if it came up and introduced itself wearing a laminated lanyard with its name in bold block capital letters.

'I'd better get back,' said Alex, dragging her from her stupor. She nodded absent-mindedly, then shook her head as if bringing herself back to reality.

'I'm afraid it won't like the shade,' she finally managed. 'If you come with me, I'll show you some plants that will love it there.' Putting one foot in front of the other was suddenly an ordeal, as if her body couldn't cope with walking away from him. She hadn't thought it was possible, but her feelings for him were becoming more intense and she knew without question that she would combust with longing if they didn't kiss soon.

Once the customer had made their selection, she went with them into the shop, to the till. That's odd, she thought, eyeing the container display. She stepped forward to inspect the arrangement more closely, but became aware of a retired couple standing next to her.

'May I help you?' she asked.

'If you wouldn't mind, dear. We were just admiring these gorgeous containers of flowers, but we can't lift them.'

'No problem,' said Dilly. 'You point to the one you want, and I'll lift it into your trolley.'

'But we can't lift it out at the other end.'

'In which case, why don't I deliver it to you?' she asked.

'We can't afford delivery.'

'Do you live far away?'

'About five miles away, in Trindlesham village.'

'In which case, if you pay for the arrangement, I'll drop it off for you tomorrow.'

'Would you, dear? Thank you. We want two, please.'

'Point them out to me and I'll leave them near Bella on the till. Please tell her that Dilly said it was fine.'

'What a pretty name. What's it short for?'

Dilly smiled. 'Daffodil.'

'The perfect name for spring, and for someone who works with plants.'

Dilly nodded happily as she went to find a trolley for the couple. As she passed the till, she explained the situation to Bella.

'What were you thinking?' hissed Bella. 'How are you going to get two planters to Trindlesham, or have you passed your driving test in the last few days and neglected to tell me?'

'I'll stick them on my trailer.'

'They'll wobble everywhere.'

Dilly shrugged. 'I wanted them to buy them, but they couldn't afford the delivery and I can't see Dave going for a free delivery. What else could I do?'

Bella shook her head. 'You know, you really should work here.'

'I'd love to,' said Dilly, wishing it were possible, but unlike Bella, she had seen the state of the nursery's finances. 'Although I'd miss gardening too much. Speaking of which, I need to place an ad. Please don't let me get sidetracked and forget it.'

'And speaking of being sidetracked, shouldn't you be taking a trolley to those people? I don't know where your mind is today.'

I do, thought Dilly as she returned to the couple. Having left the containers by the till as promised, she checked the display. There were definitely arrangements that were unfamiliar. Clearly someone else had been making up new ones. Obviously it wouldn't be Dave. He didn't have the patience or the eye to create arrangements and was generally dead set against fripperies, and prettily filled planters definitely fell into the frippery category in the world of Dave. Unless Bella had been on a secret crash course in gardening, she wouldn't have a clue. Dilly felt sick. What if Alex had let her down again and given the task to someone else? She needed this little additional income stream. He wouldn't have done that, she told herself firmly. You can trust him. You have to.

She inspected one of the containers. At least the plants were well firmed-in and thriving. She hoped Alex had done the work, although quite when he would have had the time with everything else he had going on, she didn't know. Glad of the excuse to spend a few more minutes in his company, she went to find him. He hadn't gone to the office after their flirtation in the stock beds, so she guessed the polytunnel was worth a try. She found him standing at the potting bench with a terracotta pot half-filled with plants.

'Caught in the act,' he said, his face flushing slightly.

It would have been wonderful to go back to the flirtatiousness she had enjoyed so much in the stock beds, but she needed to make sure everything was fair and above board with the containers first.

'I hope you're keeping a tally on the number and type of pots you're filling, as according to our deal, I'm taking a cut on the number of pots sold and it won't be fair if I take money for the ones you've filled.'

He looked contrite. 'There's this one.'

She put her hand on her hip. 'And how many more?'

He appeared to be searching his mind for an answer, but then he gave a little shrug.

'Alex, how many more? I won't take a cut for any of them if you don't play fair.'

He must have realised that she wasn't joking, and swiftly said, 'Eight'.

'Eight,' she repeated so she wouldn't forget. 'Right. We need to make this official. I'll count the ones I make from now on too,' she said.

'No need... I trust you,' he said.

Dilly smiled. She loved that he trusted her. Whatever she might have felt about hurting him by her own lack of trust was eclipsed by the hope encapsulated in those three little words.

They worked hard and had soon filled two trolleys with pots. All the time she was planting, Dilly's mind was on one thing. It was killing her to stand side by side with him, when all she wanted to do was kiss him. Did he feel the same? she wondered, sneaking a glance across at him while he worked. There was a slight blush, coursing its way up his neck. Be professional, Dilly, she told herself as she looked away and checked the number of containers.

'You've done another six, so that takes you to fourteen,' she said, slipping off her glove and making a note on her phone. He shook his head. 'What?' she asked.

'You honestly don't need to do this.'

'If you don't want me to make up pots, say so.' It was hardly fair now that he was capable, if time-poor.

'I didn't mean it like that, Dilly. You do so much more here than the pots. I'm more than happy to donate my share of fourteen containers to your financial pot.'

'You might be, but I'm not. This nursery needs every penny it can make, and I couldn't live with myself if I took anything more from it.'

'Thank you,' he said simply.

Relieved that she wasn't being told she couldn't help, and grateful he had agreed so readily, Dilly felt inexplicably secure. She couldn't believe it. She was up to her ears in financial worries and fighting to save the nursery she loved, while her body was running away with itself and buzzing with excitement and longing, yet she felt safe.

She sighed happily. 'What with the chair outside your back door and your fingers in the compost, Alex, I don't recognise you.'

'Is that a good thing?'

She was in the spotlight of his gaze, and she loved being there. 'It's a very good thing indeed.'

He set a terracotta pot in front of her. 'So you're saying that I didn't pass muster before?'

'Oh, you did.' Suddenly aware of his proximity, her voice lowered almost to a whisper. 'You most definitely did.'

The air between them crackled. There was no mistaking how he felt. They both wanted this. It was as if the temperature of the cold polytunnel had hit tropical humidity. She wanted to lose her clothes. Lose her mind. Lose her fear. His eyes darkened and her body turned towards him. She had no control of it. This time she knew she wouldn't run. She couldn't, even if she wanted to. She trusted this man. She knew he wouldn't let her down. He lowered his mouth onto hers. His lips gently caressed hers, as if slowly, tantalisingly, getting to know each millimetre, before their kiss deepened and she melted into his arms.

The door to the polytunnel flew open, and they sprang apart microseconds before Dave marched in.

'There you are,' he said, as if he'd been looking for an age. 'Someone in the shop wants a word, Dilly.'

Dilly's nervous energy had nowhere to go. Her body shook as her brain adjusted to what was required of her.

'Dilly?' continued Dave, as if verbally knocking on her skull to be allowed access to the world she had tumbled so blissfully into. The world she never wanted to leave.

Dilly's brain finally caught up as her body continued to pulse with longing. It was odd that Dave called them *someone*. Dave had lived in Sweetingfield all his life and it was extremely unusual for him not to know anyone's name. She couldn't look at Alex. If Dave had seen nothing when he barged into the polytunnel, crashing into their kiss, then he would certainly read what had happened if Dilly so much as looked at Alex. She rushed from behind the potting bench and left Dave to close the polytunnel door behind her.

A highly attractive blonde woman waited for her at the till. 'Dilly?' she asked, looking hopeful. Dilly nodded. Perhaps this lady wanted to offer her work. That would be the cherry on the icing on the cake, on what had been, without question, a truly magnificent day. 'I'm Tess Boylan. My parents told me they were in earlier, and you kindly offered to drop off their plants for them, but since I was passing, I thought I'd collect them for them as a surprise. I have ID.'

Dilly smiled through the disappointment of it not being a job offer. 'They're over here.'

'They're gorgeous! Are there more?'

'There are,' said Dilly, leading the way. She waited to one side while Tess selected a planter. Much as she wanted to help this woman, and in so doing, help the nursery, she longed to be back with Alex. As if hearing her body's needs, he arrived in the shop with a trolley of freshly planted containers.

'Tess?'

'Alex! What are you doing here?' She rushed forward to hug him. 'I never had you down as a green-fingered type.'

'I'm not,' he said, causing Dilly to feel awash with sadness. He was a green-fingered type earlier, when he had his hands in the compost, she thought. What had changed? Her eyes rested on Tess. *That* has, she thought. She could never be a match for a woman like Tess. It was obvious at first glance that she had the kind of effortless beauty Dilly had given up hoping for midway through her teens. She appeared to be as at home in the nursery as Dilly would be at dinner with the King. 'Tess – what *are* you doing in Norfolk?'

'I was guest lecturing at the UEA,' she explained. 'And now I'm visiting my folks in Trindlesham.'

So not only attractive, elegant and stylish, but beneath that straight, untangled blonde, slick, perfect head of hair lay a humongous brain. Dilly tried not to be intimidated, but she was only human and she sensed her confidence deflating. You and Alex kissed, her brain told her, but she remained unconvinced. The old fears and insecurities were back in force.

'Dilly had kindly offered to drop off their pots for them, but since I was passing, I thought I'd save her the job.'

Alex's eyebrows shot heavenwards. 'They'll want their delivery charges back.'

'They weren't charged,' said Tess. 'Dilly said she'd be driving past.' Now Alex really looked confused, as well he might, since Dilly didn't drive. 'So what brings you to Norfolk, Alex?' Tess asked, the pots of flowers forgotten. Dilly didn't blame her. He could eclipse all flowers, then again, so could Tess. They were one of the most striking couples Dilly had ever seen.

'Sabbatical,' he said simply.

'In a nursery?'

'It belongs to my family.' He might have said brother, but that wouldn't have been true, since he had invested so heavily in it. By saying it belonged to his family, he was telling the truth, since he was a member of his own family. At least he hadn't lied, thought Dilly. Dear, genuine Alex had the most exquisite lips she had ever kissed, and those lips didn't lie.

'So do I get a discount for being a friend of a family member?'

Alex shook his head. 'I'm afraid not. We all pay our way round here. Support small businesses and all that.'

'Worth a try. I'll take one anyway. It'll look well on my doorstep.'

Alex bent down to lift the planter she had chosen, and Dilly couldn't stop herself from checking out the strength of his body and the way his muscles responded to the weight of the container as he carried it to the till.

This is turning into a most up-and-down day, thought Dilly, a knot forming in her stomach. Alex would go back to his clever and sophisticated life with glamorous people like Tess, and she would be left with barely enough work to make ends meet and nothing to distract her from the gaping chasm left in her life by his departure, but the memory of their one kiss.

Once the Easter rush was over, and the containers and hanging baskets had been refilled for regular customers, there would be no need for her to be at The Treasure Trove at all. She needed to get back to normal. Dilly collected her bicycle from Alex's cottage and wheeled it through the stock beds, into the car park, then came to a halt. Alex and Tess were placing the containers of plants in the boot of an unfeasibly clean and smart silver car. They chatted briefly, then they hugged.

Hurt and envy coursed through Dilly's veins and there was nothing she could do to stop it. She had always accepted her lot, but suddenly a pang of pain ripped through her. Life was so unfair. Tess had two living parents, looked like a goddess, was clever, stylish and didn't have tangled orange hair, ruddy cheeks, freckles and a body that went south as soon as she sat on a sofa for two minutes. Tess was also being embraced by the arms that Dilly had spent the better part of the past few weeks dreaming of being wrapped in, and now that she had felt their strength around her, she never wanted them to let go. Realising she was staring, she spun round and hurried towards the nursery. Tess was a reminder that this wasn't Alex's life and Dilly needed to take back control of her own life before it was too late. She parked her bicycle and went into the shop.

'Hi, Bella.' She could hear a brittleness in her bravado, but she pressed on as she rummaged in her pocket for some cash. 'I've just remembered that I need to put an ad on the wall.'

'Take your hand out of your pocket, Dilly,' came a voice from behind her.

Dilly swung round. 'Dave, I'm happy to pay.'

'After all you're doing here? You have to be kidding.'

'I can't not pay. It's not fair.'

'I want to pay. You're making such a difference to this place.'

'I thought you didn't like all the bunting and frills, Dave.'

'I might not, but other people do, so who am I to argue? Look at the cost of the ad as an apology for me being an old grump about them.'

A no-frills, no-spills apology meant the world to Dilly.

'Thanks, Dave,' she said. 'I appreciate it.' And I needed it, she thought.

Being wrapped in the arms of kindness mattered. You have everything you need, Dilly, she reminded herself. You have Luke and Bella. You have all the plants and nature surrounding you that you could wish for. You have Mary and Lois and wonderful friends. And when you get home, Dilly

Pepper, she told herself firmly, you are going to phone Carl to sort out your working arrangement and put your heads together to find new ways to make money.

Dilly knew with absolute clarity that she needed to take back control of her feelings too, to protect her heart from the pain of separation when Alex left. If seeing him with Tess had taught her anything, it was that as much as he had worked wonders at fitting into Dilly's world, it was only temporary. He would leave and she would suffer. I can't put myself through that, she thought. I can't – and I won't.

As she let herself into her cottage, her mind was spinning with possibilities. The life she had believed to be safe was more precarious than she had realised. Perhaps Barry had done her a favour. Had she not lost him when she did, she might not have seen how dependent she was on the whims of others and on her own health, until she was facing tough times with an ageing body. She would find a way to shore up her earnings all year round and build something for her future. There was no question about it: she needed a new income stream.

Her phone pinged with a message from Alex, but she ignored it. Now was not the time for unsustainable highs, and what-ifs. Now was the time for deep thought and action to preserve her livelihood and future peace of mind.

She loved working with Mary and Jessica. She had always believed that wildlife and the gardens themselves were enough to sustain her, but she was beginning to realise that she thrived on interaction with other gardeners too, no matter their level of expertise. She thought of Alex. Seeing him electing to put his hands in the soil and sit on a chair enjoying his garden had been exhilarating. She had believed at the time that it was because she was pleased for him that he was connecting with the natural world, but she now realised there was a selfish joy there, too. Nurturing new gardeners and helping others to appreciate the natural world made her happy. They supported and nourished her simply by loving the world around them. It was as if connecting with nature connected them more to her. *This* was where she belonged, not in the arms of a man who was only passing through.

Chapter Thirty

At last! It was the day Dilly had been waiting for. Every year she took Luke to the lambing open day at the local farm, and having grabbed herself a couple of sought-after tickets as soon as they had become available, this year would be no exception. First though, she needed to go to Mary's to look at the nursery's seedlings and to The Treasure Trove to check the plants.

'I don't know why I didn't think of asking to sow a few seeds in Mary and Lois' greenhouse sooner,' she told the houseplants having their weekly soak in the kitchen sink. 'It's the perfect way to make sure Mary and Lois are okay, without interfering in their lives.'

Having tended her houseplants, she wrapped herself in her brightest, most joyous scarf and her bright pink hat. Today was a day off and although the sun was shining, there was frost on the pavements.

'The worst kind of weather for the plants,' she said to Mary as they inspected the seedlings together in the greenhouse. 'Frozen one minute and then sunburnt the next. It's a tough start in life.'

'And there are those people who buy their bedding plants, only to put them out too soon,' Mary added solemnly.

'I've given Bella and Liv strict instructions to let people know to keep their bedding plants protected until after the last frost, but even so, someone will probably turn up again and have to replace their purchases. It's sad. Those poor plants.'

'Their poor pockets,' said Mary. 'Dilly – are you excited for today? There's a peculiar energy buzzing from you.'

'I am. I can't wait!'

Mary chuckled. 'Not long now. How many years have you done this?'

'Thirty. And I never tire of it.'

Mary hugged her. Go and have fun. The automatic roof ventilation will make sure these seedlings don't swelter in the sun today, and I'll come and keep an eye on them for you, to make sure.'

'Thank you, Mary.'

Dilly rushed to the nursery to check on the plants there. Dave snorted when he saw her. 'So much for your day off. What time do you need to be there?'

'Noon, so not too long to wait now.'

'And will Bella be in at lunch while you have Luke, to give Liv a break?'

'That's what she said,' sang Dilly. 'So I'll spend the morning making up some of the hanging basket orders.'

'Yes, because that's not work at all,' said Dave, rolling his eyes. 'You do know what a day off is, don't you, Dilly?'

'I do. Just as you know what retirement is, Dave,' she said, winking at the man who accepted a job at The Treasure

Trove hours after retiring from his forty-five-year office-based career.

She took off her best hat and scarf, and hung them over a clean, empty basket hanging from a stand, as it was better to be cold than to get her favourite accessories dirty. There were already cars parking up on the gravel outside. It was going to be a busy day, so she was glad that she was around to offer a little ad-hoc help while she planted.

'I heard you were in.' Alex stood at the door.

She blushed, her feelings of shame at having ignored his message at odds with the need to throw herself into his arms. His face had higher colour than usual. The outdoor air was doing him good and he looked better than ever.

'I'm sorry I didn't get your message about having a drink until it was too late,' she said.

It was true. By the time she had found a way through her plans for the future and read Alex's message, Jeff had already called last orders at The Yew.

'No worries. It was only a thought.' He nodded at the stack of hanging baskets with labels tied to them. 'I can help you with some of those, if you think I'm up to it,' he said, swiftly changing the topic of conversation.

'That would be great, thanks.' Dilly was relieved, but disappointed to be back on a more professional footing. 'There's an order book here. Please can you match the hanging basket to the plant lists? That way, I'll fill them much more quickly.'

'So you don't trust me to plant them?'

'I do, but I think it'll be quicker if we work together on each basket, rather than alone,' she said.

'Teamwork?' He cocked a far too sexy eyebrow, causing Dilly to catch her breath.

'You're learning,' she managed, battling to keep her body's response to him in check.

Dilly loved working alongside him. She loved anything alongside him.

'Once these are all done, what will happen?' he asked, scrutinising the labels on the stack of baskets.

'How do you mean?'

'I can see the business makes money from them seasonally, and I can see that the Mothering Sunday display and Easter display encourage spontaneous purchases, but then what?'

'Alex Hampton! Are you becoming a businessman?'

He laughed. 'I doubt it. I'm just intrigued about what happens next.'

'Nothing happens, as far as I can see. Nathan usually makes enough from the Christmas trees and spring splurge.'

'Splurge? Is that the official term?'

'Are you thinking of learning the jargon too now?'

'I'm doing my best. I think I'm comfortable enough with your Latin plant names, but your personal quirky words throw me sometimes.'

'Ah well, take it at your own pace. You'll catch up eventually.'

'Thanks,' he said, setting a hanging basket in a large pot ready for her to fill.

She didn't want to spoil the mood, but she needed to ask. 'Has the extra expense of buying in plants caused problems?' One look at his face told her everything she needed to know. 'Ah... in which case I had a thought.'

'You did?' He sounded hopeful.

'Did you think I wouldn't?' she asked.

'Absolutely not.'

'I had an idea last night and I can't stop thinking about it.'

'Sounds interesting.'

'I hope so.' In for a penny, Dilly, she told herself as she took her courage in both hands and shared her plans. 'I've been thinking about running gardening courses or workshops here.'

'You don't need to convince a lecturer about the joy of teaching,' he said.

She felt a surge of happiness. Might she be able to protect her winter income and her future earnings by running classes? 'It would bring people into the nursery when it's quiet, and hopefully increase its turnover.'

'I'll have to...'

'Run it past Nathan?'

'It's the right thing to do, Dilly.'

'I wasn't suggesting it wasn't.' She sighed. 'Has he mentioned anything about coming home?'

Alex shook his head.

Had Nathan been so deeply unhappy in Sweetingfield, where he was surrounded by love?

'Why?' she asked, even though it was none of her business, and she mightn't like Alex's answer.

'Because it's a lot easier hiding away there than living here.' He rubbed his eyes. 'It would be a whole lot simpler if he'd come home so I could go back and live in my flat, but he needs to be alone.'

There was no hiding from the truth of what Alex had really said: he would return home in an instant if he could. The idea that he might want to leave Sweetingfield earlier than he had originally planned had never dawned on her. Now she was torn between wanting Nathan back where he belonged and was loved, and wishing he would delay his return a little longer, because while he wasn't in Sweetingfield, Alex would stay. Of course you want Nathan home, she admonished herself. Stop being so selfish.

She watered the hanging baskets she had completed and hung them on a rack. Droplets plunged from them to the floor like the tears she wanted to shed. Alex couldn't wait to leave. It was the worst news for her on her happy day off. She wanted to get out of the polytunnel – to rescue her day and make special memories with Luke, rather than dwell on Alex's desperation to leave.

'Well, if it isn't Doctor Alex Hampton, getting his hands dirty.'

Dilly glanced up to see Tess looking as striking as ever in perfectly fitting, tight blue jeans and an expensive-looking cream sweater. She strode confidently across the polytunnel towards Alex. It was the last thing Dilly needed.

'The girl on the till said you'd be out here and I didn't believe her,' continued Tess.

Dilly grabbed her scarf and hat. There was no way she was staying to witness them hugging and reminding her of where Alex truly belonged.

'I'm on my way. See you, Alex,' she said breezily. 'Hi, Tess,' she added. 'Sorry. I have to rush.' And without a backward glance, Dilly was out of the polytunnel and on her way to Bella's to collect Luke, even though they had agreed that Bella would bring Luke with her to the nursery.

'Change of plan,' said Dilly, when she knocked on Bella's door.

Bella laughed. 'You couldn't wait!'

'I'm saving Luke's legs the extra walk so we'll have plenty of energy for the farm.'

'In which case, I'll be on my way. Have fun, you two,' said Bella. 'Cuddle a lamb for me.'

'Does that mean we get to cuddle two lambs?' asked Luke.

'That *would* be a treat!' said Dilly.

The walk to Mayflower Farm took them along the high street and the edge of the village green to the church, where they passed under the lychgate, which had been decorated with cherry blossom for a wedding. They went past the church and its hall, then through the graveyard, where Dilly nodded to her parents' stone. She would have liked to have offered more than a nod to them, but she didn't want to upset Luke, and she knew her mum and dad would understand this. Actually, she thought, they would prefer us to be focussing on a lovely day out, rather than them.

The grass in the graveyard was allowed to grow until it was grazed during summer, rather than mown every week or so from spring. Snowdrop foliage was left to die down naturally and their seeds were dispersing further across the graveyard than in Dilly's childhood. Every year, this little oasis grew more beautiful and Dilly loved it, not because of the sense of loss it might evoke, but for the hope for the future she saw in the nature allowed to thrive there.

They passed through the wooden gate at the end, onto the field margins, and skirted the boundary to the lambing shed.

'Not far to go now, Lukey,' she said, as the sound of lambs bleating grew louder.

'Do you think we'll see any be born?' he asked, his eyes filled with hope.

'Fingers crossed,' she squealed, hurrying up their pace.

They arrived in plenty of time for their slot, so they sat

outside on a large hay bale in the sun, eating ice creams without sprinkles, since Luke was adhering admirably to his Lenten pledge.

A hush came over the waiting group when it was their turn to enter the large and airy lambing shed. They listened attentively to Farmer May talking about the ewe who was on the verge of giving birth to twins.

Come on, girl, thought Dilly. Suddenly, Farmer May became distracted. The ewe was definitely on the point of delivery and he went over to her as her first lamb arrived in the world. It was all Dilly could do not to cheer.

Farmer May cleaned up the lamb's mouth and checked the ewe over. 'Another one is coming,' he explained, and they all watched and waited as he reached down and was able to grab the front legs of the next lamb and help him to arrive safely in the world.

Dilly watched Farmer May. He was obviously concerned and she began to worry that something awful was going to happen. He bent down to check the ewe, then he grinned broadly. 'It turns out that it isn't twins,' he said, taking hold of the next set of legs, which were promptly followed by a black button nose. Dilly heaved a sigh of relief, as the last of the triplets was born safely.

'Yuck. What *is* that stuff on it? It's all yucky,' said Luke.

'Look, Lukey,' she whispered, having decided that a chat about meconium could wait for another day. 'The mum is cleaning her babies up.'

They watched in reverent silence as the firstborn lamb stumbled to its feet and sought out its mother's teats.

'Isn't that wonderful?' gasped Dilly, tears of joy forming in her eyes.

'It most certainly is,' said a voice behind her. Tess. Dilly's heart sank. 'Thank goodness there were triplets, otherwise we'd have missed it.'

Dilly turned round to see Alex standing behind Tess. 'I nipped out for an hour,' he explained. 'And I'm glad I did. I've never seen a lamb being born.'

'*Never*?' Luke sounded shocked. 'But you're a grown-up!'

Alex laughed. 'I haven't lived.'

'I didn't know you had tickets for lambing,' said Dilly, as she struggled to control a melange of feelings about Alex and Tess gatecrashing her special outing with Luke.

'I didn't. Tess and her friend did, but her friend's pregnant, so she can't come into the shed.'

'Are you going to cuddle a lamb?' asked Luke excitedly.

'I don't know,' said Alex, looking bemused. 'Am I?'

'*You* can,' said Tess. 'But I'm not risking ruining my Angora jumper.'

'Are you, Dilly?' asked Alex.

'Dilly always cuddles the lambs. Come and have a go, Alex,' said Luke, grabbing Alex's hand and dragging him into another area of the shed, where slightly older lambs frolicked while the ewes hung around in groups, with one eye on their offspring, like mothers at a coffee morning playdate. Luke plonked himself down in the middle of a hay bale, and Dilly sat next to him.

'Come on, Alex. Don't be scared,' whispered Luke, and with a quick glance at Dilly, Alex sat down on the other side of Luke.

'Honestly, Alex. What has become of you?' said Tess.

Dilly wished that Tess wasn't there, but since Alex wouldn't be sitting on this hay bale if she wasn't, Dilly could hardly complain, especially as Luke was delighting in having Alex join them for lamb cuddles.

A lamb was gently placed onto Luke's lap. 'It's tiny,' he whispered.

'Better than the wriggler you got last year.' Dilly reached over to stroke it. 'You're so pretty, aren't you?' she cooed.

'Do you want to cuddle one?' one of Farmer May's daughters asked Dilly.

'Yes, please, but Alex can go first,' she said, nodding in his direction.

The farmer's daughter placed a lamb in his lap, and Dilly gazed at her two favourite males in all the world, cuddling their lambs. I shall remember this moment forever, she thought.

'Your turn,' said the farmer's son, handing a lamb to Dilly.

'This is better than I'd imagined it could be,' said Alex.

Dilly dragged her eyes away from her lamb to see Alex smiling across at her. It was as if they were the only people in the world. Them, and their lambs.

Dilly felt something warm. 'Heavens, Dilly,' called Tess. 'Is that what I think it is?'

Dilly grimaced. 'My lamb's leaked,' she said, and Luke and Alex burst into laughter.

* * *

Luke was still laughing when they got home.

'I hear you got wet,' said Bella when she got to Dilly's cottage to collect Luke.

'News travels fast,' said Dilly.

'Alex was only gone for forty minutes,' continued Bella. 'And those lambs seem to have genuinely put a smile on his face. If not them, something or someone did.'

'That'd be Tess,' said Dilly.

'Ah, yes, although she wasn't there long. She showed me a cracking photo of you when she came back to the nursery with Alex. She AirDropped it to me with the others. Shall I send them to you?'

'If you wouldn't mind,' said Dilly, glad to have pictures of Luke and her having fun to look back on when he grew too old for days out with her. Her phone pinged to announce the arrival of the photos, but she didn't look at them. She wasn't ready to see the horrendous face she pulled, any more than she needed help to remember Alex's reaction to holding a lamb for the first time. She would remember *that* for the rest of her life.

Chapter Thirty-One

Dilly woke early on Easter morning. The excitement she felt at the prospect of a fun day with friends who were like family, in the village she loved, never diminished. If she lived to be a hundred, she would feel the same. She had a quick shower, then put on a cheerful lemon dress with a fitted bodice and full skirt, and topped it off with a delicately embroidered woollen cardigan. There would be no work clothes for Dilly today. There would be no breakfast either, she decided as she opened her door to find three Easter eggs and a card in the porch.

Unable to wait a second longer, she tore into her first egg. Chocolate melted on her tongue and she let out a loud, 'Mmmmm.'

'We knew you wouldn't wait,' said Bella as she appeared in the porch with scrambled eggs on toast for Dilly. 'Have something proper to eat, Dilly. You do this every year, and every year you complain about feeling sick by lunch time.'

'Spoilsport,' said Dilly, stuffing another shard of chocolate egg into her mouth. She savoured the flavours as it melted on her tongue. 'Thanks though – and thanks for the Easter egg. It's much fancier than usual.'

'I haven't given you yours yet. I thought I'd save your stomach.'

'So why are there three? Mary, Lois and...?'

Bella shrugged. 'Who's the card from?'

'I haven't checked.'

Bella laughed. 'Did you really tear into the upmarket egg without reading who it was from?'

'Guilty as charged,' she said, walking through to the porch to open the card. Colour rose in her face when she saw the signature at the end.

'Well? Who is it from?' Bella's dark eyes twinkled at the prospect of a piece of gossip.

Dilly's face burned as she read the card and she swiftly began to wrap what was left of the egg. 'It's from Alex,' she said, certain that guilt was oozing from every pore of her face.

Bella's eyes were like saucers. 'And... is there something you're not telling me, Dilly Pepper?'

'He wishes me a happy Easter, and would I please pass this egg to Luke on Easter morning.'

Bella guffawed. 'You stole upmarket chocolate from a child?'

'I'm sorry,' spluttered Dilly. 'I didn't know.'

'It's as well I came over with a proper breakfast while there was some of the egg left.'

'Please don't tell him,' whispered Dilly.

'I think he's going to notice. There's only half an egg left.'

'Not Luke – Alex. I think it'd be best if I keep this egg and buy Luke another one.'

'Was it so good that you want more?' teased Bella. 'You

can't do that anyway. The shop sold out the other day. I don't think you'll be able to replace it.'

'Tell Luke that I'll buy him a whole new fancy upmarket big egg next year.'

Bella kissed her friend. 'You will do no such thing. We can tell him you had to check it to make sure it was safe to eat.'

Dilly was hopeful. 'Will he buy that, do you think?'

'Not a chance,' said Bella, grabbing the egg from the table. 'See you later. And Dilly, don't worry – there'll be no shortage of chocolate today with the egg hunt.'

'That might appease Luke.'

'I was trying to appease *you*. Eat up and line your stomach for all of the chocolate.' Dilly's mouth was full of scrambled eggs, so she nodded her acknowledgement. She couldn't wait to check out the Easter Eggstravaganza stalls.

* * *

The village green was a picture with its pastel bunting-strewn mini-marquees and gazebos offering face painting, balloon modelling, Easter gifts and homemade cakes and jams. Dilly found Bella and Luke by the temporary tattoo stall.

'Apparently face painting is so last year,' hissed Bella, as she watched Luke hold out his forearm for a tattoo.

'I miss those bunny faces he used to get, with the hilarious comedy incisors to his chin,' said Dilly, putting her arm around her friend.

'Me too,' said Bella sadly.

Dilly tipped her head on one side to see the tattoo Luke had chosen. 'Now we get a...' she squinted as she tried to work out what it was '...ah... a dagger. How lovely.' She stuck out her bottom lip to her friend, and they silently consoled one another over Luke's passing early childhood.

'We have to treasure every minute,' said Dilly.

Bella grimaced. 'Even the dagger tattoo ones.'

'Remember when he was a toddler, hunting for eggs at the play area?' said Dilly fondly.

Bella sighed. 'Then he moved on to The Treasure Trove for a couple of years.'

'I hope Alex is coping okay with all of those children. I should have gone up there.'

'He'll be fine,' said Bella, rubbing Dilly's arm reassuringly. 'Alex and Dave will have plenty of help from the Easter Eggstravaganza committee.'

The children were now crowding around two teachers from the school, who had helped out with the Easter holiday club. Luke was hopping from one foot to the other, as if his feet would run off with the rest of him in tow if he didn't keep moving them on the spot.

'I love the way his legs look as if they're trying to trick the rest of him into believing that he's running,' said Dilly.

They stood in silence watching Luke, as if capturing this moment forever, until he carefully swivelled round to look at them, posing proudly as he held the hat he had made in position on his head so that Bella and Dilly could take photos. Everyone applauded exuberantly as he and the other children strutted around the village green wearing the monstrously tall Willy Wonka hats they had decorated with flowers, bunnies and lambs, to a soundtrack of joyous brass band music. As they passed by Mary and Lois' cottage, Dilly was delighted to see Lois sitting on a chair by the little boundary wall, with Keaton bouncing up and down beside her as if he hadn't recently had to spend time at the vet's.

Once the children had paraded their hats, it was time for the Easter egg hunts. Luke couldn't set off soon enough.

'There's no rush,' called Dilly.

'There is,' gasped Luke. 'It's further away now I'm in the sixes and sevens group. We have to go all the way to school.'

'It's likely to be a scrum this year,' Dilly whispered to Bella, fearing for Luke's safety in the older group.

When the church bell struck ten thirty, Miss Ashworth, the headmistress, called to the children.

'Ready?' she asked, and without even a get set, go, she blew her whistle and the children scattered to the four corners of the school grounds.

Miss Ashworth was beaming. She was obviously so proud of every child, and she was as generous with her approval when her students held an egg aloft as she was with her encouragement to those children who were struggling to find any at all.

'It's so different from when Luke was a toddler and we had to find the eggs for him,' said Dilly.

'I think this is more fun, though.'

Dilly nodded. It was wonderful to get a glimpse into Luke's school life and to see him having such fun with his friends. 'You haven't told him I took a nibble of his Easter egg yet, I take it.'

'I didn't get a chance. He was in such a tearing hurry to get to the village green.'

'And I guess he'll take the news better if he's already full of chocolate.' Dilly grimaced. 'I hope he'll be okay about it.'

'Dilly, he loves you. He'll be fine about it. Although I doubt he'll ever let you forget it.'

'Not quite the memory I was hoping to make.'

'It's perfect,' said Bella. 'Think about it... you feel so guilty that you'll overcompensate for years to come.'

'You're right, I will.'

'So it's a kind of investment in his future chocolate consumption.'

'I like your thinking,' said Dilly. 'Do you fancy a hot chocolate?'

'Haven't you had enough chocolate already today?'

'Not yet.'

'You're worse than Luke,' said Bella, as Luke and his friends ran towards them, keen to get to the church hall for something to drink, and in Luke's case, for an ice cream topped off with extra sprinkles to celebrate the end of Lent.

The church hall had been transformed, with all the tables covered in prettily embroidered cloths, on which stood jam jars of daffodils. Dilly was delighted and scared in equal measure to see little stacks of leaflets about talks and workshops at The Treasure Trove next to the daffodils.

'Don't these look great?' said Bella, picking up one of the leaflets. 'Very professional.'

'They are,' said Dilly. 'As soon as Nathan agreed to me doing the workshops and talks, Alex, Dave and Liv got busy with publicity.'

'They've done an amazing job at such short notice.'

'I only hope I'll live up to the leaflets,' said Dilly with a heavy sigh.

'You'll be brilliant!' Dilly wished she had Bella's confidence in herself. 'Enough about work, Dilly. We're enjoying a day off. What are you doing this afternoon?'

'I hadn't thought yet.'

'Luke has a party. Parents are invited, so I've cadged a lift with one of the other mums.'

'That's great.' Dilly hadn't thought of doing anything other than Easter things with Luke and Bella, which was a huge assumption, she now realised. She'd have to find something else to do with the rest of her day. 'I think I'll pop up to the nursery and see if they need help.'

'Can't stay away?' Bella teased.

'I want to see how my talks are selling.'

Bella winked. 'That old one.'

They vacated their table as soon as they had finished their hot chocolates and ice cream, because there was a queue of people waiting to sit down. Dilly hadn't seen Sweetingfield so busy since the previous summer and she hoped the crowds would convert to a healthy profit for businesses and village charities and societies.

She greeted villagers and visitors as she ambled along the high street to The Treasure Trove. The journey took four times longer than it usually would, but seeing everyone made her heart swell with gratitude and a greater love for her village. When she arrived at the nursery, she was delighted to see that Alex was rushed off his feet and the Easter display was looking decidedly depleted.

'Hi, Alex,' she called once he had finished pointing one shopper in the direction of the herb troughs.

'Dilly!' His eyes sparkled more intensely than ever. It was as if something had lit up inside him. Dilly was happy to see him looking more relaxed, even if it had most likely been caused by Tess' recent visit. 'I had no idea it would be this busy.'

'It'll be because the big garden centres can't open today,' she explained.

'That and the Sweetingfield Eggstravaganza Easter egg hunt.' He stepped forward to help a customer load two arrangements from the collection of Easter pots onto a trolley.

Dilly waited until the customer was on his way. 'How did it go?'

'The children seemed to have fun.'

'And did you?' she asked, rearranging the pots to cover the gaps left behind after the customer had taken two.

'Surprisingly, yes. It was chaos though.'

'As it should be.' She stood back to contemplate the display. 'It looks like you're in need of more filled containers.'

'I am. I can't get to the polytunnel to make them though.'

'I'll do it.'

He barked with laughter. 'You're not dressed to plant up pots.'

'Plants don't have dress codes.'

'I'm surprised to hear that... You apologise to them, you speak to them, you cajole them, but you don't dress appropriately for them.'

'It's Easter Sunday, Alex. If I can't dress up to say goodbye to these pots of plants now, when can I?'

'So long as there isn't a health and safety thing about gardening in frocks.'

'I'm making up containers of plants, not strimming naked,' she said, heading towards the polytunnel before she blushed at the merest suggestion of naked gardening.

Dave snorted when she wheeled a trolley of containers into the nursery later, her prettiest frock speckled with bits of compost. 'I've seen everything now,' he said.

You haven't, she thought, still embarrassed by her naked gardening comment.

'Today's been the busiest I've seen it in here,' said Dave, nodding towards the queue at the till.

'That's great,' said Dilly.

'If you say so. I'm looking forward to getting my feet up with a pint.'

'You've not got long to wait, Dave.'

Dilly was delighted by how busy the nursery was. If only Nathan were here to see it, she thought, turning to lift a container onto a display and finding that it had already made it into a shopper's trolley. 'I'd better make some more,' she said.

She continued to make up planters until after the nursery had closed and Dave had departed for his well-earned pint. She had nothing to rush home for and was happy to help, although she feared her pretty lemon frock might never be the same again. As she loaded the final container onto a trolley, the door to the polytunnel opened. There, looking more handsome, relaxed and happy than she had ever seen him, was Alex. Her heart felt as if it were skipping at a million beats per minute. She realised that no matter what happened in her life, no matter how many barriers she erected to protect herself from being hurt, she would always feel this way when she saw him.

'Thank you for your help today.'

'My pleasure,' she said, dusting the worst of the compost from her dress.

'It's still sunny and warm-ish. Do you fancy a drink in the garden?'

Dilly smiled happily. 'There's nothing I would like more.'

'Leave those. I'll move them in the morning. Let's go and grab the last of the sun.'

Dilly gladly abandoned the containers and joined Alex for the short walk to the cottage.

Having poured them both a glass of white wine, he brought out a second chair and a small café table.

'Cheers! It's been a great day.' He sounded as contented as she had ever heard him.

They clinked glasses and Dilly took a welcome sip of the refreshing white wine. 'It has... although it didn't start as well as it should have.'

'Oh?' His brow furrowed.

'I have a confession to make,' she said.

'That sounds ominous.'

'I ate some of Luke's egg by accident.'

He roared with laughter. 'How can you accidentally eat a child's Easter egg?'

'I saw it and...'

'Didn't read the card?'

'I'm sorry,' she said.

She felt terrible about eating his gift to Luke, but Alex couldn't stop laughing. 'That is the most outrageous case of seeing food and eating it I've heard in a long time. How is Luke about it?'

Dilly shrugged. 'I don't know. I left it to Bella to break the news.'

'So you ate a child's egg—'

'*Some* of a child's egg.'

'What stopped you eating it all?'

'Bella,' she said, rubbing her eyes with her palms.

'So had his mum not intervened, you'd have wolfed down the lot?' Dilly grimaced and he burst out laughing again. 'Dilly, you're brilliant! If it had been anyone else, I'd have said they might have done it on purpose, but I know it was a complete accident as you would never intentionally do anything to upset anyone, especially Luke.'

Dilly took a large, satisfied gulp of wine. This beautiful man trusted her despite his past and her hurtful mistrust of him. 'I will spend the rest of my life compensating him for the loss of egg,' she said.

'I don't doubt it.' He stood up. 'Do you fancy some olives, or will their egg shape remind you of your shame?'

'I am a bit hungry actually.'

'I'll put together a selection of things to eat.'

'Let me help you,' she said.

He nodded appreciatively and she followed him into the kitchen. Together they began to create a mezze platter stacked with baby tomatoes, cucumber, hummus, baba ganoush, feta cheese and warm slices of toasted pitta bread. Best of all were the delicate snips of delicious pea shoots they harvested from the seeds they had sown together. Her embarrassing memory of what might have been after the seed swap was being replaced with a happier one tonight. She had grown, just like the seeds. She could only hope no one would cut her down like she was cutting the pea shoots.

Assembling a meal in this way was completely within Dilly's culinary comfort zone. She was happy to help to create something delicious in the kitchen, so long as she didn't have to cook. It was a taste of holidays on a plate, and as Alex topped up their wine glasses, then placed a candle in a hurricane jar on the table, Dilly felt as if she had stepped out of her normal life and into someone else's.

'Here,' he said, handing her his stylish blue jumper. 'It's getting cooler.'

Dilly thought she might die of happiness at the thought

of her body being swathed in soft cashmere – *his* soft cashmere.

They helped themselves to their shared plate of food and Dilly pocketed every memory. The creaminess of the hummus, the tartness of the tomatoes, the clattering squawk of a pheasant, the faint citrus smell of Alex's jumper, the tickle of cashmere on her wrists. She would treasure this night forever.

'This is great,' he said. 'Being here with you.'

His eyes, lit by the sun dipping below the horizon, settled on hers as they had so many times before. And just like before, her body craved his touch. She dropped her eyes to his mouth. It was inviting and so tempting it was impossible not to lean towards it. Towards him.

She was too hot, as if the cashmere she would happily wear for evermore was too much and she needed to tear it off and rip every shred of clothing from her body so she could feel his skin next to hers. Suddenly the tiny table between them seemed vast and she wanted to kick it away. Her breathing became ragged. She lost all words. There was no gentle exploring this time. It was the deepest, most passionate kiss of her life. Pure, desperate, unfulfilled desire forced their bodies together. Dilly Pepper was finally living and loving in the moment, and giving no thought to tomorrow. Tomorrow didn't matter. The thought crashed into her brain, smashed through her body and she briefly drew away. Tomorrow *did* matter. Tomorrow was where the hurt lay. She sat back in her chair. She needed a moment to reassure herself.

Concern was written across his face, but she wasn't going to run. She was going to allow herself this moment of happiness even if the cost of it was pain.

'Dilly, I'm sorry.' He reached out for her hand. 'I didn't mean to—'

'There you are, Alex.'

His hand flew from hers. 'Nathan,' said Alex, turning away from her.

Dilly tried to catch her breath. She couldn't leave it like this. She couldn't let him feel rejected again, but there was nothing she could do right now. She watched the brothers. The relief on Alex's face would stay with her forever. Every ounce of love and concern for his brother was etched there for anyone to see. Nathan's arrival had visibly washed Alex's worries away. It was clear then that it had never been about the money for Alex. It had only ever been about brotherly love.

Dilly felt as if she was intruding on their happiness. They were two brothers who cared deeply about one another, who needed to be together – preferably not in the company of a half-cut gardener in her lemon Easter frock, who had just bodily thrown herself onto one of them.

She stood to hug Nathan. 'It's good to see you. Sit down,' she said, gesturing to her seat. 'I need to be on my way.'

'Let me walk you,' said Alex.

'Absolutely not. You two sit down,' she said firmly.

A cloud crossed his face, but she needed to get away quickly. She was scared that at any second she might burst into tears. The thing she had wanted, yet dreaded, had happened. Nathan was home.

Chapter Thirty-Two

Dilly stretched her arms and legs extravagantly across her bed to create a huge starfish. She had nothing planned, so she could spend the whole bank holiday reliving the good bits of the previous night if she wanted to. Up until the momentary blip of her pulling away from Alex for a few seconds, it was everything she had ever dreamed a kiss could be. It was, without question, the most romantic experience of her life. Then again, she thought, there wasn't much competition: Jimmy treating her to half a bag of greasy chips and a bite of cheesy garlic bread from the all-night snack van, or Drew Johnson's scrawled love notes in year six. She had never asked for, or received, much, so she supposed she had never been disappointed. Now that she had tasted romance, she wanted more. It was every bit as wonderful as she had dreamed it might be; yet still more could have happened, *would* have happened, if Nathan hadn't returned at that moment.

Her mind was whirling with possibilities and probabilities. She was frightened that her comfortable world was about to be upended again. What if Nathan was back to tell them that he wanted to sell up and move away for good? She hadn't been planning to go to the nursery today, but now she decided that she would pop over there with the excuse of checking how the talks were selling and to see if her help was needed. At least then she might have a better handle on what on earth was going on. Was she being nosy, or simply caring? she mused, as she pulled on her work trousers. There was a fine line between sticking her beak in and helping, and she wondered how she was going to work out where that line was and how on earth, given her feelings, she would avoid stepping over it.

'Here she is, the woman of the moment,' called Dave, as she pushed open the door. Her heart leapt in anticipation. This sounded hopeful. 'You've already sold out three of your talks, with a waiting list on two of them. The others only have a couple of spaces.'

'Never,' she gasped, peering at his computer screen. Sure enough, the columns were filled with names.

Dave pointed at one course title. 'Perhaps you should think about doing that one twice. There are already three on the waiting list.'

'Wouldn't that be pushing my luck?'

'With this response? You'll walk it. Here.' He handed her a red marker pen. 'I'll let you do the honours.'

She took the pen, but felt confused.

'Write SOLD OUT across the first three on the noticeboard.'

A smile flooded her face as she took the pen to the advert.

'Graffiti-ing your own poster?' called Nathan.

He was back at his desk in the office, and looking healthier and more relaxed than he had been when she saw him at Alex's flat. He was mending, and for that Dilly was thankful with every cell of her being. It was wonderful to see him back where he belonged, but she did miss his brother sitting there.

'Dave's right about offering that course twice,' he said. 'Why not find a date and we can email those on the waiting list to see if they'd be available then?'

'Great idea,' said Dilly. 'I only hope I'll be good enough.'

'You'll be amazing,' said Nathan. 'You know your stuff and people like you.'

Dilly smiled. Nathan was back in more than body. He was the same supportive man he had always been. 'Thanks, Nathan.'

'No. Thank you – for everything,' he said meaningfully.

'She's put a lot of hours in,' said Dave. 'And these classes and workshops are inspired.'

'Yes,' said Nathan. 'You've helped me out of a hole and I won't ever forget it.'

'No worries, Nathan. I'm glad you're back,' she said.

'Aren't we all?' said Dave, heading to the kitchen.

'I'm glad to *be* back,' Nathan told Dilly. 'Especially after seeing the garden at Nursery Cottage. It looks fantastic. I couldn't believe that anyone would ever sit out there again, then there you were with Alex, enjoying a warm spring evening. It gave me so much hope, but I'm worried... I didn't interrupt anything there, did I?'

Dilly sensed herself blushing. 'No. You didn't.'

'That's what Alex said too, but I couldn't work out if he was being reserved. You know what he's like.'

I did think he was reserved until that kiss, which was anything but, she thought, excitement zinging through her body at the memory of it.

'I stayed there last night,' continued Nathan. 'Alex is trying to persuade me to move in once he's cleared out all his gym equipment, but I like living off-site.'

Dilly's heart seemed to stop. 'He's going?'

'He's already gone... First thing this morning.'

Of course he has, thought Dilly, and probably because I stupidly pulled away from him at the wrong moment. She turned from Nathan before he could see her disappointment.

'I'll sort out some dates for that course,' she called as she beat a hasty retreat.

She stomped down the nursery track, barely seeing the cars that were making their way up to begin their Bank Holiday Monday shopping. She might have helped out had Alex still been in charge, but now that Nathan was back, she would no longer be needed at The Treasure Trove. Life was returning to normal. It was a shame that normal wasn't quite so joyous as it was before Alex arrived in her life. Who am I trying to kid? she thought as she tramped along the high street. He left without even saying goodbye and I feel wretched.

As she approached the village green, she plastered a smile on her face. She didn't want her sadness to weigh on other people. They had enough troubles of their own without her offloading her stupidity on them. It was her own fault. She knew he'd leave. She knew this day would come. She had caused her own heartache and now she would have to deal with it alone. No one else should have to pay the price for her refusal to see facts.

'Dilly,' called Jonty. 'Are you here to help clear up after the Easter Eggstravaganza?'

'I had been thinking of putting my feet up and watching you from the comfort of my armchair, but—'

'But you heard I'd be buying a pint for the workers?' said Steve, reaching up to unhook the roof of a gazebo.

'And no one turns down the offer of a pint on a bank holiday,' she said, unhooking another side of the gazebo, while stifling tears for what might have been.

It's best you keep busy, Dilly, she told herself, as she helped to restore the village green to its pre-Eggstravaganza state. Life here would soon look normal, as would her own life now that Alex was gone. You were perfectly happy before, she reassured herself, and you'll be happy again. Even so, her legs seemed to be made of lead and her stomach felt as if it had been twisted into a thousand painful knots of longing for what might have been.

True to his word, Steve bought the workers a pint in The Yew. As they all stood at the bar, Dave burst in. 'What a day,' he sighed. 'And what happened to you, Dilly Pepper? One minute you were there, the next...' He shrugged. 'Scarpered. Vamoosed. Vanished into thin air.'

'Hardly, Dave. I went to help with the clear-up operation on the green.'

'You might have said goodbye.'

Alex might have said goodbye too, Dilly thought sadly.

'It's getting to be a thing around here,' continued Dave. 'First Nathan, then Alex, now you.' He leant on the bar to order, but there was no need, as Jeff had begun to pull his pint the minute Dave walked into the pub. Dave nodded his approval. 'Nice one.'

'You sounded in need of it,' Jeff said by way of explanation.

'I am, Jeff, and that's no lie.'

'So where's Alex gone?' hissed Steve. Dilly shrugged. 'So

now no one's running the nursery?' His eyes were like dinner plates. 'No wonder you're worn out, Dave.'

Dave shook his head. 'Nathan's back.'

'Hallelujah!' Steve clapped his hands. 'Why didn't anyone tell me?'

'Not many people know,' said Dilly.

'So Alex has gone back to his old life?' asked Steve.

'Looks like it,' said Dilly as dispassionately as she could.

'He could have said goodbye,' said Steve.

'Maybe it's not for good,' said Jonty.

Dilly remembered his gym equipment. There was a possibility that he would be back for that and say his farewells then. She didn't relish the prospect of saying goodbye. Now, she realised, by disappearing without a fuss, he had saved her the agony of parting. Perhaps that was why he had left without warning.

'I can't imagine he won't be back,' said Steve decisively. 'Something might have cropped up in those towers of learning that needed his attention.'

'Like work?' said Dave. 'He doesn't seem to have done anything apart from nursery stuff for weeks. Some sabbatical that was.'

'Just like your retirement then,' teased Steve.

'Yours isn't much better,' said Dave.

'But I haven't gone back to work,' said Steve.

Dave took his pint. 'You may as well have done for all the time you spend running around doing stuff. The only difference is that I get paid for it.' He took a long gulp on his pint. 'Has Dilly told you about her success?'

'Ooo!' Steve clapped his hands. 'What is it, Dilly?'

'She's sold out all of her classes.'

'*All?*' gasped Dilly. 'Only three had sold out earlier.'

'Well, now you're a sellout,' said Steve. 'And if anything deserves a toast, it's Dilly's new gardening workshop venture.'

'I'm already on it,' said Jeff, proving that he never missed a thing. Dilly wondered how many secrets Jeff knew and if he realised how she felt about Alex.

'I hope I'm up to it,' she said under her breath.

Steve rested his hand on her arm. 'You're going to be amazing, Dilly, and if you want some tips on structuring your classes or workshops, ask me.'

'See? Still working in retirement,' said Dave. 'I'm beginning to think retirement is a figment of everyone's imagination.'

'Or it's something dangled before us to aspire to,' said Jonty.

'Aren't you retired?' Dave asked.

Jonty shook his head. 'Simply having a few gap years.'

'I like your style,' said Dave.

Once they had thoroughly toasted Dilly's sellout classes, she left the others at the pub. She wanted to be alone with her feelings about Alex's departure. She needed time to reflect, to hurt and to grieve. Only then would she be able to move forward. She knew that no one would cut her any slack for grieving a relationship she'd never had. It was a figment of her imagination, like Dave's retirement. Then again, like Dave's retirement, it might have happened eventually, but that day hadn't arrived in time and now it was too late.

There was nothing she could do about any of it now. Fear had won, and she had lost. She curled up in a ball on the chair in her sitting room and placed a cushion over her face so that Bella wouldn't hear her sobs through their shared wall.

Chapter Thirty-Three

Dilly's tears from the previous night eventually dried up. Life would go on. The void left by Alex's departure was agony, but she had a good life and dear friends, and for that she was thankful. Still, there was no denying the sense of emptiness, the sickness that pervaded her gut and her heart, and the sadness running through her veins. Tomorrow won't feel as bad as today, she reassured herself. At least he was still living on the same planet and he was presumably happy, since he was back in his home and doing what he loved with people who were like him. His health and happiness were what mattered. Even so, it cut more deeply than she could ever have imagined.

You knew it would hurt, Dilly told herself as she walked her bicycle out of the garage. Just be thankful that you're busy right now. Today you have two gardens to tend, and time with Carl, plus you need to run the ideas for the first of your lesson plans by Steve. It's all go. There's so much to do to get things ready for summer. Always with your head in tomorrow, she tutted, but wasn't that a good thing when tomorrow hurt less than today?

'Morning, Dilly.' She was roused from her thoughts by Bella, who looked more alive and cheery than she had in weeks.

'Where are you going at this early hour?'

'Work,' she said breezily.

It was wonderful to see Bella looking so happy. We're like those weather houses, thought Dilly. Only instead of rain and shine, we're one happy and one sad, depending on which brother isn't in Sweetingfield. 'What about Luke?' she asked.

'He's gone to school, would you believe?'

'Already?'

'He's finally decided that he's happy to do breakfast club,' said Bella. 'So that'll save you a job.'

Dilly felt wounded that someone else she loved was moving on without her. 'I didn't know,' she said, hoping her face wasn't betraying her heartbreak at this latest development.

'He decided last night, bless him. The goalposts seem to be constantly changing with him at the moment.'

'Ah well, we knew it would happen one day,' said Dilly, smiling through her regret that she might have done her last ever school drop-off and not even noticed. 'He's growing up,' she said simply.

'He is,' Bella called happily as she rushed off to work.

Luke agreeing to go to breakfast club might only be a little step, but it made a world of difference to Dilly. People were moving on. At least things were working out with Carl. He could mow the lawn, a task which gave Dilly far too much time to immerse herself in her feelings about Alex's departure and the loss of her school-run responsibilities. It left her free to focus on tasks that absorbed her. One of the many wonderful things about gardens was that they soothed the troubled soul, she thought as she wielded a sharpened hoe through a border, keeping her eyes peeled for any interesting seedlings that might be worth keeping, while trying not to dwell on the memory of doing the same task at Jessica's with Alex the first time they had gardened together.

Carl was keen to learn and it was a pleasure to work alongside him. Helping him was helping her, as he constantly asked her about plant identification and garden practices, so she didn't have much time to dwell on everything that was slipping away from her.

After a busy day in the spring sunshine, Dilly headed over to The Yew to meet Steve.

'You're looking a bit peaky, Dilly. Are you alright?'

'Peaky? After the day I've had in the sunshine?' she said, brushing aside her feelings.

'Yes. It's as if your glow's been dimmed. You're not sickening with something, are you?'

'Not so I'd notice,' she said. 'I'm probably just a bit hungry. Let's order – my treat, since you're helping me.'

'That's so kind. Thank you. I wouldn't mind trying this week's pie.'

'Two pies it is,' said Jeff, as he poured their drinks.

'Who said I was having one?' said Dilly indignantly.

'Aren't you?' asked Jeff.

'Well, yes,' said Dilly. 'But—'

'But what?' asked Jeff, handing her a pint of shandy.

'But I might have wanted something else,' she said.

'No chance.' His eyes challenged her to argue.

'I always suspected you were a mind-reader,' she said.

'Not a mind-reader, simply someone who knows his clientele,' he said, pushing the card reader towards her.

Steve and Dilly sat at a table in the bay window so that they could spread out her lesson notes. The arrival of this week's special, a vegetable balti pie, halted their work. Dilly tucked in hungrily.

'This is delicious,' she said between mouthfuls. 'I'm very taken with Jeff's new weekly pies. I can't wait to see what next week's is.'

'I think his idea is to keep us coming back for more,' said Steve. 'You'll have to do that with your talks and workshops. This plan looks so good, Dilly. I can't see why you won't be getting return visits from your students.'

'I only hope I'll be able to live up to my lesson plan,' she said, the nerves already building at the prospect of stepping outside of her extremely comfortable comfort zone.

'You'll be fine. You have a passion for your subject, a sunny disposition and a desire to help others to become better gardeners. What could possibly go wrong?'

'Plenty,' said Dilly. 'I've started to have dreams about bendy rubber desk legs, giving the wrong talk and my laptop exploding like a firework.'

'You do know that all those things won't happen in the same talk, don't you?' said Steve.

'Not according to my dream,' said Dilly.

'And you do know that dreams don't come true?' he asked.

'Yes,' she said, her mind never far from her unfulfilled dream of creating a future with Alex. 'I do.'

Chapter Thirty-Four

It was a sunny spring evening, one that Dilly hadn't been looking forward to spending alone. She was under no illusion that when Bella messaged her to suggest a trip to The Yew, she was trying to keep her best friend busy, as well as her child. Dilly had to be kept occupied like Luke did, not only because she needed distracting from missing Alex, but also because she was getting more worked-up and nervous by the second at the prospect of giving her first talk, and she needed something to divert her and calm her down.

'How often do we get to do this?' asked Bella as she shuffled onto the bench at a table in the beer garden.

'Not often enough,' said Dilly, sitting down opposite her.

Dilly and Bella both had half an eye on Luke, who was in the play area that was separated from the garden by a white-painted picket fence. 'He's getting more adventurous,' said Dilly, nodding to Luke, who was scaling the tallest piece of play equipment.

'Yes, more's the pity. Now I think it's a case of when, not if, I'll get to rush him to A and E.'

'Always look on the bright side,' said Dilly as she watched him drop from the monkey bars. 'You do know that he lands like a cat and will be fine?'

'I know no such thing,' said Bella. 'At this rate, you'll be refusing to babysit for him.'

'I'd never do that. If only you'd go out somewhere. I haven't had a chance to spend an evening sitting on your sofa and watching your telly with Luke for months.'

'I would ask you to babysit tomorrow night, but since I'd only be going out to cheer you on while you were doing your talk, I could hardly ask that.'

'No,' said Dilly, 'that would have been counterproductive. It's nice that you thought of asking me to babysit though.'

'I was going to ask you... I know it's short notice, but I was wondering if you might look after Luke on Saturday night.'

'Yes,' said Dilly, almost before Bella had finished speaking. 'I can't wait! I'll bring popcorn and we'll watch Saturday night telly and—'

'It's not a playdate, Dilly. You will remember to send Luke to bed?'

'Please let him stay up longer.'

'Half an hour, Dilly. I can't believe I'm having to negotiate this with the babysitter. You do know they're famed for wanting the kids tucked up in bed so they can have a quiet night?'

'What's the point in that? Where are you going, anyway?'

'It took you long enough to ask!' Bella leant in to Dilly. 'I have a date,' she whispered.

'You kept that quiet. Who with?'

'Nathan.'

Dilly punched the air. It felt as if every tooth, freckle and strand of hair was grinning happily in Bella's direction. She reached forward and clasped Bella's hand.

'This is the best news.' For both of you, she thought. 'I want to know everything. Tell me about him asking you.'

'He didn't,' said Bella. 'I did.'

'Go Bella!'

'I know. I surprised myself. There's definitely a spark now he's back. I've always liked him, but obviously he was married, so I wouldn't ever have let on how I felt, and then when they got divorced, he was in a bad place. Then when we did go out, and kiss...'

'You kissed?' exclaimed Dilly. 'I knew there was more to that non-date. Why didn't you tell me?'

'Because he disappeared so soon after it. I thought it was me. He's told me now why he had to go, and I know he's told you – and before you go beating yourself up over it, as you tend to do, I understand why you couldn't say anything.'

Dilly scrutinised Bella's face for any sign of hurt, but there was none. 'How do you feel about that?'

'I'm fine that you didn't say anything, and I completely understand why he had to go away to come to terms with it. Nathan feels embarrassed about taking time out like that, but I don't agree. He needed to deal with it as best he could, and he didn't want to be a burden to his friends.'

'He would never have been a burden,' said Dilly sadly. 'Why didn't you tell me about your feelings for him all that time ago?'

'I was ashamed at falling for someone I knew I could never be with.'

'You can't help your feelings,' said Dilly.

Bella smiled. 'I know. And when I found out he didn't go away because of me, it seemed like the right time to act, so I casually asked him if he fancied a night out.'

'And what did he say, apart from "yes", obviously?'

'He said he'd love to, but for him it would be a date rather than colleagues going for a drink, and would I be okay with that?'

'Which was exactly what you wanted to hear.'

Bella nodded, then raised her eyebrows as Luke came rushing towards them.

'Can I have a lemonade?' he shouted.

'I think the word you're looking for is please,' said Bella, grabbing her handbag. 'Another lemonade for you, Dilly?'

'I'd love one, thanks,' she said, smiling.

It was the best news. Although she'd guessed that Bella hadn't told her the true extent of her feelings for Nathan, Dilly could have kicked herself. She might have spotted what was going on with her friend better if she hadn't been so distracted by Alex. She wondered what Alex was doing now, then pushed the thought aside. Now was the time for Bella and Luke. Nathan was home; Alex was gone. Bella was going on a date; Dilly was staying in to babysit. They truly were the weather house of neighbours, she thought, as Luke shuffled along the bench for a cuddle.

They sat, snuggled together in the ebbing sunlight. This was a moment to be pocketed and cherished. One day, all too soon, Luke would grow out of wanting to hug her. Dilly kissed the top of his head.

'I hear that you and I are going to spend Saturday night in front of the telly with popcorn,' she said.

'Yay! Do I get to stay up late?'

'As late as your mum allows you to.'

'Is it okay with Mum that you're coming over?'

'It is. She kindly said she'd go out. Is chocolate popcorn okay for you?'

'Yessss!' he said, punching the air and catching her nose with his fist.

'Ouch!' Tears sprang to her eyes.

'I'm sorry, Dilly. Have I made you cry?'

'No, sweetheart, you haven't,' she said, wrinkling her nose. 'I'm fine.'

'I saw that, Luke,' said Bella as she carefully placed their glasses of lemonade on the table.

'I'm sorry, Dilly. It was an accident.'

'I know, Luke,' she said fondly, as he took his lemonade and gulped it down, before sliding along the bench and back to the play area.

'I guess you're right about A and E,' said Dilly, watching him go. 'Only my bet is that we'll be needing it for me, not him, now he's getting bigger and stronger.'

Bella grimaced. 'Are you still okay to babysit on Saturday night?'

'Of course I am. But I'll wear an American footballer's kit, just to be on the safe side,' said Dilly, rubbing her nose.

Chapter Thirty Five

Dilly walked into the nursery at the end of a long day at work. Nerves ranged over her skin like electric eels and she felt cold to the marrow. It was as if her circulation had given up the ghost and joined her icy feet in freezing her to stone. She had tried to eat before she left home for the evening, but she could only manage a quarter of a cup of tea, so she was running on empty and shivering, yet incredibly, her palms were sweaty and on the brink of turning into waterfalls.

How did teachers do this, day in, day out, with kids who mightn't be interested in learning? And there were so many of them in a school. Whole classrooms, chock-a-block with students with varying levels of interest, rather than a handful of folks, fascinated by gardening and keen to learn. Her brain had completely turned to mush. She wasn't cut out for this.

She set up her screen with help from Dave, who still knew his way around a presentation, thank goodness, but even his confidence and laidback disposition did little to calm her.

First through the door was Carl. He had caught the gardening bug, and he was very keen to learn.

'Please can you sit in front of me so I have a friendly face to look at?' she asked him.

He had been anything but a friendly face when she first met him. He was the face of death and destruction when it came to plants and wildlife, and potentially even poor Keaton. Now, though, their friendship and business partnership was coming together far better than Dilly could have imagined. That he had paid his own money to attend her talk about gardening for wildlife filled her with joy.

Next through the door were Tess' parents, followed by a mum from school who Dilly recognised, and then the rest were people she had never seen before in her life.

The time passed in a flurry of words, photos, examples and questions, and Dilly was surprised when the time to break for cups of tea and biscuits arrived. She hoped that everyone was learning what they wanted to know and were satisfied with her efforts.

One of the strangers approached her. 'Hi, Dilly, I'm really enjoying this, and I'm wondering if you might be able to talk at our gardening club in Truelake?'

'You've travelled all the way from Truelake?' Dilly gasped in disbelief.

The lady nodded. 'I'm on the committee of our gardening club. Obviously we'd pay travelling expenses and your fee.'

Dilly had no idea what her fee was. How could she put a value on it? To her it was a pleasure to go to a gardening club and spend the evening with like-minded people, and it felt strange to charge for the privilege, but if the situation at The Treasure Trove and Alex's reaction to her knowledge had taught her anything, it was to own her expertise with more confidence than she had in the past.

'I've always thought that you needed to value your knowledge more highly,' said Steve when she told him in the pub later. He wanted to know chapter and verse about her first experience of standing in front of a roomful of people and speaking, and she was glad to offload. She hadn't stopped shaking since the end of the talk, and had arrived at the pub, her cheeks on fire and her body shooting and fizzing with so much adrenaline that she wasn't sure if she would ever come back down to earth again. It had been a resounding success. Everyone said they enjoyed it, and a couple of participants had even asked about other classes.

'I'm not sure I can put my body through this again,' she said, still scared to lift her drink in case she sloshed it everywhere.

'You'll be less nervous next time,' said Steve.

'How do you know?'

'You seem to have forgotten I was your teacher once upon a time.'

'But you were never nervous.'

'I was when I was training. Look at tonight as your training. If you have enough talks booked in your diary, your confidence will grow, your nerves will be a distant memory and you'll have no financial worries next winter.'

A broad smile spread over her hot, red face. 'I can't believe I stood up in front of people and spoke for so long.'

Steve looked as if he might burst with pride. 'Who'd have thought it? Dilly Pepper not just stepping, but leaping, out of her comfort zone?'

'I'm so glad I did. I can see all kinds of possibilities now.'

'Well, they do say that it's outside of the comfort zone where the magic happens.'

Dilly's mind strayed to Alex. If she had been bolder and braver, and not listened to her fears, would she have hurt any less when he left? She parked the thought. Now was not the moment for regrets; now was the time to celebrate what she had achieved.

'Why don't you set up a page online to advertise your talks, so that gardening clubs can find you?' suggested Steve.

Dilly nodded thoughtfully. 'My biggest problem, though, apart from the nerves, is the travel. I can't cycle halfway across the county to give a talk, much as I'd like to, especially not in winter.'

'I'll drive you.'

'I couldn't ask you to do that.'

'You're not. I'm offering... Actually, I'm not.'

Dilly's heart sank. She would have loved to have given talks with Steve there for moral support.

'I'm insisting,' he said.

She sighed with relief. 'Thanks, Steve.'

There was no denying that her life was changing and she'd had to adapt, although how she would ever adapt to Alex not being nearby was still beyond her. She believed, deep down, that one day she would eventually spot the silver lining to the sadness she felt at his departure, but for the moment, she still hurt too much to see it. She could only keep busy and try to distract herself from the heartache – and thanks to her new teaching venture and friends like Steve, her life was filling with wonderful distractions.

Chapter Thirty-Six

Dilly had made a promise to Jessica and Nathan that she would continue to tend the garden at Nursery Cottage, so now she was obliged to go there even though she didn't want to. It was too painful to think of all the hope she had ploughed into it and the belief that her dreams would come true. She had invested so much in that little garden – not only her time and her energy, but her faith in what tomorrow would bring. Only tomorrow had brought exactly what she knew it would when Alex left – heartache.

Carl had a run of mowing jobs, so it was the perfect time for her to be at Nursery Cottage. She couldn't share this space with Carl. It was too precious to her, and she was scared that she might break down and cry, and that wouldn't be professional. If she had to be in Alex's garden, then she was better off being there alone. It was filled with memories, from that awful sugarless coffee given to her by a man who wanted nothing to do with gardening, to their last wonderful evening there, when they had laughed and relaxed together and she had basked in the glow of his attention; the heat of their kiss; the excitement of Nathan's return; and the emptiness of Alex's departure. That one little patch of earth held more painful and joyful memories than her own garden, and she knew she would be linked to it forever.

At least on a busy day, Nathan would definitely be in the nursery and she wouldn't have to see him. She could be alone with her memories. She steeled herself to get on her bike, then slowly made her way up the busy high street.

The nursery track had grown so familiar that she cycled along it, avoiding the potholes without looking out for them, yet even now she couldn't shed her shame when she saw the spot where she had been thrown from her bike. She shielded her eyes from the polytunnel as she approached it. It was home to too many memories. There, they had worked side by side to create pretty containers of plants for people to enjoy in their gardens in the hope that they would rescue Nathan's nursery and protect Alex's investment; and it was there they'd shared their first kiss. That place would never be the same now that Alex wasn't here.

She shored herself up. Everything had ended well, she reminded herself. Nathan was back. The nursery was showing signs of thriving once again. Jeff's plants would soon be delivered to him. She had increased her own income and Carl was working alongside her. He was learning more by the minute and becoming a better, more thoughtful gardener. It was all brilliant. A happy ending. Only it didn't feel that way. Her misery over Alex's sudden departure was so deep and draining that it crushed and buried any hope of lasting relief and happiness about anything else.

She leant her bicycle against the hedge, just as she had the first time she had gardened there. Now the hedge was neat and all the brambles had been removed. The bed bordering the little brick path that ran around the side of the house was a carpet of blue, purple and white aubrieta. Birds flitted from the hedgerows and the garden was alive with butterflies and bees.

The pear trees in the little orchard had taken over from the plums as star performers in the spring show and were smothered in blossom; hornbeam leaves were unfurling like tiny fans; and the clumps of tulips she had once secretly feared might have given up blooming long ago, were clad in bright pink petals and merrily strutting their stuff in joyous gaggles down the border. So much had changed since she was last there. How she wished Alex could see the merriment of the tulips and the quiet beauty of the hornbeam.

She tried not to look at the chairs on the tiny patio. She didn't need that kind of reminder of what she had lost. With a huge intake of breath, she went to get her weeding knife. She would start with the path. Having relieved it of its weeds, she would turn her attention to edging the border to give the tulips the best possible stage on which to perform, even though no one else would see them.

On her way to fetch the knife, she stopped to admire a small tortoiseshell butterfly basking on a cushion of aubrieta. She knelt down to observe it up close, taking care not to block the sun's rays. 'Aren't you gorgeous?' she said to it.

'Thanks,' came the reply. She thought her eyes might shoot out of her head as a huge smile tore across her face. She turned, still kneeling by the flower, to see him standing there, his smile reflecting hers.

'You're back,' she said softly.

He nodded. 'I needed something.'

Dilly's pounding heart sank to her boots. 'Your gym equipment.'

'Are you saying I'm out of condition?' Those moss green eyes were teasing.

'Not at all,' she said, standing up. If this was the last time she was going to see him, she wanted to etch all of his features on her brain so she would never forget a single one. His disappearance had taught her this. Had she known he was leaving so soon, she would have memorised every nanosecond of their last evening together. Now she had a chance to make good on that, and she was going to take it. 'But you do need your gym equipment,' she said.

'I don't *need* it, but I do need something else.'

'I guess you did leave very suddenly. I'm not surprised you forgot something.'

'I didn't forget anything, Dilly.'

'No, well... you're not the forgetful type. What with your big brain and everything.' What am I saying? she cringed, begging her mouth to stop talking.

He laughed. It was a fond laugh. A kind one. 'It was Tess...'

Tess? Dilly's mind felt fit to explode. What was she doing here?

'She pointed it out to me,' he continued. 'In the photos of us cuddling lambs – me, you and Luke.'

'I didn't see them,' she said.

'If you had, you might have spotted it, too.' He looked sad and apologetic. 'I've been looking at those photos a lot since I left, but I never saw myself in them. Only you.'

Dilly felt the familiar humiliation. Her lamb had wet her lap. Her face must have been awful. It was why she had never looked at the photos – that and the fact she wanted to avoid dwelling on what she had lost, in case it prevented her from healing and moving forward. 'Were they so bad?'

'No. You look as gorgeous as you always do.'

'Hardly. Especially on a cold, wet day with my hair everywhere and my pink nose and blue lips,' she said, stopping short of mentioning her saggy, soggy trousers after the snowy ditch.

'That's when you are your most beautiful – wild and alive.'

Dilly could barely believe what she was hearing.

'I've always felt stilted and dead by comparison, Dilly. Then Tess pointed out the look on my face in those photos. I felt alive and it showed. I was genuinely, deeply happy. I knew I felt it, but I looked it, too.'

'That's lambs for you. You can't help but smile when you see one,' she said.

'I might have had the cutest, fluffiest little lamb sitting on my lap, but my eyes were only on you. There isn't a single photo of me looking anywhere else. It's *you* who makes me happy and *you* who makes me feel more alive.' His voice became softer. 'Then Tess pointed out something else.'

There's more? thought Dilly, reeling with shock. She already felt like an imposter in her own dream coming true. 'Wh-what?' she whispered.

'That in every photo, you're looking at me in the same way.'

Her heart raced. She had never felt so vulnerable and visible, yet safe.

He reached over and tenderly cupped her face. How could something gentle feel so hot that it might leave her scarred? She thought she might die of longing and excitement as she gazed into his eyes.

'I'm sorry I left like I did,' he said.

'You have no need to apologise. The Roman Empire was

probably feeling a bit overlooked.' Now what am I saying? 'What with everything else going on,' she added, hoping to hide her embarrassment.

His hand hadn't left her face. His eyes hadn't left hers. 'If you speak to bees, birds, weeds and corms, why should I be surprised that you think that a vast empire that fell, over one and a half millennia ago, has feelings?' His voice was filled with tenderness.

'Are you mocking me?'

He shook his head. 'I would never do that.'

His Adam's apple bobbed nervously. She would remember that forever too, she vowed.

'I thought you were regretting the kiss, Dilly, but that kiss...' He fell silent and she waited for what seemed like an eternity. 'I can't forget it,' he said tenderly. 'You were right. I have come back for something. You. I missed you so much it physically hurt.'

The words hung in the air. Dilly wasn't convinced that she had heard them correctly, and if she had, she was so shocked that she didn't know what to do with them. For a woman who had promised herself that she would remember every little detail about their last minutes together, she was doing a fine job of missing something big. It was as if those fingers on her face had dulled everything apart from an urgent need to kiss this exquisite man.

She sensed his eyes devouring her, as if he knew, like she did, that this was the last time they would see one another. Did he feel the same way as her, or was she projecting her own emotions onto him, like she did to corms and bees? She didn't trust her judgement and she hadn't a clue what to do, so she stayed silent, thirstily drinking in the sight of him as if she would never drink again.

'I...' His eyes began to roam the garden as if he was tired, or frustrated with something. Was it with her? Had her silence bored him? She really ought to be getting back to work. The garden wouldn't tidy itself. He looked back into her eyes. 'Please can I kiss you?' He sighed. 'I don't want to get it wrong again.'

She caught sight of a weed at the side of the path. Work could wait. This couldn't. She was finally going to live in the moment. 'You didn't get it wrong last time,' she said. 'Please kiss m—'

She was talking and smiling as her lips met his. She would pocket this moment forever. She would remember every last sensation. Their kiss deepened, their tongues exploring as he scooped her up and carried her into the cottage, their lips never leaving one another's. This man would never hurt her, she knew, and as Dilly Pepper's body took over at last, her brain completely lost any ability to think.

Chapter Thirty-Seven

Alex's return to the village was big news – bigger, perhaps than Nathan's. It seemed that no one apart from those closest to him had ever doubted that Nathan would return, but the return of Doctor Alex Hampton caused all kinds of ripples of excitement, not least because with it came the reason for his return. Dilly Pepper had never, in the whole of her life, been on the receiving end of so many meaningful smiles. She had only gone to the shop to buy milk, but it seemed she had been spotted leaving the nursery earlier that morning and the cogs of the village grapevine had been cranked up to full tilt by the time she realised she had run out of milk. Had she known any of this, she would have sneaked next door and borrowed some from Bella. As it was, she was now brazening out being the centre of attention for something other than tripping over her pancake pinny, landing in a snow-filled ditch or leaving a trail of tomato soup along the high street.

Dilly returned the villagers' knowing smiles with one she was certain blinded them with happiness. There was nothing she could do to subdue its brightness. She was in love. Well, she had known she'd been in love for ages, but now everything had changed because Alex had come back to be with her. She wanted to skip along the high street to work in Mary and Lois' garden, but instead opted for walking quickly, although today it felt as if she were floating.

Keaton bounded over to her as he always did and she bent down to give him a big hug. The last time she had wrapped her arms around anyone, it had been Alex. She would wrap her arms around him again later, and she couldn't wait.

'Shall we get on with the new borders?' she asked Keaton as she snuggled into his warm fur.

'Absolutely not,' said Mary firmly. 'You will take tea with Lois and me in the back garden and tell us what's going on.'

Dilly followed Mary to the back garden, where a table was set with tea and biscuits, and Lois sat snuggled under a blanket. To see Lois outside gladdened Dilly's heart on an already joyous day. 'Here she is,' said Mary.

'Ah, good,' said Lois, those dark eyes twinkling for the first time in too many months. 'Tell us all.'

Dilly spluttered. There was no way she would do that. She sat down and stuffed a biscuit in her mouth to give herself time to think.

'So are the rumours true?' asked Mary.

Dilly chewed thoughtfully and wondered how long she could spin out eating a biscuit.

'Are you and Alex a thing?' demanded Lois. Dilly kept on chewing.

'Dilly, you have to realise that we know what you're doing with that biscuit,' said Mary.

'Please finish it and tell us, before I fall asleep,' said Lois.

Dilly nodded, still eating.

'Is that yes, you'll tell us, or yes, you have a thing?' asked Mary.

'It's a thing,' said Dilly eventually.

Mary clapped her hands and beamed at her friend. 'We couldn't be more delighted, could we, Lois?'

Lois reached over to Dilly and clasped her wrist in her skinny, gnarled hand. 'This has made me so happy, dear.'

Dilly held her eyes. 'It's made me extremely happy, too,' she said fondly.

'That's wonderful,' exclaimed Mary. 'And since good news needs to be celebrated, I'm declaring it a beach day. In any case, the weather's far too lovely to be working.'

'What a great idea!' said Dilly. 'A bit of sea air will do you both good.'

'A bit of sea air will do us *all* good,' said Mary. 'You're coming, too. And before you say anything, there's a specialist cactus nursery near the coast. Nathan told me about it. He's kindly agreed to meet me there, and you, naturally, in your capacity as my gardener, ought to be there, too. It goes without saying that I'll pay you for your expertise. I'm sorry if it's an inconvenience and throws out your plans for work on the border, but we have to grab these days while we can, and I would appreciate your advice today, especially as the nursery's plants will be moving to their new homes before long, and there's nothing sadder than an empty greenhouse.'

'It would be interesting,' said Dilly. 'But only if you're sure.'

'I'm completely certain. Jessica is bringing a picnic and since it would be a crime to go to the coast without Luke, especially as it's the last Friday of the Easter holidays, he's coming, too. Clearly I'm too old to look after him, so his mother will have to come for that.'

Dilly laughed. 'How are so many of us going to fit into Nathan's car?'

'Alex is bringing his car too,' said Mary, and Dilly blushed. 'And before you start fretting, Liv and Dave will keep the home fires burning at the nursery. Everything is under control.'

'You seem to have it all sorted out,' she said.

'Oh, we do. Jessica arranged it the minute she heard,' said Lois, and Dilly was delighted and embarrassed all at the same time at the thought of Jessica's, Mary's and Lois' happiness at the news of her and Alex getting together.

'If anyone needs a beach day, it's us,' said Mary. 'Pop home, Dilly. Bring whatever you need and we'll see you in half an hour.'

Dilly packed her bag in under five minutes. She was so excited to see Alex she thought she might burst. Having paced up and down the kitchen a few times, she decided that she needed to find something to distract herself, so she flung open the back door to go into the garden and found Alex walking towards her.

'I couldn't stay away,' he said, beaming.

Dilly's heart leapt as she threw herself into his open arms. 'I'm so happy you're here,' she cried, wrapping her legs around him as he carried her indoors, kissing her as if they had been apart forever, not just a couple of hours.

All sense of time disappeared as they devoured every millimetre of one another's bodies. Life's baggage lay jettisoned with their clothes, somewhere between the back door and the sitting room. It was hot, desperate, frenzied love-making and as Dilly lay, breathless, naked and satiated, she thought back to the snow day, when she had been frightened of her own power. Never again, she vowed, marvelling at her newly discovered fearlessness.

'I've missed you,' he whispered, his thumb softly brushing her cheek.

'You'll be bored with me by the end of the day.'

'I could never be bored with you, Dilly Pepper,' he said, kisses fluttering down her body and setting off a million new fireworks.

They were late to collect Mary and Lois. Alex took the blame, claiming to have been held up, and Dilly could see from Mary and Lois' faces that they knew exactly who had waylaid him.

Lois was soon asleep and Mary fussed with Keaton, who sat between them, proudly wearing the middle seatbelt as if he was born to car travel now he'd been treated with travel sickness tablets.

Dilly couldn't stop looking at Alex. From his strong jaw, to his green eyes sparkling in the spring sunlight, then to his strong hands holding the wheel and those long, sensual fingers. She bit her lip. Part of her couldn't believe what had happened, while another part of her never believed that anything else ever could have. How she was going to concentrate on sourcing Mary's plants with all these emotions careering through her body, she didn't know.

As it was, she wasn't required at the cactus nursery, and her suspicion that it might have been a ploy to get everyone to the beach was confirmed. Nathan had already forwarded the list of Mary's must-have plants and they were all perfect, leaving them free to spend the day enjoying themselves.

Jessica brought the biggest picnic imaginable. 'I had a lot

of baking in the freezer,' she explained as she handed out sausage rolls and cheese muffins, stopping briefly to rest her hand on Alex's shoulder and give it a fond squeeze. He didn't flinch, or look as if he wanted to be anywhere else, and Jessica smiled. That he was finally relaxing and trusting again must mean the world to Jessica, she thought, as she helped herself to food.

Dilly sat alongside Alex, their legs stretched out before them and their arms behind one another as she leant into him, her head resting on his shoulder. She watched Mary's, Lois' and Jessica's smiling faces, then glanced up at Alex and met his eyes. He must have been looking at her all along. It felt as if he had always been in her life, yet everything was so new. She wanted to tumble across the sand making love to him *and* sit there chastely, eating the picnic with everyone else, all at once. It was so confusing and exhilarating. The thrill of his muscular thigh next to her, and the powerful desire to rip every shred of clothing from his body was becoming so intense that she almost couldn't wait for the day to be over. Almost, but not entirely, because what was happening right now was precious. *Now*, when she thought she might die of longing. *Now*, when sweet temptation collided with the absolute confidence that her future promised fulfilment of her desire. *Now*, when she was surrounded by the people she loved most dearly.

Luke stood up. 'I'm going to make a race,' he said, stomping off and scattering sand over the beach rugs.

'Can I help?' asked Nathan, brushing sand off a half-eaten sandwich.

'Yeah,' said Luke, grabbing Nathan's hand to drag him to his feet. Nathan leapt into the air as if Luke was too strong, making Luke giggle. Nathan's energy levels were improving and his joyous zest for life was back. There was a bounce in his step and a bounce in those curls glinting in the sunlight.

Bella looked so contented watching Luke and Nathan plotting the race route together that Dilly was overwhelmed with happiness for her. Tomorrow's date was bound to be a huge success.

'They make a great team,' said Mary, nodding at Nathan and Luke.

'They do,' said Bella fondly, her dark eyes never leaving them as they chatted and began to build a sandcastle.

'Alex! We could do with your input on this,' called Nathan.

He laughed. 'I'm no sand sculptor.'

'You don't know until you try,' said Jessica.

'And you may as well put your historical expertise to some use so we can make this castle look a bit realistic,' added Nathan.

'Yes. Come on, Alex,' insisted Luke.

Alex shook his head and laughed. 'Okay,' he said, getting to his feet. Dilly watched him walk towards his brother and Luke, his strong calf muscles flexing and releasing with every step in the soft sand. Alex in shorts was a whole new Alex to admire, and Dilly had to check herself to make certain she wasn't drooling.

Keaton followed him, and was soon making their task more challenging. 'Muuuum,' whined Luke.

'Shall we take him for a walk?' called Dilly.

'Yes, please,' said Alex.

Dilly and Bella put Keaton on a long lead and took him for a stroll along the beach.

'At last,' said Bella, once they were out of earshot.

'At last, what?' asked Dilly.

Bella hugged her friend. 'At last, everything, I think. At last Nathan's back in our lives. At last Alex is back. And at last you have what you wanted.'

Dilly couldn't help smiling. She suspected she had been smiling ever since Alex had come home. Home, she thought. Yes, Sweetingfield was his home now and her makeshift family was his, too. He even seemed more relaxed with Jessica today and Dilly hoped that now his barriers were melting away, he would not see Jessica as his mother's twin, but as an individual, and allow her to treat him like the son she'd never had.

'So what's the story, Dilly?'

'You're as bad as Mary and Lois,' she chided, remembering their tea and biscuits inquisition.

'Alex came back. He missed me.'

Bella squeezed her tighter. 'I'm so happy for you, Dilly.'

'I'm happy for you... and for me... for all of us.'

Bella nodded. 'Alex is going to work at the nursery every other weekend so Nathan can take Luke to football.'

Dilly hadn't believed that her smile could get any bigger. 'I didn't know that. I only knew he'd be back here at weekends and when he could in the week. I'm glad. It'll be good for Nathan and Luke to spend time together.'

'Less time for Auntie Dilly though,' said Bella.

'I'll always be here for him.'

'I know,' said Bella.

Arm in arm, they stumbled happily along the shoreline, kicking the waves in the shallow water with their bare feet, while Keaton trotted along close to them on the beach, taking care to avoid getting his paws wet.

'It's doing him a power of good,' said Bella, nodding to the little dog.

'And Lois. I'm so pleased she was able to come today. I think the change of scenery is benefitting her, too.'

'I guess we shouldn't go too far,' said Bella, looking over her shoulder.

'Luke will be fine with them, you know.'

'I know that, but I'm not sure how okay they'll be with him,' said Bella.

Dilly laughed, remembering her experience in the snow ditch a few weeks earlier. Was that really only a few weeks ago? she wondered. It seemed as if the whole world had changed since then.

It was one of those balmy spring days when Dilly might easily have forgotten that it wasn't summer already. As they drew nearer the group, Dilly could see Mary fussing over Lois, who was tucked under a blanket on a beach chair. Mary sat back down on her chair next to Jessica, and the women cheered for Luke, who was competing in a complicated race involving running between piles of stones, building turrets on a castle and sprinting with buckets of water to fill the moat. Alex and Nathan vied to take a sharp corner in the race, and their buckets of water collided, soaking Alex's tee-shirt. Their laughter carried on the sea air and Dilly felt a surge of love for her newly extended family of friends.

She watched Nathan and Alex race to the sea to grab more water for the moat, laughing and shouting like competing schoolboys. It was as if she were glimpsing their past, before life had wounded them and they had become weighed down with heartache and responsibility. Any thought of filling the moat had clearly been forgotten as they splashed one another with buckets of water. She and Bella rushed forward and joined in the water fight, while Keaton made a run for the safety of Mary and Lois, his lead tumbling behind him.

Alex's hair was dripping with water. It reminded her of him fresh from the shower a few weeks ago, but now he was laughing and that generous, bright smile which reached to his playful green eyes made him more gorgeous than ever. She plunged into the sea with no care for the cold. She wanted to be close to him. She flung herself into his arms and he caught her before toppling back into the water, laughing and kissing her as he fell.

'Sorry,' she gasped as they surfaced.

'Are you apologising to me or the sea?' he asked, holding her in his arms.

'The sea, obviously,' she said.

'Don't ever change, Dilly Pepper,' he said, kissing her tenderly. 'I love everything about you, from the tiniest little freckle here—' he kissed just beneath her earlobe and she thought she might die of longing '—to the huge things you do, like making the world a brighter and more beautiful place.'

All she could think of was that Alex loved everything about her. He had seen her fall over in her banana pinny and be helped to her feet by a nonagenarian. He'd encountered her wrapped in a towel that made her look like an uncooked sausage roll and he'd seen her get more angry than she'd ever been in her life – and he still loved everything about her.

She reached up and held that handsome face in her hands and kissed him. She would never stop loving and kissing this man. Ever. She drew away from him slightly and gazed into his eyes, which seemed to reflect the turquoise of the sea and the blue of the sky.

'I love everything about you too,' she said.

His brow knitted slightly.

'And yes, Doctor Alex Hampton, I'm talking to *you*. Not the waves, the sea, the fish in it, the sky above us, or the bee in the crocus flower.'

She could have gone on, but she needed to feel his lips on hers and as they kissed again, it felt to Dilly Pepper as if all of her tomorrows had come at once.

A Note from Sarah

Thank you so much for reading *A Garden of Hope in Sweetingfield*. I had a wonderful time writing this book and spending time in the company of Dilly and Alex. If you enjoyed reading their story, I would love it if you could leave a very short review. A sentence is enough. Reading your feedback is amazing, and it will help other readers to pick up the book and escape to Sweetingfield for a few hours.

If you would like to hear about my latest releases and find out about what's happening in the countryside around the farm, please sign up to my newsletter. Your email will never be shared with anyone else, and you can unsubscribe at any time.

Thank you!

Love, Sarah x

Acknowledgments

Writing is a solitary experience, but that is not the whole truth, because I get to meet wonderful new readers all the time through my newsletter and social media. My first thank you is to you, for reading my books and reaching out and supporting me. I am truly grateful to you.

Thank you to my writing friends who are always on hand to lend an ear and share their wisdom. Susan Allan, Susan Buchanan, Anita Faulkner, Rosie Hendry, Suzanne Snow, Ian Wilfred and all of my pals in the RNA Norfolk and Suffolk Chapter and Contemporary Chapter.

To my fabulous beta readers: Susan Allan, Jill Batchelor, Helen Cook, Julie Donaghey, Alison French and Julie Vince. Thank you so much for taking the time to read an early version of this story and for sharing your thoughts. You are all stars!

Thank you to Andrew Tapp for your patience, friendship, advice and for the hours we spent discussing Dilly and the title of this book. One day, we'll go back to chatting about music and plants, I promise!

It is ten years since I first met with gardening professionals from a Facebook group called All Horts!!, and I now count a number of them as friends. Dilly's passion and her problems were inspired by All Horts!!' members, and I hope that her story goes some way towards highlighting the commitment and passion gardeners have for their work and the difficulties they face. Thank you, All Horts!!, for sharing your knowledge and experience with kindness and generosity.

Thank you to Berni Stevens for yet another extraordinarily beautiful cover, and to Perfect Prose Services for spotting the howlers, curbing my excesses and making this book shine.

Finally, thank you to my family – to my children for their unfailing support, and to Michael for loving me despite the twigs, soil and minibeasts in my hair. I love you.

Also by Sarah Shoesmith

Summer in Sweetingfield

New Beginnings in Sweetingfield

Summer in Sweetingfield

Summer Sutton stood knee-deep in soft, whispering grass and looked across a vast field dotted with buttercups, cow parsley and poppies, to where a small flock of sheep grazed in the warmth of the sun. Glad she wasn't clad in a heavy woollen coat like them, she dropped her rucksack to the ground and breathed in the fragrance of wild apple blossom. The month of May didn't get any better than this.

She left her rucksack where it was and carried on walking. Her belongings would be safe. There was no one else here apart from the distant sheep. She gave a little twirl of happiness as she walked, arms wide, her face towards the sun, then she sat down and slipped off her sandals. The grass tickled her neck and shoulders, making her giggle. She brushed her hand lightly across the top of it, her mind devoid of thought, apart from for a sheep which appeared to be lying down in the shorter grass away from the flock, kicking up its hooves and sunbathing. She had never seen a sheep do that before, but then she was hardly an expert, having always lived in the city. That sheep didn't follow the flock. It did its own thing, just like her. Taking her lead from the relaxing sheep, she removed her battered wide-brimmed straw sunhat, placed her faded blue denim jacket on the ground and lowered her head onto it to lie back on a duvet of meadow grass.

Swallows flitted in the air above her, seemingly inexhaustible creatures that travelled the globe, returning to their homes each summer and winter. They were migrants with a purpose. Summer had neither a home nor a purpose and she had reluctantly grown to accept, she probably never would. The swallows wanted for nothing. They had each other and this beautiful place. Why should she want more? She closed her eyes. The sounds of bleating, a dog's bark, and the hum of bees flitting from one open flower to another echoed in her mind as she fell happily and willingly into a light doze.

She was woken by a sudden jolt. Something had hit her in the ribs. Not hard enough to break them, but with sufficient force to send her heart racing.

'What the...?' shouted the tumbling man as he hit the floor with a thud.

Her hand automatically reached for her denim jacket where her money and cards were stored in a pocket. He hadn't robbed her.

'Sorry!' He turned back to her as he scrambled to his feet, concern written across a face so handsome it took what was left of the breath from her lungs. 'Are you okay?'

'Fine,' she blurted out automatically, even though she wasn't. She was reeling from the shock of being woken – and floored by his looks.

'Good.' He was already on his way. What was his hurry? She swiftly checked behind her, half expecting to be trampled underfoot by whatever, or whoever, was chasing him across this otherwise tranquil field, but the coast was clear, so she turned her attention back to the man and enjoyed the sight of him charging across the field, his strong legs powering through the long grass.

Still hungover from sleep, Summer dragged herself to her feet to see the man skid to a halt by the dozing sheep. He went to grab a handful of its wool, but his hand appeared to double back on itself as if it had stopped working. He must have hurt himself when he fell, she realised. Without a second thought, she abandoned her hat and jacket, and rushed barefoot to help him, her short sundress riding up her thighs as her strides lengthened.

She could see exasperation and pain written across his face as he used his uninjured left hand to roll the sheep over. It staggered to its feet before Summer reached him, and he stepped back, his eyes never leaving it.

'What happened?' she asked.

'Shh...' he whispered. 'Don't scare her.'

They stood in silence for a few seconds as the stunned creature found its bearings.

'Why did you make it stand up?' she persisted.

'Shh...'

'But it was perfectly happy.'

'She wasn't,' he hissed.

'It didn't look distressed though.'

'Shh... please let her recover,' he said through clenched teeth. He was clearly in pain. He must have had his eyes on the sheep and not seen Summer hidden in the long grass. At least she wasn't hurt, but she felt bad for him and wanted to help. She spotted him rubbing his hand. He was injured. She had to do something.

'Your hand,' she said.

He shook his head. 'Shh...'

'But what are you—?'

'What bit of shh don't you understand?' He turned to her, his eyes, bluer than the sky, sparking with fury and exasperation.

'Well, if you're going to be like that,' she said, turning away from him. Handsome though he was, life was too short to spend time where she wasn't wanted. He could stay with his beloved sheep. She collected her hat and jacket, then returned to her rucksack and pulled out a torn wristband. On it, written in drunken scrawl, was the reason she was here. '*Chestnut Cottage, High Street, Sweetingfield.*' Home to two of the loveliest people she had ever met. Kind, warm, caring, or at least they had seemed to be when she met them at the music festival last August. She just hoped they remembered her and would honour their promise to welcome her with open arms should she ever venture east to Norfolk.

So far, the welcome had been anything but warm. She had been unceremoniously torn from her sleep by a kick in the ribs, and hissed at by a man with anger in his eyes. If this was a reflection of life in Sweetingfield, she would be gone by teatime.

She watched the man assessing the sheep. Farmers could get very upset by people who didn't take care of their livestock and close gates, or who littered the countryside, but she had done none of these things. The sheep trotted back to join the rest of the flock, and relieved that it looked okay, Summer tried to calm the anxiety that was nibbling away at her self-assurance and making her question her decision to come to Sweetingfield. Surely not everyone here would be like him.

The man watched the sheep for a few moments more, then strode towards her, following the path he had flattened in his haste to get to the sheep, his dark hair shining in the late spring sunshine. Summer felt her stomach do a little flip. Yes, he had it all. It was a shame he was so angry.

She looked at his hand, which hung limply at his side. 'You're hurt,' she said.

'It'll mend,' he said, brushing off her concern.

'Let me take a look.'

'Are you a doctor... nurse... medic?'

She shook her head. 'Just concerned. I feel guilty that I tripped you up.'

'No need to be. You have every right to lie wherever you like on common land, but to explain about that ewe – she wasn't perfectly happy, as you said she was. A sheep lying down, especially one in lamb, is rigwelted, and in danger of dying because it can't get up on its feet without help.'

Sadness swamped her. She would never want to be responsible for the death of any creature. She hated the idea of hurting anything or anyone. She nodded guiltily at his hand. 'Will you get it seen to?'

He flashed her a look that told her it was none of her business. She lifted up her sunhat and plonked it on her head. It didn't matter how good-looking he was; if he was going to be like that, she had better things to do with her time.

Available in paperback and ebook

New Beginnings in Sweetingfield

Discover this uplifting small town story packed full of friendship, community and love!

Ellie Carson has invested everything she has in an abandoned farm, only to discover that living the rural dream is a nightmare. Her cosy flat has been replaced by a fourth-hand caravan in a field, her boyfriend has left her, and time and money are running out.

Heartbroken, Ellie faces financial ruin if she can't renovate a farm cottage in time for the summer holidays... and she can't do that alone.

Can she trust her fellow villagers to help, and if she does, what about Dan? Known as The Player, Dan is strikingly good-looking and full of fun. Ellie assumes that he is shallower than a paddling pool, but is she so blinded by Dan's looks that she fails to see the true beauty beneath?

Available in paperback and ebook

Printed in Dunstable, United Kingdom

78944799R00201